T0359872

INTRIGUE

Seek thrills. Solve crimes. Justice served.

K-9 Defender
Julie Miller

Hometown Homicide
Denise N. Wheatley

MILLS & BOON

K-9 DEFENDER
© 2024 by Julie Miller
Philippine Copyright 2024
Australian Copyright 2024
New Zealand Copyright 2024

First Published 2024
First Australian Paperback Edition 2024
ISBN 978 1 867 92168 0

HOMETOWN HOMICIDE
© 2024 by Denise N. Wheatley
Philippine Copyright 2024
Australian Copyright 2024
New Zealand Copyright 2024

First Published 2024
First Australian Paperback Edition 2024
ISBN 978 1 867 92168 0

MIX
Paper | Supporting
responsible forestry
FSC® C001695

Published by
Harlequin Mills & Boon
An imprint of Harlequin Enterprises (Australia) Pty Limited
(ABN 47 001 180 918), a subsidiary of HarperCollins
Publishers Australia Pty Limited
(ABN 36 009 913 517)
Level 19, 201 Elizabeth Street
SYDNEY NSW 2000 AUSTRALIA

Cover art used by arrangement with Harlequin Books S.A.. All rights reserved.

Printed and bound in Australia by McPherson's Printing Group

K-9 Defender
Julie Miller

MILLS & BOON

Julie Miller is an award-winning *USA TODAY* bestselling author of breathtaking romantic suspense— with a National Readers' Choice Award and a Daphne du Maurier Award, among other prizes. She has also earned an *RT Book Reviews* Career Achievement Award. For a complete list of her books, monthly newsletter and more, go to juliemiller.org.

Visit the Author Profile page
at millsandboon.com.au.

DEDICATION

For the trainers and staff at Dog Stars.
Thank you for helping our one-eyed Doodlebugs,
Daisy & Teddy, become all-star dogs.
Your expertise and kindness
were greatly appreciated.

CAST OF CHARACTERS

Mollie Crane—After escaping her abusive marriage, she keeps a low profile working as a waitress at Pearl's Diner. She relies on her service dog, Magnus, to help her cope with her anxiety attacks. But is her dog enough to protect her when her past tracks her down? Or will she learn to rely on the damaged detective who speaks to her heart?

Joel Standage—The KCPD detective lost nearly everything on his last undercover assignment—his life, his girlfriend and his confidence to get the job done. But a shy waitress and her goofy guard dog call him to be a warrior again.

Magnus—A misfit of a service dog.

August Di Salvo—Mollie's ex-husband.

Beau Regalio—August's bodyguard.

Kyra Schmidt—Di Salvo family attorney.

Rocky Garner—He can't keep his hands to himself.

Herb Valentino—The grouchy cook.

AJ Rodriguez—Joel's supervisor.

Jessie Caldwell—She runs K-9 Ranch.

Prologue

Two Years Ago...

"You'll always be a stupid country girl!"

Mollie Di Salvo couldn't brace for the next blow when it came. She was still woozy from the hands that had squeezed around her neck until she'd nearly passed out and collapsed to the kitchen floor. She couldn't pull her legs up fast enough and curl into a ball. She swore she heard a rib snap when Augie kicked her in the stomach.

She'd always thought anger was a fiery emotion. But as she squinted through her swollen eyelid at the eyes of her husband, she knew that anger was ice-cold.

This was the worst beating yet.

All because she'd served her granny's biscuits at the dinner party with Augie's parents, the Brewers and Mr. Hess and his date. Delicious, yes. But poor folks and country bumpkins ate biscuits. Augie was embarrassed to see them on his table. Embarrassed that the investment bankers he worked with might think he was a poor country bumpkin, too, with no sense about handling their clients' money.

Embarrassed by her.

Was she trying to sabotage this business deal? A faux pas at this level on Kansas City's social registry could cost him and his company millions of dollars.

Or something like that. To be honest, once she'd drifted away from consciousness, she hadn't heard much of his tirade.

Now all she knew was pain.

Mollie's lungs burned and her throat throbbed as she fought to catch a deep breath. She watched as Augie knelt beside her and clasped her chin in a cruel grip, surely leaving bruises, forcing her to face him. "I'm going out." His spittle sprayed her cheek. "The staff has gone home for the night, so clean up this mess. And don't wait up for me."

She watched the polished black Italian oxfords on his feet, making sure that they were walking away from her and heading out the side door into the garage. She heard men's unintelligible voices, a car door slam, and then Augie's latest fancy sports car revving up and driving away.

Mollie pushed herself up to a sitting position and leaned back against the oven. Breathing in through her nose and out through her mouth, she mentally assessed her injuries. There'd be bruises and swelling, yes—maybe even a cracked rib. But she could survive without a trip to the ER, without telling lies to the doctor and nurses, without explaining why it wasn't safe for her to talk to the police. She just needed to catch a deep breath.

She reached beneath the neckline of her dress to clutch the engraved silver locket she always wore. To her it was more beautiful than the obnoxiously large sapphire and diamond ring on her left hand. The wedding and engagement rings were all about Augie and showing off that he was wealthy and generous. But her locket was the real prize. It had been a gift from Granny. The one link left to her past when she'd been happy and the world was full of possibilities. She'd been so naive.

She had no more illusions of love. Her Cinderella story had ended just over a year ago, only five months into her marriage. The first slap that Thanksgiving night after an endless extravaganza at his parents' estate with his entire family and many of their important friends still rang through her memory. She was an introvert by nature, and the days of prepping and late-into-the-night dining, drinking, and partying had left her physically and emotionally exhausted. When they got home, Augie wanted to celebrate their successful evening. He informed her he was horny and ready for sex. She'd kissed him, explained how tired she was and promised that, after a little rest, she'd give him a very good morning.

He'd slapped her, the move so sudden she would have thought she'd imagined it if not for the heat rapidly replacing the shocked nerves on her cheek. No one said no to August Di Salvo, especially not his low-class hick of a wife. She should be grateful for every little thing he did for her. Augie took the sex he wanted that night, and Mollie knew her dream life had irrevocably changed into a nightmare.

Between the family attorney and his parents' influence, her report to the police the next day had mysteriously disappeared. And the one after that had been pleaded down to a public disturbance and dismissed with a fine.

So, she'd stopped calling the police. She stopped sharing a bedroom with her husband. And she stopped feeling hope.

Now, thankfully, Augie got most of his sex from the string of affairs he had. But Mollie didn't care that he was cheating on her.

She didn't have emotions anymore.

She drew in another painful breath. That wasn't exactly true.

She had fear.

Fear was her constant companion. If Augie wasn't with her, then she knew one of his friends or beefy bodyguards or even someone from the office or their home staff was watching her. The beautiful trophy wife who straightened her hair and dyed it blond because her husband didn't think her natural dark curls looked sophisticated. Who wore heels that pinched her feet because he thought they made her look sexy. Who'd married a man because she'd believed the Di Salvo family taking her in, and Augie supporting her through the worst time of her life, meant they loved her.

How could a smart woman be so foolish? Her loneliness and despair had led to some disastrous choices.

Her granny must be turning over in her grave to see how frightened and abused she had become. She'd grown up without parents, thanks to a rainy-night highway accident when she was four. But she'd been raised with love and enough food to eat, and she'd been taught a solid work ethic and some old-fashioned common sense by her grandmother, Lucy Belle Crane. She was the girl who'd overcome the poor circumstances of her Ozarks upbringing to earn scholarships and work her way through college at the University of Missouri. She had a degree in math education, a year in the classroom under her belt, and a semester's worth of classes toward her Master's degree.

Yet here she was, huddled on the kitchen floor of August Di Salvo's big, beautiful house, afraid to stand her ground with Augie, afraid to call the police, afraid to ask anyone for help, afraid to pursue a teaching job or further her education, afraid to leave, afraid to stay. Afraid. Afraid. Afraid.

Feeling an imagined warmth radiating from the locket in her hand, she pressed a kiss to the silver oval and dropped it inside the front of her dress. Then she braced one hand on the oven behind her and reached up to grasp the granite countertop on the island across from her.

The door to the garage swung open. Mollie gasped in fear and plopped down on her butt. The movement jarred her sore ribs, and she grabbed her side, biting down on a moan of pain and bracing herself for another round of degrading words and hard blows from her husband.

Only, she didn't recognize the man in the black uniform suit and tie who wandered into the kitchen, surveyed the entire area, then rushed to her side when he saw her on the cold tile floor.

He reached for her with a big, scarred hand. "Let me help you."

"No, I..." But he was already pulling her to

her feet. He wound a sturdy arm around her waist and led her around the island, where he pulled out a stool and helped her to sit.

"Looks like you took a pretty good blow to the head." His gaze darted to the placement of her hand above her waist. "Did you hit your side, too? Do you want me to call 9-1-1? Or I could drive you to the hospital myself."

"No. I'll be fine. I'm just—" the well-rehearsed word tasted like bile on her tongue "—clumsy."

She smiled until she saw his gaze linger on the marks she knew would be visible on her neck. "You didn't fall."

The man was too observant for his own good. The others had been trained to look the other way. Mollie realized she was still holding on to his hand, where it rested on the countertop. She popped her grip open and turned away to pull her long golden hair off her cheek and tuck it behind her ear. "You're new here."

Although he frowned at the cool wall of diversion and denial she was erecting between them, he thankfully retreated a step to give her the distance she needed to pull herself together. "I'm Mr. Di Salvo's new driver. He took the convertible out himself, said he didn't need me tonight. But I'm on shift until midnight. It's kind of chilly just sitting out in the garage waiting to work. I was told I could come into the house to get some hot coffee."

"Of course. Everything you need is right here. Regular, decaf. Cream, sugar." Moving slowly, but with a sense of purpose, she climbed off the stool and showed him the coffee bar tucked in beside the refrigerator at the end of the row of cabinets. Ever the consummate hostess, she opened the cabinet above the coffee makers, but winced when she reached for the mug above her.

He was at her side in an instant, grasping the mug and pulling it down for her. "Ma'am, you don't have to wait on me. Can I at least make you an ice pack for that eye? I do have first aid training."

Ignoring his concern, or perhaps taking advantage of it by continuing this conversation at all, she asked for the smallest of favors. "Would you pull down another mug for me?"

"Sure."

When he set the mug in front of her, she poured herself some decaf coffee and cradled its heat between her trembling hands. She scooted off to the side, leaning lightly against the counter. "Please. Help yourself."

"Thanks." He poured himself a mug, fully loaded with a shot of cream.

While he fixed his drink and took a couple of sips, Mollie felt curious enough to make note of his looks. He wasn't as tall as or movie star handsome as Augie, but then, *tall, dark, and handsome* wasn't necessarily attractive in her opinion. Not anymore.

Her would-be rescuer had brown hair and golden-brown eyes that made her think of a tiger. Despite the breadth of his shoulders beneath his black suit jacket, and the unflattering buzz cut of hair that emphasized the sharp angles of his face, the man had kind eyes. Kindness was such a rarity in her small world that the softness of his amber eyes woke a desire in her that she hadn't felt for a long time now. The desire to step outside herself and do something for someone else—the way she might once have helped a friend in need—the way no one had helped her for more than a year now. "Let me give you some advice, Mr...?"

"Uh, Rostovich." Had he hesitated to share his name? "Joel Rostovich."

"Listen, Joel Rostovich. Get out. Get out of this house. Leave your job. Get away from this family as fast as you can."

He set down his coffee at her dismissal. "You need an ice pack or a raw steak for that eye. If you won't let me drive you to the ER or a police station, at least let me make sure you get to your room safely, and I'll bring you an ibuprofen." He started to pull out a business card. "If you change your mind, you can call—"

"And if you won't get out, then stay away from me. Don't talk to me unless you have orders to. Don't smile. And sure as hell, don't you be nice to me again." She tucked the card into the pocket of his jacket and rested her hand against his chest in a silent thanks for his humanity and compassion. Then she turned and slowly made her way out of the kitchen. "It'll be safer for you that way."

Chapter One

Present Day.
Summer...

"You stupid waitress." The young man swore and shoved his chair back to avoid the milk dripping off the side of the table.

"I'm sorry, sir." Mollie Crane righted the glass she'd bumped when she'd been clearing his plate and quickly pulled the towel from the waistband of her apron to mop up the spill before any of the liquid got on the customer. This was more about saving the chair and keeping the floor dry than making sure the grumpy customer wouldn't get anything on his Arabia Steamboat T-shirt from the tourist shop down the street. Nor would he slip on any wet surface.

She always carried a towel with her now. While she was more than willing to put in the hours, step out of her comfort zone to interact with customers, and ignore her aching feet, it turned out that waitressing wasn't her best thing. She startled easily, got distracted by anything or anyone unfamiliar to her, and tended to withdraw inside her head when she got stressed. Although she'd been raised in her Granny Lucy Belle's kitchen and loved to cook, serving food outside the kitchen seemed to be a skill she was still acquiring after ten months on the job. But, it was a job, she had an understanding boss, and she needed both. And when her shift wasn't a train wreck like this one, coming in a few hours early to help out while her friend and fellow server Corie Taylor went to an OB-GYN appointment to monitor her ninth month of pregnancy, she actually made pretty good tips.

Not that this self-entitled bozo would be leaving her much, if anything, now. "I'll bring you a fresh glass of milk," she offered, trying to remember that the customer was always right— even if he was being a jerk about it.

"No, you won't." His morning must have been longer than hers to see how easily he got riled over a simple accident. She wasn't even certain this was her fault. Hadn't he been pushing his plate aside when she walked up with the glass he'd ordered to go with his pie? "You'll bring me a new plate of food. Everything here is swimming in milk. It's ruined."

Everything? The man had already eaten his patty melt, save for the bottom bun, and all but two of his French fries. And the spill wasn't anywhere near his chocolate cream pie. Mollie bit down on the sarcastic retorts she wanted to spew at him. *Ungrateful man. Scammer. Spoiled rotten.* But talking back to anyone, especially a man with a short temper like this one, had been beaten out of her long ago. She might have left August Di Salvo and her nightmarish, dangerous marriage behind, but the rules of survival were too deeply ingrained in her to do anything but apologize again. "I'm sorry if there was a misunderstanding. I thought you were done with your lunch."

"Darrell, we were almost finished." His wife or girlfriend, who sat across from him, tried to placate him with a gentle reprimand.

But with a snap of his fingers, the woman fell silent and sank back into her chair.

Oh, God. Not this. Darrell wouldn't be hurting the woman later for contradicting him in public, would he? Because of Mollie's mistake? Her body tensed and her pulse thundered in her ears at the potential for violence. She quickly dropped her gaze to the woman's bare wrists, her neck, and face, looking for any subtle signs that she was being physically abused by her husband. Mollie eased a silent breath through her nose. She didn't see any obvious bruising or that the woman was holding a wrenched joint tenderly so as not to aggravate a hidden injury. But that didn't mean he wasn't verbally abusing her.

"You don't understand the kind of stress I'm under." Augie spat the words at her, bending her backward as he tugged roughly on her hair, snapping a few strands and sending pain burning across her scalp. *She'd been dressing for dinner with his parents when he walked into her bedroom to announce he was ready to leave. He'd taken one look at her carefully coiffed hair and dragged her into the bathroom to shove her face into the mirror.* "I said I liked you blonde. Brown hair makes you look cheap."

And the bottled bleach color he insisted on didn't?

"The stylist said I needed to give my hair a break from all the dying and straightening chemicals," she whispered, even though the truth wouldn't make a bit of difference to her husband. *"My hair is breaking."*

Mollie watched the reflection of his hand down at his side to make sure it stayed there. Although dinner with Edward and Bernadette Di Salvo wouldn't be a picnic, at least she knew Augie wouldn't leave any marks on her that his parents could see. Not that they'd chastised their son or supported Mollie in the past when he'd hurt her—if anything had happened, it must have been her fault. They were old money and

*all about appearances. So, she might be safe
from his fists and feet for the time being, but
that didn't stop Augie's cutting words.*

*"Your stylist doesn't have to look at your hair
day in and day out. I do." He finally released her,
giving her a chance to ease the crick in her neck.
"You'll be wearing a sack over your head next
time I take you to bed."*

*An idle threat, since she knew he'd be sleep-
ing with his administrative assistant at the loft
apartment he kept her in in downtown Kansas
City. But the words still hurt.*

*"I can't stand to look at you like this." Augie
literally wiped his hands on a towel, as if her natural curls had contaminated him somehow. "You
used to be so smart. I don't understand why you
can't get simple things like this right." He tossed
the towel at her and pivoted to stride out of the
room. "You'll stay home tonight. I'll tell Mother
and Father you're ill."*

Mollie sucked in a shallow breath and squeezed
her eyes shut to tamp down the urge to run away
from her memories and real-life stressors to
safety. Wherever that illusion might be. Leaving her husband didn't mean leaving her fears
behind.

But she *was* smart. She was slowly amassing
the tools she needed to do better than simply sur-

vive. And beyond her own gumption, the best tool she had was right here in the diner with her.

Forcing her eyes open, Mollie looked across the diner to spot her service dog, Magnus, lying in his bed at the far end of the soda fountain counter. The sleek Belgian Malinois with the permanently flopped-over ear looked like the sharp, muscular dog that was his breed standard. But in the weeks she'd been training with him at Jessica Caldwell's K-9 Ranch just outside of Kansas City, she'd learned that, despite his athleticism, her boy was more couch potato than intimidating working machine.

"Magnus…?" She mouthed his name through trembling lips. She held out two fingers in a silent *Come* command. He was supposed to watch her, comfort her. Obey her.

Mollie frowned. Great. Magnus was facing the kitchen. He seemed to be happily relaxing, his teeth clamped around the tattered teddy bear he carried everywhere, instead of paying attention to her and hurrying to her side to calm her when she was on the verge of a panic attack, like she was now. She wasn't exactly sure what it was that Magnus responded to when she was about to lose it. But clearly, her pulse pounding in her ears, the cold, clammy feel to her skin and the short, shallow breathing weren't it.

Some therapy dog. Shouting for him wouldn't

do any good. Being deaf in one ear, he might not even hear her over the noise of clinking dishes and chatty patrons. And if he did happen to look her way and respond to the visual signals she'd been practicing with him, the former K-9 Corps washout would probably frighten some of the customers when he loped across the diner to reach her.

Mollie dropped her hand to clutch the dripping towel to her chest. When she got her break later this afternoon, she'd be calling Jessica, who ran the K-9 Ranch where Mollie had gotten Magnus, and where they'd gone through several training lessons together. Jessica and she had worked hard to train Magnus to be an alert dog for Mollie. But other than that first morning on the ranch, when the partially deaf tan dog with a black face had trotted up onto the porch and lain across her feet, indicating that he knew she needed some help—even when her own brain was too stressed out to recognize it—Magnus's responses to Mollie seemed to be hit-or-miss. Jessica said she wasn't being assertive enough, that Magnus didn't see her as his pack leader and wasn't cued in to serving her needs reliably. Mollie imagined the dog saw her as the same weak fool her ex-husband had. That she wasn't worth his time and energy to take care of, so long as she met his basic needs. In Magnus's case, that meant having food, his teddy, regular exercise, and a comfy bed to sleep in.

How did she end up so horribly alone again? She had no family, an ex-husband who'd rather see her dead than pay her one dime of alimony, no friends outside of work and dog training, and a washed-up K-9 Corps dog who seemed to think she was his service human instead of him catering to her.

"Hey!"

Now the fingers were snapping at her.

Mollie startled and swung her gaze back to the table in front of her. "I'm sorry. What?"

"Are you going to go put in the order for my lunch again?" the rude customer asked.

"No, she won't." Mollie saw the flash of movement between tables a split second before her boss, Melissa Kincaid, stepped up beside her. Although shorter than Mollie's five feet six, and looking like a fairy princess with her golden hair and delicate features, despite the scar on her face, Melissa was a tough cookie when it came to running her restaurant. "I'll happily gift you with the slice of pie, but I'm not in the habit of comping meals that have already been eaten and clearly enjoyed. Would you like me to box your pie up to go? I'd be happy to," Melissa strongly suggested. She turned and smiled at Mollie, indicating she had the disgruntled customer well in hand. "Go on. Take a break. I'm sure Herb will have another order up for you in the window by the time you get back on the floor."

"I'm sorry." She mouthed the words to her boss.

"Don't be," the older woman reassured her, squeezing her shoulders in a sideways hug before nudging her away from the table. "Take five minutes. Find your calm place. Then get back to work. We're shorthanded and I really need you."

"Thank you." Mollie quickly retreated while Melissa dealt with the demanding customer. At least he hadn't put his hands on her, she reasoned, knowing she would have had a full-fledged meltdown if he had. The public knew Pearl's Diner as an eatery with a cute, nostalgic decor that served filling, yummy comfort food and award-winning desserts from early morning until late at night. But Mollie knew the truth behind the scenes—that Pearl's was a haven for women working to get back on their feet again after surviving a difficult or traumatic situation. Melissa Kincaid's first husband had been an abuser, and the original Pearl had practically adopted her, giving her a job and a way to start rebuilding her life some fifteen years earlier. Corie Taylor had been a struggling single mother whose ex was in prison. Since inheriting the diner from Pearl, Melissa had paid Pearl's gen-

erosity forward, hiring Corie and allowing her
to bring her son to sit in a corner booth when
she needed childcare. Both women were now
happily married to good men—a KCPD detective and a KCFD firefighter, respectively—and
had started new, healthy families of their own.

Mollie had once had a dream like that. But
after her grandmother's death and her subse-
quent marriage to Augie, she was content to simply be alive and have a job. She might want more
from life, but for now, survival was all that mattered. She was grateful to Melissa for giving her
an apron after the Di Salvos had blackballed
her name and kept her from getting a teaching job—or just about any job involving education. She was even more grateful that the petite,
nearly fearless woman looked out for her when
it came to rude customers, and that she allowed
her to bring Magnus to work with her—even if
he was the worst service dog in the history of
K-9 companiondom.

Once at the sink behind the soda fountain
counter, Mollie rinsed out the milky towel and
draped it over the drying rack beneath the sink.
Then, mostly out of sight from the customers,
she knelt beside her furry partner. "Hey, baby,"
she cooed, making sure the dog was aware of
her presence before she touched him. At least,
he seemed pleased to see her. When he raised

his sleek head and focused his dark eyes on her, Mollie smiled, chiding him even as she absorbed the affection he doled out. "How's my big Magnus? Taking it easy today, are we?" She scrubbed her palms along his muzzle and scratched around his ears when he turned his head into her touch. "You know, you failed rescue dog 101 a few minutes ago. Mama needed you."

As if he understood her words and wanted to apologize, he tilted his head, turning his good ear toward her and placing one big paw on her knee. He whimpered softly and laid his head in her lap. She continued to stroke the top of his head as she absorbed his body heat and focused on the inhales and exhales in his strong chest, willing his calm, currently devoted presence to seep into her psyche.

"That's it. Good boy. That's my Magnus. Mama about had a panic attack with the rude man. She needs some of your attention." She rewarded him for his supportive behavior now by picking up his teddy bear and playing a gentle game of tug-of-war with him behind the counter. She wondered if he was losing more of his hearing, or if it was her training that wasn't working out. "We're going to review our skills tonight. I need you to put your paw on me or your nose in my hand every time I'm on the verge of losing it. You keep Mama with you in the here and now, okay? Don't let me get lost in the scary places in my head." She talked softly to him, explaining his job to him as if she were teaching a student in her classroom, and he understood every word she said. "You're being such a good boy right now. We're going learn a new word this week—*consistency*." Magnus tilted his head, as if he was curious to expand his vocabulary. "*Consistent* means every, single, time. Not just when you're in the mood to pay attention. The whole idea of being an alert dog is—"

"Hey, girlie." Herb Valentino, the perpetually grumpy septuagenarian who ran the kitchen during the daytime shift stuck his head through the order window and waved her back into the kitchen. "Stop talkin' to that mutt of yours. If you're just sittin' around, I can use some help back here gettin' orders out. I'm swamped."

Mollie cringed at the cook's nickname for any female under the age of fifty. But she'd been called a lot worse. And, it was probably better for her to stay busy and focused on something other than thoughts of Augie, violence, and a service dog who'd failed her again. Besides, she felt a sense of comfort when she worked in a kitchen—even if it was beside grumpy Herb instead of her darling late grandmother. She'd learned the old man's bark was much worse than his bite. She even had a feeling he kind of liked her working beside him, so long as she obeyed his orders and didn't mess with his recipes. Mollie gave Magnus one last pet and pushed to her feet. "Sure. Melissa only gave me a short break, but I can help get some plates out."

"Wash your hands, girlie. After pettin' that mutt, I don't want you touchin' any food."

She was already at the sink, soaping up her hands, by the time he'd finished his warning. She grabbed a towel to dry her hands and pulled on a pair of plastic gloves before moving up beside the tall, lanky man with bushy gray eyebrows and faded tattoos from his time in the Navy several decades earlier. "Reporting for duty. Put me to work."

He winked at her and did just that. Mollie spent the next several minutes loading condiments onto burgers and putting side dishes onto plates. They worked side by side, with Herb cooking and Mollie finishing plates and setting them in the warming window. She made eye contact with one of the other waitresses. "Order up!"

While the other woman filled her tray with the hot lunches and carried them out to the diners, Mollie swung her gaze over to her own section to see if Melissa was still doing okay covering her tables. She was relieved to see the rude tourist had left the diner. Everyone else at least had their drinks. She'd better get back out there to make sure their food orders were in the queue. But she stopped and stared when she spotted Melissa at the hostess stand near the door, chatting with a man who looked unsettlingly familiar.

Joel Rostovich.

Not quite six feet tall. Muscular as she remembered, yet thinner somehow. Short brown hair with beautiful golden-brown eyes that reminded her of a tiger. He needed a shave, but somehow the beard stubble that shaded his jaw and neck looked intentional—and gave his face an animalistic vibe. He wore a light blue polo shirt that exposed his beefy arms, some intricate tattoos on his forearms that disappeared beneath the sleeves of his shirt, and a mile of tanned skin that was broken up by several pale pink scars that made him look like he was no stranger to violence. He looked like a mixed martial arts fighter who'd come out of the cage on the losing end of things.

He'd worked for her husband.

He'd been kind to her.

But there was a hardness to him now. Even with the length and noise of the restaurant between them muting the actual words, she could hear a snap to his tone. She could see the wariness in his eyes that hadn't been there two years ago in the middle of the night in her kitchen prison when they'd met. And when he stepped around the hostess stand to follow Melissa to a table, she saw the badge hanging from a lanyard around his neck and the gun holstered to the waist of his khaki pants.

And she saw the cane.

Mollie frowned, a fist squeezing around her heart when she saw him move. He hadn't used a cane when they'd met two years ago. He hadn't had that slow, uneven gait, either.

She'd met him here at Pearl's Diner once again a few months back, during one of her first shifts at the restaurant. No limp then, either. He hadn't been at one of her tables, but there'd been another rude customer, a uniformed police officer who'd grabbed her, and she'd had a full-blown panic attack. Several customers had tried to come to her aid that night, including Joel. She realized he was a cop for the first time that night because he'd been wearing a standard blue KCPD uniform. She'd been too shocked to acknowledge him, although she had a feeling he recognized her, despite her different hair color, hairstyle, and working-class clothes. At least, he'd sensed something familiar about her.

Mollie gasped when Melissa turned down the long aisle of tables and booths near the front windows. *No, no, no. Do not seat him in my section. Do not...*

A compactly built man with short black hair streaked with silver at his temples stood and held out a hand to greet Joel. With a nod, if not a smile for the hostess, Joel shook the other man's hand before sliding into the booth across from him.

Mollie exhaled a worried sigh and wondered if she could get away with spending the rest of the day in the kitchen, instead of waiting tables and interacting with a man from her past.

Only, she couldn't get it out of her head that the man who'd just been seated at her table wasn't the same man she'd known before. It didn't have anything to do with him wearing a polo shirt instead of a KCPD uniform or chauffeur's suit and tie. *Softer* wasn't exactly the right word, but that man two years ago had been willing to help if she'd asked.

This man didn't look like he wanted to help anybody, like he wasn't even happy to meet the man who appeared to be an old friend for lunch. Like he wouldn't be happy to run into her again.

"Mollie." Herb's gruff reprimand made her jump and pull her gaze back to the faded gray eyes beneath his gray, bushy brows. "You're fallin' behind, girlie. Finish these plates and get back out there. Melissa's giving you the high sign."

Mollie acknowledged her boss's wave to get

back out on the floor before dropping her gaze to the three plates in front of her, all waiting for fries and a bowl of whatever side they'd ordered. She checked the computer screen beside the window and dished up coleslaw and cottage cheese. She salted the fries and set the plates in the window. "Order up!"

"What's your mutt up to now?" Herb asked. He nudged his arm against hers and nodded through the pickup window.

Mollie watched Magnus pace behind the counter, his dark eyes focused on her. He scratched at the swinging door that separated the soda fountain area from the kitchen, then raised up on his hind legs, bracing his front paws on the edge of the metal sink and stretching his neck to get his nose closer to her. He repeated the entire process, whining as if he was calling her name.

Now he picked up on her stress?

Yes, baby. Come to Mama before I completely freak out in the middle of the lunch rush.

"His job," Mollie whispered. "He's finally doing his job."

Chapter Two

Joel Standage didn't think anything good could come from being summoned to a lunch meeting with his covert division supervisor, A. J. Rodriguez.

Not that he didn't like or admire the hell out of the short, muscular man who was a legend in undercover work at KCPD. A.J. had taken down more perps in his twenty years with the department—either working his own undercover operation, or training and providing support for the younger UC operators he now supervised—than just about any other detective on the force.

But Joel was barely a cop of any kind anymore. After blowing his last assignment—losing the woman he'd loved but apparently couldn't trust, and damn near his life—he'd been relegated to desk duty at the Fourth Precinct offices. And hell, it didn't seem that he was much good at even that. Poring through case files, running background checks, babysitting perps who were cooling their heels in interview rooms, and providing info support to the men and women on the front line was what cops who were turning gray or losing their hair near the end of their careers did. Intellectually, he understood those jobs provided vital services to every person wearing a badge. But emotionally, it made him feel like he was on his way out, too.

He'd made his way back after injuries that would have taken out a man who was any less fit than he'd been. But even with months of physical therapy, he knew he'd never be 100 percent again. The trouble was, he didn't know if he was at 90 percent, 75 percent or even a lousy 50 percent. And the sad fact was, he wasn't sure he wanted to find out.

He wasn't sure he cared much about being a cop anymore.

He was pretty damn sure no one else did, either. He had no close family who cared, and certainly no girlfriend, anymore.

Joel leaned his cane against the bench beside his new knee and toyed with the rolled-up napkin and silverware in front of him as he summoned a wry smile. "So, boss. To what do I owe the honor of having lunch with you?"

A.J.'s dark eyes sparkled with an amusement Joel didn't understand. "I wanted to get you out of the office, amigo. Have this meeting someplace where you couldn't hide behind your desk or computer and act like an invalid."

"I died on the operating table, A.J. I've got more metal in me now than that cherry Trans Am of yours. Technically, I *am* an invalid."

"Boo-hoo." The black-haired man leaned forward, resting his elbows on the table and steepling his fingers together. "Frankly, Joel—I wanted to see you get off your ass and get back to being the good cop I know you can be."

Well, that was straightforward enough.

He was on the verge of telling A.J. that any faith in him was misplaced when the waitress walked up to their table.

Not just any waitress. *Her.*

Mollie Di Salvo. "Hi."

Joel tilted his face up at her quiet greeting and watched her set two glasses on the table in front of them with a barely there smile. She'd changed her hair. It was shorter, curlier, darker—earthier and more natural than the straight blond tresses he remembered. But it made her big blue eyes pop like pools of cobalt against her pale skin. He'd recognize those blue eyes anywhere.

What was the ex-wife of one of Kansas City's wealthiest men doing waiting tables in the City Market District? When he'd seen her here last October, he'd assumed it was a stopgap job until her alimony money came in or she found herself a better job. But that was nine months ago. Why was she still here?

"Welcome to Pearl's Diner." Her gaze moved carefully between A.J. and him, taking in the badges and guns they wore. And the cane. And the scars. Joel shifted uncomfortably in his seat and pulled his arms beneath the table. Did she recognize the pale shadow of the man he'd been when they met two years ago? Did she feel pity for him? "Can I get you anything else to drink? Iced tea? Coffee with cream, right? Or something from our soda fountain? It *is* hot outside."

"Mrs. Di Salvo." Joel's greeting was gruff and terse. "You know how I drink my coffee? I haven't been to Pearl's in months. And you didn't wait on me then."

She shrugged. "Actually, I remember from that night at…" The barely there smile disappeared completely.

"The Di Salvo estate." They'd talked for all of ten minutes that night. Either she had an eidetic memory, or she had the kind of brain that simply recalled random details about the people she met.

"I didn't know you were a police officer then, Mr. Rostovich." She clasped her order pad between her hands and hugged it against her chest. Although her voice said cool and polite, her posture screamed tension. Maybe even fear. "Not that it would have made it easier for me to trust you. You worked for my husband. That alone meant I couldn't trust you."

Looked like she still had her survival skills down pat. Underplay her knowledge. Hide her emotions.

Joel curled his hands into fists on top of his thighs, surprised by the urge to take her hand and give her a reassuring squeeze. Or even hug her as tightly as she clutched that pen and order pad—if that would ease the discomfort radiating off her in waves. "You were doing what was necessary to protect yourself." He reassured her verbally since touching her was out of the question for far too many reasons. "And it's Standage. Joel Standage. Rostovich was a role I was playing."

"To investigate Augie?"

"Yes, ma'am." Not that it had done them any good. In the end, August Di Salvo had walked away from his trial a free man, thanks to conflicting witness statements and a technicality that had rendered other testimony—like his own—inadmissible in court. And the DA's office wasn't willing to prosecute Di Salvo again until they could put together an airtight case against him. "I'm sorry we couldn't keep him in jail."

Her soft, rose-tinted lips pressed together in a tight frown. "Augie's parents spent a lot of money to make his troubles go away."

So, the rumors of witness intimidation and bribery were probably true. Did she include herself as one of those *troubles*? But again, why would she be waiting tables at a homespun diner if she'd been paid off with Di Salvo money?

A.J. drummed his fingers on the Formica tabletop, joining the conversation. "Di Salvo? You're Mollie Di Salvo?"

Her blue gaze swung to A.J., then moved on past him to the soda fountain at the back of the seating area. Joel narrowed his gaze when he saw the blur of brown and black fur pacing behind the counter. Was that a dog in the restaurant? He looked like one of the Belgian Malinois dogs that worked in the K-9 division. Joel's frown of confusion deepened when Mollie raised her hand beside her shoulder as if she was taking an oath, and the dog sat.

The dog's dark, nearly black, eyes remained focused on her as she looked back at A.J. "That's not my name anymore. And I'd appreciate you not repeating it out loud. I'm Mollie Crane now."

More curious and faintly disappointed than he wanted to be, Joel asked, "You got remarried?"

He glanced at her ten unadorned fingers. Although, she might not be wearing a ring because of the work she did here.

"Divorced," she answered, clutching the order pad to her chest again. "Not that it's any of your business. As you might remember, that was a… bad situation for me. I went back to my maiden name."

Bad situation was an understatement. Bruises the size of a man's hands around her neck. A black eye that was swollen nearly shut. Struggling to catch her breath against the pain of a gut punch or kick. Her husband had been a bully and a bastard with work, his staff, and the woman he supposedly loved—and Joel hadn't been able to get enough intel to keep the man in prison after his arrest for a myriad of white-collar crimes. Yeah. He remembered her *bad situation*.

Although she had shadows of fatigue under her striking blue eyes, and she needed to put a few pounds on her skinny frame, he didn't see any obvious signs of violence on her today. "You okay now?"

He was obliquely aware of A.J. watching the whole interchange with curiosity.

Mollie tapped her pad with her pen, ignoring his question. "Drinks?"

Did that mean no, she wasn't okay and needed help? Or, was she dismissing him as in, *It's none of your business, Standage*?

Joel sank against the back of the booth, wondering why he cared one way or the other about her answer. He acknowledged the flutter of concern that quickened his pulse at the idea she could still be in danger, knowing he was a man who could help her. He was equally aware of the dark cloud of colossal failure that settled like an ice-cold storm front in his brain. He had no business rescuing anybody. Not anymore.

If only he'd picked up on those signs of rejection from Cici before that fateful night. He'd felt the distance growing between him and his fiancée. He'd been working too much, and he'd suspected she'd gone back to using again. But he'd been trying to make things right. He'd been in rescue mode, determined to save her from her addiction and remind her of the relationship that had once flourished between them.

Meanwhile, Cici had been using her knowledge about Joel's job as payment for the opioids that ruled her life. And when information alone was no longer enough for her suppliers, she'd fingered him as a cop working undercover in their organization. Cici hadn't survived the hell they'd put her through for keeping his identity a secret for so long. And Joel had literally died trying to save her one last time.

Joel was lost in the painful memories when A.J. spoke again. "You're right, ma'am. It's too hot for coffee today. I'll take iced tea. Plenty of ice. No lemon."

Those big blue eyes looked at Joel, and he

nearly forgot the question. Drinks. *Get your head in the game, Standage.* "Same."

"What can I get you gentlemen to eat?" She jotted down their order, gathered their plastic menus, and left as politely and quietly as she'd come.

Joel watched her every step of the way, as she stopped and picked up some empty plates from one table, set them in a tub in a window to the kitchen, then put in their order on a computer at the far end of the soda fountain. The dog he'd noticed earlier followed her every step, then sat on his haunches beside her while she tapped the order onto the screen. Mollie's left hand slipped down to pet the dog's head. She murmured something, and the dog leaned against her. After she tapped in the last item on the screen, he watched a real smile blossom across her mouth as she dropped to her knees and hugged the dog around the shoulders. Definitely her dog, judging by the attachment the two shared.

Joel nearly smiled himself at the tender moment, when he noticed the vest the dog wore. It was more than a harness to connect a leash to. The vest had a handle, reflective tape, and the words *Service Dog* emblazoned on it.

Why did Mollie Crane need a service dog? Was she in some kind of trouble? Had she been left with a medical condition from the injuries

August Di Salvo had repeatedly given her? It wouldn't be a stretch to suspect she'd been left with some kind of post-traumatic stress after surviving that marriage, either.

Joel straightened in his seat, the rusty urge to find out what was wrong and what he could do to help sparking through his veins. Only, he wasn't really much help to anybody these days. He dug his fingertips into his rebuilt legs, remembering pain without truly feeling it. He was a thirty-two-year-old man, hobbled up like he was decades older, and unable to fully trust anybody—not even himself.

What the hell kind of help did he think he could offer the prickly waitress?

He watched the tough woman push to her feet and order the dog to his bed at the end of the counter before washing her hands and carrying a tray out to another table. She'd been clear about not wanting his help two years ago. Why should he think anything had changed since then?

A.J. drew his attention back to him. "You two have a connection?"

"We met when I was working undercover for August Di Salvo. I was his driver. She was the missus. He beat the crap out of her, and I tried to help. Without success." Joel's gaze continued to track Mollie as she moved around the diner. "I couldn't get her out of that situation. To be honest, after that first night I found her with choke marks on her neck and a black eye, I didn't have much contact with her. Di Salvo kept her isolated from staff like me. I drove her a few places, but someone was always with her—Di Salvo, his parents, security. They didn't let her say much. She must have gotten herself out of the marriage somehow after I left."

"She remembers you."

"I ran into her one more time last year. Here at Pearl's. She must have just started working. A customer—one of our boys in blue, sadly—was getting handsy with her." Joel shook his head at the memory. "Rocky Garner? He works patrol."

A.J.'s laugh held little humor. "I know him. He's not doing KCPD any favors in the PR department."

Joel knew the veteran cop's reputation, too, having researched him after the incident. He couldn't recall the exact number of times Garner had been put on report for using excessive force or being inappropriate with female suspects. But it was enough to keep him from advancing in rank. Garner had to be a decade older than Joel, and he'd yet to make sergeant or earn his detective's shield. "I tried to help, but Mollie acted like she had no clue who I was. It wasn't too long after that I went on my…last assignment." The one that had nearly got him killed, gutted him emotionally, and left him sitting at a desk at KCPD. "Didn't expect she'd still be here after all this time. I figured waiting tables was a stopgap measure for her. Until her alimony came through, or she got hired for another job." He briefly replayed that encounter in his head. "She didn't have the dog with her then, either."

Joel felt A.J. studying him and met his dark gaze with an arched eyebrow. "Think you could rekindle your acquaintance with her? Develop a friendship?"

"What?" Oh, no. His boss couldn't be asking what he thought he was. "I don't do UC work anymore, A.J. Besides, she saw me in uniform last year." He fingered the lanyard and badge hanging from his neck. "She knows I'm a cop."

"You don't have to pretend to be anything but a cop. I'm not asking you to marry the woman or infiltrate this place as a fry cook. But it couldn't hurt to chat her up and find out what she knows about Di Salvo's operation. Word on the street is that he's courting some new business associates. And not the respectable kind." A.J. leaned in again, dropping his voice to a low-pitched whisper. "We couldn't make the charges stick the last time. I'd love to have dirt on his lawyer, who got him off with a slap on the wrist, and find out how his parents got our witnesses to recant their testimony. And I'd love to find out about his dealings with Roman Hess. That guy's as dirty as they come. If we could tie those two together, we could make an arrest stick on both of them."

Joel couldn't believe what he was hearing. A.J. wasn't playing. "You want to go after the entire Di Salvo empire?"

"They play at being pillars of the community, but I think they're all dirty. At the least, they're laundering money for a half dozen criminal organizations across the country. At worst, they're making a play to control this city on the scale of Tom Pendergast in the 1920s and '30s, or the Meade family in the 2000s." The senior detective relaxed back in his seat, as if this ambitious assignment was a done deal. "I've talked this over with Chief Taylor. He's all in for launching another investigation into the Di Salvo family."

And now this meeting made sense.

"Did you know Mollie worked here when you invited me to lunch?"

A.J. didn't try to deny it. "One—you don't belong behind a desk. You've got good instincts about people—"

"That's crap."

"With the glaring exception of your ex. Otherwise, you read people. You read situations. I bet I could ask you about any person in this diner, and you could tell me their location, what they're doing, and if I need to be worried about any of them."

Maybe he could. Although, the only thing alarming him right now was this conversation. "Two—you can keep your cool when things go sideways. That's a natural talent you're wasting shuffling papers behind a desk. Three—your detective's badge is going to get rusty if you don't start actively working cases again. I don't want to lose you. KCPD doesn't want to lose you. What your woman did to you is every undercover cop's worst nightmare. But you survived. I'm sure you've got some PTSD from everything you went through—and I hope you're seeing Dr. Kilpatrick-Harrison or one of the other department counselors for that."

He was. Although he'd missed one appointment because of a conflict with his physical therapy schedule. And he had simply skipped the last two because he hated talking about the damn feelings he couldn't yet put into words.

"Did she report me for not showing up?" Joel asked, wondering if that was another reason for this meeting.

"Dr. Kilpatrick-Harrison said she was worried about you. Brought it to my attention that you keep putting off your appointments."

"Maybe I'm not interested in passing her psych eval and getting back out on the streets."

A.J. scowled. "I'm not just talking as your supervisor here, Joel. I'm talking as your friend. Don't let those bastards break you. Don't let them change the good man you are. Take this assignment. Prove to yourself that you're still a good cop. That you're still a good man who deserves to be happy. Who needs to feel useful. Who has to learn how to trust again." He paused to let his words sink in. "Like I said, this is not deep cover. You don't have to be anything but a KCPD detective. But if you could get close to Mollie Di Salvo—"

"Mollie Crane," Joel corrected.

A.J. nodded. "All I'm asking is that you get close enough to Mollie *Crane* to find out what— if anything—she knows about her ex-husband's criminal activities. If she's in the dark about him, then you're done. If you find out she can help us in any way, then we'll have another discussion about what our next step is at that time."

He'd been physically cleared to return to active duty, but he wasn't sure he was mentally ready. There was a part of him that wanted to get back into the game, but he was equally leery of misjudging the people around him so badly that he'd be setting himself up for a world of hurt. Again. Or worse, letting someone else down the way he'd failed his late girlfriend.

He visually tracked down Mollie and found

her fussing impatiently with her dog, using hand signals and looking a little flustered. "I wouldn't know how to start a relationship, anymore. Real or fake."

"Find out what she cares about." A.J. turned to follow Joel's focus as Mollie fell to her knees and petted the dog, then teased him with a large gray toy that looked suspiciously like a teddy bear. "Never mind. I think your first step is pretty obvious."

"What's that?"

A.J. grinned. "Ask her about the dog."

THE MAN WITH the binoculars merged into the shadows inside his parked car. Although there was still some sun warming the sky on this late summer night, he was an expert at blending in and being overlooked, underestimated. When he did want someone's attention, he knew how to get it. But the time wasn't right for that yet. He learned so much more, was far more successful in getting things done, when he hung back to assess a situation first—learn the players and what he might be up against. Knowledge was power. Knowing his enemy's weak points and how to exploit them gave him the control over others that he craved.

He watched the woman walking her mutt across the street, dumping the plastic bag of excrement she'd dutifully picked up in the public trash can on the sidewalk as they hurried past his position. Although her gaze was on a swivel, looking for any threats, she didn't see him.

"There you are, sweetheart." He glanced down at the crumpled photograph in his lap, then lifted his gaze to study her again. Mollie Di Salvo could change her hair color and the quality of her clothes, but she hadn't changed her face. Even without makeup, he'd know her anywhere. She exuded that natural, all-American country girl vibe that he found so prosaic. "I've got you now."

It hadn't been hard to track down her place of work. But with an unlisted, pay-by-the-minute phone number and address, it had been harder to identify where she was hiding herself these days. Her apartment was in an older, well-maintained three-story red brick building, just a few blocks from Pearl's Diner and the pocket park at City Market, where she'd exercised her dog.

His lips curled with an arrogant smile. Once, she'd been at the top of Kansas City society. Now her world had shrunk to three city blocks.

She pulled a key card from the purse slung over her shoulder before crossing the street and approaching her building. He'd get inside another time to locate her exact apartment. For now, he was learning her routine. Did she work the same schedule at the diner every day? Walk the same route home every night? Did she drive a car? Take public transportation? Was she seeing anyone? Who were her friends?

Was that mangy wannabe police dog with her 24/7?

Did she think that reject of a mutt was going to protect her? When the time came, if he couldn't distract the dog with a steak, he'd shoot the mutt. He had plans for Miss Mollie, and he didn't want to be interrupted by man or beast.

She'd dishonored the Di Salvo family. Maybe she even thought she had outsmarted them. No Di Salvo, and no one who had ever worked for them, would tolerate what she'd done for long. If she didn't know there was a target on her back, she was sadly oblivious.

He could play this game for a while. Have fun with her. Edward and Bernadette would be so pleased with his initiative. And if he wasn't amply rewarded by the people who were supposed to respect him, then he'd take what he was missing out of Miss Mollie's hide.

He might get in trouble for it. But the satisfaction would be so worth it.

Besides, he'd have to get caught first.

And no one had ever been able to take him down.

Chapter Three

Even though it was his day off, and Joel could wear jeans and a T-shirt and forgo shaving his morning scruff, he still looped his badge around his neck and strapped his gun to his belt to remind himself that he didn't have to play any undercover part. If he was going to do this, he intended to be straight up-front with Mollie Crane about who and what he was.

After locking the door to his small gray bungalow, he paused for a few moments to scan up and down the block. He acknowledged his widowed neighbor out watering the flowers blooming in a riot of pots on her front porch. He recognized the cars parked in driveways, and took note of the people driving past he didn't know. His heart revved a little and his fist closed around the handle of his cane when one young man turned in the driver's seat and made eye contact with him.

But the guy kept on driving until he turned into a driveway farther down the block. One of the teenage girls who lived there charged out the front door and hurried to climb inside the passenger side of the car. The two teens kissed, then waved to the girl's father standing in the doorway before backing out of the drive and heading on their way. Not the enemy. Not a contact from his past. Not a threat marking him for death.

Forcing his heartbeat to slow, he headed down the concrete steps and crossed to the faded red Chevy pickup in the driveway. Mentally, he knew the older neighborhood of Brookside, south of downtown Kansas City, was a decent, safe place to live. He'd hoped to move Cici in one day, get married, and start a family together. But she hadn't wanted him to save her. Emotionally, he still felt the loss of that pipe dream—she'd loved the drugs more than she loved him. He understood now not to take anything or anyone at face value. Everyone had secrets they were willing to die for—or kill for—to keep. And he wasn't going to be blindsided by putting his trust in the wrong person again.

He opened the truck door and shoved his cane across the bench seat. The plain metal stick was more of a mental crutch than a physical one these days, but when his muscles got achy from overuse or a change in the weather, he liked to have it with him to keep from limping along like an old man, or worse, falling flat on his face. He'd

briefly considered playing up his wounded warrior status to gain Mollie's sympathy and develop
a relationship in which she felt compelled to take
care of him and thus spend more time with him.

But the small print on his man card didn't
want her to see him that way—weak, damaged,
something less. He wanted to be the man he
used to be around her—sharp, confident, a few
steps ahead of everyone else in the room. He
thought Mollie was pretty. She seemed quiet and
sweet, if understandably skittish about men. And
though she wasn't acting much like it now, the
woman he'd met that night at the Di Salvo estate had a backbone of steel. All things he would
have been attracted to if he hadn't been burned
so badly by Cici—things he was *still* attracted
to if he was honest with himself. It was his faith
in his own judgment and ability to handle a relationship that he needed to shore up before he
got involved with another woman.

Not that he was getting involved with Mollie Crane.

Not an undercover op. He didn't have to
watch his back or keep an eye out for whomever might trade his life for another fix. He was
a cop, straight up. Just a cop following up on his
supervisor's strongly worded suggestion that he
strike up a friendship with one Mollie Crane,
previously Di Salvo, and see if he could get any

inside information on a man who'd gotten away with breaking numerous laws and hurting too many people for way too long. Joel had to remember to look at this as if he was cultivating a CI, a confidential informant, who might be able to help the department build a case against her ex.

This absolutely was not a date. Or the prelude to one.

But he had to admit he was a little bit excited—and a little bit nervous—about cultivating a relationship with Mollie. Not unlike the way he'd felt years ago in high school when he'd worked up the courage to ask the girl he liked out on his first date.

Not a date!

Reminding himself to stay in the moment and not worry about any suspicions or self-doubts, Joel climbed inside the pickup that was as up-to-date and well taken care of under the hood as it was beat-up on the outside. He loved how the engine purred with power when he turned over the ignition. His face relaxed with a genuine smile. At least one part of him hadn't been shredded by the incident with Cici. He loved working on engines in his spare time and had done a bang-up job restoring his truck and keeping it running like a dream under the hood. Giving himself a mental slap on the back, he backed out of the driveway and headed toward the City Market north of downtown. Ten minutes later, he was pulling into a parking space around the corner from Pearl's Diner.

Leaning on his cane, he took a couple of deep breaths. He'd timed his arrival for what he hoped was the end of the lunch rush so that Mollie wouldn't be too distracted by work. Plus, there'd be a smaller audience to see him and give him grief back at the Precinct offices, if his efforts to get better acquainted with the blue-eyed waitress crashed and burned. There always seemed to be someone from KCPD here, thanks to the diner's location, its early and late hours, and its delicious, homestyle food.

Taking one last deep breath, Joel pulled open the door to the diner and walked up to the petite blonde who was wiping down menus at the hostess stand. "Mrs. Kincaid?"

She looked up and studied him from head to toe, taking in his casual dress, his gun and his badge number before she met his gaze again. "Detective Standage, is it?"

"Yes, ma'am. I wasn't sure you remembered me."

"You're A.J.'s friend."

He smirked before correcting her. "He's my boss, actually. But yes, I met him here the other day."

"I remember." She tucked the menus away, save for one. "You're here by yourself today?" When he nodded, she turned away and headed toward a small table. "This way."

"Could you seat me in Mollie's section?" With a quick scan of the diner, he didn't immediately spot the curly-haired waitress. A brief moment of panic that he hadn't been smart enough to check to see if she was working today quickly passed when he saw the Belgian Malinois curled up asleep on his bed behind the soda fountain. He smiled. The dog wouldn't be here unless Mollie was. "I'd like to talk to her. But I'll order food if I need to. I don't want to get her in trouble."

The diner owner faced him again. "Does she know you're coming?"

"No, ma'am. To be honest, I had to work up the courage to come here and talk to her." He tapped his leg with his cane. "I'm a little out of practice with polite society."

The petite blonde crossed her arms in front of her and canted her hips to one side, studying him again. He got the sense she was looking for something different this time. "You're interested in Mollie? In the nine months I've known her, she's never dated anyone. FYI? You've got a tough hill to climb if that's your goal."

She didn't know the half of it. "We're old acquaintances. The last few months have been tough for me. I'm looking to rekindle a friendship with someone from before that time." None of that was a lie. Although, it sure sounded like he was interested in more than a friendship with Mollie Crane.

"Are you a good man?" Melissa asked bluntly.

Joel stood up a little straighter. "I try to be. I don't know exactly what kind of man I am anymore. Like I said, I'm out of practice."

"It doesn't matter what your social skills are, Detective. You're either a good man or you're not." She arched a golden eyebrow at him. "Don't be offended if I ask my husband about you."

"Sawyer?" He'd worked some cases with the decorated detective and believed the respect he felt for Sawyer Kincaid was mutual. "I think he'd give me a decent recommendation. But I'm glad you're looking out for the people who work for you. Makes me believe Mollie's safer now than she was before."

"Good answer." Her lips curled into a full-blown smile. Strong and beautiful. No wonder his coworker was so head over heels with her. "Come on. I'll seat you at the counter. You can catch Mollie when she goes on her break in a few minutes."

"Thank you, ma'am."

She waited until he was seated on the red vinyl stool before sliding the menu in front of him.

"Uh-uh. I appreciate you being polite, but I'm not old enough to be a 'ma'am.' If Sawyer vets you, and Mollie okays it, then I'm Melissa, and you're welcome here anytime."

Joel summoned a smile of his own. "Thanks."

"I'll let her know you're here."

The diner's owner pushed through the swinging door into the kitchen. She came back out a minute or so later, nodded to him, then went back to her work at the front of the restaurant.

It was another minute or so before it swung open again and Mollie stepped out. She stood there a moment before looking to her dog and summoning him to her side. The dog leaned against her thigh, and she rested her hand atop his head before taking a deep breath and finally crossing to the opposite side of the counter from him. The dog followed right beside her and sat when she stopped. "Joel?"

He stood and hooked the handle of his cane on his side of the counter. "Hey, Mollie."

Although she continued to pet the dog's head, her blue eyes tilted up to meet his. "Melissa said you wanted to speak to me?"

Joel frowned at the pulse he could see beating in her neck. "Do I make you nervous?" he asked, refusing to acknowledge that his own heart rate had increased the moment he saw her.

"Lots of things make me nervous," she confessed, twisting her lips into a wry smile. She tipped her head toward Magnus. "That's why I keep this guy with me." He was surprised when she elaborated on what exactly was making her nervous now. "I don't like surprises. I didn't know you were coming today. Is this police business?"

"Why would it be police business?" He frowned at her question. Technically, he wasn't working on an active investigation. This was more of a fact-finding mission, finding out for A.J. if there was any new, compelling information that warranted launching a new investigation. Unless *Mollie* was expecting to be contacted by someone from KCPD? "Did something happen? Do you need a cop?"

"No," she answered quickly. "If you aren't working a case, why do you need to see me?"

Joel gave himself a mental reminder that Mollie Crane was an intelligent woman who'd proved herself a survivor. She might be nervous around him—around men—but that didn't mean she wasn't smart. He had a feeling she'd see right through any story he'd try to put over on her.

Admiring her courage to explain her reaction to him, Joel gestured to the stool beside him. "Melissa said you were ready to take a break. Would you like to sit down and have a coffee with me?"

Her uneasy reaction gave way to suspicion. "You mean like a date?"

"I mean like two people getting better acquainted, maybe even becoming friends." He leaned toward her and dropped his voice into a whisper. "I have a feeling I didn't get to meet the real Mollie two years ago. I know you didn't meet the real me."

She considered his invitation for a moment before tucking a loose curl beneath the headband she wore. "I need to take Magnus out for a walk to do his business and get some exercise."

"Around this neighborhood? By yourself?" There were a lot worse places in the city. But a woman alone on the streets of K.C.? Especially during the height of the tourist season this close to the City Market when there were hundreds of strangers, including the pickpockets and muggers who often accompanied large crowds, visiting the neighborhood? Wouldn't be his first choice if he was responsible for her safety.

But…he wasn't. *Not a date!*

"It's safe enough during the day." She offered him a slight smile that blossomed into something beautiful when she pulled a fuzzy gray teddy bear from beneath the counter and the dog danced in place beside her. "Magnus. Leash." The Belgian Malinois trotted over to his bed and came back carrying his leash in his mouth. He stood still for Mollie to attach it to his harness and was rewarded with words of praise and a short game of tug-of-war with his toy. "Besides, Magnus looks pretty scary, so no one bothers me."

Scary? With a teddy bear in his mouth? Although, the toy did look pretty mangled from where Joel was standing, so anyone who accosted Mollie might take the dog's energy, sharp teeth, and the strength of his jaw into consideration before approaching them. Instead of disparaging the ferociousness of her dog, Joel picked up his cane. "May I come with you?"

"To walk the dog?"

Ask her about the dog.

Remembering A.J.'s advice, he nodded. "I like dogs. Grew up with them. Although I haven't had one of my own since leaving home. My…" *late girlfriend didn't like them.* Nope. He wasn't going there with Mollie. He suspected the fact that he hadn't been able to keep his last girlfriend safe wouldn't earn him any trust points. "I miss being around one," he said, instead, dredging up his rusty skills that enabled him to say the right thing to the right person at the right time.

Mollie must have heard enough truth in his explanation to agree to his request to accompany her. "Okay." She thumbed over her shoulder to the kitchen. "We'll go out the back way.

The alley comes out right across from the dog park where I take him during the day."

Joel nodded and followed Mollie and Magnus through the swinging door. He was inhaling the tantalizing scents of baking fruit pies and some Italian sauce sort of magic when a gravelly voice barked out, "What the hell is that mutt doin' in my kitchen? And who's this guy?"

"Language, Herb!" Joel had already stepped between Mollie and the grouchy shout when a woman with a blond ponytail waddled out from behind a bank of ovens. Her cheeks were flushed from the heat of the kitchen. She was about the same age and height as Mollie, and her arms were hugged around her very pregnant belly. She smiled at Mollie. "Whew! I wish I was going on your walk with Magnus. I feel like I'm the one baking in here."

Mollie nudged Joel aside to take the other woman's hand and squeeze it. "Didn't the doctor say you were supposed to stay off your feet as much as possible?" she chided gently. "I told you I know how to bake a good pie. My granny taught me."

The blonde woman kept hold of Mollie's hand. "Believe me, it's a lot easier to sit back here on a stool and work with the food than it is to wait tables. This little one will be here any day. I swear he's already half the size of Matt. Matt Taylor—

that's my husband," she explained to Joel. "He's six-five." She rubbed her belly with her other hand as she smiled at him. "Who's your friend?"

A lanky older man with bushy gray eyebrows and an old USN tattoo on his forearm stepped up between the women. "Not my fault. I can't keep her sittin' down like she's supposed to be." He was where the growly voice had come from. "I swear to God, girlie, if you have that baby in my kitchen, *I'm* the one they'll be taking to the hospital." The words were complaints, but Joel thought he detected more of a protective papa bear in the man's stance. "You're sure he's a friend?" he asked Mollie. "You ain't never brought a man back here before. Hell, I ain't never seen you with a man, period. He ain't forcin' you to go somewhere, is he?"

Definitely a protective papa with the women who worked at the diner. "No, sir," Joel assured him, holding up his badge. "I'm one of the good guys. We're taking the dog for a walk."

"I'd like to hear that from her," he insisted.

"He's a friend, Herb." Joel glanced over to see Mollie smile at the older man. She put Magnus into a sit position, then made introductions. "Detective Joel Standage, this is my friend, Corie Taylor—responsible for all the delicious pies you've eaten here, and she's due to give birth to her second child next week."

"Not in my kitchen," the grouch with the bandanna tied around the top of his head insisted.

"And this grump is our chief cook and all-around ray of sunshine. Herb Valentino."

While Joel wanted to savor the unexpected snark in Mollie's comment and bask in the soft beauty of what he suspected was a rare smile, he remembered he was here hoping to earn Mollie's trust. Making friends with her friends seemed to be a good way to start. He extended his hand to the older man and nodded toward the faded black tattoo on his forearm. "You're a Navy man. Thank you for your service."

Herb seemed a little flustered to be acknowledged for his time in the military. But like the Navy men Joel knew best, he was proud to claim his ties to the letters and anchor inked on his arm. He reached out to shake Joel's hand. "I served twenty years on boats. Ten years on an aircraft carrier. I ran a tight mess."

"My dad was in the Gulf during Desert Storm. Marine. Demolitions expert. Defused a lot of land mines."

Herb's grip on Joel's hand tightened with a begrudging mutual respect. "He make it home?"

"Yes, sir." By the time they released hands, the cook seemed to see him as less of an intruder in his kitchen. "He stuck with it for twenty years.

Now he's an accountant here in K.C. Just a few years away from his civilian retirement."

"You didn't follow him into the service?"

Joel shook his head. "No mom in the picture. She left when I was eighteen. I was the oldest of three boys. I raised my younger brothers while Dad finished up his commitment. Both my brothers serve now, though. Army National Guard and a career Marine."

"You serve our city as a police officer," Mollie pointed out from beside him.

"Yeah, I do." He glanced over at her and nodded his thanks for her support. "Dad remarried a few years back. Sweet lady. Another accountant in his office."

Corie pointed to Mollie and grinned. "Mollie is our numbers guru here. She tutored my son through his HAL math class, that's High Ability Learner, meaning I didn't understand his pre-Calculus, and she worked out a huge snafu in the books here at the diner. The cook who was here before Herb was ordering food on the sly to supply his own pop-up restaurant—on Melissa's tab."

"Fired his ass," Herb added. "Good thing I came along when I did. These two little ladies were trying to run this kitchen on their own. With no clue how to do it for paying customers. Slow as molasses."

Corie linked her arm through Herb's. "We make good food, but we're nowhere near as fast as this guy. Like he said, he runs a tight kitchen."

"Don't make me blush, girlie," the older man groused before shooing Joel and Mollie toward the back door. "You two get on with whatever you're doin' and get that mutt out of here."

"He's a service dog," Mollie reminded the gruff cook. "I'm allowed to have him with me wherever I go. He's never bothered anything in your kitchen."

"Well, I don't have to like it. And don't be late comin' back because I'll need your help gettin' prepped for the dinner shift." He patted Corie's hand where it rested on his arm. "I'm sendin' this one home."

Mollie nodded. "I'll help until Melissa needs me out front. And Corie? Listen to Herb. Go home if you need to. Put your feet up. I can pull the pies out of the oven and do the prep work when I get back."

"And have my darling husband hovering over me 24/7? The baby's room has been ready for a month. My grandmother-in-law gave me that great baby shower. At least here I'm allowed to do something." Corie shooed them on their way, too. "Go. No matter what this guy says, the baby and I are fine. Not my first rodeo."

Mollie glanced over at Joel and tweaked her lips into another wry expression, as if she was rethinking saying yes to spending a few minutes with him. He needed to move them along before he failed his first assignment out of the office since coming back from his medical leave. "Maybe I should—"

"We'd better get going before your break is over," Joel pointed out. "Magnus needs his exercise."

Mollie nodded. "Of course, he does."

"Don't forget your key so you can get back in," Corie reminded her.

Mollie patted her apron pocket. "I've got it."

Joel nodded to the cook and baker. "Nice to meet you both." He automatically brushed his fingers across the small of Mollie's back to turn her to the back door and tried not to take it personally when she scooted away from his touch.

She peeled off her sweater and tied the sleeves around her middle, unwittingly accenting her narrow waist and the flare of her hips, before tucking the teddy bear into the waistband created by the sweater. Giving a slight tug on the leash, she urged the dog into step between them. "Magnus, heel."

More distance. But considering who she'd been married to, Joel could understand how she'd be reluctant to have a man anywhere near her. He had his work cut out for him to earn her trust. But as long as she was willing to have a conversation with him, he'd take it as a win.

Chapter Four

Joel held open the heavy steel door that led into the alley behind the diner. Magnus leaped over the concrete step onto the asphalt and Mollie followed quickly behind him.

While he was instantly assaulted with the heat and humidity of the July afternoon, goose bumps pricked along his forearms. A potential ambush was his past talking, not the here and now. But it was second nature for him to check up and down the thoroughfare between two busy side streets, ensuring it was empty of traffic and pedestrians. The dumpster and recycling bin behind the restaurant gave easy places for someone to hide, as did the light poles and recessed doorways leading into the building across the alley.

He quickly shook off his suspicions and jogged to catch up with Mollie as she and Magnus headed toward the end of the alley at a fast clip. He couldn't help but check each hidey-hole as he passed it. But there was no enemy hidden here. And despite the sketchiness of a back alley, this one was remarkably clean. Other than a collection of cigarette butts on the ground at one back door, indicating a smoking area for employees, no doubt, there was no overflowing trash piled up beside the bins and dumpsters. And it looked like it would be well lit at night, judging by the lights on the centermost pole and above every door.

His nostrils flared with a steadying breath. He should be aware of his surroundings, but being paranoid about the bogeyman or some drug dealer's enforcer lying in wait to take him down would just mess with his head and keep him from being able to protect Mollie or himself if there was a real threat.

Of course, he wasn't here as her protector. The skills were there, but they were rusty. Thank goodness, this was all about striking up a friendship. *Not a date. Not a UC op where he had to be on guard around the clock. Just get reacquainted with the woman and talk. Then set up another time to talk again.*

Mollie looked over at him when he stepped up to the other side of Magnus. "You're moving pretty well without your cane," she pointed out.

He shrugged. "It's more for emergencies—in case my leg gives out."

"Does it give out a lot?"

He didn't want to read anything in her concerned tone. "Not really. Not anymore. I've had a lot of physical therapy to rebuild my muscle tone. It's more of a mental thing. For security."

She reached down and stroked Magnus's fur. "I understand that. Here's my security blanket." They stood in awkward silence for another minute, waiting for the light to change at the corner and allow them to cross safely. "I hope Herb didn't offend you," she said. The dog had dutifully stopped when she did, although he was panting with excitement at the outing. "It took me a while to figure out his bark is worse than his bite."

Glad for the change in topic, Joel smiled. "They're protective of you. Everyone who works at the diner is."

"We're protective of each other."

The light changed, and they waited for a black Lexus with tinted windows to turn at the corner and drive past before they stepped off the curb and crossed the street to the pocket park. A couple reading a walking tour map skirted around them on the sidewalk. An older gentleman walked his miniature schnauzer out of the dog park across the street and latched the gate behind him before heading down the opposite sidewalk. Although Magnus's head swiveled on alert to both the tourists and the dog, he remained at Mollie's side unless she clicked her tongue behind her teeth and ordered Magnus into step beside her.

Although the grassy area of the dog park was only about twelve feet deep between the fence lining the sidewalk and the brick building on the opposite side, it stretched from one end of the half block to the other. There were benches and a leafy maple tree at either end, plus a waste bag dispenser and covered trash can chained to the fence near the gate.

"An urban dog playground," he mused, watching as Mollie unhooked Magnus from his leash and gave him permission to run and be off duty for a few minutes.

"I suppose so." Mollie wound his leash in her fist and headed for the shade at one end of the park. "Local fundraisers added the fake hydrant, agility ramp, and plastic barrel just last month. I imagine every dog in the neighborhood loves to come here and sniff and mark their territory."

She perched on one end of the bench and watched Magnus check out every object that was geared toward dogs, as well as the tree and bench at the far end of the park. She busied her hands with the woeful teddy bear and gave Joel a sideways glance to see if he was going to sit beside her. Taking the cue from her guarded posture, he sat at the far end of the bench, beyond arm's reach, and she inhaled a deep breath.

At the same time, her tummy growled. "Oops. Sorry about that."

"Am I keeping you from eating your lunch?"

"No," she answered a little too quickly for him to believe her.

His concern was genuine. "I don't want to be the reason you don't get enough food to eat today." He thumbed over his shoulder across the street. "We can head back."

"I'll eat dinner before I go home. Or I'll box up something to take with me." She paused long enough for Magnus to come trotting back to her for pets before he nudged at the teddy bear with his nose. "Silly boy. Go get it." She tossed the bear across the grass and Magnus tore out after it. "I've lost weight since the last time you saw me, haven't I."

"Yeah. But you've still got curves in all the right places." She raised her eyebrows at that comment. Maybe he should apologize, but he'd meant what he'd said. When Magnus returned and dropped the bear into her lap, Joel held his hand out for it. "May I?" Dark brown eyes followed the bear from Mollie's hand to his. "Go get it, boy!" He hurled the bear halfway across the park and watched the athletic dog chase it down and retrieve it. "Not that I should be noticing. But hey, I'm a guy. And I just want you to be healthy."

She chuckled softly, and Joel couldn't tear his gaze away from her gentle smile. With coffee-colored curls catching in the breeze and drifting across her cheeks and jawline, her skin flushed with the heat, and not a stitch of makeup that he could detect, he was struck full force by her natural beauty.

He felt himself smiling, too. "What? What did I say to make you laugh?"

"I heard my grandmother's voice in my head when you said that. *Are you healthy, Mollie Belle? Are you taking care of yourself? Eating right?* She was a fabulous cook, and she always fed me too much. When I went off to college, those questions came up in nearly every conversation we had." She tossed Magnus's teddy bear one more time, then tucked those loose curls back into the headband she wore. He could guess by the smile, and how it wistfully faded away, that her grandmother was a special, yet sad memory for her. "I'm not starving, Joel. Admittedly, when I first started working here, I didn't have a lot of money in my bank account." She shook her head. "Who am I kidding? I didn't even have a bank account back then. But Melissa took pity on me. She fed me breakfast during the job interview. Hired me before I'd finished my coffee. I'm not the best waitress, but I can put up with Herb, so I think she keeps me around for that reason alone." Joel grinned as he was meant to. "Plus, she has a soft spot for a hard-luck case like me and Magnus. Pearl—the original owner of the diner—gave Melissa a break when she needed one. I hope to pay her generosity forward one day, too."

Any urge to smile faded. Where was Mollie's money from her divorce? Joel made a mental note to research some court records to find out if there was some sort of legal issue with her alimony. Or if Di Salvo's slick lawyer had gotten him out of paying anything, just like he'd gotten August Di Salvo off on the major charges that had been brought against him. But instead of pressing for info related to her ex right this minute, he asked, "You have enough money for food now?"

Mollie nodded. "I have an account at the Cattlemen's Bank extension over by the City Market now. And a studio apartment down the street that allows dogs. It's just stress. I don't always feel like eating."

"You have to eat to keep your strength up, Moll." He left his cane leaning against the bench and stood to play a vigorous game of tug-of-war with Magnus. Once he'd won, the high-energy Belgian Malinois danced and drooled, eager for Joel to throw the toy again. "Go get it!" Joel looked down at Mollie. "It was just an observation. I sure hope I don't sound like your grand-mother."

Although it was barely a noise in her throat, he loved that she laughed again. "My granny was five foot nothing. You're a giant compared to her. Heck, so was I, and I'm only five-six. She had a beautiful, melodic voice. Not like that gravelly tone you have." She nodded to the ink sticking out beneath the sleeves of his T-shirt. "And, ab-solutely no tats on Granny. So, no worries that I'm confusing the two of you." He liked that she'd noticed some details about him. He also noted that the moment she started talking about her grandmother, her shoulders relaxed their stiff posture and she'd pulled a silver locket from the neckline of her uniform and was rubbing it be-tween her fingers. "It's having somebody wor-rying about me that made me think of her."

Her smile disappeared abruptly, and she tucked the locket back inside her dress. "You look like you've lost weight, too. I mean you've still got muscles in all the right places, but…" She blushed as she realized she'd echoed the compliment he'd given her earlier. "Does it have something to do with your injuries?"

Joel grabbed his cane and sat again. The topic was bound to come up. And since he'd probed into her health issues, it was probably only fair that he share a bit of his recent past, too. "I was in the hospital for a couple of months. Multiple surgeries on both legs." He turned his left arm in front of him, pointing out the pink puckers of skin that marred the lines of tribal symbols and motivational words that curled around his forearm. "Some of the cuts got infected."

"That sounds horrible. What happened?" Gunshot to both his knees. A couple of thugs trying to butcher him alive while he was incapacitated. Beating what was left of him and then literally dumping him in the trash. He'd lost so much blood by the time he reached the hospital that his heart had stopped. Drug dealers didn't take kindly to cops who infiltrated their operation. When he didn't answer, Mollie came up with her own explanation. "Sounds like you were in a horrible accident."

"I got hurt working a case," he responded vaguely.

She looked as though she suspected there was more to his injuries, but he wasn't going to share the gory details. He was here to get her to talk— not the other way around.

But she had an inkling that he'd suffered more than a car accident. "Did Augie's men do that to you?" she asked in a strained whisper. She reached toward one of the scars but pulled away before making contact, and Joel regretted missing the chance to find out what her skin felt like against his. "He had a man who worked for him, Beau Regalio. Augie called him his bodyguard, but he could be—"

"I know who Beau is." An enforcer of the first order. He'd confiscated one of Beau's guns that he'd turned in as evidence, but somehow Di Salvo's lawyer had gotten the forensic report tying the weapon to a witness tampering crime tossed out on a technicality. "No, he didn't hurt me. I was done working your ex-husband's case when this happened." He hated the words coming out of his mouth. "Did Beau ever hurt you?"

Her skin blanched, and she shook her head. "That was Augie's prerogative. But Beau never looked away. It was almost like he…enjoyed the violence. You're the only one in that house who ever tried to help me."

Joel swore beneath his breath. "I should have done something more."

"No." He flinched when her compassion finally overcame her fear, and her fingertips brushed across his forearm. Her touch was soft and cool against his warm skin, but she didn't linger. "You couldn't risk blowing your cover and jeopardize your investigation. I know that now."

He nodded. "Plus, money buys a lot of loyalty. We couldn't make the major charges against your ex stick because witnesses changed their testimony and evidence simply disappeared."

"If I could have stopped Augie from hurting people…" A warm breeze caught her hair and dragged a curl across her cheek. Joel clenched his fingers around his cane to keep from reaching out to tuck it back behind her ear. "Defying him was never really an option. He made so many business deals that were shady. I'm a math teacher, not a forensic accountant. But I could tell that some of the arrangements made at meetings I overheard weren't legit. The numbers simply didn't add up. And some of his investors who reneged on a project…? They'd be at a dinner party at our house one night, and the next week I'd see their name in the business pages of the newspaper, losing their company or closing shops and laying off workers. There was even one man…" Her voice faded away. "I saw his name in the obituaries. He…killed himself."

Yeah, he knew about the man's suicide—and probably some other cases of violence related to her ex she *didn't* know about. He reached over and lightly wound his fingers around her wrist. Her wide eyes locked on to his. "Nothing August Di Salvo did is on you. You were a victim as much as anybody. I'm glad you got away from him."

It was on the tip of his tongue to ask her exactly how she had gotten away from the Di Salvo family. But even in the heat of the afternoon, he could feel the skin beneath his grasp chilling. Her cheeks paled and she reached into the neckline of her uniform again and tugged on the long silver chain to reach her locket.

As gentle as it was, he popped his grip open and pulled away. "I'm sorry. I remember that night in the diner a few months back. You don't like men touching you."

"That's not it. Well, that customer was a jerk." She moved her fingers and focus to the top of Magnus's brown and black fur. "Actually, I miss having someone touch me. But… I need to be in control of what's happening. I need time to know who the person is and why they're putting their hands on me."

He remembered her warning in the diner. "No surprises."

Visibly calming herself, she tilted her gaze back to his. "Granny used to hug me all the time. I miss the warmth and the comfort of that physical contact. Back when I was a naive newlywed with Augie, I liked when he put his arm around me, or when we'd make out—" Nope. He did not want that image in his head. "And then, he changed. Or rather, he let the real Augie out." He'd seen plenty of proof of the real Augie Di

Salvo. "I hate that he ruined hugs and cuddling and even holding hands for me."

With the urge to reach for her pulsing through his fingers, Joel hated that, too. Mollie Crane was a pretty woman with a wry sense of humor and a quiet intelligence that he longed to get to know better. But understanding that his touch might be more frightening than comforting, he wrapped all ten fingers around his cane and changed the subject. "That's a pretty locket. Looks antique."

"It was Granny's. She raised me. It's one of the few things I have of hers." Her nostrils flared with a deep breath as she paused. "Augie sold, threw out, or burned the rest of the things I brought with me into the marriage. Including the house where I grew up."

Clearly her grandmother had meant the world to her. "I'm so sorry."

"He didn't see cute and adorable and a tribute to early twentieth-century architecture the way I did. He saw *old*. And *small*. He said a Di Salvo would never live in a dump like that. He didn't want anyone connecting the property to him once we were married. I didn't know he had done it until after we'd been married for a while. I was feeling homesick and had driven out to see it. He took great pride in explaining how that part of my life was over, that I was a Di Salvo now, not a hick from the Ozarks."

"He can't erase your memories. Or what your grandmother meant to you."

"It was a beautiful little cottage. Granny took such good care of it. She planted a huge garden in the back. During December, she put up enough lights and decorations to rival the Plaza lights. I loved growing up there." Tears glistened in her eyes, and Magnus rested his head in her lap, nudging at her hands. She leaned over to touch her nose to the dog's, then scrubbed her hands all around Magnus's head. "I'm okay, boy. Mama's okay."

Joel wanted to comfort her, too. But while the dog's touch was welcome, his was not. He needed to keep the conversation moving before he did something stupid like hunt down Di Salvo and burn *his* house to the ground. "So, Magnus? He's your service dog?"

She nodded, sitting up straight before tossing the teddy bear and letting Magnus chase it again.

"Post-traumatic stress?"

"He alerts when I'm about to have a panic attack. So I can get somewhere safe, make sure I pull over if I'm driving, or to comfort me to keep it from happening, like he did just now. He's supposed to, anyway. He's still in training, I guess. I feel safer when he's around, too. He can be scary when he gets fired up. Although, he's hard of hearing. He misses a few things. That's why he couldn't qualify for KCPD's K-9 Corps." Magnus trotted back and dropped the slobbery bear into her lap. "I'm sorry. I'm going on about stuff you're probably not interested in."

"Mollie, I'm interested in anything you have to say. You can talk to me. Tell me things. I'm not the bad guy here."

"I didn't think you were." She glanced up at him. "Why *are* you here?"

Suddenly, this assignment he hadn't wanted was becoming way too personal. How much truth did he share without blowing the most interesting and meaningful fifteen minutes he'd had since the night he'd lost everything? Partial truths weren't exactly a lie, were they? "I was surprised to see you still working at Pearl's Diner. I wanted to know how you've been, if you're okay. Just because I haven't seen you in a while doesn't mean I haven't thought about you. I felt guilty that I didn't do more to help you."

"I'm okay," she answered quickly in a tone he didn't quite believe. "I honestly never expected to see you again. I thought I'd left Augie's world behind me. That's my goal."

"I'm not part of that world. I'm a cop. A detective with KCPD."

"I know that now."

"You seeing anyone?" Well, hell. Where had that question come from?

She shook her head, stirring the curls against her jawline. "I don't socialize much. I go to work, go home. Go to dog training or run errands, go home again." Her question proved even more surprising. "Are *you* seeing anyone?"

That made him go to the dark side. "My girl-friend…died."

"Oh, Joel. I'm so sorry. Was it the same accident where you got hurt?"

She held his gaze for the longest time as he worked through his personal hell to find some civilized words he could share about that night. Before the words about betrayal and loss and a wasted life could come, Joel was startled from his thoughts by Magnus rising on his hind legs and propping his front paws against his chest. Instead of blue eyes, he was looking straight into the darkest of brown eyes and feeling the dog's warm pants of breath against his face.

"I'm so sorry. Magnus! Sit!" Mollie tugged on his leash, but the dog plopped down on Joel's feet and rested his head atop his thigh. "You're *my* comfort dog, you big goof."

Pulling a rusty laugh from his throat, Joel scrubbed his hands around the dog's ears and neck. "He's okay."

"I'm sorry. He must have sensed your distress." Her bottom lip disappeared briefly between her teeth as she offered him an apologetic smile. "Honestly, I could, too."

"I do get stressed thinking about Cici and everything that happened. She had an addiction to opioids. Wish I could have saved her. Wish I'd done a lot of things differently the night I lost her." He was talking to the dog as he continued to pet his warm fur. He was beginning to see how a good therapy dog could truly help someone dealing with tragedy and trauma. A warm, living, breathing distraction. Something to focus on besides stress and pain. "Good boy. Thanks. Go to Mama." Nudging the dog's muscular shoulder, he guided Magnus back to Mollie. "I thought service dogs were supposed to focus on their owner."

"They are. Apparently, I've got the one reject who can't seem to remember that his job is to take care of *me*."

"Shouldn't he be more reliable than that? If he's supposed to protect you?" Maybe he was doing Mollie a disservice by interacting so much with Magnus. But he was smart, all boy, and pretty hard to resist.

"I'm meeting with our trainer tomorrow to see if there's more I can do to make him bond with me. He's deaf in one ear." She explained the flopped-over ear that seemed at odds with the Belgian Malinois's sleek lines. "I wonder if he's losing hearing in the other ear, as well. If he's looking at me and focused on me, he does fine. But he gets distracted too easily."

"I think he's just a friendly guy with a big heart. Trying to help as many people as he can."

"That's not how he's supposed to work."

"Look at how he's rubbing against your hand," Joel pointed out. "He's devoted to you."

"I guess. I'm still taking him in for a refresher course at K-9 Ranch."

"I've heard of the place. Just outside the city." He'd heard the owner had recently married a sheriff's deputy who sometimes helped KCPD with investigations that crossed jurisdictions with the county. "They do good work there. Rescuing dogs. Training them to be companion or service animals."

"I went there looking for a small dog, a little noisemaker who fit my little apartment and could give me the help I needed. But this big guy latched on to me from almost the moment I set foot on the ranch."

"He picked *you*."

"That's what Jessica, the ranch's owner, said, too. Sometimes I think he was just anxious to be adopted, and I was the first sucker to come along who'd take him."

"Don't sell yourself short." He leaned over to

pet Magnus again. "This guy's a smart dog. I don't think he'd make a mistake and choose the wrong person."

She rolled her eyes in a *Whatever* retort, and Joel got the idea that Mollie Crane had once been full of wry humor and attitude—before August Di Salvo had beaten the spirit out of her. Parts of his body that hadn't cared about much of anything for a long time perked up at the idea that he could get to know the old Mollie—the real Mollie—if he played his cards right. He was actually excited by the challenge of proving to her that he was someone who was safe enough to be herself with.

With anticipation still sparking through his veins, he stood as Mollie checked her watch and hooked up Magnus's leash. He needed a plan. He needed to spend more time with her. He needed to be the man who could rise to the challenges that A. J. Rodriguez and Mollie herself had unknowingly set before him.

"My break is almost up, and Magnus has done both his businesses," she announced. "I'd better be getting back before Melissa sends out a search party."

Joel helped clean up after the dog. He was racking his brain to come up with something more they could talk about as he held the gate open for an elderly couple bringing a pair of miniature poodles into the dog park. The three dogs sniffed each other as if they were all old friends, and the couple exchanged polite greetings with Mollie. Once she gave the order to *heel*, though, Magnus came right to her side and followed her through the gate. They crossed to the curb and stepped between two parked cars, waiting for the traffic to stop.

Not ready to end their conversation yet, Joel asked, "Melissa is married to a guy I know at KCPD. Sawyer Kincaid?"

Mollie nodded, watching the cars, as well as the pedestrians on either side of the street go by. He was glad to see her be so aware of her surroundings. "He comes in a lot. Sometimes with their kids, sometimes with his partner. He's very protective of her."

He detected the note of wistfulness in her voice and tamped down the urge to be just as protective of Mollie. It wasn't his place. It might never be. "I've seen her at police functions, like the softball game with KCFD."

She smiled, her gaze watching every vehicle that drove past. Gray car. White car. Public works truck. Car with out of state plates. "Yeah. We've got a friendly in-house rivalry at the diner. Melissa is married to a cop, and Corie is married to a firefighter. They've all come in to eat after a game. They tease each other a lot.

I don't always like big, rowdy crowds like that. But it's all in fun. And the tips are great."

He could imagine. "You're more the stay home and read a book or watch a movie on TV kind of gal?"

"I used to enjoy a good celebration. But now I like quiet and predictable, which I guess makes me sound pretty boring, so yes."

Sounded a little bit like undercover work. "Too many people to be on guard against in a crowd, right?"

She looked up at him, perhaps surprised at his understanding, and nodded.

Blue minivan. Gray SUV.

"Still, those softball games are a hell of a lot of fun. You should come watch one." He thumped his thigh. "Not that they're going to ask me to play on the team again anytime soon."

For the first time since he'd known the dog, he heard Magnus growling a low-pitched warning in his throat.

At first, he assumed Magnus was making his presence known to one of the other dogs. But his dark eyes were tracking movement out on the street.

Joel felt his own hackles rise to attention. Black car driving slowly past. Tinted windows. Sunglasses and a lowered sun visor kept the driver's face from being visible. The car flashed its left turn signal and paused at the light. *Yeah, buddy, I notice it, too.*

"Magnus?" Mollie tugged on the dog's leash to turn his attention to her, and the growling ceased. "I don't know what's wrong with him."

"He's protecting you."

"From what?"

Joel was too paranoid to ignore anything suspicious in the people around him. Maybe if he hadn't ignored the danger signals when he'd run to Cici's aid that night, she'd be alive and he'd still be the cop he once had been. The black car stopped at the traffic light and he instinctively put his hand on Mollie's back and urged her forward. "Let's go."

When she arched her back away from his touch, he quickly pulled away. "I don't mean to flinch every time you touch me."

"My fault," he quickly apologized. "Didn't mean to startle you. Shall we?"

Even without sharing contact, she was moving across the street beside him. "It was good to see you again, Joel."

"Same here." He made sure the car turned the corner and drove away before relaxing enough to continue their conversation. "Is it okay if I stop by again to see you?"

"Why? You've checked up on me." She stopped at the end of the alleyway. "No bruises. No abuser.

I'm fine. I don't blame you for anything that happened to me, so you shouldn't blame yourself." She gestured to the cars on the street. "I'm assuming you parked somewhere around here? You don't need to walk me back to the diner."

"Uh-uh. A man makes sure the lady gets safely inside before he leaves her." Especially when the hairs on the back of his neck had been standing on end ever since Magnus had growled.

"Okay, Sir Galahad," she teased. "You may walk me to my alley door."

He fell into step beside her. "While I appreciate you letting me off the hook, I've enjoyed our conversation. I'm fascinated by your dog, curious to know if his training works out. And, I don't want this to come out as an insult—but I feel comfortable with you."

"Why would that be an insult?"

"I should be telling you how pretty you are. That I like your dark hair better than that fake blond look you were sporting two years ago. I should tell you how brave I think you are." He shrugged. "Something more personal and profound than you make me feel comfortable."

"Do you feel comfortable around a lot of other people?"

He pondered her insightful question and gave her an honest answer. "No. Not anymore."

Mollie stopped and tilted her gaze up to his.

"Then that was a compliment. And I'll take it as one. Thank you." He saw the whisper of a smile before they walked beside each other once more. "You're welcome to come by the diner anytime. We're a public place, and you can't deny the food is delicious."

"As much as I love the burgers, I actually want to know if I could come to see you."

"Oh. Like a date?"

"Maybe you'd let me take you out to lunch or grab a coffee."

"I'll think about it. I haven't dated anyone since Augie."

They passed one door and then another. "It wouldn't have to be a date. But we could hang out. Talk some more. Be comfortable together."

They were nearing the dumpster behind the diner when she finally nodded. "Okay. But just as friends. And you can't surprise me like you did today. I don't do well with surprises."

"Magnus will save you."

"I'm not holding my breath."

"Give the guy a chance. He might surprise you." Why did that feel like he was trying to sell his own worth, and not the dog's? Joel stopped and pulled out his phone. "Could I have your number? That way I can call or text before I stop by, so it won't be a surprise."

Mollie studied the badge at the middle of his

chest, then met his gaze. "I suppose that's the smart thing to do." She pulled out her phone. It was a cheap, pay-by-the-minute style, but it got the job done. "Now text me, so I can program your name and know it's you."

The message he sent was simple and honest. And maybe a little bit hopeful.

You can trust me, Moll.

Her shoulders lifted with a deep sigh. His phone dinged when she texted him back.

I'll try.

Any attempt to confirm that they now qualified as something more than acquaintances fell silent when Magnus barked and lunged forward. "Magnus! What is he doing?" Mollie jerked on his leash. "Magnus. Come."

Oh, he was loving this misfit of a dog. Magnus had sensed the threat even when Joel's guard was down.

The same black car had pulled into the far end of alley. "Do you know that car? Who drives it?"

"No. I—"

"I'm going to take you by the arm now," Joel warned, so Mollie wouldn't be startled. "Get your key out. Walk faster."

Although she quickened her pace and didn't

pull away from his hand above her elbow, she still questioned his concern. "Joel, what's wrong?"

"I see that car one time, I don't worry about it. I see it twice, I dismiss it as somebody circling the block because they're lost or looking for a parking space." The windshield reflected the afternoon sun, blinding him to the driver or any passenger inside. "But three times?"

"He's following us?"

The car revved its engine, shifted into gear, and hurtled down the alley toward them. Joel cursed. "Move!"

They ran. But they weren't going to be fast enough. The car nearly clipped a dumpster as it drifted toward their side of the alley.

"Get the door unlocked." He tossed his cane aside, clamped his hands at either side of her waist and lifted her onto the concrete step. While she worked to jam the key into the lock and turn it, he pressed up behind her as the car barreled toward them. "Hurry!"

Magnus nearly tore the leash from her hand as he lunged toward the approaching car. His furious barking echoed off the brick walls like a pack of hounds warning off an intruder.

"Magnus!" Mollie clamped down on the leash to keep the dog from bolting, turning her attention from the door.

"Mollie—lock!"

Leaving the relative safety of the recessed doorway, Joel scooped the dog up in his arms. And with seventy pounds of squirming dog sandwiched between them, he pushed them all forward the second he heard the key turn the lock.

The steel door swung open and the three of them tumbled inside as the heat of the car rushing past swept over them like a crashing wave.

They landed in a tangle of legs and fur on the kitchen floor. He cursed the *oof* of air from Mollie's chest as he landed on top of her. Magnus woofed and scrambled to one side as Joel rolled to the other. When he saw the dog clambering to his feet and heading for the door, he kicked it shut. "Magnus. Stay." He gave the order, having no idea if the dog would obey him or not. "Mollie?"

Joel reached for Mollie to see if she was injured, but she was already pushing herself up to her hands and knees. She glanced over her shoulder, breathing hard, maybe from adrenaline as much as any physical exertion. "Are you all right?"

"Are you?" She'd lost her headband in the fall, and he reached out to push her hair off her face. She snatched his wrist to pull his fingers from her silky curls. "I'm sorry."

"What is going on?" He jumped at the worried female voice above his head. "I heard the commotion at the door and tried to get back here to open it as fast as I could, but…baby belly." Corie Taylor's cheeks blanched as they heard the squeal of brakes and the unmistakable sound of a car jumping the curb and painting rubber across the pavement as it made a sharp turn at high speed. "What is that guy doing? Is he drunk? He could have hit you."

Mollie squeezed Joel's wrist before she pushed him completely away. "Go, if you need to." She turned her head the other way. "Magnus?"

"I got the mutt." Herb had joined the party and had the dog's leash wrapped around his bony fist. "He's fine."

Mollie reached for her dog and wrapped her arms around his neck before nodding to Joel. "Go."

He pushed to his feet, ignoring the twist of pain above his right knee at the sudden movement. He nailed Corie with a look as the pregnant woman leaned over to squeeze Mollie's shoulder. "Stay with her. Make sure she's all right." He gave the next orders to the Navy vet. "Keep this door locked. I'll knock when I'm ready to come back in."

"Okay. Should I—"

But Joel was already out the door, giving chase, pushing his rebuilt legs as hard as they could go. The car was already out of sight, but he easily followed the tire marks where the car had turned left across traffic. The noise of horns honking and the jumble of cars in the intersection told him the car had cut through a red light. But which way had it gone?

Joel ran to the corner. He held his badge up and stepped between the cars to reach the center of the intersection. He was breathing hard, and the nerves in his right thigh were sparking through his muscles like a shot from a Taser. Joel spun three hundred sixty degrees, looking down every street. But the car had disappeared. The angle had been wrong to even glimpse a license plate number between the parked cars along the sidewalk and uptown traffic.

But he knew cars. And a late-model four-door Lexus RX with tinted windows, gold trim, and a 6-cylinder engine under the hood wasn't one he'd soon forget.

The lights changed and horns honked. He waved an apology to the vehicles that were waiting and jogged back to the sidewalk. He kept his eyes peeled for anything else that pinged his suspicion radar as he hurried back to the diner.

After he checked to make sure Mollie and Magnus were okay, he needed to get to Fourth Precinct headquarters to see if he could get a hit in the system with just a make and a model. He needed to know who was driving that car, and why the driver had been watching Mollie.

Because that "accident" was no accident.

Chapter Five

"Something's wrong with Magnus." Mollie unhooked the dog's harness and sent him off to play with the boy who was tossing balls across the backyard for some of the residents at K-9 Ranch before turning to their training supervisor, Jessica Bennington Caldwell.

The older woman carried two glasses of iced tea across the deck, where it had become their habit to sit for a few minutes and chat after one of Mollie and Magnus's training sessions. Jessica shook her silvering, blond braid down her back and eyed the Belgian Malinois racing ahead of a Black Lab and an Australian shepherd to retrieve the ball. "Wrong? He looks fine to me."

"Penny! Tobes!" The nine-year-old boy called each dog by name and tossed a ball, so each dog had the chance to run and retrieve successfully. Magnus skidded to a stop in the grass and almost knocked the boy down in his enthusiasm for playing the game. "Good boy, Magnus."

"You're doing a good job, Nate," Jessica called

out to her foster son. He beamed at the praise and went back to exercising the dogs. Then Jessica handed Mollie one of the glasses and invited her to sit in one of the deck chairs. She leaned down to pet her own service dog, Shadow, a German shepherd mix with a graying muzzle, who seemed content to supervise the activity from his shady spot on the deck, before taking the seat beside her. "Do you think he realizes he's helping me with a chore to earn his allowance?"

Mollie couldn't help but smile at the boy's joyous laughter as he rolled on the ground with the dogs licking his face and silently pleading with Nate to throw the balls again. She looked across the deck to watch Jessie's foster daughter, a sweet blonde girl named Abby, pet and feed treats to a spotted Australian shepherd puppy as she mimicked the training she'd seen Jessie do with the other rescue dogs in her care. "Nate and Abby are two lucky children to have found a home here." She'd heard some of the story of how Jessie had found the two runaway children and taken them in as foster children, and how she had guarded them like a fierce mama bear from a home invasion. "How's the adoption going?"

"We've jumped through all the hoops and filled out more paperwork than you can imagine." Jessie's face softened with a serenely beautiful smile. "But our attorney says they'll be ours before Christmas."

"That's wonderful. Congratulations." Mollie toasted her with her glass. She'd given up on having a family of her own. She had too many hang-ups to manage even a healthy relationship with a man, which she considered a prerequisite to starting a family. But she would dearly love to at least get back into a classroom to surround herself with young people again. If only she didn't have the specter of the Di Salvo family hanging over her. "I have to admit I'm a little jealous. You have this beautiful property, your amazing dogs, two children to love—and let's not forget the hunky deputy sheriff you married last month."

"You ladies talking about me out here?" The back door opened again and a tall, well-built man wearing a sheriff's department uniform walked out. Garrett Caldwell pulled a departmental ball cap off his spiky salt-and-pepper hair and leaned down to trade a kiss with Jessie. Then another one. Mollie politely looked away from the love shining between them.

"You're home early." Jessie's tone was happy, but her expression looked vaguely worried.

"Relax. Nothing's wrong." He pressed his thumb against the dimple of his wife's frown to ease her concern. "The county is relatively quiet today. I'm the boss of my department, so

I decided to grant myself permission to spend an extra hour with my beautiful family." Mollie looked back as Jessie's husband straightened and pulled the tea from his wife's hand to steal a long swallow. "Mollie. How are you doing today?"

"I'm fine."

Garrett dropped his gaze to Jessie and the two exchanged a look. He handed off the sweating glass and put his cap back on his head. "I'll keep an eye on the kids. Looks like you two were in the middle of an important conversation."

"Thanks, sweetheart."

He winked a goodbye to Mollie, then headed over to Abby to scoop the giggling little girl up in his arms. He carried her down to the grass where he traded a fist bump with Nate and listened patiently as both children recounted the highlights of their day.

Jessie had inherited the seven-acre property that had once been a working farm and converted it into a dog training facility, as well as a spacious country home, allowing them the distance they needed to share a private conversation. "So…" Jessie sipped her tea. "You don't think Magnus is working out as service dog? I thought your training session went well today. Especially with the nonverbal cues. His reactions to you were spot-on."

Mollie nodded. It was hard to explain the difference in Magnus's behavior when he was here on the ranch to when he was with her in the city. She didn't want her boy to be labeled a failure any more than she wanted to feel like one when it came to their working relationship. "Do I need to get his hearing tested again? He doesn't always seem to be aware when I need him unless he's looking right at me."

"And...?"

"And what?"

"He's barely two years old. Just out of his puppyhood. Maybe it's taking him longer to mature, but I don't think so." Jessie turned her head to point out how responsive Magnus was to Nate's commands as he showed off his skills for his foster dad. "He's a clown, but he can also turn on work mode faster than any dog here. He wants to work. He wants to have a job and do it well. He wants to please you."

Mollie reached down into her bag beside her, where she'd hidden Magnus's toy. "What he wants is his teddy bear."

Jessie laughed. "That, too. He's definitely more reward driven than treat driven." The older woman set her glass on the table between them and leaned a little closer. "We can take Magnus to my vet again, if you think his hearing loss is a legitimate concern. But we already knew he was going to be more responsive to visual cues.

Is he not answering your verbal commands when you're away from the ranch?"

"He went to this guy I was talking to yesterday and put his paws on him. Laid his head on his lap just like he does with me." Mollie wasn't sure if she was explaining her hit-or-miss success with Magnus clearly enough so that the other woman would understand her fears. "*I* was stressing because I don't always handle social situations that well anymore. I was sitting right there, and he ignored me. He's supposed to be *my* dog, and he went and comforted someone else."

"Was this a one-on-one situation, or something with more people, like the diner when there's a run of customers?"

"I was exercising Magnus. He asked if he could go with me to talk. It was the two of us and the dog."

"Hmm… Maybe you weren't as panicked about being with *this guy* as you thought you were. Maybe there's something about *this guy* and having Magnus with you that made you comfortable enough to be with him."

Comfortable. There was that word again. Joel said he felt comfortable with her. But did she feel the same? Joel was a man—an attractive one at that, if a little beat up around the edges. And he knew about her time with Augie. How could she possibly feel comfortable with a man connected to the past she could never truly move on from?

Jessie's gray eyes narrowed as she pondered Mollie's story. She glanced out into the yard to see the three panting dogs sitting in front of Garrett and the children, eagerly waiting for the balls to go flying again. Magnus's razor-sharp focus was impossible to miss. Once the dogs took off, Jessie looked over at Mollie, nodding as if she had some kind of answer for her. "Was *this guy* in distress? Could he have been having a panic attack like you do sometimes?"

It was Mollie's turn to carefully think over her response. She'd asked Joel about his injuries, but he'd skimmed the details, either protecting her sensibilities or protecting himself from reliving a painful memory. He'd made a joke, but his knuckles were white where he gripped his cane. And then he'd mentioned his girlfriend dying. His tone had sounded so bleak. His golden-brown eyes had seemed so distant. And she thought he was going to snap that cane in two. That was when Magnus had targeted him. She'd had the urge to comfort him, too. If she was a toucher, she would have squeezed his hand or offered him a hug. But Magnus had stepped up and done what she hadn't been willing to do. "Yes. He was very stressed at the moment."

"It's rare for a service dog to respond to anyone but the human he's bonded with. Maybe our boy here is so smart, he responds to anyone in distress. My Shadow does that with the kids." Mollie sat up a little straighter, watching her dog with a sense of pride. Maybe there wasn't anything wrong with Magnus. Maybe her boy was smarter than she'd given him credit for. "Is there a personal connection between you and this *guy*?"

Surprised by the question, Mollie swung her gaze back to her friend. "Personal? With Joel?"

"Joel. Okay, at least I don't have to keep calling him *this guy*." Jessie smiled. "This Joel—have you been dating him? He's not your brother or a family friend, is he?"

"I don't have any family."

"So, you are dating?" Jessie continued before she could correct the misassumption. "Magnus may see you as a family unit, and he's responding to you both because he wants to protect his entire pack."

"I'm not dating him," Mollie blurted out. "I sat and had a conversation with him for fifteen minutes. Sure, we discussed some surprisingly deep stuff, but that's just where the conversation went. I've met him a couple of times before, and he was always nice to me. He doesn't look nice—I mean, he looks more like a thug or a street fighter or something dangerous like that. I think he must look that way for his work. But he was always nice to me."

Picking up on her rambling discomfort, Jessie reached across the table to touch the arm of the chair, where Mollie squeezed her fist. "I'm not your therapist—I rehabilitate dogs, not people. But it sounds like you have feelings for him."

Did she? How could she?

"I… I guess we share a connection." She vividly remembered Joel tackling her and Magnus when that car had nearly run them down. And when he'd come back after chasing the car, he'd come right up to Mollie to make sure she was all right before he called the near hit-and-run in to someone at KCPD. He apologized for the bruises on her knees, even though she assured him they were quite minor compared to the injuries she could have sustained if that car had hit them. As frightened as she'd been of that car racing toward them, she hadn't completely shut down in panic when he'd lifted her to safety and shoved her and Magnus into the kitchen ahead of him. Then she'd given him her phone number because he'd revealed some things that made her think he was just as broken as she was, and, like her, was trying to move on with his life and find his new normal. "I *am* comfortable with him. Yes."

He'd said those words about her, and now she was saying them about Joel. They both had a lot of emotional baggage to deal with, but it hadn't seemed to matter when they'd sat down and talked. It had all felt so normal, and she hadn't shared anything *normal* with a man for a very long time.

Jessie patted her hand before pulling back. "I'm not trying to put you on the spot, but I do need to understand what's happening so that I can evaluate Magnus's behavior and figure how to retrain him. Or if it's truly necessary."

"That makes sense." She thought she understood the point Jessie was making, even if she didn't find it completely reassuring. "Magnus protects my world. And if someone is part of that world, then Magnus thinks he has to protect that person, too?" Jessie nodded. "But Joel and I are friends. Barely that. I need Magnus to be there for *me*, not everyone else."

Jessie stood and crossed to the deck railing to watch the dogs interacting with her husband and foster children more closely. "Can you ask Joel to come to a training session with you? I'd like to observe the three of you together. Then I could tell if Magnus is switching loyalties, or if he's just being a typical Mal—" Jessie's nickname for the Belgian Malinois dogs she worked with "—who's looking for a bigger, more demanding job to do."

"You want me to invite Joel here?" Mollie wiped the icy condensation from her glass, then palmed the back of her neck beneath her hair to cool her skin. The late afternoon was hot with the sun high in the hazy blue sky. But it was the mix of nervous anticipation and a familiar dread at purposely developing a relationship with a man that made her temperature spike.

"Yes. If you're nervous about it, just remember that I'll be with you the whole time. Do you feel safe with Joel? I can make sure Garrett is home when you're here." Jessie turned to face Mollie, leaning her hips against the railing. "The kids will be here, of course, since they're off for the summer from school. That reminds me. Have you given any more thought to tutoring Nate on his math skills? He qualified for the HAL program in math. But since this is a new school, I don't want him to feel like he's out of sync with the other students when he starts fourth grade this year."

Mollie finally set down her glass and joined Jessie at the railing. "Sure. I'd love to repay you by helping him with math. I miss working with students."

"Good. Then I'll see you, Joel, and Magnus tomorrow. If that time still works for you?"

Mollie tried not to feel like she was being rushed into this. Impulsive behavior had been smacked out of her by Augie years ago. And the secrets she'd kept since her divorce demanded she be cautious about her dealings with people.

"I'll have to check with Joel to see if his schedule allows him to get away in the afternoon."

Reaching over, Jessie squeezed her hand where she clutched the railing. "Make it happen. It's as important for Magnus as it is for you that we get this problem straightened out. Some dogs can't be trained to be more than the family pet. And that's okay. Being the family pet is an important job. But I've never met a Mal who couldn't be trained to do more. Even without his hearing, he's a high-energy dog. We need to focus that energy, or he could become difficult to control. Might even become dangerous to himself or to others."

Mollie pictured Magnus going after that black car yesterday in the alley behind the diner. No one on the outside needed to know that her dog was a happy boy who loved his teddy bear and a good tummy rub. He looked and sounded dangerous when he perceived a threat to her.

Augie had always driven black cars. For a brief moment in that alley yesterday, her stomach had bottomed out at the idea that not only had he tracked her down—a nightmare she'd suspected would eventually happen—but he'd violated one of the few details of their divorce agreement by getting close to her again and threatening her.

Of course, the dangerous driver in the alley could have been a drunk driver. Maybe he thought he was still on one of the main streets. Or maybe the impatient driver had taken a shortcut and driven so fast the car had been nearly out of control.

Augie had always been an impatient driver.

Even before that first time he'd assaulted her, she'd seen glimpses of road rage when he was driving. She should have gotten a clue about his selfish, irrational, violent behavior long before that Thanksgiving night. His mother, Bernadette, had insisted he use a driver on staff as often as possible to protect the heir to the Di Salvo fortune—keeping Augie from behind the wheel in order to keep his name out of traffic court records and keep him in one piece.

A staff driver reminded her of Joel and the few months he'd worked for the family. Although he'd been at the periphery of her world, other than that first night they'd met, she'd sensed even then that he was a good man. Someone she should be able to trust. Someone who wanted to keep her safe.

He seemed a harder version of that good man now. Something about the accident he'd glossed over, as well as the girlfriend he'd lost to drugs had changed him. Not just the limp or the visible scars—but the scars on the inside. Oh, he was still very much a protector. The way he'd shoved both her and Magnus out of the path of that reckless driver, then run off to see if he could identify the man, proved that.

But was he still the man who'd spoken so gently to her, who'd tempted her to lean into his strength and allow someone stronger to stand between her and Augie? Mollie had sensed the reticence in him today. Maybe it was sorrow or guilt. Self-doubts that he'd failed the woman he'd loved. He'd been dealing with a lot of emotional stress. Clearly, Magnus had picked up on that, too.

"Mollie?" Jessica touched her arm. She startled but didn't shy away.

Magnus was staring at her from the middle of the yard, and when she made eye contact, he trotted up the steps to push his head into her hand and lean against her thigh. Mollie instantly breathed easier at the warm contact. She scratched around his ears and knew he'd become much more than her service dog. Maybe that was why she was honestly afraid that his loyalty wasn't to her. She had no one in her life beyond a few work friends and this dog. She needed someone or something to belong to her—someone who wanted her to belong to them, too. "Good boy. You're my good boy."

"You were a million miles away." Jessie asked permission before she petted and praised Magnus, too. "I don't think you need to worry about Magnus being your dog. But I still think it would be a good idea to bring your Joel to a training session tomorrow."

Her Joel?

She hadn't thought she could do a relationship again. So why wasn't she correcting Jessie's assumption about her friendship with Detective Standage?

"I'll talk to him. I really want Magnus to work out as my service dog. I… I'm getting attached to this big goof."

"I'm glad to hear that. Come on. Let's run him through one more set of commands before you head back to the city. Hook him to his leash, and we'll go out to the barn, away from the distractions of playing children."

They went through one more session of basic dog commands, using both verbal and visual cues. Then there was another round of pets from Nate, a shy hug from Abby, and Mollie had a worn-out Magnus loaded into the back seat of her car where he stretched out on his blanket and cuddled with his teddy bear while she pulled out her cell phone.

She waved to Jessie and her family and held up her phone to show them she'd be sitting in their driveway for a few minutes while she contacted Joel.

Mollie stared at the blank screen of her phone for a full minute, working up the courage to text Joel. She hadn't purposely contacted a man for several months now.

When she heard a whine from the back seat, she lifted her gaze to the rearview mirror and saw that Magnus had raised his head to look at her, tilting his head as if to ask if she needed him. Mollie smiled, then reached back to pet him. "I sat here too long without speaking or moving, didn't I? I didn't mean to worry you." When she reached his flank, he stretched out and gave her full access to a tummy rub. "You're mama's good boy. You go ahead and rest now. You've earned a break."

When she faced the steering wheel again, she breathed out a determined sigh. She could do this for Magnus. She fingered her locket, summoning the confident young woman her granny had raised. Then she pulled up Joel's number. With only a few numbers on her phone, it was easy to find. She typed before self-doubts and second-guessing could get in her head again.

Hey, Joel. Is this a good time?

Only a few seconds passed before he answered.

For what? Miss my scintillating charm already?

Are you still at work? I can text you later if you're busy.

Sorry. Ignore my sarcasm. I try to be funny when I get nervous.

Why would you be nervous?

Because a pretty woman I like just texted me.

Mollie glanced at her reflection in the rear-view mirror. Her hair was a windswept mess from spending the past two hours outside. Her cheeks were flushed from the sun, and the only makeup she had on was some pink gloss to protect her lips. Shorts, sneakers, and a faded Worlds of Fun T-shirt she hadn't even bothered to tuck in completed her look. She was a far cry from the perfect beauty Augie had demanded she be.

So why did Joel Standage saying she was pretty make her smile when Augie's praise had only made her feel trapped and on edge?

His three blinking dots turned into a message before she could answer.

I'm not taking it back. You're pretty. I like you. And you texted me. You can't argue with that logic.

I don't know what to say to that.

You don't have to say anything. Things are winding down here on my shift. This is a perfect time to chat. What's up?

She glanced back at Magnus. Her boy had fallen asleep already, with his muzzle lying on top of his bear. Poor guy had put in a full day. She needed to take care of him.

I need to ask you a favor.

Clearly, he'd been texting while he waited for her response.

I didn't have a LP# to ID the owner of the car that played chicken with us yesterday. But I did find out that Edward Di Salvo and your ex both own that make of car.

LP# must mean License Plate number. Sure, she could go off on a tangent with him. Besides, she'd already suspected that yesterday's incident had something to do with Augie. Confirming her worst fear or having another rational explanation for nearly being run down would at least tell her what she was dealing with.

Augie always valued what his parents said. If Edward said that was the kind of car someone of their station would own, then Augie would get one, too.

Sadly, they aren't the only drivers in the state who own that make of car. I can't even say for sure it belongs to a K.C. resident.

So, you're saying it's not much of a lead.

It's not even enough to get a warrant to look at their cars to see if they have the kind of scratches and alignment issues it would have sustained from jumping curbs and turning at the speed that guy was going.

Mollie shook her head. She really wanted it to be a drunk driver. She might not be able to identify who was behind the wheel yesterday, but she had a feeling she knew who'd sent him.

What's the favor? You can ask me anything.

Right. She didn't really want to be talking about the Di Salvos right now, either. She typed in her request.

Would you be willing to come to a training session with me and Magnus tomorrow at K-9 Ranch?

Yes.

She huffed a sound that was almost a laugh at his easy acquiescence.

Don't you want to know what time? Or why I need you?

I enjoyed our time together yesterday. Before someone tried to run us down. My schedule is flexible, so I'll make it work. You need me? I'm there.

Magnus is the one who needs you.

I'm still in. You two are a package deal. Besides, I like the guy. Wait. Is he okay?

He's snoring in my back seat right now.

:) Go Magnus. Play hard and sleep well.

Jessie—our trainer—wants to see how Magnus interacts differently when you're around. Why he doesn't focus on me when you're there.

He's your dog, Moll. I'm sorry if I screwed up his training.

It might be nothing. Maybe you're a distraction. Maybe he's creating his own job. Jessie can't help me until she sees the three of us together.

What time?

4 p.m.?

Yes. Do we drive together? Should I pick you up someplace? Work? Your apartment?

I don't know if I'm comfortable being alone in a car with you. It's not you. It's my own hang-up.

Augie hadn't even let her drive after the first few months of their marriage. She'd thought it was sweet at first, that he was taking care of her. But she eventually realized he was controlling where she went, and making sure she was never alone. And the punishment he meted out hadn't been limited to the closed doors of the estate, either. Being trapped in the back seat of a car with Augie wasn't an experience she cared to remember.

Her phone dinged, dragging her out of her thoughts.

I'm not your ex. But I can drive separately.

Making even a simple decision like sharing a ride had been taken out of her hands when she'd been Mollie Di Salvo. No more.

I don't want to be paranoid for the rest of my life.

I don't want you to be afraid of me. Ever. If that means you don't want to be shut up in a vehicle with me, that's what we'll do. I'll drive my truck and meet you there.

No. She was braver than this. Granny Crane would be pointing a stern finger at her right now if she let Joel think she was afraid of him, specifically. Inhaling deeply, she typed away.

Change of plans. Would you mind driving the three of us? I don't think we'd all fit in my compact car very comfortably.

You sure?

Yes. She could do terse and direct, too.

Magnus can sit in the seat between us.

Deal. She texted him her address. Just pull up in front of the building. We'll be waiting in the lobby and will come out when we see you. We'll need twenty minutes to get there.

I'll be there. Red pickup truck. It doesn't look like much on the outside, but she's a peach on the inside.

Sounded a little like Joel himself.

While she was smiling at that revelation, the surprisingly chatty detective texted her a new message.

See you tomorrow at 4. Thanks for asking me. It means a lot to me that you want me to help.

It means a lot to me that you said yes.

Are you driving?

Not yet. I'm still at K-9 Ranch.

Put your phone down and get yourself safely home. I'll see you tomorrow around 3:30.

See you then.

As if he knew she was still looking at her screen, savoring their rambling conversation, another text from Joel popped up.

Phone down. Drive safely. See you tomorrow.

Bossy much?

You have no idea.

Before she gave in to her curiosity to ask him to explain that response, Mollie stuck her phone into the cup holder between the seats and started her car. She replayed their conversation in her head as she drove down Highway 40, heading into Kansas City. She smiled when she realized that had been the longest conversation she'd had with a man in ages. Yeah, they'd covered some serious stuff, but they'd been silly, too. It felt good. And normal.

She liked normal.

She liked Joel, too.

She was still smiling as she parked her car in the private lot behind her building. She gave Magnus a few minutes in the grassy median, then they ran up the stairs to her second-floor apartment.

That's when the smiling stopped.

Mollie froze at the top of the stairs, pulling Magnus to a halt beside her. There was a newspaper tacked to her door—the weekend society page from the *Kansas City Journal*, with a picture and headline announcing the engagement of August Di Salvo to a woman she recognized, one of the family's attorneys and his longtime mistress, Kyra Schmidt. Kyra looked as blonde and beautiful and dressed to highbrow perfection as she'd once done for Augie.

But seeing her ex's face on her front door wasn't the thing that made her blood run cold. It was the message scrawled across the paper in black marker.

You know what I want. Make this right. Don't ruin this for me.

The door itself wasn't quite shut. She could tell by the scratches on the lock that it had been jimmied open. "Magnus, sit. Stay." Avoiding both the newspaper and the knob, she nudged it open with her elbow. The old, walnut-stained wood door creaked open to reveal careless destruction. "Oh, God."

Her apartment was small. The only interior doors were a closet and a bathroom. But they both stood open. The mattress where she slept had been flipped off the bed, the pillows cut open. And every drawer and cabinet were open or overturned on the floor. Even Magnus's bed had been torn open, its stuffing strewn about like cotton candy.

She heard Magnus whining beside her and looked down to find his nose tilted up to her. Right. Stay in the moment. Freezing up in panic wouldn't do her any good. She bent down to pet the Belgian Malinois around the head before patting his flank and pulling him away. "Magnus, with me."

Mollie instinctively touched her locket through her T-shirt as she retreated. When her back hit the opposite wall, she yanked the chain from beneath her shirt and opened the locket. She breathed out a sigh of relief when she saw the tiny, folded piece of paper opposite her granny's picture inside. Then she reached down and fingered the small pocket in Magnus's harness, nodding when she felt the small object hidden there. "Good boy. Good boy, Magnus."

She knew what the intruder was looking for. He'd never get his hands on it as long as she was alive. Keeping it well hidden and out of Augie's reach was the only thing *keeping* her alive.

Make this right? As if. August Di Salvo was never getting his hands on it. It was the only bargaining chip she had.

Why was this happening now? What had changed in Augie's world to prompt him to come after her like this? His engagement? While she pitied Kyra for saying yes to his proposal, Mollie was more than happy to see him move on to another woman and leave any connection with her behind. This had to be related to the car that tried to kill them yesterday. Or maybe the goal was to scare her. Or make her retreat so far into her fear that she'd be an easy mark for someone to complete the job.

But he wasn't getting his hands on what she'd taken from her ex-husband. It was the only leverage she'd had to get away from him, to get his signature on the divorce papers, to keep him from hurting her ever again. Augie didn't get to win this time.

She was deep into her mental pep talk when she heard the clanging of a ring of keys and an old metal toolbox coming down the stairs from the third floor. "What the...?"

Mollie cringed at the building manager's reaction to her door. She yelped when Mr. Williams swung around to face her.

"You okay, Miss Crane? Looks like somebody busted in." He set down his toolbox and moved closer to the door, inspecting the same damage she had. "I've been upstairs all afternoon working on that broken pipe between 304 and 305. I never heard a thing."

He scratched the back of his thinning gray

hair. "How'd they get inside the building without one of the residents' key fobs?"

"Don't touch anything!" she warned, shaking herself out of her terrified stupor. "There may be evidence."

"You're right, ma'am. Goll-darnit." He unrolled the sleeve of his gray coveralls to cover his fingers before pulling the door closed again. "They busted my lock." Right. Because that was the worst of what had happened here today. "Good thing you weren't home, Miss… Miss Crane?"

Mollie was already charging down the stairs, swiping away the tears that threatened to fall so she could dig her phone out of her back pocket and pull up a familiar name. When she reached the bottom step, she perched on the edge of it and typed.

Joel? I need a cop.

She stared intently at the screen, waiting for his response. Then she startled so badly when her cell rang that she dropped her phone. She quickly scrambled to pick it up from between her feet, sending up a silent prayer of thanks when she read the name and answered. "Joel?"

"What's wrong?" His gruff voice didn't sound at all like the jokester she'd been texting a half hour earlier. She threw her arm around Magnus's shoulders and reminded herself of the decision she'd made during that conversation. Joel Standage was a good man. Beat up by life and rough around the edges, but he made her smile, he liked her dog, and he made her feel safe. "Mollie?"

"I'm here."

Joel cursed. "Don't scare me like that. Where are you? Are you hurt? Are you in danger?"

She answered each question as quickly as he'd rattled them off. "My apartment building. No. I'm not sure."

"I'm on my way to you now. Tell me what's going on."

"He broke into my apartment."

"He? Di Salvo? Is he still there?"

"I don't think so." She heard a siren in the background of the call. Joel must have one of those portable models he stuck on the roof of his vehicle. "Augie or someone who works for him was here. They left a message, and it looks like they went through the whole place. I don't have much, but I think everything has been touched."

"Do you have something he wants?"

She glanced around the empty foyer and tuned out the voices in the hallway above her as Mr. Williams knocked on doors and asked the other residents if they'd had a break-in, too. She knew the answer was no. This wasn't a break-in. It was a targeted search. After nearly a year of so-called freedom, Augie was coming after her.

"Mollie?"

"Yes. I have something. He…he didn't find it. I didn't hide it in my apartment." She could hear a siren close by now. A black-and-white pulled up out front, sliding into the fifteen-minute loading zone at the curb. She didn't think detectives drove squad cars. "What are you driving?"

"My truck. Red pickup."

"Did you call for backup? There's already a police car here."

Mr. Williams and his rattling toolbox came down the stairs. "*I* called them. I read that heinous message on your door." He leaned over to pat her back or squeeze her shoulder, but Magnus put himself between her and the super and growled.

"Magnus!" She tugged him back to her side.

Mr. Williams gave them a wide berth as he stepped down to the foyer. "That dog's a menace. When I said you could have a pet, I didn't mean an attack dog."

"He can tell I'm scared. He's protecting me. You may have startled him because that's the side he can't hear on. He won't hurt you unless I tell him to." At least, she hoped he was that disciplined of a dog.

Joel's voice shouted in her ear. "Who's that? Who are you talking to?"

"The building super. He called 9-1-1."

"Don't talk to anyone until I get there. I'm only a few minutes away."

When she saw the two uniformed officers getting out of the car, she gasped and pulled her knees to her chest, instinctively folding herself into a smaller presence. "Joel?"

"Right here, babe."

"Remember that police officer who wouldn't keep his hands to himself at the diner last October?"

"Yeah. Rocky Garner. What about him?"

"He's here."

Joel swore again. "Do not talk to him. Magnus with you?"

"Yes."

"Good. Keep him between you and Garner."

"Okay."

"I'm in your neighborhood now. I'll be there shortly. You're going to be okay, Moll. You're stronger than Augie. You survived him. You'll survive this, too."

"You have a lot of faith in me."

"Hell, yeah, I do."

She took a deep breath at his words and pulled her shoulders back. "Don't get hurt driving over here. I'm okay."

"Damn right, you are."

She almost smiled. "You know, Joel, you cuss a lot when you're fired up."

"That going to be a problem for you?" Did that mean he was an emotional hothead? She wasn't a big fan if that was the case. Or was the problem that he intended to be around her more often?

She hoped it was the latter. "As long as you're not cussing at me."

"Never."

She watched Rocky Garner and his partner climb the front steps to the building. The handsy officer adjusted his protective vest, his gun, and his hat before he made eye contact with her through the glass. Then he smiled. He remembered her, too.

Mollie shivered. "Joel?"

"Yeah, babe?"

"Hurry."

Chapter Six

There wasn't a ball small enough Mollie could curl into. Officer Rocky Garner removed his hat and made a beeline toward her spot on the bottom step. "You the one who had the break-in, sweetheart? Are you okay? You're not hurt, are you?"

The words were right, but the person saying them, and the slick way they were said, was wrong.

Mr. Williams stepped in front of Rocky before he could reach her. "I'm the one who called it in, Officer. We don't get a lot of break-ins here, but this one's serious."

Officer Garner seemed confused, then displeased, to have the gray-haired man impede his progress toward Mollie. But he pasted a smile on his face before patting the man's shoulder. "You the manager here?"

"Yes, sir."

"Fine. That's just fine." Officer Garner stepped back and gestured to the Black officer, who appeared to be his partner. "Why don't you give your statement to Darnell there, and I'm going to talk to the victim."

"I dunno. Miss Crane is a little shaken up. She knows me. I could stay…" Mr. Williams glanced back at her, then seemed to think better of going against Garner's suggestion and left Mollie to fend for herself.

"She's in good hands with me." The smarmy officer assured her super before propping his elbows on his holster and utility belt and facing her with a deceptively casual stance. "Mollie, isn't it? You're a mite prettier out of uniform. Sorry this happened to you. Want to show me your apartment where the break-in happened?"

She glanced out the glass doors at the front of the lobby, hoping Joel would make a miraculous entrance and save her from having to talk to Rocky Garner. But no such luck. The street was in the throes of rush hour traffic, and there was no place to park on either side. If he parked in the back of the building, he'd have to knock hard and flash his badge to get someone to let him in. If that didn't happen, he'd have to run around to the front, where Mr. Williams or one of her curious neighbors who were gathering to see what the police being there was all about, could admit him.

But no red pickup. No Joel. No miracle.

"Ma'am? Let's go." Any deception about casual or friendly disappeared when he leaned toward her and latched his fingers against her elbow. "You on the main floor or upstairs?"

Mollie jerked her arm, but couldn't immediately break his grasp. At the same time she breathed in his coffee and mint-scented breath, Magnus growled, low in his throat.

Officer Garner released her and held both hands up in mock surrender. "Your mutt has a mean streak in him. I'm afraid you're going to have to muzzle him or lock him in a neighbor's bathroom, so I can walk through the crime scene with you."

Mollie shook her head. "He stays with me. Always."

"Bet that puts a damper on your love life, don't it?" He snickered at his own joke.

"Please don't touch me again, Officer. I have panic attacks. I do better when the dog is with me."

His dark eyes narrowed at her attempt to stand up for herself. "You a mental case?"

She cringed at his crass comments. Either he thought he was being funny and was woefully mistaken about his level of charm or he was legitimately one of the biggest jerks she'd ever met. And that was saying something.

Anger surged ahead of her fear, and Mollie

pushed to her feet, holding Magnus's leash tightly in her hands. "Are you married, Officer Garner?"

"Nope. Divorced twice."

"I can see why," she muttered under her breath, ducking her head.

"Excuse me?"

"I said this way," she answered in a stronger voice. With his blatant innuendos and touchy-feely hands, it didn't surprise her that marriage wasn't a strength of his. But she kept her comments to herself and headed up the stairs. "My apartment is on the second floor."

She felt the officer's gaze like laser beams on her backside as he followed her to the second floor. "Why'd you ask? You interested? You always seem like such a prickly thing at Pearl's. But I'm willing to try anything once."

Her granny would have slapped the man's face by now and lectured him up one side and down the other. Mollie was sorely tempted to do the same. Instead, she kept her cool and pointed out her front door before stepping aside and putting Magnus in a sit between her and the police officer. "That's my place."

He let out a long, low whistle before pulling his phone out and snapping a few pictures of the newspaper and threat. "Make *what* right? You know this Di Salvo dude? Looks like he's pretty pissed at you. Why would he threaten you?"

Threaten? Mollie blinked back the images that tried to sneak out of her memories. Hair literally pulled from her scalp. Vile words. A punch to the mouth if she dared to talk back.

The memories blended with the commotion down in the lobby, her neighbors whispering in the doorways, and Officer Garner pushing open her door. "Boy, he sure did a number on your place." He snapped a few more pictures. "You're lucky you weren't here. What did he take?"

Magnus was leaning against her leg and pushing his cold nose into her hand when she heard footsteps on the stairs and turned with an audible sigh of relief at the sight of Joel's muscular shoulders and golden-brown eyes. Magnus's tail thumped the floor with a similar anticipation. "Joel."

"You two okay?" were the first words out of his mouth. He crossed straight to her, his limp barely slowing his stride. For a second, she thought he was going to touch her face or hair with his outstretched hand. But at the last moment, he reached down and scrubbed Magnus around his ears. "Good boy. You keeping Mama safe?"

She wondered what his fingertips would feel like against her skin, and she acknowledged a moment of envy that he'd petted her dog instead. But she was beyond happy to see him here and felt herself take a normal breath under his watchful eyes. "We're fine." She glanced around at the neighbors peeking from their open doors before nodding to Rocky Garner and the officer talking to the super and more residents downstairs. "It got crowded pretty fast."

"And you don't like crowds." He raised the badge hanging from the lanyard around his neck and flashed it to the other residents. "I'm Detective Standage, KCPD. I need you all to go back to your apartments and lock your doors." He might look like he'd just climbed off a Harley with his tattoos and beard stubble, but he spoke with an authority that got the others moving from being curious onlookers to respecting her privacy. "Everything is fine. Miss Crane and her dog are safe and so are all of you. Thank you for your cooperation." He dropped his warm brown gaze back to her as the others did as he requested. "I didn't lie to them, did I?"

Mollie shook her head. "I'm okay. Magnus is, too. He's been great." She dropped her voice to a whisper. "He growled at Officer Garner when he tried to take my arm."

Joel grinned and reached down to give Magnus the praise he loved. "Good dog."

He gave her a nod before turning to the uniformed police officer standing in her open doorway. "What are you doing here, Garner?"

"What are *you* doing here? I answered a call from Dispatch about a B&E."

Joel looked beyond him to the open door and muttered a low curse. "And making terroristic threats. That's clearly a personal message on her door."

"Whatever. You may be schtooping the victim, but this is *my* call."

Joel moved toward the bigger man. "Watch your mouth, Garner."

"Butt out, you has-been."

"You're a patrol officer, not an investigator. Do. Your. Job."

Rocky Garner was a good four of five inches taller than Joel, and he was squaring off as if he was looking for a fight. "I will be an investigator. I'm the one who's up for a promotion in two months. You're on your way out."

Mollie moved up behind Joel and brushed her fingers against the fist at his side, not wanting to be a part of any more violence today. She gasped when Joel's fist opened, and he laced his fingers together with hers and clasped her hand firmly in his, keeping her behind him out of Garner's line of sight, but maintaining the connection. Instead of panicking or pulling away, she followed her first instinct and tightened her grip in his.

"Your job is to secure and control the scene, calling for whatever backup you need. Not to go all cowboy and stomp all over the crime scene yourself. Be smart, man. You had at least seven witnesses on the scene besides Miss Crane. Do you know their names? Their locations? Did they see or hear anything? Are any of them traumatized by what happened here? Are they suspects?"

"Are you calling me stupid?" Mollie's breathing rate increased right along with Officer Garner's. He turned red in the face as his anger consumed him. "Telling me I don't know how to do my job?"

"I'm trying to keep the peace here, which is what you should be doing. Not upsetting people." Joel remained surprisingly calm, which made her feel better, but only seemed to aggravate the uniformed officer. "Especially not Miss Crane."

"I heard about you, Standage," Garner taunted. "How you blew your last assignment. People died."

Joel's grip pulsed around hers.

Uh-uh. She wasn't letting this man denigrate Joel or make her nervous any longer. She threaded Magnus's leash through the belt loop on her jeans and tapped 9-1-1 on her phone.

When the Dispatcher answered, she apologized for not knowing exactly who to call and gave the woman her name and address. "Yes, ma'am. There's a police officer who's arguing with a detective. I think he's trying to start a fight."

"Mollie…" She wasn't sure if Joel was warning her he didn't need her help, or if she was making things worse.

But she identified the threat when asked and read the badge number off Rocky Garner's chest. "I'm the victim whose apartment was broken into, and he's saying crude things about me. It's not the first time he's harassed me. Who can I report this to?"

Officer Garner broke his stare-down with Joel and nailed her with an accusatory glare. "Who are you talking to, lady?"

"9-1-1. They're giving me the number to call to file a complaint." Joel squeezed her hand, hopefully applauding her initiative in making the call.

"A complaint? Screw you, lady. I came here to help you. It looks like you've got some bad juju headed your way, and I put my life on the line to protect you. You should be grateful I answered the call." He shoved Joel away, cursed as Magnus shifted to his feet and growled, and headed down the stairs to the lobby. "C'mon, Darnell. We'll wait outside and let the mighty detective handle the hysterical female."

They both watched until Officer Garner stormed out the front door. His partner made some sort of apology to Mr. Williams before heading out after him.

"I'm not hysterical," Mollie whispered. "I'm pissed off." She raised her voice to a more normal tone and called after the retreating cop. "And who says 'bad juju' anymore, anyway?" She practically growled herself as her emotions surged through her. "He's so old-school. And not in a good way."

"There's a good way?"

"Yes. Chivalry and kindness. Not, men rule the world and women are their minions to do with and talk to as they please—and then expect us to be grateful for that kind of attention."

"I'll take angry over scared any day." Joel chuckled and held his hand out for her phone. "May I?"

"Oh." She felt her cheeks heat with embarrassment. "I forgot she was still on the line. Sorry."

Mollie handed it over and Joel took over the call, giving the Dispatcher his own badge number and explaining the situation. "The threat has been neutralized," he assured her. "A disagreement on jurisdiction. I've already called in for backup. I appreciate your help in calming my witness. Yes, ma'am. I think she's going to be just fine." His gaze remained locked on hers the entire conversation, reassuring her that, despite

Garner's taunts and her outburst, he did, indeed, have the situation under control. "You bet."

Joel ended the call, and she tucked her phone back into her pocket. "Did I overstep?" she asked. "Make things worse for you?"

"For me? Hell, no. I hate the way Garner talks to you. To any female from what I've heard. I'm guessing the sensitivity training we all have taken hasn't rubbed off on him yet."

"I guess not." She huffed out a relieved breath that the officer had gone.

"That was cool to see you stand up to him."

Mollie shook off the compliment. "I didn't like how he was talking to you, either. I could only do it because you were standing between us. I would have been in full-on panic mode, hugged around Magnus and unable to think of any way to help if you hadn't been here."

Those tiger eyes gleamed with some sort of secret light as he held her gaze. "I'll take that job, standing between you and the Rocky Garners of the world."

She sensed he meant something more than simply protecting her from the crude cop. But she was too long out of practice to believe her intuition when it came to a man's words. "What happens now? I'm assuming since you're a detective, you'll want to ask me some questions or do some investigating?"

Joel shook his head. "Not me. I called in re-inforcements. They should be here any minute." He held up their hands between them and grinned as if he was surprised to see her still clinging to him. "I won't lie and say that KCPD isn't interested in nailing your ex for a myriad of crimes. Not that what happened here isn't upsetting, but, they'd like to pin something bigger than breaking and entering and threatening his ex-wife on him."

Mollie felt the warmth in her body drain out through the soles of her sneakers. "That makes logical sense. Augie has been indicted before without much success." She glanced at the threat on her door. "But you'll still make a report on this, right? I know in abuse and stalking cases, it's important to document, document, document. Show a pattern of behavior."

"I hate that you know that." His smile disappeared. "My friends will actually be the ones looking into this. I'm probably a little too close to the situation to be objective."

"Too close? What does that mean?"

"You and me?" He shrugged, clasping both hands around hers now. "I'm feeling something here. Between us. It's new, and we're still getting to know each other better. I'm more likely to do whatever is best for you than whatever is necessary to solve the case and arrest whoever did this. So, I called an objective third party—my boss and his partner. Two veteran detectives. They'll get answers."

"Joel, this is too much. When I called, I just… I wanted some backup. A friendly face who knows a little about me and what I went through with Augie." She was shaking her head as she spoke. "I'm not comfortable being caught up in the middle of a big investigation. I don't know why he's coming after me like this now. I don't care if he gets married again. The terms of our divorce won't change."

"He doesn't pay you alimony?"

"God, no. I want nothing from that man. I just want him to leave me alone." Maybe she was shaking. Maybe she'd gone pale. Maybe she was obsessively fixated on the angry threats. *You know what I want. Make this right. Don't ruin this for me.*

It sounded like a reckoning was coming her way.

Keeping their hands linked together, Joel pulled her aside and hunched down to put his face in front of hers. "Hey. Look at me, not at that message on your front door. Mollie?"

When he said her name, she stopped fidgeting and met his gaze. She tilted her head to keep her focus on him as he straightened. "I didn't know who else to call. Maybe because we just had that long text conversation, but you were the first person I thought of."

"I'm glad. That's what friends do. You need me? I'm here." He rubbed his thumb across the back of her knuckles, and the warmth of that simple caress seeped beneath her skin and calmed her, allowing her to stay in the moment and think more rationally. "Maybe I'll need your help one day, and I'll call you to return the favor."

"What could I possibly do for you? I'm a waitress with post-traumatic stress. I'm perennially broke and scared of my own shadow."

"No, you're not. If you were weak, you wouldn't let me stand here holding your hand when I know physical contact can be a trigger for you. You wouldn't have stood up to Garner and stopped him from being a bully." A grin reappeared in the middle of his scruffy face. "You made him go away. I'll always be grateful for that."

She pooh-poohed his joke, and she almost laughed. "That's all I'm bringing to the table? My ability to make a phone call?" And then understanding dawned. "Oh. My connection to Augie." She tugged against Joel's grip. "That's why you want to be my friend. Because you think I can help you build a case against him."

He released her hand the moment she struggled but refused to back up. "Hey. Hear me out.

Please. Maybe that's why I approached you initially. But that's not why I'm here today."

She eyed his hands as he held them out to either side without touching her. Even now he was respecting her need to be cautious about physical contact. That alone made her want him to touch her. But she petted the top of Magnus's head instead. "Why are you here?"

He scanned the hallways, perhaps making sure they were still alone before he continued. "You make me smile. You asked me to help your dog." He reached down to pet Magnus, too, and the tips of his fingers brushed against hers. "You just showed me you can think on your feet, even when you're upset. That's strength, Moll, and I admire that. You make me want to be the man I used to be. No, you make me want to be better than that guy."

She didn't pull away when he slid his hand over the top of hers.

"I can feel your hand growing cold under mine. You're holding yourself so still right now, I'm guessing you're trying to placate me and not draw any attention to yourself." His mouth hardened into a thin line. "You probably did that with your ex. A survival mechanism. And I hate that. I hate that you think I could be anything like him."

"I know you're not Augie." Those words were

true. "But I still don't understand what you think you can get out of a relationship with me if it's not part of some plan to capture my ex-husband."

He slipped his fingers beneath her palm and pulled her hand away from the dog's head. She didn't resist when he gently chafed it between both of his to bring some circulation and warmth back to her fingers. "The short version of the story is… I think I need you."

"You think?"

He glanced up and down the hallways before turning his focus back to her. "I'm a man looking for a reason to get up in the morning. A man trying to make sense of the past few years of my life and where I go from here."

"And you're saying *I'm* that reason?"

"I don't know. But I know I've felt more excited about the last two days of my life than I did the last two years before that. It's because I got to see you and talk to you and get to know you. Knowing that you like me enough—trust me enough—to ask for my help with Magnus or when you're scared or overwhelmed, tells me that I need to be strong again." When Magnus heard his name, he raised his nose and nuzzled it against the clasp of their hands. Joel released one hand to pet the dog and praise him for being so attentive. "I need to care about something beyond the guilt and anger and resentment swirling around in my head 24/7."

"Guilt, anger, and resentment?" Mollie gave Magnus some attention, too, centering herself before asking, "Are you okay?"

"I'm working on it. But not like I should." Joel pulled her fingers from Magnus's fur and clasped them within his own again. When she didn't protest, he tightened his grip ever so slightly. "Talking to you makes me feel a little less broken, a little less useless."

"You're not useless."

"My last girlfriend betrayed me. She disappeared one night. I thought I was going to save her, but it was a trap. She was already dead from an overdose of opioids laced with fentanyl, and I got hurt because of her. I literally died and had to be resuscitated because of her."

"Died?" Her hand squeezed around his again. "Joel—"

"I'm not telling you this for sympathy. Just the opposite, in fact. It's nice to have someone who believes in me enough to call me when she's afraid and needs a favor. Not someone who's using me or setting me up to get hurt."

She uttered a breathless apology. "But I *am* using you."

Mollie felt the callused pad of his thumb gently stroking her hand again. Did he even realize he was doing it? Was it weird to feel this sensual pull to the man simply by holding hands? Maybe it was the way she felt cocooned between him and Magnus and the rest of the world. Maybe it was the fact that his touching her wasn't sending her into a panic. Maybe it was the fact that she hadn't been touched so caringly in a long time.

"Asking me for help is not using me." Joel's voice dropped to that gravelly timbre that sounded so masculine to her. "Telling a drug lord that I'm a cop working undercover in his organization in exchange for your next fix is."

Her mouth dropped open, aghast at the meaning behind the words he'd so casually shared. "She did that to you? The woman you loved?" Her gaze dropped to his muscular forearms, and she traced one of the puckers of scar tissue there with her fingertip. "Is that how you got hurt?"

When she looked up again, his jaw was tight and he simply nodded. She suspected there was a lot more to his story he wasn't sharing. "Cici didn't need me. She needed her next fix. My life, my heart, meant no more to her than a wad of cash. The dealer and his thugs she was working with explained that to me in very painful detail. I was the most convenient way to get her drugs."

Mollie needed a moment to process what he was telling her. Because of his limp and scars, and hardened personality, she thought he'd been in a traffic accident. But he'd been attacked, viciously, possibly by more than one person. More than the miracle of him surviving, he'd managed to get back to his normal life and become a cop again.

She'd finally stood up to Augie. She'd put together a plan, and finally made her escape. But she hadn't moved forward from her trauma the way Joel seemed to be trying to.

"Did the police capture them?" she asked quietly. "Were they arrested?"

He answered with a scary lack of emotion. "Cici's murder? The attempted murder of a cop? Any number of lesser crimes? They're in prison for the rest of their lives."

He'd found justice for the monstrous crimes committed against him. He'd survived, got justice, and was trying to move on. She wanted to do the same. She wanted the proof of Joel coming back from deception and violence and shattered hopes and dreams to inspire her to do the same. To do better than simply survive the way she had been. "Sounds like we're both searching for what's next or closure or something to make us feel a little less broken. Augie didn't need me, either. Lied to me all the time. He wanted a trophy wife who fit the standards of what he considered beautiful and accomplished to be a benefit to his career. To show his parents that he could find a good girl and settle down and take over the family business." The more she talked about what she'd been through, the easier it was to talk about it. "And the parts of me that didn't fit—my rural upbringing, a job he considered beneath him, sarcasm, brown hair—he changed or eliminated."

"He's an idiot for not embracing and protecting the treasure you are." *A treasure? Right.* She hadn't felt like anybody's treasure for a long time, and Joel's vehement defense made her a little uncomfortable. He must have sensed her retreating from him, and hastened to add, "Just continue to be real with me. Don't hold back your snark on my account. Don't lie about what you're dealing with or how you feel. Trust me to be there for you. To be enough to take care of whatever you need. I'll do my best to earn that trust. That's the only favor I ask."

"I'll try." She shook her head. "I don't know if I'm enough for anyone anymore—"

"That's your ex talking."

"—but *you* are." She reached down to pet Magnus, who seemed more relaxed now that she was alone with Joel. Smart dog. *She* was more relaxed with Joel here, too, even with the difficult conversation they'd just shared. Then, with that same hand, she reached up and rested it against Joel's chest. She felt his skin quiver beneath her touch, the warmth of finely sculpted muscle. She watched his nipples tighten into hard nubs and push against the cotton T-shirt he wore. The instinct to pull away from his body's natural reaction to being touched, to brace herself against the possibility of an unexpected blow blipped through her mind but quickly dissipated. This wasn't Augie. This was Joel. Her friend. He wasn't going to hurt her for reaching out. She could do something as normal as give him a reassuring pat on the chest, and she would be safe. "I will try to be the friend that you need, too. I promise. But I don't know how much help I can be with Augie. That's scary territory for me."

When she would have pulled away, Joel reached up and covered her hand with his, keeping it resting gently against him. "We'll figure it all out. Whether we stay friends or become something more? Who knows? Just give me a chance, okay?"

She considered what he was asking of her. And though they'd gotten off to a rocky start, she had to admit she wanted that same chance with him. "You didn't have to tell me about KCPD investigating Augie. You could have kept quiet and just used me to get what you needed."

"I'm not using you," he stated without equivocation. "The department isn't going to use you."

She heard a low-pitched conversation punctuated by a laugh and nodded to the two men coming up the stairs behind Joel. "The decision may not be yours."

Mollie pulled away from Joel and reached for the comfort of Magnus instead. She recognized the short, wiry man with the graying sideburns as Joel's friend from the diner. But the man with him was as big as a house. His blond hair receded slightly at the points of his forehead, but the creases beside his eyes were laugh lines. She tried to focus on those, and that he'd been laughing a moment ago, and not on the fact that he towered over both the dark-haired detective and Joel.

Joel turned to greet them. "Relax. I know these guys, and they're the best detectives I've ever worked with." He extended his arm to shake hands with both men.

"Boy, you don't get out much, do you, Standage," the big man teased. "Better introduce us quick before your lady friend decides big ol' me is one of the bad guys."

"I don't think that." She didn't sound very convincing even to her own ears.

Joel reached back and snugged his hand around hers, somehow finding her hand without even looking, as if a magnet drew his hand to hers. As if he felt that same connection she'd imagined earlier, too. As if they hadn't just shared a conversation that had knocked her sideways and given her a whole lot to think about. "Don't give her any grief, Josh. Rocky Garner was just here being his usual pleasant self. This is Detective Josh Taylor, and his partner—my supervisor—Detective A. J. Rodriguez. This is Mollie Crane."

"I apologize for anything Garner said." The big blond man nodded a greeting before tucking his hands into the pockets of his jeans and assuming a casual stance. "Please know he's not representative of most of KCPD. Guys like him on the front line give the rest of us a bad name."

Mollie arched one eyebrow. "He's not doing you guys any favors."

Josh Taylor laughed. A. J. Rodriguez smiled. And Joel looked at her as if he was proud that she'd let her sarcasm peek out from her typically closed-off demeanor.

"I appreciate you two taking the lead on this," Joel said. "On the surface it looks like a typical B&E. But the picture, the threat, and the way it has been tossed inside makes me think the intruder was looking for something. Full disclosure? Mollie is August Di Salvo's ex-wife." Knowing it was necessary to share that information, she still shivered at being tied to the biggest mistake of her life. "With complications like that, I'm not ready to handle my own investigation."

"That's a crock—"

"I also have a certain prejudice against Di Salvo." Joel cut off his supervisor's protest. "If he is behind these terroristic incidents, as I suspect, then I want to make sure we build a case against him that can't be thrown out of court this time. I can provide any backup you need, but I feel better knowing you're running the show."

"Backup?" Josh smirked at A.J. "You going to set him straight, or should I?"

A.J. was clearly the more subdued partner. He nodded. "Josh, you see to Miss Crane, and I'll have a chat with our *amigo* here about resigning himself to being a paper pusher for the rest of his career."

Joel nodded toward Mollie. "This is too important for me to screw anything up."

A.J.'s face lost a bit of its cool demeanor. "You're gun-shy, Joel. Not incompetent. You need to find that badass cop I know you are again."

"This is gonna be an unpleasant conversation. Ma'am?" Josh gestured toward the apartment door with his big hand. "Have you had a chance to look around to see if anything was taken?"

She was hesitant to go with the larger man, even though he seemed polite and professional enough. "I didn't want to mess up the crime scene. I don't have much. The things I do value were with me."

"That's good." He thumbed over his shoulder to her apartment. "You want to just come hang out with me and skip the fireworks?" When Mollie didn't immediately respond, Josh Taylor nodded. "That's okay. I'll go scope things out and wait for a team from the crime lab to get here." With a nod from A.J., the blond detective took pictures of the newspaper and threats, as well as the splintered wood and scratches around the lock.

A.J. decided to postpone his lecture to Joel and turned his dark eyes on Mollie. "I'm not sure how long the crime lab will need to process the scene. Unfortunately, since the Di Salvo name is involved, this could be connected to other crimes we're looking at. You got a friend you can stay with tonight, ma'am?"

Other crimes. Oh, yeah. She knew Augie and some of his associates were involved in crimes far more serious than breaking and entering. But she wasn't ready to volunteer that kind of information. Her silence might be the only thing keeping her alive.

Although that threat on the door seemed to indicate that her time might be running out.

She pulled herself from the abyss of her thoughts and heard Joel answering A.J.'s question for her. "She'll be staying with me. Once the scene is cleared tomorrow or the next day, I'll come back with her to salvage what we can and clean up the place."

Mollie tugged on Joel's hand. "Do I get a say in this?"

"Give me a minute, A.J.?" The older detective nodded. Joel pulled her aside. "Told you I was bossy. You weren't saying anything, and I thought maybe this was all getting to be too much. I should have asked and not decided for you. And after I just dumped all my emotional baggage on you, you may not want to spend any one-on-one time with me. *Do* you have a friend where I can drop you off tonight?"

"Corie's due date is tomorrow, so I'm not calling and imposing on her."

"Melissa?"

"They're at a family reunion with Sawyer's mom and brothers and their families this weekend. And Jessie Caldwell isn't really that kind of friend. Maybe more of a mentor, but I don't want to put her out. She's already helping me with Magnus." She didn't know if she was sad or embarrassed when she added, "I don't know who else I could impose upon."

"You're not an imposition. I have a fenced-in backyard. Plenty of room for Magnus to run off-leash. It's a safe neighborhood. My coffee maker works, and I've got beer in the fridge."

"Trying to sell me on your offer with beer and coffee?" Her gaze dropped to his waist and chest before meeting his eyes again. "I suppose you do have a gun and a badge."

He smiled at her subtle teasing. "There is that."

Mollie's hand found the top of Magnus's head, and she drew in a calming breath, her decision made. "Do you have a spare bed?"

"Yes. Nothing fancy, but it's clean and comfortable."

"I come with a dog. I don't need fancy." She peeked around Joel's shoulder to A.J. "I'll be staying with Detective Standage tonight. You can call me there or on my cell phone if you need me."

"Sounds good." A.J. offered her an apologetic smile. "I really do need you to do a quick walk-through with Detective Taylor to see if you think anything is missing, or if there's another message besides what's on the door. Pack a bag if you need to. He'll let you know what things are safe to touch. I need to talk to Detective Standage for a few minutes." She nodded and headed for the door. "Sorry, but, the dog should probably remain out here. So, he doesn't accidentally disturb anything."

Her pulse leaped in a moment of panic. She

didn't want to face anything Augie had left for her on her own. "But Magnus is my service dog."

Joel held his hand out for the leash. "I'll keep an eye on him—if you'll be okay without him for a few minutes. You've got this, Moll." She debated for a moment, then put her precious boy's leash in his hand and ordered the dog to stay. "We'll be at the door, so he can keep an eye on you."

Trust me to be there for you. To be enough to take care of whatever you need.

Baby steps, Mollie. She'd made huge strides in reclaiming some of her confidence and independence over the past two days. If she didn't want to be the prisoner of her fears the rest of her life, she needed to keep taking those steps forward. She could trust this man with her dog, at least. Right? "Okay."

Carefully finding her way around overturned chairs and food dumped from her cabinets and refrigerator, Mollie entered her apartment. She looked back to see Joel in a terse sotto voce conversation with his boss. About the crime scene? About her? About Augie?

Although the conversation was slightly heated, Joel sensed her looking, and turned to make eye contact with her. He winked before glancing down at Magnus. Her Belgian Malinois was lying down like a sphinx in the doorway, his tongue lolling out the side of his mouth as he panted, his dark eyes following her as she moved through the apartment after Detective Taylor.

Relaxed. Not concerned. Surrounded by people he seemed to trust.

Could she trust these men, too?

She was spending the night with a man. She hadn't done that since her divorce. And those first few weeks when she'd been staying at a homeless shelter, trying to save enough money for the down payment on this apartment, was the last time she'd had any kind of roommate besides Magnus.

She wasn't worried about staying with Joel. She didn't fear that he would try to hurt her, didn't worry that he had an ulterior motive for being kind to her and Magnus. She didn't dread the idea of sharing a meal with him and dropping her guard enough to be able to sleep.

Joel Standage was her friend. He'd answered her call for help twice today. And she got the feeling that he was just as leery of where this relationship might be going as she was. She was honest enough with herself to admit that there *was* a relationship developing here. And that was okay. With her. With Joel. And apparently, with Magnus.

Chapter Seven

The After Dark gentlemen's club wasn't in the best part of town. But the appointments of green leather, mahogany, and etched glass gave it the feeling of wealth and privilege. The place had been raided and closed down more than once in its checkered past, but under the new management of entrepreneur Roman Hess, After Dark had become less of a strip joint, and more of a place where wealth and discretion were the norm. The liquor was top-shelf, and the booths were appropriately secluded for meetings such as this one.

The host shooed away the server who had brought their drinks and welcomed the big man who slid into his seat on the far side of the table.

The big man downed his whiskey in one gulp, then wiped the back of his hand across his lips as he leaned back against the green leather with a self-satisfied sigh. "That went well."

"Is the cop you saw her with going to be a problem?"

"No. He's gimpy and washed up. I hear he's been stuck behind a desk for the past few months. He got lucky with the car yesterday. If you'd wanted me to actually hit them, I could have." He smirked a laugh. "Should have clipped the dog, though. I'm not a big fan of that mutt."

Although the host wanted to be there to witness firsthand how Mollie Di Salvo got knocked off her high horse each and every step of the way, there was the practical matter of distancing oneself from the crimes to maintain plausible deniability. That's what willing employees like this one were for. "How did she look when you saw her today?"

"Scared out of her mind."

"Serves her right. I haven't had a moment's peace since she dared to defy the Di Salvo name."

The big man rested his forearms on the table and fisted one hand within the other. "I didn't find what you're looking for."

No apology was necessary. "I didn't think you would. That country bimbo is smarter than she looks. I imagine she has more than one copy and a couple of contingency plans to keep them hidden."

A smug smile spread across the big man's expression. "I did put my hands on everything she owns in that ratty little apartment—from dumping out the dog food to slicing up her boring cotton panties."

"She really has fallen a long way from the life she once had with us."

"I'll bet she misses everything she gave up."

"Threw away, you mean." It was hard to compare the beautiful, polished blonde who'd lived at the mansion for two years with the ragamuffin brunette who waited tables at a diner—poorly, too, if reports were accurate. "I've worked too hard to get where I am. I'm not about to let her get her grubby waitress hands on any of it. And I won't allow her to ruin what the Di Salvo family has built."

The big man nodded his agreement. "What's the next step?"

"We keep her off-balance, punish her for her disobedience. When the time is right and I do get my hands on her, I want her to fall apart and beg to give me everything I want."

"Right before we kill her?"

The host gave a firm no. "I'm not getting my hands dirty. That's what I'm paying you for."

"I appreciate you giving me this opportunity. Done wonders for my bank account. I'll be waiting for my next assignment."

"Soon. I'll let you know." An envelope thick with cash exchanged hands. "I reward loyalty like yours. Mollie Di Salvo doesn't know the meaning of loyalty. That was her mistake. Keep up the good work."

The big man tucked the envelope inside the front of his jacket, understanding that he was being dismissed. "What about her dog?"

"Expendable."

"And the cop?"

"Also expendable." The host held up a hand for the server to return with another drink. "All that matters is getting what's mine. And making her pay for causing me so much trouble."

MOLLIE STOOD ON the front porch of Joel's gray bungalow as she hugged her arms around herself and watched the rain fall from the night sky. Lightning flashed, momentarily lighting up the clouds above her, and the drumbeat of thunder rumbled in the distance. The hairs on her arms pricked to attention with the electricity in the air.

Some people might find the storm unsettling or even frightening, she supposed. But she loved being out in nature like this. After the intense heat of the past few days, a thunderstorm had been inevitable. She loved the normalcy of it all. Hot, moist air rose into cooler air higher in the atmosphere. The moving air charged the atmosphere. Water vapor formed as the air cooled, lightning flashed, and rain fell from the sky. The process repeated itself over and over. Everything felt right in Mother Nature's world tonight.

She missed nights out in the trees and hills of the Ozarks, where she could smell the rain and feel cocooned from the rest of the world by a summer storm. Her vandalized apartment had no balcony, and the metal fire escape outside her window wasn't where she wanted to stand when there was lightning. And outdoor activities beyond a stuffy garden party were generally frowned upon at the Di Salvo estate. Joel's home might still be within the city limits of Kansas City, but the old neighborhood with the charming small houses and well-tended yards felt a lot closer to the country than where she lived in the City Market area north of downtown.

She breathed in the ozone-scented air, closed her eyes, and savored the damp mist from the rain splashing her cheeks and frizzing her hair.

"I'd feel better if you two came inside." Joel's gravelly voice matched the rumbles of thunder and darkness of the night.

She smiled at the unexpected sense of familiarity and security she felt here. She spread her fingers across the limestone rocks that still held some of the heat from the day. "I love your front porch. These rock pillars make me think of Granny's house. We used to sit out on her porch when it rained. It was always so cool and refreshing. No central air."

"It's not the storm I'm worried about."

"Oh." She turned to see him waiting in the shadows behind the screen door. He was leaning heavily on a metal cane tonight. She wondered if the same barometric pressure changes she'd been enjoying made his injuries ache more than usual. "Do you really think Augie's men are out in this?" She pointed to the porch lamp beside him. "I left the light off."

"Good call." He pushed the door open wider and gestured for her to come in. "But my gun and badge still think inside and out of sight is a safer place for you to be until we can figure out what your ex is up to. Come on, boy." Magnus immediately rolled to his feet and trotted indoors to find a drier, softer place to snooze, no doubt. Mollie hesitated at the threshold, saddened to be reminded that every decision in her life seemed to go back to her ex-husband and his impact on her life. "Unless you're afraid to be alone in the house with me."

"That's not it." Mollie tilted her gaze to Joel's, marveling at how his beautiful eyes gleamed in the lamplight from inside his living room. She couldn't help but notice, too, that while she was dressed in sweatpants and a long-sleeved shirt in deference to the weather and the air-conditioning in his house, Joel wore a pair of gym shorts and a faded gray KCPD T-shirt that clung to his biceps and gave her a glimpse of more of the tattoo swirling around his left arm. Her pulse beat at a faster tempo as she imagined pushing his sleeve out of the way and tracing her fingers completely around the intricate markings.

Good grief. She'd never been obsessed with any man's body the way she was with Joel's. Not even Augie's back when she'd been happy with him. When she realized her nostrils were flaring as she breathed in the clean, spicy scent of his skin and damp hair after his shower, she turned away and hurried through the front door.

She sat on the tweedy black and tan plaid couch where she'd been reading a book while he showered and changed after dinner. The throw blanket he'd offered her earlier was piled on the oak floor beside her feet, and Magnus was stretched across it with his head resting on his teddy bear. With Magnus's dog bed out of commission, Joel had been kind enough to give the dog permission to make himself at home with his things, although she'd drawn the line at letting the dog up on the couch. Dog hair and drool weren't the easiest things to clean up.

Mollie heard the screen door latch and two locks engage on the interior door before Joel spoke again. "Then what is it? Do you need something? I'd rather not run to the store in this weather, but I will. I can loan you a sweatshirt if you're cold. Or, I've got a spare toothbrush from my last trip to the dentist if you forgot yours."

Wincing in sympathy, she watched pain jar through his clenched teeth as he limped around the black leather ottoman that served as a coffee table and practically fell into his seat at the far corner of the sofa. He leaned the metal cane against the armrest and immediately dug his fist into the scars of his thigh above his right knee. "How much pain are you in?" she asked.

"Answer my question first. Are you okay being in here with me tonight?"

"Joel," she protested.

"Moll," he mimicked right back.

She would have laughed at his teasing delivery if she wasn't worried about him. "On a scale of one to ten, what's your pain level right now?"

"You're not my nurse."

"No. But I do have some experience dealing with healing fractures and sore muscles."

Joel nailed her with a look that conveyed a depth of anger he thankfully held in check. "I'm never going to let that man touch you again."

Yeah, yeah. Augie was a monster who'd screwed up her life and left her a fragile shell of her former self. But one thing she *could* still do well was focus on someone else, especially if that someone was in pain, and she could help. "One to ten?"

The grin that softened the angles of his face made her think she'd imagined the anger from a moment before. "You were a handful for your granny growing up, weren't you. Sarcastic. Stubborn. Strong. That's the real you, isn't it."

She faced him on the couch, settling her back against the armrest and curling her legs beneath her. She plucked at an imaginary piece of lint on the butt-hugging sweats she wore and nonchalantly responded. "I can neither confirm nor deny any worrisome late nights I might have caused Granny."

He laughed out loud.

THAT WAS THE moment when Joel realized he was in deep trouble with this woman.

At first glance, Mollie Crane was fragile and scattered and in need of a rescuer—just like Cici Martin had been. And yeah, she triggered his need to help and protect her, to be needed by someone. But unlike Cici, who'd lost her way to drugs and a quick fix for her pain, Mollie had courage and a sense of humor and was fighting for her own salvation every step of the way. She turned to a dog, not drugs, to cope. She worked hard at a job she might not love, found herself a decent place to live, bought herself a rattletrap of a car he fully intended to check out before he let her drive another centimeter in it, and made her own way in the world. She'd escaped her violent prison, and still had the strength to make a joke and care about others. He'd seen her interact with the people she worked with at the diner. It felt as if she might even care a little bit about him.

"That's the Mollie I like. Do you mind if I put my feet up?" She didn't protest when he turned sideways and stretched his legs across the couch. It was a big piece of furniture, and with her curled up like that, his toes barely touched the edge of the cushion where she sat. "Storms like this and changes in the weather wreak havoc on my rebuilt knees. Plus, I lost my favorite cane in your alley yesterday, so I've been walking and running without it too much today. I'm probably at a four or five. The hot shower helped. I'll take a couple of ibuprofens when I go to bed. Mostly, I just need to get off them for a while."

"Do you have enough room to stretch out?" she asked.

"Yes. Now, answer my question." He was really hoping for an answer that wouldn't make him feel guilty for issuing the invitation earlier that evening. "Are you okay here? Or is being with me stressing you out?"

"I'm fine."

He suspected as much after she'd put her foot down about his pain and teased him with a silly answer about her childhood, but he still breathed a sigh of relief to hear her say the actual words. "I'm glad."

"I certainly don't want to be in my apartment with a busted lock tonight. Even with Magnus, I wouldn't feel safe. I'm sure I wouldn't sleep." She shrugged. "I don't know if it's the house or the storm isolating us from the threat that's out there, or you, but I feel safe. I enjoy our conversations. I know there are some heavy issues we have to discuss regarding Augie. But I appreciate that you're not pushing me. To be honest, I haven't felt this…normal…with a man in a long time."

"Normal?" Was that akin to *comfortable*?

"It's hard to explain." She tucked a dark curl behind her ear and caught her bottom lip between her teeth in a soft smile that zinged straight to his groin. He wanted to taste that bottom lip for himself, soothe the spot where she nipped it with the stroke of his tongue. But she continued to talk, and he wasn't going to do a damned thing to scare her away from the easy conversations they'd been sharing all evening. So, he continued to rub at the knotted muscles in his thigh and pretend that this was how every evening between them might go. "The storm reminds me of where I grew up. I love your house. It's small, but it feels like a home. It's easy, relaxed here. I don't feel I have to dress for company or choose the right fork to eat with."

"We had pizza and beer and used our fingers," he reminded her. "I'm not that fancy."

She patted her tummy, indicating that she was still full from the takeout meal they'd picked up on the way here. "My ex-mother-in-law would have had a coronary if she caught anyone eating on the couch watching the ball game like we did tonight. And pizza was food for the hired help, not the Di Salvos. If Bernadette caught me eating anything but a canapé or hors d'oeuvres with my fingers, she would have told Edward. Edward would have told Augie. Then there'd be a conversation about me forgetting my station and embarrassing him."

"Did your in-laws live with you?" She was talking about her past. This was the information he needed. He knew he should keep her sharing intel about her previous life, but hell if he wanted to talk about anything except the two of them.

"The Di Salvo estate where you worked for a few months belongs to Augie's parents. *We* lived with *them*. Separate wings of the mansion, but still…" She sighed heavily. "Unless they were traveling, or he was on a business trip, Edward and Bernadette were there."

"Nothing says *honeymoon* like having your in-laws on the premises."

But his joke didn't elicit a smile. "Edward and Augie had offices in the city. But they conducted a lot of their business at the house. Dinner parties were contract negotiations. Business associates would stay in a guest room and use the home office for strategy meetings. Late-night drinks were for problem solving."

"What kind of problems?"

"Augie could be a loose cannon." Obviously. "He'd alienate clients with a temper tantrum or sleep with someone's wife. I learned too late that marrying me was supposed to clean up his reputation." She pumped her fist as if she was repeating a familiar cheer. "Sweet, all-American girl. No family to speak of, but a straight-A student who hadn't gotten herself knocked-up before graduation or caused any scandals. Pretty enough to be arm candy, but not ambitious enough to be a threat to the family." She shook her head, no doubt recalling what a sham her marriage had become by the time he'd met her. "I was in a vulnerable place when I met him. Granny had just died. I thought I was gaining a devoted husband and a loyal family who cared about me. But I was just window dressing. Once I got to know the real family, I became a prisoner, a puppet to play whatever part they needed from me."

"I'm so sorry. You deserve so much better."

She nodded. "Because I was so unhappy, *I* became the problem sometimes."

"You?" Since she'd been isolated from him during most of his assignment there, he hadn't realized just how much of the family business pertained to her. She could be a gold mine of information for KCPD. But the more he got to know her, the less he liked the idea of looking to her for a lead on their investigation. "What possible problem could they blame on you?"

She plucked at that invisible piece of lint again. "Volunteering for the wrong charity. I'm trained to teach. I wanted to volunteer with schoolchildren, but that didn't have the client base the Di Salvos were looking for. I needed to schmooze with wealthier people. Set them up for meetings with Augie."

"I'll bet you're a good teacher. Do you miss it?"

She gave him half a smile. "I keep my hand in it by tutoring Corie's son, Evan, and Jessie Caldwell's foster kids."

"Why are you waiting tables? Isn't there a demand for good teachers?"

Her gaze dropped to the dog snoring at the foot of the sofa, and he knew he'd hit a sensitive spot for her. But before he could turn the conversation to something less upsetting for her, she answered. "Edward is friends with one of the school board members. He got a note slipped into my personnel file that says I'm a danger to children. That I'm mentally unstable."

"No way." Joel fisted his hand on the back of the sofa and scooted closer to her. "You have panic attacks brought about by a traumatic marriage that they're responsible for. People with disabilities work in schools all the time, and yours is minor compared to some of the stuff I've heard about. They're all good people. Good teachers. Just because they're in a wheelchair or blind or need a service dog doesn't make them a threat to anybody."

She gaped at him through his entire defense of her. Too late, he realized he was probably scaring the crap out of her.

"I'm sorry," he quickly apologized. He opened his fist and pulled it back into his lap. "What you said pissed me off. I didn't mean to yell at you."

"You weren't yelling at me. You were angry on my behalf. I can tell the difference." She didn't leave the room. She didn't reach for her dog. She didn't even flinch away from his toes pressed against her knee. His brave, backbone-of-steel girl simply nodded and quietly answered. "That's the kind of power they have. If they want something, they know someone or pay someone to make it happen. Or they pay someone to make it go away."

"Like you?"

She was silent for so long, Joel thought he'd pushed too hard, got too emotional, and the conversation was over. But her words surprised him. "I left on my own terms. I didn't take a penny from them." Her fingers rubbed against the outline of the locket she wore beneath her long-sleeved T-shirt. "The break-in at my apartment? I'm sure they were looking for something I took from Augie." She reached down to pet Magnus now, as the conversation became more stressful for her. "I had to blackmail him to get him to sign the divorce papers and then leave me alone. He threatened to kill me if I ever left him. And I believed him. I had to do something to get the advantage over him."

Blackmail? Forget the fact that technically Mollie had committed a crime if what she was saying was true. This could be the mother lode of information A.J. thought she could give them. "What could you possibly take that would inspire the kind of violence you've seen the past couple of days?"

"Evidence of illegal activities. Money laundering. Payoffs. Intimidation tactics."

Bingo.

But there was a catch. She nibbled on her bottom lip again, and it was all Joel could do not to slide across the sofa and take her in his arms and tell her she never had to talk about any of this again. "I know that's what you want from me. That's what A.J. and Josh want from me. But I can't give that to you. The moment I hand over the information I have, I lose any leverage I have over Augie and his family. They'll come after me. They'll silence me. The only advantage I have is that they don't know where I've hidden the information, or how many copies I've made, or who I've arranged for it to be distributed to should anything happen to me. I'm sorry, Joel, but I can't do it."

Magnus sat up and laid his head in her lap, no doubt sensing the same fear he felt radiating off her in waves.

"You have evidence that can implicate the Di Salvos?" Joel felt compelled to point out the same facts A.J. and Josh would. "Withholding evidence is a crime."

She continuously stroked Magnus's head, but her pretty blue eyes were focused squarely on him. "So is blackmail. If it helps any, I never took any money from them. Just the divorce and my freedom. Arrest me if you have to, but keeping the evidence hidden is how I'm staying alive."

And that's where the facts he needed for this investigation ended.

After a few moments, Mollie gave Magnus permission to lie down again. "Good boy. You go night-night with Teddy, okay?" Joel imagined the dog was giving him the stink eye for upsetting his mama before the Malinois stretched out again on the floor in front of the couch.

That was probably his cue to shut up and get to bed himself before he said or did anything else that would scare Mollie away from the tentative trust they shared. "I'll recheck the windows and doors, make sure everything is secure before we turn in."

"You're not going to ask me any more questions about Augie?"

She was frowning when he met her gaze. She didn't yet understand that her well-being was more important to him than any investigation. "No."

Joel started to pull away. But Mollie grabbed his ankles and stopped him. "The round, puckered scars on your knees. Are those bullet wounds?"

He tugged against her grasp. "You don't want to hear my story tonight."

Her grip tightened almost painfully, and he suddenly had the insight that maybe she needed to talk about something else besides August Di

Salvo so she could fall asleep and not have night-mares. Or simply fall asleep at all. Once she realized she was still holding his legs, she eased her clutch on him and stroked her fingers along the sides of his calves. Her fingertips felt like heaven against his skin. But she suddenly pulled them away. "Is it okay if I touch you?"

He nodded. "You don't have to ask. You can touch me anytime you want."

"But you're so respectful of my needs. You always ask, or make sure I know it's you."

"Those are your boundaries, and I'll respect them as long as you need me to. Mine are different. Not everybody gets permission, but you do." He held out his hand until she rested her fingers against his palm. "Yes. I've been shot in both legs."

Her grip tightened around his for a moment before she pulled away to settle her hands back against his legs. "You've had surgery to replace both knees?"

"Yes."

"You sound so cold and clinical when you talk about your injuries."

"My therapist says that, too." Her eyes opened wide at the news he'd been seeing the KCPD psychologist. Well, that he was supposed to be reporting for more sessions with her. "But that's how I cope. I keep my emotions pinned down, so they don't get in the way of doing my job."

She arched a skeptical eyebrow. "Your job pushing papers?"

He poked her knee with his big toe. "Smart-ass."

Thankfully, she let the topic drop and resumed her curiosity and concern about his pain.

"I always found that alternating a hot wash-cloth and cold compresses helped when my injuries were healing." She climbed up onto her knees and scooted between his feet, forcing his legs apart. "Once the bruising had faded, a good massage stimulated the blood flow and helped the aches feel better." She leaned forward and wrapped her hands around the thigh he'd been rubbing himself. When she dug her thumbs into the ligaments and muscle above his knee, he winced. But it was a good kind of pain. The initial rebellion of his knotted muscles calmed a bit with each pass of her fingers across his skin. "Wow. You're tight as a crossbow. You've been overcompensating for your painful joints. No wonder you're limping."

"Crossbow?" he bit out through his tightly clenched jaw. Her strong hands and nimble fingers created a friction that warmed his skin and settled into his muscles. The massage hurt at first, but he exhaled sharply when the cramp unknotted itself and the pain finally eased to an ache rather than the stabbing sensation that had practically crippled him.

She inclined her head to the book on the ottoman. "You had a copy of the first Bonecrusher Chronicles on your bookshelf. I love that series."

He nodded. He liked that they were both fans of the high fantasy series. "Larkin Bonecrusher carries a crossbow."

She smiled in a pretty apology as she continued to work the kinks out of his leg muscles. "Don't take this the wrong way, but you don't look like a reader. Yet you've got a ton of books over there."

Genuinely curious now, he asked, "What does a reader look like?"

"You know. Skinny. Glasses. Socially awkward." She slapped a hand over her mouth and blushed. "I am so sorry. That was a terrible stereotype." She went back to the massage, focusing intently on her work and refusing to meet his gaze. "Readers come in all shapes and sizes and personalities, of course. I just meant that you seem more like a man of action, that you prefer to be outdoors rather than curled up on the couch reading like I was." He grinned when she waved her hand at him, indicating his face and body, without looking at him. "With all your badness and spiky hair and scars and scruffy face and all."

His badness? Joel chuckled and extended a hand toward her. "May I?"

She nodded when she understood his intent. "You don't have to ask every time you want to touch me, either. As long as I know it's you."

"Thank you." He reached out with one finger to tap her chin and tilt her gaze up to his. "I'm an old pro. I had a lot of time to read during my recovery. Besides, that's how I got my brothers to sleep every night. I'd read stories to them. It's still how I get myself to sleep most nights."

"I like that. I read, too, to escape reality long enough to calm my thoughts and relax."

He pulled back and leaned against the arm of the sofa, savoring her willingness to touch him and truly appreciating the massage. "I don't know what kind of badass you think I am. Blending in and looking like every other guy on the street is my stock-in-trade. Yeah, I work out and take care of myself. But I've always had a forgettable face. Brown hair, brown eyes. I'm easy to overlook. Makes me a perfect candidate for undercover work."

Her hands stilled above his knees. "That's not true."

"No, I was pretty good at UC work. Right up until my last case."

"What I meant was that there's nothing about you that's forgettable. Your eyes are more golden than brown. That first night I met you, I thought of a tiger. And tonight, they're reflecting the light the way a cat's would. Your voice is sexy— low and gravelly, like you just woke up or you just had…"

Her eyes got wide, and she blushed. *Sex.* She was thinking about him and sex together in the same sentence.

Joel adjusted his position on the couch to hide his body's reaction to her innocently provocative words. He was in more trouble than he thought. He wasn't just attracted to Mollie's sass and vulnerability. He was falling hard and fast for a woman who'd been so damaged by her previous relationship that she might never be able to love again.

She curled her fingers into her fists and pulled away to hug her arms around herself. Just as quickly, she was gesturing to him again. "You're funny one minute and over-the-top manly the next. You've got muscles and tats. Not everyone is into those, but they give you that bad boy vibe—unless those words on your arm are a Shakespearean sonnet."

"They're not. If you want to read my ink, all you have to do is ask. I just didn't think you were the kind of woman who would be into tattoos."

Her eloquent hands landed on her hips, and she gave him a confused look. "What kind of woman do you think I am?"

"Very high-class. Out of place in a working-class neighborhood like the City Market or Brookside. A lady through and through. Way out of my league."

"And you claim I misread *you*?" Any trace of embarrassment was gone. Now she was just huffy, and it was cute as hell. "Joel Standage, I was raised in the country by my granny. Not my grandmother or my grand-mama. We lived in a little town in the Ozarks. I went from kindergarten through twelfth grade, all in the same building. I can make biscuits and gravy from scratch that would make your daddy weep. I can change my own tire on a car and fix a toilet. I played second base on my high school softball team, and we made it to State my senior year and I had the best double-play completion stats in the entire state that year. I had a twang in my voice until I met Augie in college, and he convinced me I could go further in life without it. But it sneaks back in now that I don't have to watch every word I say. I try to be a lady, but I'm not some prissy girlie-girl with a stick up her butt like you're describing."

Food. Cars. Softball. Snark. He was so hot for her right now.

He realized his mouth was hanging open, and he snapped it shut. "You can make biscuits and gravy?"

She puffed out a breath that stirred the wavy bangs on her forehead. "That's what you got out of my impassioned speech?"

"I love biscuits and gravy."

She smiled and shook her head. "You come off as a streetwise bad boy, most of the time. But you're just a little boy inside."

"A little boy who likes biscuits and gravy," he mock pouted. She laughed out loud, and Joel smiled, thinking she didn't do that nearly often enough. "And if I'm around, you won't be changing your own tire or fixing the damn toilet. You don't have to change who you are to meet some society standard that the Di Salvos want you to be. That's not what makes you a lady."

She uncurled her legs from beneath her and scooted back to the far end of the couch, pausing as she considered his words. He could see the expression on her face change when she made a decision.

Leaning toward him, she rested her hand lightly over his shinbone. "Do you want me to fix you breakfast in the morning?"

"Yes. If you can find something more than a box of cereal in my pantry, I would love to eat anything homemade."

"You don't cook?"

"I fix cars."

"Huh? I don't get the connection."

"I never learned how to cook. Mom left us, remember? I learned how to fix cars. I'm good with engines, not ovens."

"How did you feed your brothers when you were taking care of them?"

"I can grill burgers or hot dogs outside, and whip up a mean box of mac and cheese. And I can zap anything in the microwave. But I don't have the kind of skills you're talking about."

He was suddenly, vibrantly aware of her hand on his leg. "I'm sure you have other useful skills, Detective."

Well, hell's bells. Was that sexual innuendo from Mollie Crane? Or did he just want it to be? The part of him swelling inside his shorts voted yes. Joel swung his feet to the floor, grabbed his cane, and stood before he embarrassed her with his physical reaction to her. "It's late. You must be getting tired. Does Magnus need to go out one more time? When do you need to get up for work? You can use the alarm on your phone, or I've got an old clock in my dresser."

Mollie stepped over Magnus and hurried to block his path on the other side of the ottoman. "Did I say something wrong? You act like you're trying to make a quick getaway."

When this whole assignment started, he promised himself not to lie to her. He wasn't going to start lying now. Feeling like the luckiest man in the world to know she'd given him permission to touch her, he reached out to capture a tendril of rich brown hair that had fallen over her cheek. He watched the tendril curl around his finger before he brushed it back and tucked it behind her ear. Then he sifted his fingertips into the silky weight of her hair at her nape and cupped the side of her neck and jaw. "I like you, Mollie Crane. More than a guy you need as a friend should. Some of tonight feels like flirting, like we're on a date and really getting to know each other because it's leading to something... I'm trying to be a good guy and walk away while I still can."

"A date? Can you imagine how out of practice I am at picking up signals and flirting after being married to Augie? And you have no idea how good it feels to have somebody touch me, and be able to touch him, and not freak out." Instead of pulling away, she turned her cheek into his palm. Her skin was warm and soft against his. "I'm sorry if I made things awkward or you thought I was leading you on."

"I don't. You have nothing to apologize for."

She smiled at being let off the hook so easily. "I've been scared for so long, it felt good to relax with you tonight and be comfortable enough with you to resurrect a little of who I used to be. I mean, I do have brains and a personality. I have history besides being a Di Salvo. I care about people. I haven't always lived from one panic attack to the next."

He picked up on the same word he'd been feeling since the moment they'd reconnected at the dog park. "You're *comfortable* with me?"

"Yes. I'm surprised at how quickly I'm learning to trust you. It's like I've known you for a lot longer than a couple of days and a couple of random meetings in the past."

"It's like fate kept trying to push us together, but we weren't in the right place in our lives to do anything about it until now."

Nodding her agreement with his fanciful notion, she wound her fingers around his wrist, holding his hand against her face, linking them together. "Full disclosure? I think I also have the hots for you, and I'm wondering if I can ever be *normal* with a man again. If I can build the kind of trust necessary to be intimate with someone."

Joel burned with the implication of what she was saying. "Did Di Salvo…?"

"Yes. He forced me. Whether or not I was in the mood didn't matter if Augie wanted sex. Thankfully, he always had a girlfriend or two on the side, so it didn't happen too often."

Not too often? That didn't make it any easier to hear how that bastard had brutalized her. "I'm going to kill that son of a bitch."

She shifted her hand to cup his unshaven jaw, mirroring the hold he had on her. "No. You're not. If I'm lucky, you're going to be very patient with me, and you're going to conduct a thorough police investigation. And then we're going to put him away in prison, where somebody else can kill him for us."

Joel's eyebrows rose at the quick addendum. She'd not only calmed his need for retribution, but she'd said *we* and *us*, letting him know that she was feeling the bond growing between them, too. "Yes. To all that. I shouldn't like your vindictive streak, but I do."

She glanced down at the tent in his gym shorts and pulled away without putting any distance between them. "Thank you for being stronger than I am tonight. Maybe one day you won't feel you have to hide that from me, and we can make out on your couch. Hopefully, I won't freak out on you and be a disappointment."

"No way could you disappoint me. We're *comfortable* with each other, remember? That's our motto now. Making out with you will blow my mind, I'm sure. Anything beyond that will be a true gift. And if it never happens, that's okay, too.

We'll go as hot and heavy or slow and careful as we need to, and I will treasure every moment."

He was surprised when she grasped his forearm and turned it so she could read the words inked there. "Are you sure this isn't a sonnet on your arm? You spout some pretty sweet poetry when you want to."

"Nah." He pulled up his sleeve so she could read the full message. "It's part of the Armed Forces prayer. I got it in honor of my father and brothers."

She read the words out loud. "'Teach us not to mourn those who have died in the service of the Corps, but rather to gain strength from the fact that such heroes have lived.'" Tears glistened in her eyes when she tilted her gaze back to his. "Oh, Joel. This applies to you, too. It's beautiful. Your family must be so proud." She stunned him when she leaned in and kissed the words above his elbow. Then she lifted her gaze to his. Keeping her hand braced against his bicep, she stretched up to gently kiss his stubbled jaw, his cheek, and finally the corner of his mouth.

He couldn't have held back the groan of desire that rumbled in his throat if his life depended on it. Mollie was kissing him. Battered by life, but never broken, she sweetly, boldly slid her lips against his. She'd put her hands on him and stirred his body to life. But her soft, sweet lips were stoking a fire deeper inside.

Joel dropped his cane to the rug and cupped her face with both hands, tunneling his fingers into the silky weight of her hair. He kissed her chastely at first, pressing his closed mouth against hers, not wanting to frighten her just as much as he *did* want to claim everything she offered him. She didn't protest when he angled her head from one position to another, seeking the perfect link between their lips. And each new taste was as perfect as the last.

He felt each fingertip digging into the muscles of his arm, and her open palm skimming along the textures of his scratchy stubble and the short, damp hair at the back of his head. When her lips parted to capture his bottom lip between her own, Joel felt his temperature spike. In response, he stroked his tongue along the plump arc of her lower lip and the sculpted arch of her pliant upper lip, asking for permission to enter. Her warm gasp across his skin was more of a turn-on than the most seductive words. Her lips parted and her tongue tentatively reached out to touch his. Their tongues danced around each other for a few seconds before he slipped inside her mouth and claimed the generous gift of her willing mouth.

He tasted a slight tang of beer on her tongue, or

maybe that was his own. He breathed in the delicate flowery scent of whatever lotion or soap she'd used on her face. Their bodies never touched. It was hands in hair and lips and tongues, exploring and claiming, giving and demanding, and absolute heaven.

This woman was brave yet fragile. She was strong but delicate. She was generous yet cautious. She was more than everything he wanted in a woman. With this kiss? This moment? He knew that she was everything he needed.

With a nervous chuckle in her throat, Mollie broke off the kiss. He felt the gusts of her uneven breaths against his neck and knew he was breathing just as erratically. But he didn't try to re-engage her. He didn't pull her into his body the way he longed to. He didn't tug on her hair to tip her head back so he could kiss his fill of her. Any physical contact between them needed to be on her terms.

Mollie tilted her dark blue eyes up to his. "Sorry. I liked that. I loved it. I've never kissed a man with beard stubble before. It's…sexy…like a hundred extra little caresses against my skin." Her hands had settled on his shoulders, and her gaze dropped to his lips. "You're a really good kisser. Or, maybe I've never been kissed right before… You probably wanted something more, but I'm feeling a little overwhelmed…"

"Hey." He pressed his thumb against her slightly swollen lips to silence her rambling and keep her nerves from spiraling out of control. "Treasure. Every. Moment." He whispered the heartfelt promise before planting a silly kiss on the tip of her nose and another to her forehead, where he lingered long enough to inhale the fragrance of her skin and hair once more. "I don't think I've ever been kissed that right before, either. Thank you."

He bent down to pick up his cane. His gaze swept past her taut nipples poking against the thin cotton of her shirt and he smiled. It was nice to know he wasn't the only one whose clothes felt a little confining right now.

Mollie stepped back and called Magnus to her side. "Magnus is fine for tonight. I'll use my own alarm. Good night, Joel."

He reached out and tucked her short hair behind her ear, tracing his fingertips around her delicate earlobe before pulling away. Knowing he could touch her like this soothed him, even as the possibility of getting closer to her excited him. "Good night, Moll."

She gifted him with a smile before turning away and ordering Magnus to heel. Joel watched her walk down the hallway to the guest bedroom. He was still leaning on his cane and watching as her door snicked shut behind her.

What the hell was he doing here? He wasn't

the best man for Mollie's protection detail. He probably wasn't even the best man to be her friend. She needed someone who wasn't as broken as he was. She needed better.

But after tonight, after getting close to her, he wasn't giving the job to anybody else.

So, he was damn well going to figure out how to be a better man for her.

Protector, friend, dog walker, lover—whatever she needed, he wanted to be able to give that to her.

And that meant getting rid of his cane, getting out from behind a desk, and getting back to being the cop—and the man—he'd been before his world had imploded.

Chapter Eight

Joel holstered his weapon, counted down from three, then pulled out his Glock and fired the last three bullets in rapid succession into the outline of a man on the downrange target.

Then he dropped the magazine from the butt of the gun and opened the firing chamber to make sure both were empty before setting them on the shelf in front of him. He was aware of the dark-haired man waiting patiently behind him in the booth at the firing range in the basement of the Fourth Precinct building. But he wanted to complete this round of training to make sure he was good enough to be responsible for Mollie's safety. He was trying to find his way back to being good enough for her, period.

He'd known when A. J. Rodriguez had slipped into the back of the booth a few minutes earlier, but he was focused on the task at hand. He appreciated his boss's inimitable patience and knew that was half the reason A.J. had earned his legendary reputation at KCPD. Joel removed his safety goggles and earphones and pushed the button to bring the target forward.

A.J. pulled off his earphones and hung them on the hook beside Joel's safety gear. "Working off some steam? Or getting your skills in shape so you can go back to your real job?"

"I'm trying to come back from being an idiot and dying. I *need* to come back."

Joel studied the paper target hanging in front of him. Most of his shots hit center mass. But there were three wide shots that would only wing a perp he was trying to bring down or annoy him with the boo-boo on his arm.

A.J. stepped up beside him to check the results, too. "Looks like your aim is drifting a shade to the right. You still favoring that leg?"

Joel felt almost normal right now, but he hadn't gone for his morning run or taken the stairs to the third floor more than once today. He was still relishing the fabulous, unexpected massage he'd gotten from Mollie last night. Although he hated knowing how she'd become such an expert in pressure points, pinched nerves, and massages, she could do some amazing things with those hands. "It's doing better. I don't think it's a hundred percent yet. I don't always need the cane. I just have to be careful about wearing myself out."

"You'll get there."

"Or I'll learn to compensate."

A.J. waited while Joel reassembled and reloaded his gun and secured it in his holster. "I got your message you wanted to meet. Is this about Miss Crane, or you?"

"Both."

"Walk me to my office?" A.J. pushed open the door and gave a salute to the officer on watch while Joel checked out of the range. "We can talk on the elevator ride up."

They walked past the locker rooms, and Joel remembered hiding out there his rookie year when a tornado had come through the city. The building had gone through an extensive remodel since that time, both for architectural and security purposes. But for a long while, it had been just a place to stow his stuff and hang out before his shift upstairs. But that was about to change. He wanted to get back out into the world and be a cop again. Maybe he wasn't ready for the pressure and isolation that came with undercover work. But he could be a detective. He could run an investigation. He could help Mollie.

He followed A.J. into the empty elevator and waited for the doors to close before he spoke. "I talked to Mollie Crane last night. She does have evidence against August Di Salvo."

"Yeah? She tell you what she has on him?"

This was where Joel needed to tread carefully. "It sounds like something in a file or on a flash drive. She took it to blackmail Di Salvo into signing their divorce papers."

Although his posture looked relaxed as he leaned against the back railing of the elevator, A.J.'s full attention was zeroed in on Joel. "She gonna work with us?"

Joel shook his head. "Mollie is in a very vulnerable position. I don't know if we should continue working this investigation through her. There has to be another avenue we can pursue."

"We tried that already. We couldn't get any witnesses to stick to their original testimony against him. His attorney, Kyra Schmidt, got him off on time served and a fine for obstruction of justice. We need hard evidence and a reliable witness."

Imagining Mollie up on the witness stand while Di Salvo stared daggers at her, and Kyra Schmidt glibly made her look like she was too scared to know her own mind, wasn't an easy picture to stomach. "If she turns it over to us, what's to stop him from going after her? He's threatened to kill her more than once. She claims it's her only leverage to keep him out of her life."

A.J. straightened as they neared the third floor. "Keep him out of her life? What do you think the car in that alley and the break-in at her apartment are about? I'd say Di Salvo or someone who works for him is back in her life already."

The elevator stopped, and Joel followed A.J. through the check-in desk and cubicles of detectives to reach his office in the back hallway. "Those are the angles I want to pursue. If we can tie either one of those crimes back to Di Salvo, we can at least get an arrest warrant and get that guy off the streets so she can breathe a little easier."

A.J. unlocked his door and invited Joel to one of the chairs in front of his desk while the supervising officer circled around to his own chair. "You're going to need a lot more than a B&E and reckless endangerment to keep a Di Salvo behind bars."

"But if we have more than just what she brings to the investigation, doesn't that lessen the threat to her?"

A.J. eyed him for a moment before sitting. "How close are you getting to her?"

"She's staying at my house."

"You up for a protection detail like that?"

Joel paced to the window and looked down on the parking lot below. He scrubbed his hand over the trimmed stubble on his chin that he'd decided against shaving off completely this morning because Mollie had said she liked how it felt against her skin when he'd kissed her last night.

He considered A.J.'s question. Clearly, his emotions and desire were already getting tangled up with Mollie Crane. But was he ready to put his life on the line to save someone he cared about again? His heart would do anything to protect her. But his brain wasn't so sure he was the best man for the job. "I don't know, A.J. I've been sittin' a desk for a few months now. That's why I was at the shooting range this afternoon. I know there's a gap between being fit for duty, and being fit enough to hold my own on the street the way I used to."

"Maybe you're a step slower than you used to be. Or you hurt more at the end of a long day. But you were one of my best operatives out on the streets. A lot of people are serving time because of the work you've done. Even the cowards who tried to kill you. You can think on your feet. You're aware of everything going on around you. You know when to hide, when to run, and when to fight." A.J.'s dark eyes drilled into Joel's gaze, making sure he understood what the veteran detective was saying to him. "Even beat-up around the edges, you're a good cop. You need to own that."

Joel returned to his seat across from A.J. He braced his forearms on his knees and clasped his hands together. "The instincts are still there, but I find myself second-guessing almost every decision I make. I'm not sure I know who to trust. I'm not sure I even trust myself."

"Let your training get you past those doubts. You trust me?"

"Yes, sir."

"Then I'll be your handler. I'll get you whatever you need as fast as I can." A.J. picked up the phone on his desk, as if he was about to make a call and get the ball rolling on him becoming an active investigator again. "You trust Mollie?"

Joel hesitated.

A.J.'s thumb ended the call before it had even connected. "It's your decision. You want me to assign someone else to work the case? To protect her?" He leaned back in his chair. "I think Rocky Garner's available."

"That's a low blow." He pushed himself upright. His boss probably wouldn't be giving him a hard time on this if he didn't think he could handle himself successfully.

"Think on it, Joel. Until Miss Crane decides to give us and the D.A. a statement on this evidence she has, Di Salvo will always be a threat to her. What if she decides never to let us help her nail her ex? Can you be on alert 24/7 the rest of your life?"

"If that's what she needs."

"You have to sleep sometime. You're gonna need some backup." A.J. pointed the phone at him, sending the message that even though he was supportive of his team, he was still the man in charge. "I'd have a lot easier time budgeting the extra manpower with the brass if we were getting useful intel from her."

Joel leaned back in his chair, still needing some time to make his decision. "What did you and Josh and the crime lab determine about the break-in at Mollie's apartment?"

"I believe it was as much about intimidation as it was finding this evidence you say she has. It wasn't just a search—it was personal. No more written threats, but…"

Joel wasn't sure he wanted to hear the details, but he needed to. "But what?"

"The intruder went through her lingerie and shredded it. A picture of an old woman with Miss Crane had been cut up, too."

"Her granny?" Joel cursed. "He's trying to break her. He's trying to get in her head and punish her for having the strength and resourcefulness to outwit him and play hardball with him so that she could get away from the family." The only time he'd seen an obsession like the one Di Salvo had for Mollie was when he witnessed Cici's addiction to drugs firsthand. The thing he wanted the most—to hurt Mollie—was the most important thing in his life. "He probably believes that if he can victimize her again, make her afraid, he can force her to give up the evidence and stop anything incriminating from getting to us and the D.A."

"You think her ex can break her with his intimidation tactics?"

"No. She's a strong woman. I just don't think she always believes it."

"Sounds like somebody else I know, *amigo*." A.J.'s dark eyes narrowed with a piercing stare before he waved him on his way. "Now, get out of here so I can get some work done."

Joel rose from his chair and crossed to the door. He paused with his hand on the doorknob. "May I ask a question?" A.J. nodded. "I heard that you went undercover with your wife, before you married her. Because she was a witness to a murder?"

"That's right." A.J.'s gaze drifted to the picture on his desk of his wife and two boys. "Claire and I met when I was working that case. She was the only person who could identify the hit man."

"Would you have trusted her protection to anyone else but you?"

"That was a different situation. She was already under my skin, and I was falling in love with her. It was my honor and my duty to protect her."

"Would you put her life in anyone else's hands?"

Dark eyes studied his. "No." Then A.J. opened

a file and picked up his phone, already going back to work. "Talk to her. See if you can get her to open up to you. And watch your back out there." Knowing he was dismissed, Joel nodded, stepped out, and closed the door.

Under his skin and falling in love. That was exactly where he stood with Mollie.

His decision was made.

JOEL ENJOYED THE training session with Magnus and Mollie. And now, as he watched Jessie and Garrett Caldwell's foster son, Nate, play with Magnus and a myriad of other dogs of all sizes and breeds—from a lumbering Newfoundland to an active Jack Russell terrier, who was darting amongst the other dogs in search of the balls the boy was throwing—he could see the benefits of having a pet or partnering with a working dog.

He drank a long swallow of the tea Jessie had served to the four adults watching the dogs and boy play from the back deck. "Man, I miss having dogs around." He took a seat in the Adirondack chair next to Mollie and pressed the icy glass to his forehead to cool off from the ninety-degree heat. "I wish I could bottle that work drive. I would have graduated from physical therapy and been cleared for active duty a month sooner if I could have focused like Magnus does."

"You recently suffered a trauma, too, Detective Standage?" Jessie asked.

Back to reality. His lighthearted mood vanished. He'd been treating this early evening session like a date when he should have been thinking about how to move the Di Salvo investigation forward while keeping Mollie safe.

The thick, humid air weighed heavy in his lungs as he took in a deep breath and set his drink down. "Yeah. I was injured in the line of duty."

Garrett Caldwell was still wearing his Jackson County deputy's uniform since he'd gotten home from work just before the training session had ended. "Sorry to hear that. What happened?"

Mollie reached over and squeezed Joel's hand. He was grateful for the gentle touch and lightly curled his fingers around hers. Jessie noticed the contact, too. Since he'd figured out that these training sessions were like therapy for Mollie, he wanted to help her get the answers she needed about Magnus. That meant opening up about himself, too, apparently. Still, he opted for sharing the barest of bare-bones versions of his story. "I was working undercover. Got made as a cop."

"That's rough," Garrett sympathized. Judging by the silver in his hair and the chevrons on his badge, he'd had considerable experience in law enforcement. He understood the dangers a man with a badge faced when meeting the enemy face-to-face.

But Jessie wanted details. "What else?"

Joel pinned her with a look. That woman was as intuitive about reading people as she was dogs, it seemed. He must have been staring at her for too long because Garrett moved to sit on the arm of the chair beside his wife and drape a protective arm around her shoulders. "Jessie's just trying to understand the complete picture so she can make an accurate assessment of what's going on with Magnus."

"Sorry." His grip pulsed around Mollie's, and his raw feelings settled to a manageable level with that simple connection to cling to. "I was betrayed by my last girlfriend. She set me up with her dealer. Told him I was a cop."

Mollie leaned forward to add, "She's gone, too. Drug overdose. Joel tried to save her."

A stark look temporarily darkened Garrett's gray eyes, and he leaned down to kiss Jessie on the crown of her hair. The older woman's hand squeezed her husband's knee, and she gazed up at him until he nodded, and the fiercely protective expression finally eased. "Yeah. Drug dealers can be tough SOBs to deal with."

Joel nodded, thinking Garrett and Jessie and possibly that little boy they were both studying so tenderly now had some personal experience with a drug dealer. Jessie inadvertently confirmed it when she looked up at her husband. "They're okay now, Garrett. Just remember, Nate and Abby are going to truly be ours by Christmas."

"Damn right, they are." He tipped Jessie's chin up and kissed her gently on the mouth. Then he stood, apparently satisfied that his wife was safe without him beside her. He pointed to the house. "I'm just going to check to make sure Abby and her puppy are doing okay upstairs." Joel stood when the older man extended his hand. "Good to meet you, Detective. Mollie."

After he'd gone into the house to see to their foster daughter, Jessie smiled. "Garrett's such a protective father. That little girl isn't going to be allowed to date until she's well into her thirties if he has his way."

Joel smiled as he was meant to, although he felt a little lost when Mollie released his hand. Jessie stood and invited both of them to join her at the railing to watch the dogs eagerly chase the balls and bring them back to the boy, who rewarded them with pets and praise and throwing the balls again. "So, what's the verdict, ma'am?" Joel asked. "Magnus seemed to work just as well with me as he did Mollie, once she showed me the commands. Am I a bad influence on the dog? Am I preventing him from helping her?"

"I don't think so. Mollie, you said Magnus stayed by your side when you had the break-in?"

She nodded. "And he growled at the man who made me feel so uncomfortable."

Jessie tilted her gaze to Joel. "And Magnus came to comfort you when you were telling your story to Mollie."

"That's right."

Jessie pulled her long, blond braid from her shoulder and tossed it behind her back. "I think I know what's going on."

"Please tell me," Mollie urged.

"Magnus sees Joel as part of your pack, and he's protecting the pack," Jessie explained. "Mals are overachievers. Why just take care of one human when he can take care of two? He sees the two of you together as a unit he's in charge of. Basically, he wants to be a service dog for you both. He wants to please you both. I hope you two are serious because he thinks you are."

"Serious?" Mollie echoed. "Like a couple?"

"Yes."

Joel reached down to capture her hand again and lifted it to his lips to kiss it, taking a moment to rub his chin across the back of her hand, giving her some of those hundred little caresses she'd liked so well last night. Her blue eyes darkened, and her lips parted with a sharp intake of breath. Yeah, that kiss last night hadn't been a fluke. These feelings that were hitting him hard and fast seemed to be mutual. "We're working on it."

Mollie's gaze locked on to his. "We are. We have some issues we're still working through, but I care a great deal about Joel."

"Ditto."

She rolled her eyes in that beautifully snarky way she had at his eloquent response, but she was smiling. Then she looked out at Magnus charging across the yard to reach the ball first. "So, you think he's okay? There's nothing wrong with him?"

Jessie shook her head. "I'd keep up your regular training—both of you now. And let him do his job. I think he'll continue to alert when you have a panic attack and—" Jessie glanced up at Joel "—he'll offer you comfort when you're stressed about work or events in your past. And he'll probably be protective of you both."

"Okay. Then I'll try not to worry." Mollie stepped in front of Joel and embraced the other woman. "Thank you, Jessie. I was so worried that either I was a failure or Magnus was."

Joel settled his hand at the small of Mollie's back as they hugged, letting his fingertips slide beneath the T-shirt she wore to touch a strip of soft skin above the waistband of her jeans. Mollie didn't flinch at the modest contact, and since she seemed okay with it, he didn't pull away. But they'd just crossed an emotional hurdle by admitting they cared about each other, and he needed to touch her as much as she needed to hug the woman who had given her a way out of constant fear and stress with Magnus.

"No way is either of you a failure." Jessie smiled, and he was pleased to see Mollie smiling back as the women parted. He was even more pleased to feel Mollie slide her arm behind his waist and hook her thumb into the belt loop of his jeans. "You just have a very smart dog," Jessie continued. "You know, sometimes, I think with his hearing loss, that Magnus feels broken, and he feels he has to do more—be more—to prove that he's important and loved and necessary."

"I understand that," Mollie said, surprising Joel. "I think that's why the two of us bonded."

"You're not losing that bond," Jessie assured her, squeezing Joel's arm to include him. "You're just enriching it by adding Joel to your pack."

Was she talking about dogs or his relationship with Mollie now?

Mollie seemed to ponder the same question for a few seconds before she pulled away and gave Jessie another quick hug. "We'd better get going. It's dinnertime and you have hungry children to feed. Thanks so much."

Jessie frowned. "This isn't the last time I'm seeing you, is it?"

"Of course not. You and your family have a standing invitation at Pearl's Diner. I make to-die-for milkshakes that your kids will love."

"I'd love one, too."

Mollie nodded toward the aging German shepherd mix that had been napping by Jessie's chair. "And bring Shadow with you. Service dogs are welcome there."

"I will."

"Magnus! Come!" Although the Newfoundland had tired of playtime and lain down in the middle of the yard, the other dogs were running circles around him and Nate.

When the Belgian Malinois didn't immediately respond to Mollie's summons, Joel thrust his tongue against his teeth and let out an ear-piercing whistle. The dogs all stopped and turned as one. "Magnus!" Joel put two fingers down at his side, and the black-and-tan dog came running right to him. He touched his wet nose to Joel's fingers, then sat beside him, heavily panting from his exertion. When he saw Mollie crossing her arms and glaring up at him, he quickly apologized. "I didn't think he heard you."

"I can see we're going to have to work on exactly who the pack leader is," Mollie teased before handing him the dog's harness and leash.

Jessie laughed along with Joel. "As long as it isn't Magnus, you two will be okay. Come on, I'll walk you out to your truck."

Chapter Nine

Following another round of goodbyes and a promise to keep in touch, Joel pulled his truck past the gated entrance and security cameras and turned out onto the road leading to Highway 40 into Kansas City. Since there was no center console on the wide bench seat of his truck, Magnus was stretched out between him and Mollie, resting his head on Mollie's lap. She stroked her left hand along the dog's back, more out of habit, he hoped, than any nervousness she was feeling about being alone with him again.

He waited at the light before turning onto the highway. Because they were headed into Kansas City, they were driving against the rush hour traffic heading out to the countryside and small towns east of the city. And since 40 was a divided highway out here in the county, they were pretty much the only vehicle on their side heading west.

He replayed the words she'd said to Jessie. *I care a great deal about Joel.*

Ditto might not have been the snappiest response, but he meant it. He cared a great deal about Mollie. And he had an idea that Magnus had spotted right away what the two of them had been reluctant to recognize, much less act on. He and Mollie meant something to each other. And if she gave him the chance, they were going to mean something to each other for a long time to come—maybe for the rest of their lives.

But he'd start small. He had a feeling knowing when to be patient and when to push would be key to any long-term relationship with Mollie. "Speaking of dinner…" Not the smoothest start to a conversation, but he had Mollie's attention. "We'll drive past about any kind of fast-food restaurant you want when we get to K.C. We can drive through one of them and get dinner to eat at home. Are you in the mood for anything in particular?"

"You're not going to zap something in the microwave for me and show off your cooking prowess?"

He loved it when she teased him. It felt healthy. Normal. A special way to communicate between just the two of them. "Nah. I'm saving that for our third or fourth date. I don't want to spoil you."

She laughed with him. "So, we're dating now?"

Joel sobered up, not wanting any misunderstanding between them. "I'd like to. Maybe I just needed Jessie to put things into perspective for me, but I like you, Moll. A lot."

"You said that last night."

"Yeah, well, maybe it's more than a lot." He glanced across the cab to find her listening intently to his words. "When you told Jessie you cared about me, something seemed to click inside." He skimmed the rearview mirror and took note of a couple of cars on the highway behind them before turning his focus to the road in front of them. "Even when you were still married to the jackass who hurt you, I was attracted to you."

"I was black-and-blue, and I had a split lip and cracked rib."

"You were glorious. Strong. Brave. Not afraid to set me straight when you told me the rules of the house." He glanced her way again. "Di Salvo would have made things worse for you if I had tried to help you then, wouldn't he."

"Yes. He would have hurt you, too. If not physically, you'd have lost your job, for sure. Of course, I didn't know then that chauffeuring wasn't your real job."

"I was involved with Cici then, so I wouldn't have acted on my attraction. I felt guilty for not being able to help you then, but I admired you." She turned away to look out the side window, and he took note of the SUV behind them, slowing and turning left into a tire and auto repair business between the east and west lanes of the highway. With the hills, curves, and trees along the highway, there was only one other vehicle in sight behind them, and that one disappeared into a valley, and they were alone again. "Then I met you again that night at the diner when Rocky Garner put his hands on you, and I was struck all over again by how much I was attracted to you. I wanted to punch his lights out for upsetting you like that."

"I was a mess, Joel," she reminded him. "I'm still a bit of a mess."

He shook his head. "You're a work in progress. So am I. We've both been through some stuff, but we're getting better. The chemistry between us gets my blood pumping, just like it always has. You mentioned that you miss human contact. But when you hold my hand or reach out to me, it soothes something inside me. Knowing you trust me enough to be the man you can do normal, touchy-feely stuff with makes me feel like a stud."

She chuckled at that description. "You *are* a stud, Joel Standage."

He tried to explain himself in a way that didn't make him sound so egotistical. "Spending time with you makes me feel better about myself. I feel grounded. You settle things inside me."

"We're comfortable with each other."

"Yeah. I think *comfortable* for us means we're good for each other. Maybe I sensed that potential bond when we first met two years ago." He shifted his grip on the wheel, wishing he wasn't doing so much of the talking here. "Please tell me I'm not the only one feeling this connection between us."

"You're not," she answered quietly.

"We're both free of our exes now, in one way or another. We can do something about how we feel."

"I'm not free of Augie."

"You can be."

He heard her pained gasp above the hum of the truck's tires on the pavement. "If I turn over what I know to you and KCPD."

"Think about it, Moll. If we could get him behind bars where he belongs, and you've got the evidence to keep him there, then you'd be free of him. His parents are only going to bail him out so many times. His lawyer can't charm a judge or dispute hard evidence. His so-called business associates won't let the Di Salvos touch another dime of their money if he goes to prison." He remembered her vindictive wish from last night. "They might not want him alive in prison if they think he's going to turn state's evidence and implicate them in exchange for a lighter sentence."

Magnus whined in her lap now, and Joel hated that he was causing Mollie any kind of distress. "What about those weeks or months between handing over the flash drive that got me out of that house and testifying against him? He'll kill me, Joel. Or he or his father will hire someone to do it for him. Then you've got no witness, and Kyra Schmidt can refute or discredit any evidence you got through me, and I'll still be dead."

He wanted to reach across the seat and be the one she turned to when she needed comfort. But he kept his hands on the wheel and let Magnus do his job.

"I'd be with you the whole time. We'd go to a safe house. There'd be backup in place. A.J., Josh, a SWAT team. Whatever we need to get you through the trial and sentencing. I'll keep you safe. If you'll let me." He took a deep breath and put his heart on the line. "I want a future with you. We can move as slowly as you need to, and I'm okay with that, I swear. As long as I know you want that future, too."

"I do." Her words were hushed, but he heard them loud and clear. "But I'm scared, Joel. So much."

Her blue eyes were hard to look away from to concentrate on his driving. "You think I'm not scared? I lost everything once. But I'm falling in love with you, and I don't want to give up without fighting for us."

"You want me to fight for us, too." It was a statement, not a question.

"Can you? Will you give us a chance?"

She considered his challenge for several seconds. "Will you give me some time to think about it?"

The volume of his sigh of relief was almost embarrassing. Magnus's tail thumped against his thigh, and he considered it a good sign. "I'll give you as much time as you need—"

His gaze caught a blur of movement in the rearview mirror, and he swore. How the hell had that car caught up to them so fast? The driver must be breaking all kinds of speed limits.

And then it topped the hill behind them.

"Son of a…"

"Joel?"

Black Lexus. Gold trim. A dent in its fancy grill from where it had bounced over a curb at high speed.

He pushed a little harder on the accelerator, needing to put some distance between them. "Moll, are you buckled up?"

"Of course."

"Magnus is in his harness, secured in the seat?"

"Yes." Those questions naturally made her suspicious. "What's wrong?"

"We're being followed. I know that car and he's gaining speed." She whipped around to look behind them, but he urged her to face forward again. "Don't look. I don't want to alert him that we're onto him yet." He nodded toward her door. "Check your side-view mirror."

She looked out her window and sat up straighter. "That's the same car that tried to run us down in the alley. What is he doing?"

He tightened his grip on the steering wheel and channeled every bit of training he'd had into doing what was necessary to get them out of what he suspected was about to happen. "Any chance you can get a read on the license plate?"

"Uh. It's a Missouri Bicentennial plate, with the red and blue squiggly lines?" Her fingers curled beneath Magnus's harness, and she braced her other hand against the dashboard to steady herself as they picked up speed to peer more closely into the mirror. "He's coming up awfully fast." She glanced back at Joel. "How fast can this old truck go?"

"This old truck can outrun that engine he's got any day of the week. He looks stylish, but I've got substance."

"That's right. You fix engines."

"Can't cook an omelet like that one you made this morning, but I can make this baby run like a Mack truck."

Their words came out faster and louder as they raced up one hill and down another. She leaned over Magnus and rested her fingers on his forearm. "I like substance."

"Me, too, babe. License plate."

"M-X—I don't know if that's a three or an eight." They hit a bump and all three left their seats for a split second. "I lost him behind that hill."

"Grab my phone off my belt." He gave her the security code to unlock it. "Find A.J. in my contacts. Give him our location, the three digits you got off the plate, and tell him we're being pursued." Joel swore as the car reappeared behind them. He couldn't make out the driver through the sun reflecting off the windshield, but he could see the arm and the gun sliding out the driver's side window. "Tell him there's going to be shots fired."

"What?"

"Do it!"

He nudged Magnus's butt to get him to sit up and move over, and Mollie curled her arm around him while she rattled off information to A.J. like a seasoned dispatcher. "He's sending backup and calling the sheriff's department. Says he's not clear on jurisdiction."

"Tell him to notify Garrett Caldwell." They sank into their seats at the bottom of the next hill before the truck kicked into a stronger gear and flew up the next hill. "We may need a friend to smooth things over for us because this is about to go down outside city limits."

He saw the first flash of a gunshot and knew the driver had fired his weapon. They were going too fast to get an accurate aim—he hoped. Hell. He *heard* the next pop of gunfire and knew the guy was getting too close.

"Shots fired, A.J!" he yelled for his boss to hear. "He's going to try to run us off the road."

"He says 'Affirmative.'"

Lowering his voice, he risked sliding his hand over hers where she clung to Magnus. "You okay?"

"No. I'm scared out of my mind. But I'll do whatever you tell me." She checked her side-view mirror again a split second before a bullet shattered the reflection. She jerked back in her seat. "Joel!"

He eyed the road up ahead. This guy had a plan. But Joel was onto his game. He had a plan, too. "He waited for this straight, empty stretch of road. We need to do this before we hit that curve at the end and those trees up ahead."

"Do what?"

"Hang up. Hold on."

"Gotta go." She ended the call and tucked his phone into the front pocket of her jeans. The black car swerved into the left lane and crept up beside his truck. "Damn it." The passenger side window was open. Was there a second shooter in the car? Or was the driver going to pull the incredibly foolish stunt of shooting through the car at breakneck speed and risk a ricochet inside the vehicle if his aim was off? "Get down!"

"Down, boy." Mollie pulled Magnus down and leaned into the middle of the seat with him while Joel reached for his holster. When he couldn't immediately free his Glock, he felt nimble fingers brush against his and unhook the clasp to free his weapon. "Be careful, Joel."

He breathed deeply—once, twice—then steeled himself for the coming confrontation. "I got this."

Mollie squeezed his thigh. "That's what A.J. said."

And then there was no talking. There was speed and gunfire. The black Lexus drifted onto the far shoulder, then the driver overcorrected and nearly clipped the side of the truck. He heard one ping off the bed of the truck. Another bullet smacked into the door panel. *Damn that loser. He's messin' up my truck!* Mollie gasped as another shot shattered his mirror and he felt the nick of something sharp pierce his forearm. *And you're scaring my woman!*

The truck sat up higher than the Lexus so he couldn't see into to car to know who was shooting. But he knew the guy was firing wild. A stray bullet could come right through his open window if the shooter leaned over far enough to angle his shot up. But that wasn't happening at this speed.

But that also meant *his* shots wouldn't hit their intended target, either.

Plan B. Think on your feet. Know every detail of your surroundings. That's what A.J. said he had over other cops. They were barreling toward the curve and the thick grove of trees beyond. No cars up ahead. No vehicles close behind. What he wouldn't pay to be a lefty right about now. But he could make this work.

"This is gonna be loud," he warned Mollie a split second before he eased up on the accelerator and the black car surged ahead of them. The shooter had actually done him a favor by taking off his side mirror. It made it easier for Joel to twist his body and brace his right hand outside the doorframe. He took a bead on the black car and fired off five shots in rapid succession.

He hit his target with bullet number four.

The right rear tire exploded, sending the Lexus into a tailspin. The car swerved from one side of the road to the other, leaving traces of rubber and sparks from the bare rim on the pavement. When it sailed past the shoulder and hit the ground that had been softened by last night's rain, the car flipped over and rolled three times before it plowed into the trunk of one of the stately pine trees that had been planted ages ago when Highway 40 was still a two-lane road.

Joel pumped his brakes to a stop and pulled off onto the side of the highway, turning on his warning blinkers before he shut off the engine. He ripped off his seat belt and holstered his gun before reaching down to palm the back of Mollie's head. "You can sit up now, babe. Are you okay?" She was pale and breathing hard as she pushed herself upright, but Mollie nodded. Spine of steel, this woman. He spared a quick scratch around the ears for Magnus. "How about the big guy?"

"He's fine. We're both fine." She reached up to cup the side of his jaw. "Are you okay?" Then she saw the blood trickling down his forearm. "Joel!" She grabbed his wrist and pulled it across his lap to inspect the small cut. "You *are* hurt."

"It's just a scratch." He could barely feel the sting with her hands moving so tenderly around the injury.

"No more bullet holes or shrapnel wounds, okay?"

He wished he could make her that promise.

"First aid kit?"

"Under the front seat. I'm good for now," he assured her, pulling her fingers from his arm.

"Can't say the same for my truck, but I can fix that. I need to check the other driver."

She'd been so helpful in following his orders when he needed to keep her safe, that she hadn't seen the devastating crash. But she saw the aftermath. Her fingers went to the locket that hung inside her shirt and she whispered a soft prayer. Gouges of sod were torn up along the car's tumbling path. Scratches of silver bled through the black paint. A headlamp and part of the grill had snapped off and were scattered along with a hubcap and shreds of the rubber tire in a debris field. Steam or smoke was spilling out from the crumpled hood.

There was no sign of the driver. But whether he was unable to get out of the car, or he was lying in wait to shoot them, Joel couldn't know until he got eyes on the perp.

He was relieved to see the color flooding back into her cheeks. "Should I call 9-1-1?"

Joel nodded. "Backup is already on the way, but we'll also need an ambulance and someone to reroute traffic around the accident."

"I can do that."

He massaged the back of her neck and let his fingers tangle in the curls of her hair for a moment before releasing her. "Stay in the truck with Magnus."

She pulled out his phone and handed it back

to him before unbuckling and pulling her own phone from the back pocket of her jeans. "We're good, too."

Taking the woman at her word, Joel opened his door. His gun was in his hands, and he was carefully making his way to the wrecked vehicle.

"KCPD! Drop your weapon and put your hands out the window where I can see them." He should have put on the protective vest he kept in his go bag in the back of the truck. But he hadn't planned on making a traffic stop today. And this guy—this loser—was definitely stopped. With the tinted windows in the back still intact, he steeled himself for approaching the car. "KCPD! I said to get your hands…"

The last of his adrenaline whooshed out on a frustrated curse. The driver wasn't lying in wait to shoot him. The driver wasn't doing anything ever again.

He identified the location of the man's gun on the floor in front of the passenger's seat. Then he holstered his own weapon and reached in to press his fingers against the man's neck. The driver had been battered around inside the car. The blows to the head or even his chest smacking against the steering wheel would have been enough to stop his heart.

Joel wasn't sure if he was angry or saddened by the loss of life. It had been a damn foolish stunt to try to pull off. But he needed to know why this particular man had been targeting Mollie.

He spared a moment to reach inside the car and turn off the engine before stalking back to his pickup. He opened the door on Mollie's side of the truck and held out his hand for her phone. "We're not getting any answers out of him."

"I'm handing you over to Detective Standage, ma'am," Mollie explained to the Dispatcher before surrendering her phone. "He's dead?"

Joel nodded. He requested to be patched through to Deputy Caldwell. He was amused, and stunned again by Mollie's determination, to see her open the first aid kit to clean and doctor the cut on his arm while he talked on the phone. Once he explained the situation to the deputy sheriff, he felt a shade better about what he needed to ask of Mollie. "Thanks, Garrett. I'll see what I can find out. See you in a few. Standage out."

Joel waited in the open triangle between the open door and the body of the truck while she taped gauze over the cut and tucked her phone back into her jeans. "Jessie's Garrett is coming?"

"We're still in the county. We're not in KCPD's jurisdiction. But I want someone I know backing us up on scene." Perched on the seat above him, Mollie had watched him through the entire conversation. He braced his palms on the seat on either side of her thighs. "How squeamish are you?"

Her eyes got wide, then narrowed with a question. "After surviving Augie? Not much."

"Any triggers?"

"A few." She looked beyond him to the car and understood what he was really asking. "If you're worried about a lot of blood, though, I'll be okay."

"I really need you to confirm the ID on this guy."

"Is it Augie?"

Joel shook his head. But if he was right, she wasn't going to like what he'd found.

"Can I take Magnus?"

"Yes. And you'll take me."

"Then I'll be fine."

She scooted to the edge of the seat to climb out the door, but he stopped her and planted a quick, firm kiss on her lips. "Bravest woman I've ever met."

Her gaze skimmed across his face, his shoulders, and chest, before blue eyes met his. "Kiss me again, Joel."

Although he was surprised by the request, he didn't hesitate to tunnel his fingers into her hair and lean in to cover her mouth with his. Her taste was sweet. Her touch was tender. And Joel knew he'd never shared a kiss that meant as much to him as these few stolen moments of shared support did. She stroked his face as she pulled away. "This grounds me, too," she whispered. Then she braced her other hand against his bicep and climbed down. "Magnus, come."

He waited for the dog to take his place beside her, then captured her hand in his and led them to the wreck.

When they reached the passenger side of the crumpled vehicle, Joel took her by the shoulders and turned her to look at him a moment. "Take a deep breath." She did. "It's not pretty. Looks like he hit his head more than once."

"You're positive he'd dead?"

More than. "Yeah, babe."

Mollie inhaled another deep breath before she stepped up to the driver's window. She quickly spun away and buried her nose against his chest. "Oh, my."

Joel willingly wrapped his arms around her and pulled her farther away from the body. "Tell me that's who I think it is."

Shock seemed to chase away her fear when she looked up at him. "Rocky Garner. He's not in uniform, but that's him."

"There's been some bad blood between him and me, so I didn't want to make the identification. And I'm not touching the body until the M.E. gets here."

"Garner's been after me? I mean he's a jerk, but...trying to kill me? Us? That doesn't make any sense. Can a cop even afford a car like this?"

Joel pointed to the sticker on the rear window. "It's a rental. Stay here." He circled around to reach through the open window of the passenger door. He pulled the rental agreement from the glove compartment. He read the information and cursed. "Leased to Kyra Schmidt. The lawyer who makes trouble go away for Augie."

"And his new fiancée."

Chapter Ten

Mollie awoke to a cold nose nudging her hand, followed by a whine and several warm licks across her skin.

It wasn't the first time Magnus had awakened her in the middle of the night. But it was the first time she hadn't been in the throes of a nightmare when he forced her out of her horrific memories and fear that sometimes never left her, even when she slept.

The moment her eyes opened, Magnus crawled up on the bed beside her and licked her cheek. He was whimpering in earnest now, and Mollie wondered if she'd been dreaming something awful and had simply forgotten it the moment she was awake. Only she wasn't covered in a cold sweat, and she wasn't shaking with the terror that usually accompanied the panic attacks that could take hold of her even in her sleep.

She sat up to embrace the dog. His eyes were almost invisible in the blackness of his face and the darkness of the room, but she could feel his strength and warmth and smell his treat-scented breath. "I'm okay, good boy. Mama's okay. Did I scare you? What's wrong?"

And then she heard the headboard in Joel's bedroom thump against the wall of the guest room where she slept.

This time she did startle and jumped to the middle of the bed. "What the...?"

She petted Magnus, timing her breaths to each stroke and slowing both until she was fully oriented in the bedroom that was illuminated only by the bathroom light Joel had left on for her across the hall. Her sweats had been pushed up to her knees and the long sleeves of her T-shirt were nearly up to her elbows. Maybe she'd gotten hot during the night, or maybe she had been unsettled in her sleep.

But when the headboard thumped against the wall again and Magnus woofed, she knew she wasn't the one in distress tonight. The dog gently mouthed her hand, urging her to move. Someone less accustomed to violence and nightmares might have thought she was overhearing the sounds of sex. But she was far too attuned to the insidious ways fear could overtake one when they were at their most vulnerable in sleep.

"I'm coming. I'm coming." She pushed Magnus off the bed and scooted to the edge. She shivered when she stepped onto the cool wood beyond the small rug and blanket where she'd been sleeping. Tugging her sleeves down to her wrists and smoothing her pants down her legs, she put her hand on Magnus's head and followed him down the hall to Joel's room. "Show me."

Magnus led her unerringly through the shadows to the open door of Joel's bedroom. She stopped to let her eyes adjust to the near total darkness. "Magnus!" she called in as loud a whisper as she could without disturbing Joel.

Instead of sitting next to her when she stopped, the dog trotted into the room and propped his front paws on the bed. He dodged and dropped to the floor when Joel kicked his foot out from the covers twisted around his legs, but he had his paws right back up on the bed a moment later. Magnus wasn't the only one concerned about the man who was thrashing in his sleep as though his life depended on it. Besides the sounds of him twisting in the bed and pummeling his pillows, she could hear guttural vocal sounds coming from his throat that nearly broke her heart. That had been her more nights than she could count.

"No. Stop." Those words and her name were words she could make out.

But it was the strangled whimpers that had her whispering his name from the doorway. "Joel?"

Magnus trotted back to her and tugged at her

sleeve again. Not sure exactly what she was supposed to do in this situation, she listened to her heart instead of all the damaged memories in her head. She let Magnus pull her into the room. "Good boy. You're Mama's good boy."

She cautiously approached the bed and raised her volume to something more than a whisper. "Joel."

She turned on the lamp beside the bed, blinking against its soft illumination. Wow. Joel Standage, in the middle of summer, at least, slept in nothing but a pair of gym shorts. And with the covers down around his ankles, she could see every inch of muscle across his chest, and the whole of the tattoo circling down his left arm. He had an innie belly button and those V-shaped muscles at his hips that pointed down to that most masculine part of him. Mollie gulped at the hard beauty of his body and felt an answering heat of feminine awareness between her thighs and at the tips of her breasts. How could this man ever call himself *forgettable*?

And how had she ever believed that she'd never be attracted to a man again? Her body, her heart—and her dog—kept drawing her toward this one.

But hearing the keening sound in his throat and watching him clench every muscle in his body against the terrors in his mind shook her out of her hormonal stupor. "Joel," she called in a louder, firmer tone. Still no response. But she knew who had a stronger voice. "Magnus, speak!"

At the same time Magnus barked, Mollie touched Joel's shoulder. "Joel—"

Suddenly Joel was awake. She screeched in surprise when he snatched her wrist and flipped her beneath him on the bed. Her breath lodged in her chest at the weight of him crushing her, the feel of her wrists cinched within his grip and his hips cradled intimately against hers. She knew a brief moment of panic. But that awareness was followed just as quickly by the realization that she wasn't caught in a bruising grip, and there were certainly no insults or profanities being hurled at her. *Not Augie. Not Augie.* "Joel?"

Those golden eyes blinked, then opened wide in horror.

She inhaled a deep breath as Joel scrambled off her. "Damn, Mollie. I'm so sorry. Did I hurt you?"

"Startled me." She slowly sat up, curling her legs beneath her. "But I'm okay. I'm more worried about you."

He slid to the edge of the bed, his head bent, elbows on his knees, his fingers raking through his short hair. "I had you pinned under me. I didn't bruise your wrists, did I?"

His voice sounded as agonized as those sense-less mutters in his throat had.

"I'm okay."

"I didn't remind you of him, did I?" His tor-tured gaze sought out hers.

No. No way could this rough-around-the-edges man with the sense of humor and addic-tive variety of kisses ever remind her of the cold polish and selfish evil of August Di Salvo.

She scooted to the edge of the bed beside him. She caught the wrist closest to her to pull his hand from the punishing assault on his head. He flinched with the instinct to pull away, but he purposely relaxed his arm against his thigh as if he might hurt her by struggling, and she kept hold of him. She reached out with her left hand to cup his stubbled jaw and turn his an-guished face to her. "Joel. Look at me. Take a deep breath. I'm okay."

He did as she asked, much the same way he'd calmed her in the past. "I'm sorry I woke you. I never want to add to your stress."

"You woke Magnus. He was worried about you and came to get me." He glanced down at the dog trying to wedge himself between Mollie and Joel's knees. Mollie moved her hand to the middle of Joel's back and rubbed what she hoped were soothing circles there. "Do you think I'd feel better knowing you were in here suffering, fighting some demon in your sleep, all alone? Magnus did what he was supposed to do. He sensed you were in trouble, and when he couldn't take care of you, he went and got help."

"But *I'm* supposed to be taking care of *you*."

"No. You're supposed to be *protecting* me. And I do feel safe with you. But I'm not an invalid, Joel." She kept one hand on Joel's back—his broad, smooth, incredibly warm back—and petted Magnus with the other. "One of the things I like about you is that you treat me like a normal woman. I've had some experience with nightmares, and I'm a terrific listener. I *am* someone who can help. Please let me. Now praise your buddy here. He did his job."

Joel reluctantly reached down and scrubbed the dog around his ears and muzzle. "Good boy, Magnus. Good boy." Magnus's tail thumped against the floor at the bit of roughhousing. She was relieved to see the hint of a smile at the corner of Joel's mouth. It reached the other corner when Magnus pushed his head into Joel's hands, and they shared some more gentle wrestling. "That's my good boy."

She let the boys bond for a few moments before asking, "Do you need to talk about your dream? It seemed pretty violent."

Joel shook his head. When the wrestling stopped, Magnus stretched out across their feet.

She suspected that Joel appreciated the contact as much as she did. "Should you talk to your therapist about it?"

He glanced at her, then focused on the dog again. "I stopped going."

That might explain why his emotions had manifested themselves in his dreams. "I'm willing to listen to anything you want to tell me. I care when you're hurting like this, but a police psychologist would be able to give you some specific strategies for coping. I talked to a therapist at the shelter where I stayed for a while." She pointed to her canine savior at their feet. "Hence, the service dog. Would you do me a favor and call tomorrow morning to make an appointment?"

He considered her request for a moment, then nodded.

"Thank you."

Joel brushed the backs of his fingers across her cheek and played with her hair, smoothing the tendrils that refused to stay in place off her forehead. While she enjoyed the soft caresses, he seemed to think better of touching her and pulled away. "The nightmare was about you. It was you in that car, battered and bleeding, not Garner. I couldn't save you. Then it was you in that drug house where I found Cici, and they were hurting you." His gravelly voice was raw with emotion. "And then you were in that dumpster with me, and I couldn't save you. I'm going to fail you the same way I failed Cici."

"That's a crock," she muttered. "You *did* save me, Joel. You have saved me. More than once." She pulled her toes from beneath Magnus's warmth and faced Joel, lightly clasping his forearm. "Today on the highway. In that alley. Two years ago when you were undercover. When I was too scared to function, you came, and suddenly I could think again and do what I needed to do. The fact that I'm sitting here with you now and I'm not panicking is a testament to how many times you've saved me. You've given me back the gift of human touch. You've reminded me that I once was a pretty sweet catch."

He folded his larger hand over both of hers. "You still are in my book."

"Nightmares are wicked things, preying on our fears and worries and stress. Our lives haven't been easy. But we're here. And we're both okay." She turned her hand to link her fingers together with his. "Sometimes, you just need the reassurance of someone holding your hand or hugging you or making love, to *feel* that you're safe and cared for. That you're going to be okay."

One eyebrow arched when she said the words *making love*, but he didn't comment on it. "Magnus does that for you. You ground yourself in reality when you pet him or hug him, or he nuzzles his cold nose in your hand."

She smiled at how well he knew her and her dog. "May I do that for you tonight?"

"You want to nuzzle your cold nose in my hand?" His stab at humor reassured her more than anything else that he had recovered from the nightmare and was feeling more like the good man she cared for so deeply.

With that thought foremost in her mind, Mollie asked, "Could I sleep with you and hold you while you sleep?"

"Only if I can hold you, too." He lifted her hand to his lips and gently kissed her fingers. "I'd really love to *feel* that you're safe, even when my mind is trying to tell me otherwise."

Mollie nodded and crawled to the middle of the bed, where she straightened the mess he'd made of his pillows and sheets. Then she lay down and patted the mattress beside her. "Do you have a preference which side you sleep on?"

"The one where you're within arm's reach." He urged her to lie on her left side and snuggled in behind her. With one arm under his head on the pillow, he curled the other arm around her waist. He tugged at the hem of her shirt, and she gasped when she felt his warm, callused fingers splay across her bare skin underneath. "Is this all right?" When she didn't immediately answer, he started to pull his hand from under her shirt. "I'm sorry."

"Don't." Mollie caught his hand and laced her fingers with his to put it right back on her belly and hold him against her. "I like the feel of your hands on me. It's not sex, but this feels intimate to me. I miss intimacy. Lying like this feels good to me."

She felt his lips near the crown of her hair. "Me, too."

They lay together like that, as close as two people who still had their clothes on could be, for several minutes. Mollie felt her own heart rate calm to a contented rhythm, and she relaxed against him, eventually feeling the tension in him begin to fade, too.

Soon after, Joel's voice vibrated against her eardrums. "You know, as much as I love holding you—as much as I need this to settle myself down—I'm having a little trouble with an audience watching us sleep."

Mollie blinked her eyes open to see Magnus resting his head on the bed, those dark, steady orbs indeed watching them. She laughed softly and smiled at the dog. "Give me your hand." She put both their hands on Magnus's head. "Good boy, Magnus. Your pack is safe."

"Good boy," Joel echoed, as they pulled away. "I owe you one, buddy."

"Night-night, Magnus." If a dog could pout, she had a feeling that's what the whiny sound he made meant. "Go night-night, you big goof."

Joel raised his head, and in his firm, gritty tone ordered, "Magnus, night-night."

The dog finally got down, and she could tell by the scratching noises and circling flag of his tail that he was gathering up the throw rug on her side of the bed and making himself a nest to lie down in. Once the dog had obeyed and settled close by, Mollie rolled onto her back and looked up at Joel hovering beside her in the lamplight. She gently poked his chest and chided, "*My* dog, Standage. I don't like that he responds to your commands faster than he does mine."

He captured her hand against his chest, and she felt the heat of his skin branding her. "*Our* dog, Crane. *Our* energetic, overachieving, too-smart-for-his-own-good dog."

She smiled, more than happy to keep her hand pressed against the ticklish dusting of chest hair and the warm skin underneath. "Maybe it means I'm getting better. That taking care of me isn't enough work for him, anymore."

"Are you still willing to go to the Precinct offices tomorrow morning and talk to A.J. and Josh and the assistant district attorney?"

Her nostrils flared with a deep breath, and she dropped her gaze to where her fingers clung to a swell of pectoral muscle. They'd had this conversation in one form or another several times. She'd done her best to make Joel understand the risk she'd be taking by surrendering her evidence against Augie to the ADA. And he'd done his best to make her believe that she would never be alone against the Di Salvo family again. She met Joel's gaze again and nodded. "I haven't made my decision yet. But I'm willing to talk to them. As long as you make that phone call to your therapist in the morning."

"I will. I promise. I need to do better taking care of that part of my recovery."

"Thank you." She raised her head to press her lips against his, rewarding him with a gentle kiss. She lingered when his lips moved tenderly against hers and reached behind his neck to slide her hand across the spiky mess of his hair. He touched his nose to her face and moved his lips along her jawline, inhaling deeply as if he was learning and memorizing her touch and scent. He nipped at her earlobe, and the zing of desire that arrowed down to the juncture of her thighs caught her off guard. Who knew she had an erogenous zone there? After Augie, who knew she had any erogenous zones left?

Sensing her sudden hesitation, if misreading

the cause, Joel pulled away and flopped down on his back beside her. "Maybe this isn't a good idea. I can't guarantee that the nightmares won't come back. I'd never hurt you if I was fully conscious. It kills me to think that I could frighten you or be too rough with you when I don't know what I'm doing."

But Mollie wasn't going anywhere. "I'll have Magnus to protect me."

Joel pushed up on his elbow beside her to talk over her and the edge of the bed. "You take my head off if I hurt her in any way, buddy." Magnus answered with a stuttered snore. Laughter vibrated in Joel's chest beneath her hand. "Yeah, that's backup I can count on," he muttered sarcastically. "Still, if I did anything to remind you of him…"

"You don't remind me of him at all." Mollie dropped her voice to a whisper and purposely brushed her lips against his ear. "Augie never liked to cuddle."

She knew Joel got the message behind her words. His eyes glittered with something possessive just before he turned her to her side, slid his arm around her and pulled her into his chest. Her butt nestled into his groin and his legs tangled with hers. "Do you need the covers?"

She shook her head. "You'll keep me warm."

She clutched his forearm between her breasts

and sighed at the gentle press of his lips against her hair. "Sleep well, my love."

She smiled at the whispered word and dipped her head to kiss his hand. "You, too."

It was too soon for her to fully believe that she could fall in love again and trust her heart and body to another man. But it wasn't too soon for her to know that when she was ready, it would be with this man.

They fell asleep holding each other, with the cadence of a snoring dog curled up on the rug filling the room with a quiet sense of security.

MOLLIE HAD AWAKENED from the best night's sleep she'd had in ages. The only way she and Joel could have been closer was if they'd been lying skin to skin. And she was surprised to realize that the idea of being with Joel in that way didn't frighten her. She was nervous about being that intimate with any man again, but if the erection pressing against her bottom when she woke hadn't bothered her—and, in fact, had made her feel cherished and desirable—then she had a feeling making love with Joel would be a good experience for her. If he'd enjoyed cuddling so closely with her through the night as much as she had, then she knew he'd be patient with her. Possibly even more patient than she'd be, judging by her own off-the-charts reactions to the man's damn fine body.

But that was this morning, cocooned in the homey sanctuary of Joel's Brookside house, where Joel and Magnus were the only personalities she had to deal with. She trusted both implicitly, and she felt safe with them.

Here, in the tight confines of the Fourth Precinct conference room, surrounded by some heavy hitters in Kansas City law enforcement and the district attorney's office who were analyzing her life and breaking down every detail that could possibly be used against the Di Salvos, she was having a much harder time holding on to that sense of calm and security. It almost felt as if she'd been summoned to a command performance at a Di Salvo dinner party, where she was expected to say certain things and play her part well. Only, these guests weren't talking big bucks and making themselves look good in the worlds of business and culture and KC society. These men and one other woman were strategizing ways to build a case against her ex-husband and redeem the fiasco of the last time they'd gone up against Augie in the courtroom.

There was a big, stocky man in a suit and tie. And though Chief of Police Mitch Taylor's graying hair and authoritative demeanor confirmed that he was the man in charge, he leaned back in his seat at the opposite end of the long, heavy table from her and slowly rubbed his fingers back and forth across his chin while he listened to the intense conversation around the room.

The Black man next to him, Joe Hendricks, was the captain of this Precinct. Apparently, he and the chief were old friends, as he'd been sharing pictures of his grandchildren with Mitch before the meeting started.

The woman, Assistant District Attorney Kenna Parker-Watson, looked like the woman Augie and his parents had tried to transform her into. Straight blond hair. Tall and poised. Her tailored designer suit said she had money, and her pointed comments and quick wit put her on equal footing with the men in the room. She was also happily married, judging by the gold rings on her finger and the smile and kiss she'd shared with a handsome dark-haired detective out in the third floor's main room when she'd arrived.

Of course, she recognized A. J. Rodriguez and Josh Taylor, who was somehow related to the chief of police. She'd missed the exact connection in the flurry of introductions. A.J. was fixated on his laptop on the table in front of him, while Josh paced back and forth, occasionally stopping to jot something on the whiteboard on the wall across from the door.

Joel sat in the chair beside her, doodling pictures on a yellow legal pad and drawing lines from one symbol to the next before scratching the whole thing out, flipping the page and starting the design all over again. Magnus sat in the space between their chairs, his head resting atop her knee. So many big personalities. So much talking. She clung to Magnus's leash and burrowed her fingers into the fur on his warm head. She didn't even care that he was panting, and some drool was trickling down the leg of her jeans and seeping through to her skin.

In fact, she found herself tuning out much of the conversation and focusing on the sound of the dog's breathing and the warmth of him against her when she got too stressed. The air conditioning in the room was working just fine. But Magnus was slightly overheated and panting because he was working so hard to keep her calm.

Joel circled two of the doodles on his paper several times and tapped the pad with his pen sharply enough that she looked over to see what he had drawn. "I found a tracker on my truck when I was checking the damage. There was one on Mollie's car, too. Mine has only been there a few days. It's still shiny new. Hers was there for some time. It showed signs of salt damage from driving in the winter." So, the doodling was how he organized his thoughts? "I removed them both and bagged them as evidence."

The blonde ADA on the other side of Mollie leaned forward. "If the crime lab doesn't come back with Garner's prints on one of them, we can't prove he put them there."

Mollie realized that Joel had drawn a map of every location where she'd had an encounter of some kind with the man they now suspected was Rocky Garner. He could be placed at the diner, the alley behind it, the dog park, her apartment and Hwy. 40, where he'd met his death trying to kill them. Joel pointed to the symbols where he'd written *RG*. "Then how else do you explain him lying in wait for us when we left K-9 Ranch? We were fifteen miles out of the city, and I know he didn't follow us there."

Kenna leaned back in her seat, shaking her head. She glanced around the table to include everyone in her question. "What else do you have?"

A.J. looked up from his computer. "Garner recently bought himself a thirty-thousand-dollar fishing boat. Paid for in three installments of ten thousand dollars each. The last one was paid yesterday." He turned the screen around to show an invoice from the sporting goods store where Garner had bought the boat. "He's bleeding money in alimony payments to his two ex-wives. No wonder he was keeping the payments out of any bank account. Their attorneys could go after him for more."

"Can we trace the cash?" Kenna was persistent in documenting each fact.

"Not yet. It's already changed hands a number of times. The dealer deposited the payments in his account, and it left the bank shortly after that." A.J. turned the computer back to him and pulled up a different screen. "We can trace the car rental agreement back to Kyra Schmidt. She charged almost six hundred dollars on a credit card to have the car for a week."

Mollie's fingers flinched around the leash. "He's been following me that long?"

"Possibly longer." A.J. looked apologetic when he met her gaze across the table. "There's evidence of other deposits to Garner's account— five hundred dollars, a thousand—some more, some less—over the past two years. It's not overtime pay, because that's direct deposited like his paycheck. It's not from moonlighting as security for a reputable company like a store or sporting venue. The deposits came from Garner himself. That means he took cash to the bank."

Joel reached across the arm of her chair and covered her trembling hand with his own. "Any chance there was a deposit nine months ago?" he asked his supervisor. "That's when he was harassing Mollie at the diner."

"Last October?" A.J. scrolled through the numbers, then nodded.

Mitch Taylor pounded the table with his fist and Mollie jerked in her chair. "I had a dirty cop on my force?" He pulled out his cell phone. "I'm calling Internal Affairs to do a deep dive into Garner's financials."

Joe Hendricks seemed equally disappointed by the proof of Garner's misconduct. "They already have a file of harassment complaints leveled against him."

Mitch muttered a curse. "I have over two thousand employees on the payroll here. And it just takes one bad seed like Garner to give us all a bad rep."

Mollie could appreciate how Garner's actions were an embarrassment to the department, but she had a bigger threat to worry about. "But nothing about Officer Garner ties back to Augie? August Di Salvo?"

It was Joel who answered. "Not yet."

She felt the eyes of everyone in the room looking at her, possibly with pity, but mostly with expectation. It was more than clear that without her help, the Di Salvos would remain untouchable. She tightened her grip on Joel's hand and stroked the top of Magnus's head. "They're setting Kyra up to take the fall if things go south. It's a classic Di Salvo move. With Garner's death, if he was the man they paid to follow me, I think we can safely say things have gone south."

"We'll need a court order to look at Kyra Schmidt's financials." The ADA nodded in agreement with Mollie's assessment. "I'll work on that today. If she's paid Garner to do odd jobs for her and the Di Salvos from her personal account, we can track the timelines to see if they match Garner's deposits. But she could just as easily have paid him petty cash from her law firm, and investigating the firm's financials would be a harder sell to a judge."

Josh Taylor had made a list of crimes on the board. "So, we can prove Garner is guilty of harassment, breaking and entering, and the attempted murder of a police officer and potential witness. We can prove he had some kind of working relationship with Schmidt—"

"Who could get her connection to him tossed out of court by claiming he stole the rental car. Or that she had no idea what he was going to do with it when she hired him for a different job, like escorting an important client to the airport," Kenna countered. "He can't defend himself, thanks to your detective here."

Mollie spun her chair toward the attorney. "Joel saved our lives. If Officer Garner hadn't been driving so recklessly—"

"Easy, Mollie," Kenna apologized. "I'm just

repeating what Kyra Schmidt would probably say in the courtroom."

"Don't insult Joel when I'm around. Please. He's a good man. And a good detective. He does whatever is necessary to protect the people he cares about."

"It's okay, Moll." Joel squeezed her hand. "We're just talking through what we know on the case, looking at what all our options are." Then he leaned in more closely and whispered against her ear. "But thank you for sticking up for me."

If they'd been alone, she imagined he would have added something about Cici choosing her drugs instead of protecting him. But they were hardly alone.

"I didn't mean to upset you, Mollie," Kenna apologized, and her blue eyes looked sincere. "I could use someone like you on the witness stand. You speak from a place of strength. You don't come off as someone who's angry or frightened and desperate. You have a calm demeanor."

"Calm?" When was the last time anyone had used that adjective to describe her? "That's because of Magnus."

"It's not just because of the dog. But you could have him in the courtroom with you. You were clearly the wronged party in your marriage, yet you don't sound bitter or brokenhearted."

"I'm more embarrassed that I fell for him in the first place. Trust me, he was easy to get over."

Joel chuckled behind her. Kenna smiled and rolled her chair closer. "I think I like you." For the first time, Mollie felt as if the attorney was speaking to her woman-to-woman, and not as the secret weapon who could make or break her case. "I'd like to take a look at your divorce papers."

"The ones I printed off the internet?"

Kenna nodded. "Sounds like you negotiated yourself a hard deal. And you said it was vetted by an accredited attorney and filed properly, which was a smart move on your part. But maybe I can do better by you."

"I don't want anything from Augie."

"She'd like to be able to teach again," Joel interjected. "Can you get the false report on her record cleared with the school board?"

"I'll waitress for the rest of my life if I have to. I just want my freedom."

"Do you feel free of him?" Kenna asked. "Or are you going to be looking over your shoulder for the rest of your life?"

"Kenna…" Joel warned.

"I'm sorry, Detective. But if I'm going to prosecute this case, and win, I need more than what any of you have shown me." She turned to include everyone in the room. "Garner, I could have put away with my eyes closed. But the DA doesn't prosecute dead men. Maybe I could get Kyra Schmidt fined, or even disbarred, if I could tie her to Garner's harassment campaign. But I've got nothing—nothing—that conclusively links any of this to the Di Salvo family."

"Except me." Mollie felt a little like a soldier being prepped for a suicide mission.

"Look," Kenna began, "I've been in a situation where I wasn't safe. That's how I met my husband, in fact. He saved my life. Twice. That whole situation convinced me to leave the dark side of defense and go to work for the prosecution." She laid her hand on the table close to Mollie, understanding and respecting that she wasn't comfortable being touched by someone she didn't know well. "My point is, I understand your reluctance to put yourself in a position where you feel threatened again. Let me play devil's advocate for a moment. Do you think you're the only person the Di Salvos have threatened? Cheated? Or worse? What about those people who will continue to be hurt by them if nothing is done to stop them?"

"I feel for them, but… Augie said he'd kill me if I left him. I countered with the offer to keep what I took from him out of police hands, so long as he let me leave. And live. If anything happens to me, I've willed it to go to KCPD and the DA's office."

"You're not going to die before we take that bastard down," Joel griped.

But Kenna Parker-Watson seemed eternally cool and unruffled. "It doesn't sound as if he's keeping up his end of the divorce agreement."

Suicide mission. "*If* you can prove he's behind the harassment and Garner trying to kill Joel and me." Mollie offered another explanation. "Kyra Schmidt might have decided to eliminate me to protect her new fiancé and all the money she stands to gain by marrying Augie."

"Possibly," Kenna conceded. "But that just means she knows there's something there she has to protect. You know, the thing about bullies is that they only keep their power when no one stands up to them."

Mollie had heard that argument before. She believed it herself once. "Yes, but the person who stands up to the bully usually gets the crap beat out of them, or worse."

Kenna's hand inched closer. "I'm willing to stand up with you against your bully. You wouldn't be alone this time."

Mollie looked to Joel. He tucked a stray strand of hair behind her ear. "You know I'm with you all the way."

There was a chorus of support from around the room, from A.J. and Josh, as well as the two senior officers. Finally, Magnus put his head in her lap and turned his dark eyes up to hers, promising his unflinching support.

Mollie smiled down into those faithful eyes. Then she lifted her gaze to Joel's handsome golden eyes. She wasn't alone against the Di Salvos. Not anymore. *Not a suicide mission.* Instead, she was the veteran survivor who could lead this makeshift army into battle. She just prayed she wouldn't be a casualty along the way.

She turned to Kenna's blue eyes and nodded to the yellow legal pad in front of her, warning her to get ready to write. "I have documented evidence of money laundering and racketeering from internal servers on the Di Salvo computers. I can show payoffs to enforcers and bribes to officials that probably coincide with the witnesses who backed out of testifying against Augie in his previous trial."

This part was harder. She turned to Joel but couldn't quite meet his eyes. Her gaze landed on the Armed Forces prayer inked into his arm and she replayed the words in her head. *Teach us not to mourn those who have died in the service of the Corps, but rather to gain strength from the fact that such heroes have lived.*

She had to be the hero now. But could she trust that these people would be there for her when she needed them?

Joel tapped a finger beneath her chin and tilted her face to his. "What else, Moll?"

"I don't want you to see them. But I have dated pictures of my injuries and my copy of the first police report and medical exam that disappeared after the first assault. And, there's an audio recording of one of the times Augie...hurt me. There's no video. I hid my phone in a drawer, but it was running the whole time."

She heard deep-pitched curses in two different languages, and gasps of admiration for her and contempt for the Di Salvos from around the room. But her eyes were glued on Joel and the muscle ticking in his jaw at the evidence she'd described. "Hell, babe, you had the presence of mind to record him?"

"That's how desperate I was to get away from him."

His gaze caressed her face. "Strong as steel."

"It's in a lockbox at my bank." She patted Magnus's shoulder. "I keep the key with me at all times. And the false account numbers are in—"

"Your locket." She nodded at Joel's deduction. "And Magnus guards your key." His eyes remained shrouded in sadness, but he smiled. "Brilliant, brave, and beautiful."

There was a respectful moment of silence before Kenna spoke. "Please tell me you'll let me see that evidence."

She hadn't looked away from Joel. "You'll keep me safe?"

He pulled her into his arms and hugged her as tightly as the chairs allowed. "Twenty-four seven."

"He'll have the backup of the entire Precinct," Joe Hendricks promised.

"Of the entire department if needed," Chief Taylor added. "I'll assign a SWAT team to you to and from the courtroom."

"Are you afraid to testify against your ex?" Kenna asked.

"Yes. But I'll do it anyway. I want…" She reached over to squeeze Joel's hand. "I want to fight for *us*, too."

Chapter Eleven

Joel's head throbbed with a mixture of fatigue and forcing his eyes to concentrate on the pages of the book he wasn't really reading.

For the umpteenth time that night, he let his gaze slide over to the opposite corner of the couch, where Mollie was curled up with her book. He could tell she was deep in thought because she hadn't turned a page in the last ten minutes.

Giving up the pretense, he set his book aside and clicked on his phone to check the time— 11:00 p.m. He also pulled up his messages to see if there was any news on what progress the DA's office was making in going through the flash drive, photos, and recording Mollie had turned over when they'd opened her lockbox at the bank the afternoon after that strategy meeting at Precinct headquarters. Nothing there.

He typed a quick text to the undercover officer stationed somewhere outside the house to make sure the neighborhood was as quiet as it seemed to be. Nothing to report there, either.

"Any news?" Mollie finally closed her book and set it on the ottoman in front of them. He hated that there was no hope in her eyes when she looked at him, just polite curiosity.

"No." He tucked his phone into the pocket of his shorts and stood. "It's getting late, though. Maybe we should turn in."

She nodded. "I do have an early day tomorrow."

Mollie had barely slept the past three nights, even with Joel's arms wrapped around her and Magnus snoring on the rug on her side of the bed. There'd been an officer somewhere near them around the clock, and a squad car made regular passes through the neighborhood throughout the night. When they left the house, they both put on protective vests, but here, he thought they were safe enough that they could stay indoors without the vests. Still, he checked the locks on the doors and windows to make sure everything was secure while Mollie roused Magnus and headed back to his bedroom.

He wished there was something more he could do for her to ease the seemingly endless wait for justice to happen.

All she did was work at Pearl's, lie in bed with him, where he'd distract her with kisses and some making out until she fell into an exhausted, if troubled, slumber, and run Magnus

through his training paces in the backyard while
Kenna Parker-Watson pored over each piece of
evidence. Every time she called with a follow-
up question, the ADA assured Mollie they were
putting together arrest warrants and restraining
orders that should put the Di Salvos away for a
very long time and give her back the normal life
that her marriage had denied her.

Earlier this evening, Joel had declared she
needed a break, and he had driven her to Saint
Luke's Hospital to visit Corie Taylor and meet her
new baby boy, Henry Sid Taylor. Somehow, Chief
Taylor and his wife were there visiting, too. But
Joel knew the timing was about more than visiting their new grandnephew. Mitch Taylor was
armed when he told Joel he'd stand watch outside the room while they visited with Corie, her
husband Matt, older son Evan, and baby Henry.

It was a treat to watch Mollie hold Henry,
who was a strapping eight pounds and twenty-
two inches long, and chat about some of the adventures Corie was missing at the diner. Herb
was grumpier than usual with the change in his
routine, now that Mollie had stepped in to take
over pie baking duty and help with morning prep
work. Melissa was looking to hire two new waitresses, with Corie going on maternity leave and
Mollie finding a home she was better suited to
back in the kitchen. The tourists weren't tipping

as well as the regulars, and—thanks to some scheduling by Captain Hendricks—there seemed to be three or four more police officers than usual coming in for lunch or dinner this past week.

Joel loved seeing Mollie smile and laugh with her friend. And watching her hold baby Henry twisted his heart with longing. Mollie would make a great mother with her intelligence, strength, and gentle ways—and he desperately wanted to be the man who put a baby in her belly. If she could ever trust him enough to let him love her.

He'd kept his promise and gone to see Dr. Kilpatrick-Harrison to talk about his nightmares and fears that he wasn't the man that Mollie needed to get through this investigation and trial. Mollie seemed genuinely pleased and relieved that he was taking care of himself.

But it killed him to see the shadows beneath her beautiful blue eyes. Mollie wasn't thinking about babies and a future with him. Until this nightmare was settled, and the Di Salvos were no longer a threat to her, her world was a tiny, confining thing filled with fear and anxiety about living long enough to testify against her ex.

After letting Magnus out for one last run and securing the back door, Joel followed Mollie back to his bedroom. By the time he finished brushing his teeth and pulling off his T-shirt, Mollie was sitting up on the edge of the bed. He walked past her to plug his cell phone into his charger on the bedside table and secure his Glock and holster with his badge in the drawer there.

"You want to get up at 4:00 a.m. again?" he asked, setting the alarm.

She nodded. "I'm still not used to getting to the diner so early. I don't trust myself to wake up on my own."

He smiled down at her. "Then we'd better get to bed now."

She scooted back to the middle of the bed. "You don't have to stay with me. Herb will open the kitchen, and you can drop me off and go on to work or come back home for a nap while I help with prep."

"Twenty-four seven, remember? Where you go, I go." Joel settled in beside her and pulled her into his arms. He loved that she didn't even hesitate to curl against his side and rest her cheek against his chest. When she started tracing lazy circles across his chest with her fingers, he had to capture her hand and spread it flat against his heart to stop his body from reacting to her innocent caresses.

He lay in silence for several minutes, waiting for the tension to leave her body and for her to finally drift off to sleep. But she wasn't relaxing. And neither one of them were sleeping.

"Make love to me, Joel," she murmured against his chest.

"Looking to relieve some stress?" he teased.

But she didn't laugh. "I feel so disconnected from the life I wanted for myself. A career, a man who loves me, a family, a home. I'm this brittle, wishful shell of everything I used to be. But I feel connected to you. I feel closer to who I'm meant to be when I'm with you."

"And you think making love will strengthen that connection?"

"I wouldn't be using you to escape what I'm feeling." She pushed herself up to rest her chin where their hands were clasped and look him in the eye. "I want to be with you because you make me feel stronger."

"Are you sure?" He released her hand to tuck a coffee-colored tendril behind her ear. "Sex could be a trigger for you, and I don't want to make you afraid of me."

"I'd never be afraid of you," she vowed. "And, something might trigger a horrible memory. But I've never wanted to try with anyone else. I've never wanted any man the way I want to be with you."

"I feel the same way. I would be honored— and ever so grateful—to make love to you."

"I can't guarantee I'll be any good."

He pressed a finger to her lips to silence that nonsense. "We're both a work in progress, remember? I might not be any good, either."

She rolled her eyes. "I doubt that. All you have to do is kiss me, and I want you."

"I get the same feeling when you put your hands on me." He raised his head to kiss her gently. She joined the kiss as he rolled her onto her back and he positioned himself beside her. "I expect there to be a lot of talking while we do this. You tell me what you like, and you, for sure, tell me anything you don't like."

"I will." She swept her hands along his biceps and across his shoulders before cradling his jaw between her hands and rubbing her palms against his stubble. "But you need to tell me stuff, too. I want it to be good for you."

"It will be." When she started to protest that he couldn't know that, he silenced her with another, deeper kiss that required several minutes of heated contact before he could pull back and explain. "Because it's with you. Because you trusting me with this is the biggest turn-on and best gift I've ever been given."

She stroked her fingers across his jaw and his heart raced with desire. Her brows arched with an apology. "Protection? I stayed on the pill while I was with Augie because I couldn't imagine bearing his child. But I went off them when I ran out. I've never been with another man, so there was no need to pay for them."

He smoothed his thumb across each eyebrow until she relaxed. She had nothing to apologize for. He'd be honored to take care of her protection in this way, too. "I have condoms."

"Thank you." Her lips were slightly swollen and a seductive shade of pink from their kisses. "I want this so badly. But it scares me, too."

"If you decide you don't want to go through with it, I'll be fine. I'll cuddle with you all night the way we have been."

Her gaze ran down his chest to his belly before she met his eyes again. "Could I touch you?"

"You *are* touching me, babe."

"I mean..." Her hand followed the path her eyes had taken, skimming over his stomach toward the evidence of his arousal tenting his shorts. *"You."*

"You touch me however you want."

He loved it when she laughed like that. He loved when she bravely pushed the boundaries of her growing self-confidence, too. "You'd give me that kind of power over you?"

He loved her, period. "Yes. Don't you know, babe? You always have that kind of power over me."

"You'd better kiss me now, Joel."

"Happy to oblige."

The next thing he knew, her bold hand was slipping inside his shorts and curling around his manhood.

Joel sucked in a harsh breath and gritted his teeth against the jolt of anticipation thundering through his blood. He rested his forehead against hers while he tried to even out his breathing.

She smiled, showing him the woman she'd been before her ex and violence had ever touched her life. "I think we have on too many clothes."

Joel made love to her mouth with his and pulled up the hem of her shirt, taking his time to learn the shape and feel of her breasts plumping beneath his hands. She squirmed beneath his touch, then gasped and arched against him when he plucked her rock-hard nipples between his thumb and palm.

When he lowered his head to lick the exposed peak and draw it into his mouth, her fingers stroked along his shaft. Joel's mind blanked for a moment at the absolute perfection of Mollie's hand on him. "You're going to be trouble for me, aren't you?"

He reclaimed her mouth and gave himself over to her needy hands.

Yeah. So much trouble.

THE MOMENT MOLLIE stuck her key into the back door to the kitchen at 4:50 a.m. the next morning, she knew something was horribly wrong.

It wasn't locked.

She looked up to the man beside her, fearing the worst. "Joel?"

He pressed a finger to his lips, warning her to be silent, even as he unholstered his gun. He pulled his phone from his belt and pressed it into her hands. "A.J. Backup. Now."

Mollie nodded her understanding. She was as afraid now as she'd been that first night Augie had assaulted her. Only this time, her fear was for Joel and the unknown threat that might be waiting on the other side of that door. He gave Magnus a silent hand signal to stay by her side, then wrapped his fingers around the door handle.

She grabbed his arm before he could open it. "Be careful. I don't want to lose you."

He mouthed two words. *"Love you."*

Then he nodded to the phone, pulled open the door, and disappeared inside.

She gaped at the steel door for a moment, processing those last words. Then she snapped herself out of her stunned freeze, galvanized by the emotion filling her heart and spilling over into every cell of her body. Joel loved her.

She loved him.

The rightness of that revelation chased away the self-doubts and second-guessing that had ruled her life for too long. She was fighting for her future, fighting for the man who loved her. She pulled up A.J.'s number.

He answered on the first ring. "Rodriguez."

She didn't bother with a greeting, either. "Pearl's Diner. Something's wrong. Joel armed himself and went inside to check it out."

"Are you safe?"

"Joel is in there by himself." She articulated every desperate word.

"Easy, Mollie. Backup is en route." He said something to someone on his end, and she pulled the phone away from her ear at the shrill of a siren. "Josh is notifying the UC man assigned to you this morning. We're spread a little thin. Josh and I and a SWAT team are at the Di Salvo estate to take your ex into custody. We've got Mom and Dad in a squad car, but there's no sign of August, Beau Regalio, or the lawyer."

Mollie's heart sank when she heard the jumble of overlapping voices from inside the diner. "That's because they're here."

She jumped back from the door when she heard Joel shouting. "KCPD! Drop your weapon! Hands where I can see them!"

She heard three distinct gunshots. Magnus leaped to his feet and barked. She heard a crashing sound, some indistinct voices…and her name, shouted in a voice that was sickeningly familiar. "Mollie! Where is she?"

She wrapped Magnus's leash around her fist.

"Mollie?" She heard A.J.'s voice over the phone again.

"He needs help. Now!" she shouted.

She disconnected the call and pulled open the door. "Magnus, heel!"

The drops of blood on the floor leading from the back door to the freezer didn't frighten her as much as seeing Beau Regalio dragging Joel's limp body. Was that blood on his shirt beneath the edge of his flak vest? Was this his blood on the floor? Where was Herb?

"Joel!" She would have moved to help, but the gun pressed against her scalp froze her in place.

"There's the little woman." Augie stood at the stainless-steel sinks, wiping his hands on a dish towel. "You've caused me a lot of trouble."

There was no teasing, no love, no regret in his dark eyes as he crossed the kitchen toward her.

The feeling was mutual.

Magnus growled and lunged to her left, nearly pulling her arm from its socket as she fought to keep him at her side. The gun was jerked away from her head as Kyra Schmidt dodged the Belgian Malinois in full protector mode. "I hate dogs!" The blonde backed up several steps until her back hit the row of ovens. "August. We need to take care of business and get out of here now. We need to get to the airport."

"Shut up and keep your gun on her."

Kyra circled around until she was standing in front of Mollie, well out of the furious barking dog's reach.

It was enough of an interchange for her to see Beau dumping Joel inside the freezer and shutting the insulated door. "Joel! What did you do him?" she demanded.

That was definitely blood on the sleeve of Beau's jacket as he pulled up the back of his suit jacket and tucked a Glock 9 mm—probably Joel's gun—into the back waistband of his slacks.

"Did he shoot you?" she taunted. "Maybe Herb went after you with one of his kitchen knives."

"You don't get to talk unless I ask you a question."

She saw it coming, but there was no way to dodge the fist that came flying at her face. Mollie stumbled back from the blow, and would have landed on her bottom if Magnus hadn't been tugging so hard in the opposite direction. She immediately put her hand up to cup the pain blooming across her cheek. "The police are on their way, Augie. You can't escape."

"I said no talking." He might have hit her once, but Magnus wasn't going to let him hit her again.

Augie cursed. "Get that dog away from me!"

"Shut up, mutt!" Beau kicked Magnus, knocking him off his paws. But he was instantly up and lunging for the bigger man this time.

"Don't you hurt my dog!"

"Put him in the cooler with the others," he ordered Beau. But when the Di Salvo bodyguard tried to grab Magnus's leash, the dog bared his teeth and snapped at him.

When Beau pulled his gun to shoot the dog, Mollie put up her hand, pleading for mercy. "I'll put him in the freezer."

Augie grabbed Kyra's gun and pointed it at Magnus. "Try anything funny and I'll shoot him myself."

Although Magnus fought her every step of the way, she led him through the kitchen. Beau was close enough that she could feel the heat of his big body when he reached around her to open the freezer. When she glanced inside, she saw Herb Valentino lying on the floor, unconscious. There was blood oozing from the bandanna tied around the top of his head. Her heart lurched when she saw Joel lying face down on the floor beside him. A small pool of blood stained the floor beneath him. He was still wearing his protective vest, but one of those gunshots could have hit him in the neck or caught him low in his belly beneath the bottom edge.

Please God, don't be dead. I love you, too.

He'd been shot and left to die once before. Even if she didn't make it out of this, she prayed that backup would come, and Joel would get whatever medical help he needed.

"Quit mooning over your dead boyfriend. Get rid of the dog now!"

Augie's command spurred her into action. "I'm sorry, baby," she apologized to Magnus, forcing him to go against months of training that told him to stay by her side, to be there for her whenever she needed him. "You stay here with Daddy."

He was still barking and lunging for the armed men when Beau shut the freezer. Then he was on his hind legs, frantically scratching at the door to get back out.

Augie grabbed her by the hair. But since she kept it short now, he lost his grip and she fell to the floor. That only seemed to anger him further. Before she could scramble to her feet, Augie took her arm in a painful grasp and dragged her through the kitchen.

"Nobody's coming to save you, Mollie. You're mine. I told you what would happen if you left me."

"Shoot her," Kyra insisted, hurrying after them, her high heels clicking on the tile floor. "We need to make this clean and fast and get out of here."

"I told you to let me handle this."

"I'm a damn good lawyer, August. But even I can't refute a former Di Salvo testifying against you."

"Shut up!" He swung around and backhanded Kyra. *Welcome to the club, lover girl.* "That cop you paid off couldn't finish the job, but I will. I want her to suffer for the embarrassment she's caused me. I lost investors. Father threatened to disinherit me if I didn't get that evidence back. If I'm convicted, we all go down." He barked an order to Beau. "Bring the car around. We'll finish her off at the dump site. Then make sure the charter jet is waiting for us. I intend to be in Belarus where they can't extradite me before any other cop finds me."

Augie's first mistake was that he didn't kill her outright.

His second mistake was in thinking that Magnus was just a dumb, annoying animal of no consequence.

His last mistake was underestimating how determined Joel was to keep her safe.

The emergency latch inside the freezer suddenly unfastened and the door swung open. In three long strides, Magnus was across the room. He leaped at the man holding on to her, his vicious snarl even making Mollie cringe. He hit Augie in the chest with enough force to knock him to the floor and free Mollie. His long teeth clamped around Augie's wrist as he grabbed the dog to fight him off. The gun went flying, clattering across the kitchen and sliding beneath the sink.

"Shoot him! Shoot—" Augie's command ended in a high-pitched screech as teeth tore through flesh.

Beau trained his gun on the dog, but pulled it back just as quickly. "I don't have a shot!" He swung the weapon around at Mollie. "Call off your damn—"

Beau crashed to the floor with a hard thud as Joel tackled him. "Joel!"

The two men fought for control of the weapon. Beau landed a punch in Joel's side that made him groan. But then Joel was on top. He hit the bigger man once, twice, in the jaw, stunning him long enough to flip him onto his stomach, drive his knee into the middle of his back and handcuff him.

Then he pulled his own gun from the bodyguard's belt and turned to Mollie. "You okay?"

She moved behind him as he aimed his gun at Augie. "I'm fine. You got shot."

"Clipped me in the side. Second shot hit my vest and knocked me down. Hit my head. Magnus licked my face. He was quite insistent that I get my ass back out here to protect you."

Augie cried out again.

"Better call him off."

"Magnus! Come!" When the dog didn't immediately respond, she spoke in a louder, firmer tone. "Mama's okay. Come!"

Augie cradled his bleeding arm and writhed in pain as Magnus trotted back to Mollie's side and sat. She picked up his leash and praised him. "Good boy, Magnus. Good boy."

As Joel trained his gun on Augie and ordered him to roll over and put his hands on top of his head, Kyra made a run for the back door. But she was knocked flat on her ass when the door swung open and five fully armed SWAT officers streamed in. They were followed closely by A.J. and Josh, who quickly moved to cuff both Kyra Schmidt and Augie.

Standing down from superdetective mode, Joel holstered his weapon. He reached for Mollie, but she was retrieving a clean towel from the sink shelf. And instead of returning his hug, she pressed the folded towel against the wound in his side. "You're not dying, understand?"

"I'm okay, Moll." He gently grasped her shoulders.

"No, you're not. This is blood. Your blood."

A.J. pulled a whining Augie to his feet while the SWAT team secured the kitchen and the rest of the diner and helped Herb out of the freezer.

"I see you got yourself shot again, Standage," A.J. commented dryly.

Joel chuckled. "Any bullet you can walk away from…"

"You two, stop it!" Mollie didn't find their cop-to-cop teasing very funny at the moment.

"Don't worry." A.J. handed Augie off to another officer. "An ambulance is on its way. I doubt the bullet hit anything vital or his color would be off, and he'd be unconscious by now. I'm guessing your ex is in worse shape with the damage your dog did to him."

"Magnus did his job. He was protecting me."

A.J. held his hands up in apology. "You'll get no complaints from me. I'm putting that dog in for a medal." Then his eyes darkened with sincere admiration. "Thank you for saving this guy. I need him on my team."

Mollie nodded. "Thank you for being here to back him up."

"Thanks, A.J." Joel pried her hand away from the towel and kept it in place there himself. "Come on. Let's go out front and have a seat somewhere out of the way while they secure the scene."

When she saw that he was limping again, she slipped her shoulder beneath his arm and helped him through the swinging door. Magnus saw his familiar bed at the end of the counter, and she released him so he could sniff it out and lie down if he wanted. Mollie guided Joel to one of the vinyl stools and climbed up on the one next to him.

When she started fussing with the abrasion at his temple, he caught her fingers in his free hand and kissed them. "I'm fine. You just sit here with me and keep the towel pressed against my wound." He frowned when he saw her face, and brushed her hair away from the bruise he must already be able to see discoloring her swollen cheek. "I want them to look at you, too."

"A souvenir from Augie. I've had worse."

"Not on my watch, you haven't."

Tears stung Mollie's eyes as the fear and adrenaline left her body. "You told me you love me, and then you got shot and I thought you were dead."

Joel gently cupped her cheek and swiped away the tears that spilled over with his thumb. "I've been dead. Didn't like it. I've never been more alive than when I'm with you."

Then he slipped his hand behind her neck and pulled her closer until he could cover her lips with his. Mollie reached up to stroke his stubbled jaw and returned the gentle kiss with all the love and hope blossoming inside her. A few moments later, she pulled away to look him in the eye and speak her truth. "I love you, too. I can't wait to testify and put the Di Salvos and their greed and evil out of my life forever. Because I want to start a new life with you."

He smiled. "You want to be part of my pack, Mollie Crane?"

"You'll be part of *my* pack, Joel Standage."

"I accept those terms."

A cold nose nudged her arm, and a warm, furry head nestled in her lap as Magnus squeezed between the two of them.

They both laughed and reached down to pet the dog who had brought them together. "Fine, you big goof," Mollie conceded. "We'll both be part of *your* pack."

* * * * *

Hometown Homicide

Denise N. Wheatley

MILLS & BOON

DEDICATION

To my aunts, Sharon and Glenda. I love you!

Denise N. Wheatley loves happy endings and the art of storytelling. Her novels run the romance gamut, and she strives to pen entertaining books that embody matters of the heart. She's an RWA member and holds a BA in English from the University of Illinois. When Denise isn't writing, she enjoys watching true-crime TV and chatting with readers. Follow her on social media.

Instagram: @Denise_Wheatley_Writer
Twitter: @DeniseWheatley
BookBub: @DeniseNWheatley
Goodreads: Denise N. Wheatley

Visit the Author Profile page
at millsandboon.com.au.

CAST OF CHARACTERS

Nia Brooks—An ambitious former 9-1-1 operator turned rookie police officer in small-town Juniper, Colorado.

Drew Taylor—A ten-year veteran Juniper police officer.

Ivy Brooks—Nia's younger sister, who is considered the black sheep of the family.

Bruce Mitchell—Juniper PD's chief of police.

Officer Martin Davis—A rambunctious Juniper police officer.

Shane Anderson—Juniper's newest bachelor, who has his eye on Nia.

Ethan Rogers—A prominent businessman who is a member of Legacy, a prestigious men's social club.

Vaughn Clayton—An attorney running for senator and who is also a member of Legacy.

Prologue

"9-1-1. What is your emergency?"

"Someone's trying to break into my house!" a woman screeched into the phone.

Operator Nia Brooks shot straight up in her chair. The buzz within Juniper, Colorado's communications center was louder than normal as the phone lines had been dead for hours. Increasing the volume on her headset, she scanned the computer screen for the caller's location.

"What is your address, ma'am?"

"Three eighty-two Barksdale Road."

"And you said that someone is trying to break into your house?"

"*Yes*. A man has been banging on the back door and fighting with the knob for several minutes now. I'm here alone, and…"

The woman fell silent. A loud thud penetrated Nia's eardrums, followed by a deep, muffled howl.

"Do you *hear* him?" the woman hissed.

"I do," Nia replied, forcing a calm tone as her fingers flew across the keyboard. "I'm already in contact with the police dispatcher alerting them to the situation. Law enforcement should be heading your way. Just stay on the line with me—"

"Listen," the woman interrupted, her voice breaking into a jagged whisper. "I told you I'm here by myself. I don't have any weapons. If this maniac makes his way inside my house, I have no way of protecting myself. So *please* tell the authorities to hurry up!"

She paused at what sounded like a bat pounding the door.

"Leave me alone!" the woman screamed. "I'm on the phone with 9-1-1 and police are on their way!"

"Yes, they are," Nia assured her. "I can see that law enforcement is en route to your house. And they're aware that this is a high-priority emergency situation."

Quivering sobs rattled Nia's headset as the woman whimpered, "They need to hurry up and get here. This man is about to break down the door. When he does, he might try to kill me!"

"Are all of your windows and doors locked?"

"I think so—yes. I turned off all the lights, too, hoping that would somehow run him off. Obviously it didn't work."

"Well, the secured windows and doors should keep him at bay until police arrive. In the meantime, I'll be right here on the line with you. What is your name, ma'am?"

"Linda. Linda Echols."

"Okay, Linda. When the knocking first began, did you happen to take a look outside and get a glimpse of the man?"

The woman paused, only the sound of her unsteady breaths swooshing through Nia's headset. "I—I did. Just once. When the banging started. I looked out to see what all the commotion was about and tried to tell him that he had the wrong house, not realizing he was trying to break in. He insisted that he was exactly where he was supposed to be. But he's dressed in all black and looks to be wearing a mask and—*wait!* I think he might be…"

She went silent again.

"Linda, talk to me. Tell me what's going on. I don't hear anything."

"Yeah, neither do I. Maybe he finally decided to stop—"

Boom, boom, boom!

Nia cringed at the rapid succession of thumping.

"Linda?"

Silence.

"Linda! Are you okay? What is he doing now?"

"He just picked up one of my patio chairs and is slamming it against the window! He's gonna break it and get inside. I need for the police to get here. *Now!*"

Just as Nia enlarged the map on her screen and

checked the responding officer's location, a message from dispatch flashed below it.

Inform the caller that police are on the way, but due to construction they've been rerouted, causing a delay.

Clenching her teeth, a frustrated grunt gurgled in Nia's throat. This was the hard part of the job—the part that she couldn't control. It pained her, being on the front line with the victims from behind a desk as opposed to in person.

"Where are the cops?" Linda rasped. "Are they almost here?"

"They're still on the way. But there's roadwork near your home that's blocking the direct route. So as soon as they get around that they'll arrive at your house. And like I said, I'll be right here with you until they—"

Crack!

Nia jerked in her chair as the sound of shattering glass pierced her ears, followed by Linda's guttural scream.

"He's getting in!"

Inhaling sharply, Nia asked, "He's getting inside the house?"

"Yes! He just smashed the sliding glass door!"

Nia pounded the keyboard with an update to dispatch while clambering footsteps stuttered through her headset.

"I'm still here with you, Linda. What's happening now?"

"I'm running upstairs to hide inside my bedroom closet. *Please* tell the cops to hurry up and get here!"

A faint shuffling echoed in the background.

"He's inside the house!" Linda whisper-screamed as the sound of shoe soles squeaked across the floor.

"Hey!" a gravelly voice roared. "Get your ass back down here!"

"Linda," Nia began, struggling to maintain her composure, "are you inside the bedroom yet?"

"I am now."

"Good. Make sure you lock the door. Can you push a dresser or a chair or some sort of heavy object in front of it?"

"I can try, but I don't think I can move this chest of drawers across the carpet!"

Eyeing the map on her screen, Nia checked the responding officer's location. Her chest tightened at the sight of the vehicle's marker. It was at a standstill.

The intruder's demands boomed in the distance, followed by Linda's hysterical cries.

Bam!

"He's forcing his way inside the bedroom!"

A throbbing pain pulsated over Nia's left eye. She pounded her fist against the desk, watching helplessly as the responding officer's vehicle finally began to move.

"Linda, the police are making their way to your

house. Is there anywhere inside the bedroom you can hide? The closet? Or bathroom?"

The other end of the call went silent.

"Hello?" Nia called out. "Hello! Are you still there?"

"I'm gonna kill you," she heard a man grunt. *"Linda!"*

A jarring thump preceded heaving gasps.

"I'm gonna kill you," the man muttered again over the sound of gut-wrenching gurgling.

Nia's body weakened at the thought of Linda being killed.

Come on! she wanted to scream after seeing that police were still several blocks away from the victim's house.

Just as she typed another message to dispatch alerting them to the severity of the situation, the call dropped.

Chapter One

Officer Drew Taylor kicked in the cracked wooden panels hanging from the door of Shelby's Candy Factory before stepping inside. The place had been closed for years and sat abandoned on the land bordering Juniper and Finchport. Since it was in Juniper's jurisdiction, the town had made plans to demolish the property last year and build affordable housing in its place. But then protestors had stepped in, insisting that the historic landmark merited preservation.

The powers that be agreed to halt demolition after activists promised to renovate the building. Their plan to turn it into a multipurpose community center, however, had yet to happen after fundraising efforts failed. In the meantime, the factory remained vacant—and dangerous.

Teens had been using the space to throw wild parties while squatters saw it as a place to hang out, drink and sleep for days on end. Law enforcement did their best to keep out the riffraff. But the moment they drove away, loiterers and partygoers sneaked right back onto the scene.

Shelby's had become a point of contention for most Juniper residents. The quaint town of just over 10,000, located right outside Denver, prided itself on a welcoming spirit, solid family values, neighborly kindness and tight-knit bonds. Many of the cafés, boutiques and service businesses had been passed down from generation to generation. The hardworking community strove to maintain a glowing reputation, which was vital considering many of Denver's tourism dollars trickled over into Juniper's agricultural museum, vintage car shows and antique mall.

Most residents felt as though Shelby's had become a stain on the town. Nothing good had come of allowing it to remain standing—especially now, as Drew had been called there to investigate a dead body.

He and his partner, Timothy Braxton, walked across the dilapidated main level in search of the crime scene. Layers of dust covered the 3,000 square feet of cracked cement flooring. Shards of glass were scattered everywhere as large holes marred the cloudy picture windows. Pulleys once used to lift heavy candy-filled cauldrons were still in place, as were a few of the cooling tables and taffy-spinning machines.

"Officers, over here!"

Drew and Timothy made their way past a row

of drop roller machines toward the back of the factory. The stench of decomposing flesh hit before Drew even laid eyes on the victim.

"Oh my God..." Timothy uttered, holding his hand to his nose.

A deceased woman's body sat propped up in a metal folding chair. She'd been bound and gagged. Dried blood had pooled around her neck and chest.

Drew's stomach lurched at the sight. Juniper rarely saw crimes this brutal. Thefts, drug deals and bar fights were the norm—not vicious murders committed by demented killers, who, the officer feared, would kill again.

The victim looked to be in her mid to late twenties. Five foot six if he had to guess, and about 135 pounds minus the postmortem bloating. Her long, dark brown hair was a tangled mess. If he hadn't seen the back of her white T-shirt, he would've thought it was a reddish brown as the front had been completely soaked in blood. Layers of duct tape were wrapped around her wrists and ankles. While her dark blue jeans appeared to be intact, she wasn't wearing any shoes.

"Any word on who the victim is?" Drew asked Officer Davis.

"Yep. Her name is Katie Douglas."

"So she had ID on her?"

"No. When the call came in over the radio that a body had been found, whoever tipped off law enforcement knew the victim but asked to remain anonymous."

Drew bent down and studied the woman's skin. Judging by the green discoloration, along with the mixture of blood and foam leaking from her mouth, she'd been dead for a few days.

He pulled a handkerchief from the pocket of his black cargo pants and waved off several blowflies before holding it to his nose. "Have you found any evidence that might contain DNA?"

Officer Davis held a brown paper bag in the air with a gloved hand. "So far, just a piece of duct tape with a bloody fingerprint that I spotted near the victim's feet."

"Good. Let's make sure we get that sent off to the crime lab as soon as possible."

"Will do. Oh, and there was one more thing…"

The officer handed over a brochure. Drew slipped on a pair of latex gloves before taking it. "What is this?"

"An event calendar for Latimer Park's recreational center. We found it stuffed inside the victim's hand."

"Hmm, interesting…"

In between the blood stains, Drew studied the activity details. There was a wide variety of them, from pumpkin-carving contests to crafting classes. "I wonder if she's somehow affiliated with the park. But I don't see her name listed as an instructor or host on any of the events."

Peering over his shoulder, Timothy asked, "Are there any handwritten notes on it? Or phone numbers?"

"Nope. Nothing. We'll send this to the lab as well. See what DNA might be detected. We should also stop by Latimer Park and pick up a calendar on the way back to the station. I wanna have that on hand just in case we can somehow trace the victim to the park."

Drew made his way toward the back wall. A door that was normally boarded up had been yanked from the hinges. "Hey, Davis, where's the forensic team?"

"They're on the way."

"And the medical examiner?"

"She's at the hospital wrapping up an autopsy. She should be here soon."

"Can you let me know when she arrives? I'd like to speak with her."

Officer Davis's eyelids lowered, as if he wanted to question Drew. Instead he replied, "Uh…yeah. Sure."

Ignoring his confusion, Drew pulled out his cell phone and took several photos of the scene. After nearly ten years on the force, his colleagues still didn't seem to understand his behavior once he slipped into investigative mode. Drew had a habit of taking over, oftentimes making a list of duties for his fellow officers while collecting forensic evidence on his own. Today would be no different.

As he began filming a video, Drew contemplated what the victim had gone through before being murdered. Had she been drugged and kidnapped? Did she know her killer? Was it someone she'd trusted?

He squeezed his eyes shut, thinking of how this could have been someone he knew. The thought sent a streak of anger through his chest that pushed past his lungs and out his mouth in the form of a loud grunt.

"You all right?" Timothy asked, following him into the alleyway behind the building.

"No. I'm not. I've gotta do something here. As a matter of fact, I don't wanna wait on the forensic team. I've got my kit in the trunk of the car. I'll let the medical examiner handle the processing of the body while I collect whatever evidence I can find. Fingerprints, shoe prints, blood trails—anything I can get my hands on. I've got a bad feeling about this one, Tim. If we don't catch the suspect soon, trust me, he *will* kill again."

DREW STOOD OUTSIDE Chief Mitchell's door gnawing at his bottom lip. The chief never called him to his office. At least not for a one-on-one meeting. Usually when he wanted to talk he'd call Timothy in with him. This time, he specifically asked to speak to Drew alone.

Just as he raised his fist to knock, the door flew open. Officer Davis came charging out.

"Hey, man!" he said, giving Drew a hearty slap on the back. "Listen, great job at the crime scene today. Way to step up and take the lead. Oh, and congrats!"

"Thanks. But wait, congrats on what?"

"The chief will tell you. I'm late for an appointment. Let's catch up tomorrow!"

Remaining planted in the doorway, Drew's brows furrowed as the officer darted down the hallway.

"Hey, Taylor!" Chief Mitchell called out. "Come on in. That damn Davis has such a big mouth. He never could hold water, could he?"

"Not since I've met him, sir, which was during our days at the academy. But what is he supposed to be keeping from me?"

"Close the door and have a seat. That's what I need to talk to you about."

Drew made his way inside the cluttered office. While pulling out a worn burgundy tweed chair, he eyed the cardboard boxes stacked against the empty filing cabinets. Framed pictures and certificates that had yet to be hung were propped against the wall. Containers of unopened supplies hugged the side of his desk. No one would know the chief had taken over the space almost thirty years ago considering it looked as if he'd just moved in.

"So," Chief Mitchell began, his chubby jowls quivering, "Officer Davis just updated me on the crime scene at Shelby's. Such a shame, finding Katie like that. Poor girl…"

"Sir, are you okay?" Drew asked after the chief's voice broke.

"Yeah, yeah. I'm good. I went to high school with the victim's father. So I feel somewhat connected to this case. Her dad called me this afternoon and the man was inconsolable. I promised him we'd do everything in our power to catch the sick son of a bitch who did this to his daughter. Which is where you come in, Officer Taylor."

Drew nodded, his eyes drifting toward the stack of boxes sitting directly behind the chief. The one on top caught his attention. "Linda Echols" was scribbled across the side in bold black letters.

It had been almost a year since her murder occurred, leading to one of the toughest investigations Drew had ever worked. No viable evidence was found at the scene of her home invasion. With the house being in an isolated area, no witnesses came forward and no security footage surfaced. Every lead hit a dead end. Eventually, the case went cold.

Since Linda's death, not a day had gone by that Drew didn't think about it. He'd grown extremely close to her family while working the investigation. After speaking to Linda's mother on an almost daily basis, he made a promise to catch her killer. When that didn't happen, he'd considered quitting the force. But it was Chief Mitchell who had encouraged him to remain onboard.

"You'll never make an arrest if you're no longer a member of Juniper PD," the chief told him. When Drew expressed feeling like a failure after making a promise he couldn't keep, his boss stopped him. "Listen, son. This was your first lesson in understanding that sometimes, working in the field of criminal justice means playing the long game. Hell, some cold cases don't get solved until twenty or thirty years down the road. But the key is, if you work hard enough, they eventually will. So keep your head up and hang in there."

Those were the words that kept Drew on the force, prompting him to pin a photo of Linda inside his cubicle as a reminder to never give up on trying to solve her case. And now, after hanging a picture of Katie next to hers, Drew hoped the investigation would somehow come full circle and lead him to Linda's killer. He had to consider the possibility of the cases being connected, considering both women's throats had been slashed and Linda's attacker was still on the loose.

"Well," Chief Mitchell said, pulling Drew from his thoughts, "let's talk about why I asked to meet with you. When Officer Davis and I were discussing the crime scene, he mentioned how you really stepped up and took on a leadership role with getting the reports completed, holding critical conversations with the medical examiner and forensic team, and gathering evidence. Then of course there were the photos and videos you captured... Keep this up and you'll be stepping into my shoes once I finally decide to retire."

"*Wow.* That's, uh...that's quite the compliment coming from you, Chief. Thank you."

"Of course. It's a compliment well-earned. And the reason I'm saying all that is because I'd like for you to head up the Katie Douglas murder investigation."

Drew sat straight up, turning his ear in the chief's direction. "I'm sorry. I think I misheard you. What did you just say?"

"I said I'd like for you to be the lead investigator on the Douglas case."

The weight of the request sent him slumping in his chair. Hundreds of thoughts flew through Drew's mind. There were at least three other officers who were more qualified than him. Officers who'd been with the Juniper PD way longer and weren't still carrying the burden of Linda Echols's cold case.

"I—I don't know what to say," he stammered. "This is such a huge investigation, and—"

"Wait, are you saying that you don't want to take this on?"

"No, no. It's not that. I'm just thinking about all the other officers who have more seniority than I do. Like Nelson or Harper or Adams—"

"Officer Taylor. I'm asking *you*. Davis wasn't

the only one who came to me with great feedback on the way you handled that crime scene today. I received calls from the medical examiner and head of forensics. They both sang your praises. Not Nelson's, Harper's, or Adam's. Nor anybody else's on the homicide team. *Yours*."

Pulling in a puff of air, Drew leaned back, his eyes glazing over as he stared into the speckled drop ceiling. Moments like this were the reason he'd joined the force. This was his time—his opportunity to prove he was capable of getting a murder solved.

"So what do you say, Officer Taylor. Are you in?"

Gripping the arms on his chair, Drew slid to the edge and looked Chief Mitchell directly in the eyes.

"Absolutely, sir. I'm in."

Chapter Two

Nia pulled a mirror from her drawer and checked her reflection. The beach waves she'd carefully flat-ironed through her long chocolate brown bob that morning were still intact. But her T-zone was shiny and lip gloss had faded.

Glancing at the time on her laptop screen, she saw that the special officers' meeting called by Chief Mitchell was set to begin in ten minutes.

"Just enough time to freshen up," she muttered, grabbing her makeup bag and swiping powder across her nose and gloss over her lips.

A knock against her cubicle's frame sent her jumping in her chair.

"Good morning, Officer Brooks."

Nia spun around, rolling her eyes at her smirking work bestie and former 9-1-1 colleague, Cynthia Lee. The pair had grown close while working together in the emergency services department. After Linda Echols's devastating murder last year, Nia was hit with the desire to serve a bigger purpose. Within days she submitted a transfer, and with Chief Mitchell's blessing, joined the police academy.

"Good morning, Cyn. What are you doing away from the call center this early?"

"Well, I've been here since five this morning. So I'm on my break. But here's a better question. What's with the flowing curls and face full of makeup? You got a hot date or something?"

"*Please.* Don't start with me. I'm just making sure I look presentable for the officers' meeting."

"Yeah, right. Presentable would've been a neat ponytail and dab of lip balm, like *I* normally wear," Cynthia quipped, propping her hands underneath her cherubic freckled face. "But you look like you're getting ready for a photo shoot. It's not like you even need all that with your gorgeous skin, those modelesque cheekbones and incessant gym visits. I mean, you keep the men's heads turning around here." She paused, glancing over her shoulder before whispering, "Could all the primping have anything to do with *Drew*?"

Nia grabbed her arm and pulled her farther inside the cubicle. "Will you lower your voice? Better yet, cut that talk out altogether. You know I'm not into Drew like that."

"Oh, do I really? Because last time I checked, you've been pining after that man ever since you started working for Juniper PD."

"*Lies,*" Nia rebutted, checking her reflection one last time before slapping her compact shut.

"Now I may have mentioned that Drew is a hand-some guy—"

"Juniper's very own Boris Kodjoe to be exact."

"But you know my rule. I don't date cowork-ers. Plus Drew seems like such a grump. Like he's always in a bad mood. Not to mention he's never paid an ounce of attention to me."

"First of all, most people meet their partners at work, so you need to toss that rule out the window. Secondly, how would Drew even know you're in-terested in him? It's not like you've ever gone out of your way to talk to him. Or say hello even."

"Isn't your break over yet?" Nia asked, pushing away from the desk.

"Nope. I've still got five minutes left."

"Well, I need to get to the conference room. So we'll have to table this conversation for later. Or better yet, just forget about it."

"Look," Cynthia said, stopping Nia before she brushed past her. "Do me a favor. At least try and sit next to Drew during this meeting. Maybe start up a conversation. Say good morning. *Something*."

"Enjoy the rest of your morning, Cynthia," Nia retorted before rushing down the hallway.

"Hey! Are we still on for lunch?"

"Yes, see you at noon!"

The conversation was out of Nia's head before she reached the conference room. All eyes were on her when she walked through the door. Gripping her notebook tighter, she ducked her head while searching for an empty chair.

The majority of the other officers were already there—including Drew. Cynthia hadn't been totally wrong in her assessment of Nia's feelings for him. She had been crushing on the officer ever since her first day of work. Aside from his ruggedly handsome good looks, there was a kindness behind his brooding, intense gaze. Drew was popular among their peers, oftentimes managing to drum up a few laughs despite his no-nonsense attitude. That, along with his impressive career accomplishments, made him one of the most well-respected officers within the department.

But Nia never allowed her crush to go too far. And while she had no intention of breaking her "no dating colleagues" policy, it wasn't as if he was available anyway. Rumor had it he'd been seeing someone for years.

Tables for two were set up alongside the conference room walls. The only empty space left was directly behind Drew. Just as he glanced in her direction, Nia dropped her gaze to the floor. Her calf muscles burned as she rushed past him and plopped down into the chair. Hoping he hadn't seen her ogling him, she flipped to an empty page in her notebook, then nervously bounced her pen against the table.

Drew turned slightly. He didn't look directly

at her, but judging by the curl in his downturned lips, something was annoying him.

The pen, she thought. *Stop banging the pen!*

The second Nia's hand froze midtap, Drew turned back around and faced the front of the room.

Her jaws clenched with embarrassment while he proceeded to talk to his partner, Timothy. When he spoke, the indentations in his biceps flexed as he waved an arm in the air. Tim's jokes sent him twisting in his chair, those gleaming white teeth lighting up the entire area. Nia's lips parted after he ran his strong, nimble hands over his freshly cut hair. She couldn't help but wonder what they'd feel like pressed against her body.

Just as her thoughts trickled from her head down to her tingling chest, a commotion erupted near the doorway. The room grew silent when Chief Mitchell approached the podium.

"Good morning, everyone. I'm sure you're wondering why I called this meeting on such short notice. But don't worry. I'll get right to it, then let you go as we've got a lot of work to do. I recently received a call from Finchport PD's chief of police, and he was telling me about a mentoring program that he's implemented within the department."

"Ugh," Drew grunted, slumping against the wall. "Here we go. Something else to add to my plate that I don't have time for…"

When a series of groans rippled through the room, the chief held up his hand. "Hold on. Before you all go shooting down my idea, just hear me out. I know we're all busy, but none of us are too busy to help out a fellow officer. Now, Finchport's chief has partnered his veteran officers with rookie cops in order to help them adjust to working on the force. As many of you know, being out on the street feels a lot different than training in the academy."

Drew leaned toward Timothy, whispering, "If anybody on this force can't navigate the streets of Juniper, then they need to rethink their career choice. It isn't like this is LA or Chicago."

"Maybe," Timothy replied. "But what about the Katie Douglas murder? Or Linda Echols for that matter? Both of those incidents reek of big-city crimes."

"True. However, cases like those are such a rare occurrence around here. Or so I hope…"

"Listen," the chief continued. "The more Chief Garcia and I discussed his mentoring initiative, the more I thought about our department and how vital a program like that could be for us. We've talked a lot about mental health here and the benefits of checking in with one another to make sure we're all in a good headspace. While the higher-ups have provided a variety of resources, I think a mentorship program would be a great addition to the work we're already doing to improve the team's overall well-being."

Chief Mitchell signaled Officer Davis, who began placing white envelopes in front of each officer.

"I've already taken the liberty of assigning mentees to each of the veteran officers. The name of the person you've been teamed with is inside the envelopes that Davis is passing around."

Nia's legs bounced underneath the table as she anticipated who she'd be paired with.

"Ouch," she hissed when her knee hit the metal edge.

Once again, Drew's head turned slightly toward her. That look of irritation had reappeared. This time, Nia wanted to say, *Stop taking your frustrations out on me!* But instead she pressed her hand against her knee, attempting to rub the pain away without making another sound.

As Officer Davis neared their section, Drew's head adamantly shook from side to side. "I highly doubt that the chief would ask me to mentor someone. Not when I've just been chosen to head up the biggest investigation of my career."

"That's *exactly* why he would've assigned you to a mentee," Timothy argued. "What better way to learn the ropes than to watch a pro catch a killer firsthand?"

"Thanks for the reassurance," Drew deadpanned.

"But *no* thanks to a rookie getting in the way of my work—"

He paused when Officer Davis approached his table.

"Hey, Officer Taylor, congratulations again on landing that Douglas case."

"Thanks, man. I appreciate you putting in a good word for me."

"No problem. The accolades were well-earned after the way you took charge of that crime scene."

Nia held her breath when Officer Davis handed him an envelope.

"Oh, no," Drew huffed, refusing to take it. "That can't be for me. I was just telling Tim that Chief Mitchell wouldn't have assigned a mentee to me. I've already got my hands full."

Officer Davis flipped the envelope over and eyed the name on the front. "I don't know what to tell you, other than the fact that this clearly says 'Officer Drew Taylor.'"

Emitting a low grunt, Drew snatched it from his hand. "Fine. I'll talk to the chief once this meeting is over."

"Suit yourself. But I think you'd be an excellent mentor to one of our rookies."

"I couldn't agree more," Timothy added.

After Officer Davis moved on to another table, Nia noticed Timothy push Drew's envelope toward him.

"Aren't you gonna open it?" he asked. "See who you've been assigned to?"

"Nope. Because it doesn't matter. I can't be a part of the program. And it's not that I don't think this is a great idea. It's fantastic. I just don't have time for it."

Nia wished she were bold enough to interject. To tell Drew how having a rookie by his side to assist in his investigation would be an asset rather than a disruption. An extra set of eyes on case files, surveillance footage and crime scenes would only bring him closer to solving Katie's murder. But rather than intervene, she remained silent for fear of him biting her head off.

"So what are you gonna do if Chief Mitchell insists you take on a mentee?" Timothy asked.

"Quit."

"Yeah, right."

As the officers broke into laughter, Nia muttered, "That is so messed up."

Both men slowly swiveled in their chairs.

"I'm sorry," Drew said. "What did you just say?"

Nia's mouth fell open. She hadn't intended for those words to slip out of her head and through her lips.

"You weren't listening in on our conversation," Drew probed, "were you?"

"No! Of course not. I was… I was just—"

He reached back and tapped his hand against

her table. "Calm down, Officer Brooks. I'm only kidding."

When he pulled away, his fingers brushed against hers. The rush of electricity that shot up her arm sent Nia falling against the back of her chair.

Just as Drew threw her a strange look, Chief Mitchell banged his knuckles against the podium.

"All right, everybody, let's quiet down for a second so I can wrap this up. Now that you've all had a chance to find out who you've been assigned, I'd like for you to get to know your mentorship partners better. Go out for coffee or lunch. Take time during your breaks to go on ride-alongs together. Share investigative stories. Mentors, be generous in offering up guidance to your mentees. Find ways to help them get acclimated to the department, the community and the rules of the Juniper PD. Most importantly, work on creating real, lasting bonds. Remember, you are your brothers' and sisters' keeper. Now, before we go, does anybody have any questions?"

Drew raised his hand. "Yes, sir. I do."

"Go ahead, Officer Taylor."

"What about those of us whose workloads are too heavy to take on a mentee at this time? Can we withdraw our names, then jump back in the next time around?"

"There is no such thing as a workload being too heavy. We're all swamped. It's called sacrifice.

And you'd be the perfect mentor, Officer Taylor. Especially with this case you're currently working. Three sets of eyes are better than two. Consider yourself lucky to be adding another person to your team of investigators. Now," Chief Mitchell proceeded, looking around the room without giving Drew a chance to respond. "Any other questions?"

"When does the program start?" Timothy asked.

"Immediately. And I expect for the mentors to take the lead. Reach out to your mentees first. You all are the more experienced of the two. So lead by example. Set something up, then get moving on the mentoring." He paused, glancing around once again. "Anything else?"

A quiet murmur swept through the room as officers spoke quietly among themselves.

"Okay, then," Chief Mitchell said, "this meeting is adjourned. As always, my door is open if anyone would like to stop by and talk in private."

Drew pushed away from the table and jumped to his feet. "Yeah, I'll be the first one doing just that."

"Let it go, Taylor," Timothy said. "The chief has spoken, and I don't think he's going to change his mind. Not to mention I think he's right."

"Yeah, well, we'll see about that. He may be singing a different tune once we talk one-on-one about all the pressure I'm under." Drew snatched up his unopened envelope and shoved it inside his back pocket. "I'll let you know how it goes."

Nia watched as he trudged out of the room. She'd been so wrapped up in his and Timothy's conversation that she hadn't noticed Officer Davis slide her envelope onto the table.

She stared at it, praying that she'd been assigned someone who, unlike Drew, would be enthusiastic about the program and happy to mentor her.

Timothy stood as she tore it open. "Who'd you get, Officer Brooks?"

"I don't know. Let's see…"

Her stomach dropped at the sight of the bold black letters typed across the page.

"So?" Timothy said. "Who's the lucky mentor?"

She turned the paper around. He leaned forward. "'Officer Drew Taylor'? Oh, no. And of course you'd be sitting right behind us. I'm sure you overheard our entire conversation."

"I did." Nia shoved the sheet back inside the envelope. "No worries. I'm sure after Officer Taylor has his conversation with the chief, I'll be assigned to someone else."

"Judging by the tone Chief Mitchell took when Drew gave him pushback, that's highly unlikely. But either way, good luck."

"Thanks. I'm definitely gonna need it."

Chapter Three

It'd been almost two weeks since Drew had been assigned as Nia's mentor. And he'd yet to reach out to her. Timothy had been on his case about it, insisting that he set something up before Chief Mitchell stepped in. But Drew wasn't worried. He'd scheduled a reminder to contact her one day this week. For the time being, his mind was focused solely on the Katie Douglas investigation.

The chief had put in a call to the head of the crime lab down in New Vernon to prioritize the evidence collected at the scene and the results were in—neither the blood nor fingerprints matched any offender profiles in CODIS.

Drew was beyond disappointed as he was certain they'd find a pairing. In his mind, Katie's death was too violent an act for the killer not to have any priors. The officer still believed his suspect had murdered before. He just hadn't been caught yet.

The only clue Drew had to go on was the Latimer Park event calendar. He was convinced there was some sort of message behind it. After he and Timothy stopped by the park and picked up a new brochure, they'd pored over every past and upcoming event. They had even spoken with Katie's friends and relatives to find out if she was somehow connected to the park or any of the activities. As far as they knew, she wasn't.

Drew questioned whether there was a husband or boyfriend in the picture. There wasn't. Katie was single, never married and hadn't fallen out with any exes or friends as far as they knew.

The current state of the investigation had left Drew frustrated and stuck back at square one. The case was all he could think about. He didn't want to drop the ball and watch the case go cold, which meant keeping himself completely immersed in it.

But then there was that damn mentoring program, looming in the back of his mind. Drew imagined getting on Chief Mitchell's bad side and losing the case altogether after stalling on contacting Nia.

Just do it, he thought, spewing a string of curses before rolling over to the other side of his king oakwood bed and grabbing his cell phone.

He checked the time. It was almost 6:00 a.m. Nia usually didn't arrive at the station until a little after eight. Drew had no idea why he knew that. Nevertheless, he sent her a text in hopes of finally getting their first meeting over with.

Good morning, Officer Brooks. Officer Taylor here. Are you free for coffee this morning before work? If so, we can meet up at the Cooper's Cake and Coffee on Motley Boulevard near the station at 7:00 a.m. Does that work for you? Let me know.

Drew sent the message, then made his way through the spacious primary bedroom, the soles of his feet cushioned by the warm cork flooring. He lived in the ranch-style home he'd grown up in, which he'd moved into after his parents left for North Carolina a few years back. Once he was convinced that they were in Charlotte to stay, Drew sold the loft that he'd owned across town.

He thought letting go of the place would be tough. He'd owned it since senior year of college and it held a lot of memories—the most recent being one that he'd rather forget.

Stepping inside the white marble bathroom, Drew turned on the shower and grabbed his toothbrush. His mind drifted to the day that his ex-fiancée moved into the loft. Ellody was the one who'd assured him that his bachelor days were over. His home quickly became theirs as she added her own personal touches, leaving an indelible mark on both the decor and the energy.

After their breakup, he knew he couldn't stay there, which was why he'd jumped at the chance to rent out the loft and set up shop in his childhood home. The eventual sale of his place felt cathartic, confirming that he had finally gotten over his ex.

Drew's pinging cell phone pulled his eyes toward the screen. It was a response from Nia.

Good morning, Officer Taylor. Nice to hear from you. Yes, I'm available to meet. I'll see you at Cooper's at 7. Looking forward to it.

Despite the irritation rumbling through his chest, he replied, Great, see you then.

"You're getting thirty minutes, tops," Drew said to himself before composing a message to Timothy.

Hey, meeting up with Brooks for coffee at 7. Let's connect at Latimer Park afterwards. I wanna take a look around the place. See if we can figure something out on the Douglas case. Does 7:45 work for you?

He hit Send, then jumped in the shower. Anxious to get to the park, he decided to give Nia twenty minutes instead.

DREW ENTERED COOPER'S a few minutes late and glanced around for Nia. The 1950s-style café was packed. He moaned at the sight of the line that was practically out the door. Every shiny red table and booth was occupied. Drew had passed on brewing a pot of coffee at home since he'd expected to grab a cup here. But from the looks of the crowd waiting to place their orders, he'd have to get through the meetup without it.

"Officer Taylor!" someone called out from the back of the shop.

Through the throng of patrons, he spotted Nia waving her hand in the air. He acknowledged her with a nod, then made his way across the black-and-white tiled floor toward her table.

As he got closer, Drew noticed how nice she looked. Nia normally wore her hair pulled back into a bun. Today it was down, with soft curls cascading around her slender face. Red lipstick set off her bright, sexy smile. And she wasn't in uniform. Instead, she was wearing a fitted cream cashmere sweater and tight gray jeans.

"Good morning, Officer Taylor," she said, extending her hand. "Thank you again for meeting with me. I've been looking forward to this since…well, since Chief Mitchell assigned you as my mentor."

"Yeah, sorry for the delay in reaching out," he uttered, taking her hand in his. "As you know, I've been working the Katie Douglas case. Things have been tough, considering it's not going as I'd hoped."

"Hmm, I'm sorry to hear that…"

Several seconds passed before Drew realized he was still holding on to Nia. For some strange reason, he couldn't get past the soft sensation of her palm pressed against his.

Gesturing for Drew to have a seat, Nia asked, "What's going on with the investigation?"

As they settled into the booth, something about her warm tone and concerned expression lowered his guard. "Well, we got the results back from the crime lab, and nothing matched up with a criminal profile in the database..." Drew's voice trailed off when a server placed two drinks and a tray filled with food onto the table. "Wait, what's all this?"

Nia's lips spread into that alluring smile she'd greeted him with. "I got here about fifteen minutes early and noticed it was getting pretty crowded. So I decided I'd better hurry up and order something for us. That way we wouldn't have to wait." She slid a cup and two items wrapped in plastic in front of him. "I didn't know if you'd be hungry. So I ordered a spinach omelet wrap for you. And of course I had to get us both slices of Cooper's famous cinnamon swirl crunch cake."

"Wow. And here I was thinking I'd have to pass on my morning dose of caffeine. Thank you. For all of this." Pulling the lid off the cup, Drew took a sip. "Hold on. How did you know my coffee order? You must've texted Tim and asked him."

"Nope. I've heard you around the station mentioning how you can't get your day started without a cup of dark roast with a splash of soy milk and one packet of raw sugar."

"Hmph, I didn't realize you were paying that much attention to me."

"I—well, I guess I just have good ears, or…" Nia hesitated, wringing her perfectly manicured hands.

"I'm kidding," Drew said, chuckling at how easy it was to throw off the rookie. "Don't worry. I know you're not stalking me or eavesdropping. Even though you *did* jump into my conversation with Tim during that mentorship meeting."

Her tense expression broke into a slight smirk.

"So is this how it's gonna be?" Nia asked. "Are you going to haze me throughout our entire mentorship?"

"I might…" Drew quipped, relaxing against the padded seat cushion. "No, but seriously. I appreciate this. I'm gonna have to take it to go though. I'm meeting Tim at Latimer Park and need to leave soon."

"Oh…okay."

The disappointment in Nia's soft tone was apparent. But her wide eyes appeared hopeful, as if she was waiting for an invitation to ride along with them. Drew wasn't totally against the idea but decided to hold off on extending an invitation.

"What time are you and Officer Braxton meeting up?" she asked.

"About seven forty-five." Drew pulled his cell from his black leather jacket. "Speaking of Tim, he never did confirm. That's not like him."

"Maybe he's sleeping in late?"

"I doubt it. He usually hits the gym every morning at five, and it's almost seven-fifteen. I'm sure he'll get back to me soon. Anyway, why don't we talk a little bit about your past experience and what made you want to become a police officer?"

Nia's brows lifted as she slid to the edge of her seat. The glimmer in her eyes reminded Drew of the excitement he'd felt during his time as a rookie.

"Well," she began, "as you know, I worked as a 9-1-1 operator for eight years before joining the force."

"Right. I did know that."

"There was something about those calls I'd receive and the rush of adrenaline pumping through my body whenever I'd send emergency services out to assist the victims. It made me feel vulnerable and helpless in a strange way. Like there was more I could be doing. Eventually the desire to serve a bigger purpose hit, and I began contemplating making a move to the force."

"Really? Why is that? Our 9-1-1 operators are vital. They're the first point of contact between the victims and law enforcement. Without them, we'd be completely uninformed and disorganized."

"I agree. But for me, I felt the need to be more present. Out there on the front lines, assisting firsthand rather than sitting inside the call center."

"Okay. I feel you on that…"

Drew's voice trailed off when a deep frown overtook Nia's cheery expression.

"There's, um," she began, her tone almost a whisper. "There was one call in particular that really turned things around for me."

"Oh? Which call was that?"

"Linda Echols."

Nia's response disarmed Drew's cool disposition. Recoiling at the pull in his chest, he nodded stiffly. "Yeah… That was a tough one. Were you the operator who handled it?"

"I was. I'll never forget how powerless I felt on the other end of that call, struggling to keep Linda calm while trying to send help. But the responding officers had trouble getting to her house. The attacker got to her before they could. I can still remember the shrill intonations in her screams, and how she kept saying that if he makes his way inside, he's going to kill her." Nia paused, clawing at the napkin underneath her coffee cup. "I was devastated when I heard she'd been found inside her bedroom closet with her throat slashed."

"I hope you're not blaming yourself for any of that."

"I try not to. But I did. For a long time. That guilt is what prompted me to join the force."

"Well I know for a fact that Chief Mitchell was thrilled to welcome you to the department. I mean, he *really* sang your praises in particular. Every chance he'd get, he would talk about how you're an excellent addition to the squad."

"Yeah, that was really nice of him," Nia murmured, her lush lips curling into a half grin.

The sight of her spirits lifting motivated Drew to continue. "I don't know if you're aware of this, but we'd hear little tidbits about which recruits were doing well and standing out. Your name was always at the top of everyone's list. Your sharp instincts, high level of intelligence, dedication to the Juniper community...nothing but good things were spoken about you. So remember that whenever those feelings of guilt start to hit. Let those traits be a reminder that what happened to Linda was in no way your fault. You did all that you could to try and save her. And hey, you never know. Now that you're on the force, maybe you'll get an opportunity to help solve her cold case."

Sitting up a little straighter, Nia's eyes connected with his gaze. "You know what? You're absolutely right."

A loud rumble floated through the air. Drew grabbed his stomach and glanced around the café, hoping no one else heard it. When a soft giggle slipped through Nia's lips, he realized she had.

"Why don't you take at least one bite of that wrap?" she suggested. "Because clearly you're hungry."

He peered down at his phone again. Still no word from Timothy. "Might as well." After noticing she hadn't unwrapped hers, Drew asked, "Aren't you going to eat?"

"I will. Once I get to the station."

"Why don't you eat now? Tim hasn't gotten back to me yet, so I've got time."

Wrinkling her nose, Nia tapped her fingers against the table.

"What's wrong?"

"Nothing. It's just…a little embarrassing."

"What's embarrassing?"

"I'm too nervous to eat," Nia murmured through tight lips.

"Nervous? Why?"

"Is that a real question? I don't think you realize how intimidating you can be, Officer Taylor."

He dropped his wrap and searched her face for a sign of humor. There wasn't one. "I had no idea anyone thought of me as intimidating. Would it help if you start calling me Drew instead of Officer Taylor?"

"It might…" she replied while slowly peeling the plastic off her wrap.

"Good. So tell me, Officer Brooks. When it

comes to this mentorship program, what are you expecting from me?"

"Now hold on. It wouldn't be fair for me to call you Drew if you don't call me Nia, would it?"

"I guess it wouldn't be, *Nia*. So go on. I'm listening."

"Well, aside from all the things Chief Mitchell mentioned during the meeting, I'd love to just shadow you. If that wouldn't be too much trouble..."

"It wouldn't be. And before you continue, can I just apologize for whatever you overheard me saying to Tim at that meeting? I'd just been assigned the Douglas investigation, and—"

"You don't have to explain anything. I get it. I figured I'd find a way to win you over eventually. Hopefully the coffee and breakfast was a good start."

"Oh, this was an excellent start. By the way, how much do I owe you?" he asked, reaching for his wallet.

"You don't owe me a thing. Consider this a thank-you for taking the time to meet with me."

A streak of guilt stabbed Drew in the gut. He'd been so resistant to meeting with Nia, and she had turned out to be more gracious than he ever could've imagined. "You're welcome. Next time is on me. Now, back to you wanting to shadow me."

"Yes. I'd love to help out with the Katie Douglas case however I can. Of course I wouldn't get in the way of things or overstep my bounds. But it would be great if I could experience the ins and outs of a murder investigation firsthand."

"I don't think that would be a problem. But let me talk to Tim first. He's my partner, and out of respect for him, I should figure out what role he's going to play beforehand. Is that cool?"

"Of course. And just know that I'm willing to take on whatever role I can, no matter how big or small."

"I'll keep that in mind…" After checking the time on his cell again, Drew scrolled through his notifications. Nothing from Timothy. "We should probably head out. I still wanna take a look around Latimer Park before I check in at the station."

Nia was slow to gather her things. Judging by her fallen expression, Drew sensed she didn't want to leave.

"Thanks again for inviting me to coffee," she said. "This was good. I think it may have been the most we've ever spoken since I started working for the Juniper PD."

"Oh, now you're trying to make me out to be some standoffish introvert," he joked, following her toward the exit.

"That could not be further from what I'm saying!"

As he held open the door, Drew couldn't help but

notice the sway in Nia's curvy hips. She brushed up against him, her touch sending an electric shot straight to his groin.

Don't even go there...

When they reached Nia's silver Acura, she clicked the alarm. "I'll see you back at the station. Good luck at Latimer Park. I hope you and Officer Braxton find something useful."

"Yeah, about that. I still haven't heard from Tim. And as Chief Mitchell likes to say, two sets of eyes are better than one. So, if you want, you can follow me to the park."

Pressing her hands together, Nia replied, "I'd like that," before the words were hardly out of his mouth. "I've got my evidence collection kit in the trunk, too. So if I stumble upon anything viable, I'll be prepared to collect it."

Drew couldn't help but chuckle at her enthusiasm. It was actually endearing.

You're doing it again, he thought before backing away.

"Sounds good," he told her. "I'll lead the way."

"Hey!" Nia called out just as he reached his car. "I forgot to mention that I know Latimer Park's recreation manager. If she's there, I'll see if we can get in and talk to her about that event calendar you found on the victim. Maybe she knows something."

"That would be awesome. Thanks."

Drew climbed inside his car and glanced in the rearview mirror, making sure Nia was behind him before pulling out. When she waved, he gave her a thumbs-up, then left the lot. As he drove down Sandpiper Road, wise words from his father popped into his head.

The universe works in mysterious ways...

Considering Nia's unexpected involvement in the investigation, Drew thought of how interesting it would be if she became the catalyst to solving the case.

Chapter Four

Nia eased up on the accelerator, realizing she'd been tailing Drew's car way too closely. But she couldn't help herself. The thrill of working the Douglas case had her emotions coursing full speed. Determination surged the strongest as she was eager to prove her capabilities, and hopefully, solidify her spot in the investigation.

Drew's cool, laid-back attitude had come as a pleasant surprise. Nia assumed it would take weeks, if not longer, to crack his hardened demeanor. But their meetup, albeit brief, gave her hope that his mentorship wouldn't be nearly as dreadful as she'd expected.

The get-together did nothing, however, to quell Nia's feelings for him. If anything, they'd intensified. Oddly enough, she didn't feel as though the sparks were one-sided. There were several moments when Drew appeared a bit flirty. The way he'd wink at her after saying something funny or flash a suggestive half smile while agreeing with a point she'd made. Those small gestures hadn't sent warm sensations stirring through her center for nothing.

Hold on, Nia told herself mid-thought. *Don't go getting ahead of yourself...*

Drew's bright taillights pulled her back into the moment as they drove across the Sparrow Lane Bridge. Nia's heartbeat quickened when Latimer Park appeared in the distance.

Cottonwood and Early Richmond cherry trees were scattered along the outskirts of the lush, sloped landscape. Stay-at-home parents bordered the playground as children rode the merry-go-round and climbed monkey bars. Tennis lessons were in session, and several young men were practicing their free throws on the basketball court.

It was hard to believe that such a beautiful, active space was now tainted by a possible connection to Katie Douglas's murder.

Just when Drew made a slight turn onto Candlewood Avenue, he reached out the window and signaled to Nia, then quickly pulled over. She parked behind him, craning her neck to see what was going on.

After waiting for him to get out of the car, Nia peered through his rear windshield and saw Drew's cell phone glued to his ear. A few minutes later her phone rang. It was him.

"Hey, what's going on?" she asked.

"Chief Mitchell just called. We need to get back to the station. Something's happened to Tim."

"*What?* Is he okay?"

"I don't know. But judging by the chief's tone, it sounds serious. He just got a call from Tim's mother saying that he's been rushed to the emergency room. Hopefully Chief will know more by the time we get there."

"Got it. I'm right behind you."

NIA AND DREW pulled into the station's parking lot and charged into the building. While he headed straight for Chief Mitchell's office, she stopped at her desk.

"Keep me posted!" she told him.

He spun around, his brows wrinkled with confusion. "Wait, you're not coming with me?"

"I—I didn't know if you wanted me there."

"I definitely want you there. Whatever's going on, I could use all the support I can get."

The officer's worried expression almost prompted Nia to wrap him in a warm embrace. Instead she nodded, following him to the chief's office.

They barely reached the doorway before Drew asked, "What's going on with Tim? Any updates since we last spoke?"

Chief Mitchell ran his hands through his thinning gray hair. "Have a seat, you two."

While Nia sat directly across from the chief, Drew paced the creaking wood floor.

"Chief, you're scaring me," he said. "What happened to Tim?"

"He, uh…he was in a really bad car accident on the way home from the gym this morning. It was a hit-and-run. According to a witness, another vehicle that was driving behind him accelerated, then rammed into the back of Tim's car. He spun out of control and slammed into a tree."

"Oh my God," Drew moaned, slumping into the chair next to Nia's.

"He was thrown from the vehicle and suffered several injuries," Chief Mitchell continued. "A concussion, broken bones, a punctured lung…"

"Is he showing any signs of brain damage?" Nia asked.

"They're not sure yet. The doctors are still running tests. But the good news is Tim's breathing on his own. He's been put in a medically induced coma just in case he experienced any brain swelling and to give his body a chance to heal."

"Was the witness able to get a license plate number?" Drew croaked.

"No, unfortunately. But he did say that the collision seemed intentional. Instead of going after the driver, he went to help Tim and call an ambulance."

"I should probably go to the hospital," Drew said. "Check on his family and make sure they're doing okay."

The chief nodded in agreement. "Good idea.

I'm sure his mother would appreciate that. And I hate to bring this up, but now that Tim is out of commission, what are we going to do about the Katie Douglas investigation?"

"Yeah," Drew uttered, running his hand along the back of his neck. "I can't head that up alone. I'm gonna need a partner."

"Do you have anyone in mind?"

The question straightened Nia's back. Her head swiveled from Chief Mitchell to Drew, then back to the chief.

"I do, actually," Drew responded. "Officer Davis was the first person I thought of since he and I worked so well together at the crime scene."

The chief's gaze drifted toward Nia. She bit down on her jaw, desperate to throw her hat in the ring. But she held back. She'd been on the force less than a year. Officer Davis had way more experience. Nia knew she didn't stand a chance against him.

"What about Officer Brooks?" Chief Mitchell asked.

Huh?

She perked up, her face growing hot with anticipation while awaiting Drew's response.

"I'm sorry," he muttered. "Come again?"

"I said, what about Officer Brooks?"

As Drew remained silent, Nia held a hand in the air. "Should, um…should I leave, or—"

"No, no," the chief said. "You should stay. Maybe

help plead your case on why you'd make a good partner on this investigation."

She turned to Drew, cringing at the slight scowl on his face.

"That won't be necessary," Drew huffed. "Because it's not gonna happen. Now I agreed to the whole mentoring thing. But this is where I draw the line. I need a veteran officer by my side who's familiar with crime scenes and evidence analysis. Someone who can put leads and tips and pieces of the investigative puzzle together to get this case solved."

Chief Mitchell kept silent while sipping from his World's Best Granddad mug. His lack of a response seemed to set Drew off as the officer sprang from his chair, continuing his rant while pacing the floor once more.

Holding her hand to her chest, Nia pulled in a sharp breath of air and peered over at Drew. The intensity in his wild eyes and erratic hand gestures were jarring. He was speaking about her as if she weren't even in the room. His behavior was far from that of the cool guy he'd appeared to be at Cooper's—the one who seemingly welcomed her into the investigation. Now that things had gotten real, the chief's suggestion sent him spiraling.

"Please, Officer Taylor," Chief Mitchell said. "Calm down. Have a seat. Let's talk this out. Do you need some water, or coffee—"

"No," Drew interrupted, throwing himself into

the chair. "I'm fine. I'm just worried about Tim. And the investigation, of course."

"Which is all perfectly understandable. Do you still think you're capable of handling the case considering the news about Tim? Because if you're not, I can always pass it on to another officer."

"Of course I am, Chief. Regardless of what's going on around me, I'm completely up for it."

Tension sucked the air from the room. Nia clenched her toes inside her combat boots while awaiting Chief Mitchell's response. But he just sat there, patting his fist against the desk. Judging by the look on Drew's poker face, he was done pleading his case.

Finally, after several moments of pained silence, the chief said, "Officer Taylor, keep in mind that Officer Brooks isn't new to the Juniper PD. She's worked within the department for years."

"Yeah, as a 9-1-1 op—"

"Hold on. I'm well aware of her former position. My point is, Officer Brooks is familiar with this town, the rules of the department and the inner workings of crime and apprehension. She won Telecommunicator of the Year five years in a row. That award isn't easy to come by."

Chief Mitchell paused, as if waiting for Drew to reply. But the officer remained silent.

"What I'm saying is, Officer Brooks is special. She's sharp. Her attention to detail is uncanny. Her communication and leadership skills are exceptional. The level of care and respect she's shown to victims is unmatched. She has helped solved crimes by simply asking the right questions during 9-1-1 calls. You don't come by those traits easily or often. When you do, you have to utilize them. What better way to do that than to partner with Officer Brooks on this case?"

"With all those accolades," Drew grumbled, "maybe you should just assign the case to her."

"Keep it up and I just might."

That's it, Nia thought, no longer able to withstand the awkward conversation. Just as she grasped the arms of her chair to stand, Drew emitted an exasperated sigh.

"Fine. I'll partner with Ni—I mean Officer Brooks. Not that I have a choice in the matter," he added under his breath.

"Good decision," Chief Mitchell said, ignoring the second half of Drew's response. "Officer Brooks, are you good with this?"

"I am, thank you. I really appreciate your kind words as well as this opportunity."

"Of course you do," Drew whispered toward his feet.

Nia glared in his direction, that crush she'd had on him fading by the minute.

"It's all well-earned," the chief told her. "Now, I'll be expecting a report from you two on the Douglas case in the next few days. Officer Taylor, maybe you can take Brooks down to Shelby's

Candy Factory so she can assess the crime scene in person. Who knows—maybe she'll come across something that you and the other officers missed."

It was obvious that the chief was baiting Drew. Nia braced herself, waiting to see if he'd bite.

"I'd love for that to happen," he responded, holding his arms out at his sides. "If she does, that just means we'll be one step closer to solving the case."

"Now *that's* what I like to hear," Chief Mitchell boomed. "Teamwork. It makes the dream work, right?"

"Oh, please…" Drew hissed through clenched teeth.

"All right, you two," the chief continued. "Unless you've got something else for me, I think we're done."

Charging to the door, Drew said, "I'm going to the hospital to check on Tim. I'll have my phone if anyone needs me."

"Hey!" Chief Mitchell called out. "Be sure to check in with me as soon as you can. Let me know how he's doing."

"Will do."

Drew left the office without giving Nia so much as a glance. Ignoring the uncertainty banging against her temples, she slowly stood.

"Thank you again, Chief. I promise I won't let you down."

"I know you won't. That's why I assigned this

case to you. Now get out there and prove Officer Taylor and anybody else who may be doubting you wrong."

"Yes, sir."

Those words were all it took to send Nia back to her cubicle with her head held high. Just as she sat down, someone approached from behind. It was Drew.

"Here you go," he said, slamming a file down on the desk. "This is everything I've got on the Douglas case. I would advise you to read through every single word of it and examine those crime scene photos from top to bottom. We'll make plans to go to the candy factory in the next day or so. For now, I just need to make sure Tim is okay."

"Understood. Please send Tim my well wishes. And hey, Drew? Just so you know, I'm really looking forward to working on this investigation with you. I may not be the most experienced officer on the force, but I promise I'll do everything I can to help solve this case."

He responded with a grunt before walking away.

"Nice chat," Nia mumbled.

Shrugging it off, she reminded herself that getting justice for Katie was all that mattered, whether Drew wanted her help or not.

Chapter Five

Drew felt like crap as he pulled back into the station. Seeing Tim connected to all those tubes while surrounded by machines, concerned doctors and worried loved ones had been devastating. It was a reminder that anything could happen at any given moment. And there were bigger concerns in life than him being partnered with a rookie cop.

The hospital visit was a wake-up call that left him feeling ashamed of his meltdown. The disrespect he'd shown toward Chief Mitchell and Nia was unacceptable, making his first order of business a talk with his boss, then his newly appointed partner.

Drew entered the department and made a beeline for the chief's office. The door was open. He approached it cautiously, knocking lightly on the frame.

"Hey, Chief, you got a sec?"

"I do," he replied, without looking up from his cell phone. "But hang on. Chief Garcia from Finchport is gonna be calling me any minute now.

He wants an update on how our mentorship program is working out. Speaking of which…" He paused, finally peering up at Drew. "How's the mentoring going between you and Officer Brooks? Last I heard you two hadn't connected yet."

"Actually we did connect. Over coffee this morning."

The chief set his phone to the side. "Well, that wasn't what I expected to hear. But it certainly makes me happy. Is it safe to assume you two got along okay?"

"Yes. We got along just fine."

"Good. Because after the way things went during that meeting earlier…" Chief Mitchell hesitated, then pointed at Drew. "You're one of our main leaders around here, Officer Taylor. And I expect for you to act like it. At all times. The behavior you displayed in my office earlier today in front of Officer Brooks was disgraceful. You're better than that. So I'm hoping to never see that side of you again."

"That's actually why I stopped by, sir. I wanted to apologize. You're right. And you have my word that it'll never happen again."

"Apology accepted. Was I your first stop since returning to the office?"

"Yes, you were."

"I'm guessing you know what the second stop needs to be?"

Drew shoved his hands inside his pockets and walked back toward the doorway. "Yes, sir, I do."

"Good. Trust me, Officer Brooks is gonna be a great asset to your investigation. Now get to work. Oh, and thanks for the update on Tim. I'm glad to hear the doctors are planning to reduce the meds that are keeping him in the coma. Did they say what they're expecting to happen once the dosage is lowered?"

"They're hoping he'll open his eyes. Respond to sights and sounds. Grip his mother's hand. Things like that."

The conversation was interrupted when Chief Mitchell's phone rang. "That's Chief Garcia. We'll catch up later. In the meantime, you know what you've gotta do."

"I do. And I'm on my way to do it now."

Drew sauntered toward the rookie cubicle area. Heads turned as he appeared to be talking to himself. But he was practicing which version of an apology he would give to Nia.

When he approached the desk, her chair was empty.

Good, he thought, realizing he wasn't quite ready for a face-to-face just yet. The day had already been heavy enough. Plus he couldn't seem to mentally compose a decent enough apology.

"Hey, Officer Taylor," a soft voice murmured behind him. "Were you looking for me?"

Dammit...

"Yuh—yeah," he stammered. Noticing she'd gone back to the formalities, he contemplated reminding her that she could call him Drew. But he resisted. After the way he'd behaved earlier, he didn't blame her for shutting down their friendly rapport. "Do you have a minute?"

Nia set a freshly poured cup of coffee on her desk and sat down, pointing to a chair in the corner. "I do. Please, have a seat. How is Officer Braxton doing?"

"He's already showing some slight signs of improvement. I was just telling Chief Mitchell that the doctors are hoping to start pulling him out of the coma tomorrow."

"Oh, good. I've been putting in my fair share of prayers all morning." She went quiet, her dazzling deep brown eyes searching Drew's face. "How are you holding up?"

I don't deserve your kindness, he almost blurted. The amount of concern this woman was showing toward him was inexplicable.

"I'm holding up okay. Knowing that Tim is getting better has me feeling cautiously hopeful. Thanks for asking."

Drew rocked back in his chair, suddenly lost for words. The fragmented apologies he'd just mentally rehearsed completely slipped from his mind now that he was in Nia's presence.

Freestyle something, he told himself, glancing over at her. She stared back expectantly, making no attempt to fill in the awkward gap of silence. He didn't blame her. This situation was on him to fix.

"Nia, if it's okay that I still call you that, I need to address the way I behaved this morning during our meeting with Chief Mitchell. I don't wanna use Tim's accident as an excuse, but hearing that he'd been hurt sent my mind reeling. Then after finding out how bad off he was, I honestly didn't think he was going to make—"

His voice broke underneath the weight of his words. When Nia reached out and clutched his hand, warmth radiated from her smooth skin, easing his pain like a soothing balm. "Look, I'm getting off track here. I want to apologize for the way I treated you. You didn't deserve that. And just to be clear, I have no doubt that you'll be an asset to this investigation."

"Thank you, Drew. I appreciate you saying that. Apology accepted." She held his gaze, flashing that same bright smile that had caught his attention when he'd entered Cooper's. "Listen, why don't we forget about what happened earlier and start over with a clean slate?"

"I'd like that."

"Good." She opened the case file and flipped through the police report. "Now that we've gotten all that out of the way, come closer. I'll go over what I've been working on since you've been gone."

"Oh? So you've been working my case without me?" he teased in an attempt to lighten the mood.

"I've been working *our* case without you. But anyway, I was looking through these notes and saw that Katie Douglas's family found her cell phone inside her apartment, which they turned over to law enforcement."

"Right. Officer Mills is downloading and researching all the data now. Once he's done, he's gonna provide me, well, now *us*, with all the pertinent info. So we'll find out who she'd been calling, texting, messaging on social media…those sorts of things."

"Yes, I spoke with Officer Mills about that. He confirmed that he'll be tracking her digital footprint as well, which is good. I'm curious to know where she'd been prior to her murder. In the meantime, I asked if I could take a look at the apps on her phone. One that stood out was the Someone for Everyone dating app. Did you know she was a member?"

"No, I didn't. But after speaking with her family, I did find out that she wasn't seeing anybody."

"As far as they knew."

Hunching his broad shoulders, Drew leaned in and studied the notes. "That's true. I just assumed they would know. Especially her sister. They seemed pretty close."

"Trust me, that doesn't mean a thing. Take my younger sister Ivy, for example. I used to think we were as tight as could be. Then one day I found out she'd been dating some guy for an entire year who I knew nothing about. People oftentimes hide things from those they're closest to. Especially when it comes to relationships."

"You make a good point. With that being said, we should reach out to the app's administrator as soon as possible."

"I'm already on it," Nia responded before flipping open her notebook. "I reached out to their customer service department requesting access to Katie's account. We need to know who she'd been in contact with and whether she made plans to meet up with anyone before her murder. Since so many people communicate solely through the app, there may be information we won't find in her emails, text messages and call log."

"Wow. You really are on it. I love the way you're taking such strong initiative." Drew hesitated, fiddling with the crown on his stainless steel watch. "Wait, you seem to know an awful lot about this whole dating app thing."

Nia ignored the remark. But her subtle smirk let him know she'd heard him loud and clear. "So anyway, I'm still waiting to hear back from the company. I had to contact them through the app since I couldn't find a phone number. I'll let you know as soon as they reach out."

"Sounds good. Nice work on all this—"

"Oh, wait!" she interrupted. "Before I forget, I

got ahold of Latimer Park's recreation manager. Her name is Dawn Frazier by the way. She said that Katie's name doesn't ring a bell. After searching through the activity database, she found that Katie had never registered for any classes or programs. So as far as Dawn knows, she was in no way connected to the park. But Dawn did say we could come by anytime to speak with her and search the premises."

Drew eyed Nia while fidgeting with his goatee. He would've expected the average rookie to passively wait for him to return from the hospital, set up a meeting, then sit down together to discuss the next moves. But not Nia. Clearly she was well above average, proving every word that Chief Mitchell had spoken about her to be true.

Two traits he'd failed to mention, however, were her tenacity and assertiveness—characteristics Drew found to be most attractive in a woman.

"Again," he said, "good work. Thank you."

"No problem. I was thinking—maybe you should send a patrol car out to Latimer Park to keep an eye on things. You know, just in case the killer left that event calendar at the crime scene to hint at what might be coming next."

"That's not a bad idea. Even if Katie isn't directly linked, there could still be some sort of connection. We'll run it by Chief Mitchell and see what he thinks. If he gives us the okay, I'll get someone assigned to the job as soon as possible."

"Excellent."

Drew reached for one of the crime scene photos just as Nia closed the file. Their hands met. His fingers slid between hers, rousing a heat so intense that he lurched in his chair.

"Sorry," he uttered, slow to pull away.

Nia's narrowing eyes drifted from his hand to his lips. "So…what's next?"

"Why don't we head to the candy factory so you can check out the crime scene. Then we'll stop by Latimer Park if there's still enough daylight."

Rolling away from the desk, she grabbed her tote. "Sounds like a plan."

"Cool. I'll get my stuff and meet you out front."

While Nia headed toward the lobby, Drew watched her walk away, his pupils shifting to the swing of her graceful stride.

Turn around, he thought, tearing himself away from the hypnotic sight.

The officer couldn't decide which was more impressive—Nia's beauty or her savvy. Either way, he was glad to have her on his team.

Chapter Six

Nia stretched out on her cream leather sofa, kneading her fist into her quads after an intense spin class. The day had been long. She'd stayed at the station way past six, then stopped by the grocery store before heading to the gym.

Cozying up against a green suede pillow, Nia was hit with a bout of loneliness. The chilly autumn night left her wishing she had someone to come home to. It'd been almost two years since she had been in a serious relationship. In the past week, she and Drew had spent countless hours together, which only magnified her single status. It almost felt like punishment, working so closely with the man she'd been pining after for years.

Landing a case of this magnitude early in her rookie career was a dream. Nia had hoped that fact alone would hold her attention so that she wouldn't be laser-focused on Drew. Yet the complete opposite had occurred. Seeing him in uniform, taking charge and handling the investigation with such skill and ease, only made him more appealing.

Once the pair had teamed up, Nia realized she'd only scratched the surface of who really Drew was. Underneath the tough exterior was a thoughtful man who always took her thoughts and theories into consideration. That had been pretty surprising after the meltdown he'd had in Chief Mitchell's office. But aside from his investigative acumen and meticulous critical thinking skills, it was Drew's appreciation of her contributions that impressed Nia the most.

The drawback, however, was that her feelings for Drew were growing beyond her control. Her slight crush had been manageable. But these new emotions were beginning to get the best of her. And it was frustrating that she couldn't do anything about it.

Nia closed her eyes. Mulled over the moments alone she and Drew had been spending together. Just that afternoon when they were inside the cluttered evidence room he'd slipped past her, his hard chest pressing against her back. She'd gasped and spun around, her breasts brushing against his taut bicep as he reached out to steady her.

Self-control left her body when she quivered within his grip. Drew just stood there, his parted lips indicating he'd felt her reaction. Those massive hands lingered on her hips. Their mouths were so close that as he exhaled, she inhaled the sweet scent of cinnamon espresso on his breath.

Nia's desire for Drew no longer appeared one-sided. But dating a colleague was still off-limits. Being a Juniper police officer meant everything to her. If she and Drew got together, then broke up, her dream job would become a nightmare as Nia knew she didn't have the stomach to face an ex every day.

"Oh, well," she sighed, turning up the volume on the Tennis Channel. As Chanda Rubin reviewed the day's top matches, she grabbed her phone and swiped open the Someone for Everyone app. There were several messages, but none from the administrator in response to her Katie Douglas request.

Drew had been right about one thing—Nia did know her way around the dating app. What he didn't know was that she'd been a member for almost a year.

After Linda Echols's murder, Nia had grown depressed. She became obsessed with work and began isolating herself socially. Friends insisted that she needed to get out more and start dating, if for nothing else than to help take her mind off the tragic death. It had taken quite a bit of convincing on their part. But after they assured Nia she could easily connect with the perfect match through a dating app as opposed to a bar or club, she gave in and joined Someone for Everyone.

Nia had only been out with a few of the members. Two of them lived in nearby towns and one resided in Denver. None had worked out. But she hadn't given up hope just yet.

After swiping through several lackluster profiles, Nia clicked on her inbox and scrolled through the messages. She stopped at the sight of a man's profile picture. He appeared tall, his slim-fitting navy suit tailored to a tee. His flawless deep brown skin glowed as he flashed a sexy, mischievous half smile. His dark, piercing eyes looked as though they were staring right at her. The gaze was somewhat haunting, but at the same time intoxicating.

"Hmm…" Nia murmured before opening his message.

Hello, beautiful. My name is Shane Anderson, and I am new to the Juniper area. I just stumbled across your profile, and I must say, you are quite lovely. I would love to get to know you better. If the feeling is mutual, please feel free to respond to this message. I hope to hear from you soon… xx, Shane

Nia reread the message at least three times. It may have been short, but it was one of the more gentlemanly introductions that she'd received. Most men asked what her plans were for the evening and whether she was available to hook up. And by *hook up*, it was clear they weren't referring to dinner or drinks.

Curiosity coursed through Nia's fingers as she clicked on his profile. The headline read, Shane,

38. Always up for meeting great people and experiencing new adventures. About Me: Works hard as a wealth management advisor Monday through Friday so that I can venture out and explore the world on weekends. Loves to laugh. Hates Brussels sprouts. Might challenge you to a dance-off in the middle of the club.

A soft smile teased Nia's lips as she took a sip of Merlot. "So you're handsome, smart and seem to have a good sense of humor. Nice start."

She scrolled down and continued reading.

What I'm Looking For: A woman who isn't afraid to laugh at herself, loves to travel, doesn't mind dog cuddles, is confident and secure, and knows what she wants. If we're a match, she would totally be down to explore this thing called life with me.

"I think this one might have potential," she said before opening his photo album. There was a picture of him sitting out on a massive backyard deck, a golden retriever nearby. Then one of him rock climbing inside the Pier 48 Fitness entertainment complex. From the look of his cut physique, he spent a fair amount of time in the gym.

The rest of the album contained an array of travel photos—from deep-sea fishing in Cabo San Lucas to skydiving along the Amalfi Coast. As his profile headline stated, Shane did indeed seem to live an adventurous life. Nia wondered if she could keep up. Aside from becoming a police officer, the most daring thing she'd ever done was take a midnight ghost tour through downtown Colorado Springs one Halloween weekend.

Deciding that Shane had potential, Nia replied to his message.

Hello, Shane. Thank you for your message. It's nice to "e-meet" you. My name is Nia, and as a lifelong resident of Juniper, I do hope you're enjoying my hometown thus far. To answer your question, yes, I would like to get to know you better. I'll start things off. After viewing your profile, I saw that you are quite daring. Have you found any fun activities here in town that have satisfied your adventure-seeking spirit? If not, I've got a few ideas. Looking forward to hearing from you...xx, Nia

"Now I just need to google thrilling things to do in Juniper."

Soon after she hit Send, Nia's phone pinged.

"That was quick."

A mix of hope and excitement simmered in her chest as Nia reopened the text thread between her and Shane. There were no new messages.

"What, what's happening here?"

She refreshed the page. Still nothing new.

Then an email notification appeared at the top of the screen. The message was from Drew, and the subject read "Case Report for Chief Mitchell—Final."

Nia's mind immediately shifted to thoughts of

the investigation. The pair had spent the majority of the day composing the report. It had gotten late, and Drew knew she didn't want to miss her spin class. So he was kind enough to let her go while he stayed back and added the final touches.

Hey Nia, the message read. I hope your class went well. I've attached the final case report for the chief. Take a look and let me know what you think. If you don't have any changes, we'll send it first thing in the morning. Looking forward to hearing from you. Have a good night. Drew

Nia clicked on the attachment and scanned the report. They'd started off by bringing Chief Mitchell up to speed on their visit to Shelby's Candy Factory. For over two hours, the officers combed the area where Katie's body had been discovered. Just when they were about to give up, Nia found a piece of cardboard underneath the cold pressing unit. It contained a dirty shoeprint impression that looked to be the sole of a size eleven in men's. Luckily for them, the distinct treads with beveled edges and slanting lugs were clearly visible. Drew took photos and sent the fiberboard off to the crime lab for testing.

Through a shoe-sole pattern classification system database, Nia discovered that the print belonged to a Lacrosse AeroHead Sport hunting boot. Despite knowing the print could belong to anyone as there had been plenty of people in and out of the factory, she and Drew were hoping that the print would prove viable in helping to track down their killer.

Next was a summary of their visit to Latimer Park. After inspecting the area, nothing appeared suspicious. Dawn, the recreation manager, wasn't able to share much more than she already had during her phone conversation with Nia. Their brief meeting ended with her promising to keep an eye out and let law enforcement know if anything strange occurred.

After getting the okay from Chief Mitchell, Drew had assigned Officer Davis to patrol the park. Days went by with no abnormal activity. Davis questioned whether the crumpled event calendar found at the crime scene was relevant to their case.

"Don't give up," Drew had told him. "You never know what we may find."

But nothing could convince Officer Davis that the Latimer Park stakeout wasn't a waste of time. He didn't think the killer would make a move with a patrol car present. Nia and Drew felt his presence would deter the killer from making a move at all. In the midst of the debate, Davis requested that the stakeout be called off. So Drew wrapped up the report asking that Chief Mitchell make the final decision.

Nia replied to the email confirming the report was good to go, then took another sip of wine. She needed a break. Ever since the chief partnered her with Drew, the case was all she thought about. It was difficult enough knowing there was a killer on the streets of Juniper terrorizing the community. But the pressure to prove herself while struggling to not overstep her bounds had become an even heavier burden to bear. The search for balance was beginning to wear on Nia and a reprieve was in order—which was why the message from Shane had come at the perfect time.

Just as she grabbed the remote and turned to the Oxygen channel, her phone pinged again. This time, it was a text from Drew.

Hey, it's me again. Thanks for the green light on the report. On another note, Officer Davis talked to Chief Mitchell this evening, and Chief decided to stop the surveillance on Latimer Park. I'm really disappointed as I'm sure you are too since we both believe that the event calendar is no coincidence. I'll talk to the boss in the morning and try to change his mind. Fingers crossed. Have a good night.

Dread poured over Nia as she slammed her phone against the couch. Of course the calendar was no coincidence. But trying to defend their hunch without further proof, signs of suspicious activity or a viable connection between Katie and the park seemed impossible.

Nia stared at Drew's message, rereading it a couple more times before composing a response that wouldn't reflect the anger ringing inside her head.

Thanks for the update. I'm really disappointed to hear that as well. Let's just hope that Chief Mitchell is right and nothing comes of the calendar being left at the scene. Hope you have a good night as well.

After sending the message, Nia opened the Quick Eats app and ordered a buffalo chicken sandwich with a side of loaded fries instead of the salad. News of the canceled stakeout left her craving comfort food.

Just as she refilled her wine glass, her cell pinged again. Nia assumed it was Drew and swiped open her phone without checking the notification. The Someone for Everyone heart-shaped icon flashed on the screen, indicating she had a new message.

She sat straight up and opened it. A text from Shane appeared.

Hello Nia. It's nice to "e-meet" you as well. Beautiful name, btw. Thank you for your quick response. Did I mention that I love a woman who's prompt? But anyway, as I'd stated in my previous message, I'm new to town. I recently began working for a brokerage firm, and let's just say I've been earning every single penny! Once my schedule frees up a bit, I would love to meet you in person, maybe for a nice dinner or some live jazz music. Until then,

I hope we can keep the conversation going here. That way, once we finally do meet, it'll feel as if we already know one another. That said, it's lights-out for me as the alarm is set for a 4:00 a.m. training session at the gym. Have a wonderful night, gorgeous. Looking forward to hearing from you again soon...xx, Shane

Nia's pulse began to throb as she reread the message. She debated whether to respond now or wait until the morning. After a mental back-and-forth, she decided to hold off so as not to appear too eager.

The minute she set her cell down, thoughts of the investigation crept back into her head.

Enough, Nia told herself. She'd dedicated enough of her day to the case. It was time to focus on something a little more pleasant—like the message exchange with Shane.

Thanks to him, her evening was ending on a high note. "So let's keep it there," she murmured, grabbing her phone and scrolling through his photos once again.

Chapter Seven

Drew floored the accelerator, flying across Sparrow Lane Bridge, then tearing down Candlewood Avenue. He tried Nia's cell again. The call went straight to voicemail.

"Nia," he huffed. "I've been trying to reach you for the past hour. I hope you're getting my calls and texts. I need you out at Latimer Park. *Now.* A couple of joggers found a dead body on a bench over by the duck pond. Chief Mitchell and the forensic team should already be there. I'm pulling up now. Call me when you get this message."

After parking along a side street near the tennis courts, he sprinted across the freshly cut grass. Panic swirled through his lungs as he choked on shallow breaths of air.

It was a little past six-thirty in the morning—too early for the recreational areas to be occupied. *Thank God.* The last thing Juniper PD needed was for people to catch sight of the gruesome scene.

Yellowish-orange light broke through dark clouds as the sun began to rise. A few of the officers who'd worked the overnight shift were already there, wrapping yellow Police Line tape around lodgepole pine tree trunks. In the center of it all was a shallow duck pond. Birds were splashing about, their fluttering wings flipping over banana water lilies in response to all the commotion.

On a black wrought-iron bench right across from the water sat a woman's body. Her head was slumped over, and just like Katie Douglas, her throat had been slashed. Blood drenched her off-white bomber jacket. Her hands and feet were bound with duct tape. And a piece of paper was stuffed inside her right hand.

"Hey, Taylor!" Officer Davis called out. "I just got a text from the chief. He should be here any minute. Any word from Officer Brooks?"

"No, not yet. I've sent several messages and left voicemails. Her phone must be out of juice because she never turns it off."

The thought of something happening to Nia flashed through Drew's mind. *Don't do that*, he told himself, gritting his teeth in frustration.

As he approached the victim, Drew's grip on the evidence collection kit tightened, his stomach turning at the grisly sight. The woman looked to be no older than twenty-five. A long dark braid hung down her back. From what he could tell, her height and weight appeared to be almost identical to Katie's. The similarities between the two crime scenes were uncanny. Either they were dealing with a copycat killer, or their suspect had struck again.

"So what do you think?" Officer Davis asked. "Is it possible we might have a serial killer on our hands?"

"Not only is it possible, but in my opinion, it's highly likely. And apparently he's got a type. Notice the parallels between this victim and the last?"

"Yeah, I do. You know who else comes to mind when I compare the two?"

"Let me guess. Linda Echols."

"You got it."

Staring down at the ground, Officer Davis dug his heel into a clump of grass before emitting a forced cough. "Hey, uh… Officer Taylor? There's something I need to say to you. I feel terrible after insisting that Chief Mitchell take me off the park surveillance job. You're the lead investigator on this case, and I should've listened to you and believed that hunch you were feeling about the clue left at the last crime scene. You knew it might lead to something like this. But I got impatient. Blew it off, thinking the killer was playing some sick game rather than tipping us off."

"Actually, it was Officer Brooks who was adamant that we keep watch on the park. I just wish I'd been more aggressive in trying to convince Chief Mitchell to change his mind. But the reality is neither of us can do anything about what's happened here. What we *can* do is put every effort into catching this maniac before he kills again."

"Agreed." Shoving his hands in his pockets, Officer Davis slowly backed away. "But I just can't shake the guilt of knowing this victim's blood is on my hands. I could've prevented this. From here on out, trust that I've got your back and will follow your lead until we get this case solved."

"Thanks, Davis. I appreciate you saying that."

"Officer Taylor!"

The sight of Nia running toward Drew eased his tense shoulders.

"Hey, where have you been? I was starting to worry about you."

"I'm so sorry I didn't call you back," she panted. "My phone battery died right after your first text came through. So what's the latest? Are the joggers still here? Have they been questioned yet?"

"They were questioned briefly by responding officers but weren't able to offer up much info. I'd like for us to interview them more thoroughly down at the station."

Drew followed Nia's gaze as she pointed toward the street. "The medical examiner just pulled up. I'd better slip into some protective gear before we get started. I'll be right back."

As he watched Nia hurry off, Officer Davis nudged Drew's shoulder.

"What's up?" Drew asked him.

"Yeah, that's my question to you. What's up?"

"What do you mean?"

Nodding in Nia's direction, Officer Davis replied, "What's going on between you and Brooks? I noticed how quickly your mood lifted the second she ran over here."

Drew's eyes narrowed at the officer's sly smirk. "I'm just glad to know she's all right after not hearing back from her earlier."

"You sure that's all it is?"

"Yeah. I'm positive." Drew broke the officer's inquisitive stare and pulled on a mask and gloves. "Look, we need to get started on the crime scene analysis while the medical examiner processes the body. I wanna move on that ASAP so I can take a look at whatever's inside the victim's hand."

With a slow nod, Officer Davis caught the hint and dropped the subject. "You got it, boss."

DREW EASED INTO a seat inside Earl's Steakhouse and waited for Nia to arrive at the table. She'd been stopped near the entrance by a group of old friends from college. After being introduced, he had stood around waiting as the girl talk commenced. But once they began discussing bridal showers and TikTok makeup tutorials, he excused himself and followed the hostess to their booth.

After he and Nia had spent the day processing the crime scene, Drew offered to treat her to dinner. Sending her home alone straight from the station just didn't feel right. As her mentor, he wanted to make sure she was okay and offer up a little moral support over a nice steak and glass of cabernet.

Drew peered over the top of the menu, watching as Nia's friends fawned all over her. Whatever she was saying had them completely captivated. Nia had that effect on people wherever they went. When she walked into a room, everyone took notice. Whenever she spoke, those around her stopped and listened. Nia was a natural-born leader who had that *it* factor. Her beauty only added to her appeal. The more she and Drew worked together, the deeper his admiration grew. And if he were being honest, his attraction as well.

The moment she pivoted and headed toward the table, Drew dropped his head, diverting his attention back to the wine list. Before doing so, he caught a glimpse of her fading smile. There was a look of agony behind her tired eyes. He wasn't surprised, considering they'd spent hours at Latimer Park, scouring the crime scene for evidence. This being Nia's first encounter with a murder victim, her discomfort showed—the slight gagging, watering eyes and excessive fidgeting. He'd recommended she work on completing the police report while he processed the scene. But she refused, insisting she was fine.

Drew appreciated Nia's endurance as she ended up being an essential part of the analysis. She was the one who had initiated the fingerprint search, dusting the bench with a dark powder and using clear adhesive tape to lift the prints. She'd spotted a muddy shoeprint near the victim's feet that the other officers missed. To record that pattern, she and Drew used a sheet of rubber layered in gelatin to lift it off the soil's surface. And then there was the cigarette butt Nia had found floating near the edge of the duck pond that she'd retrieved before the birds got to it.

It was quite a rousing sight, watching the awe on their colleagues' faces as they observed Nia's work. They'd never seen her in action since this was her first time processing an active crime scene. Drew on the other hand was accustomed to her procedural acumen. But even he was impressed when she immediately recognized the pattern on the shoeprint. It contained the same beveled edge treading as the Lacrosse hunting boot impression found at Katie Douglas's crime scene—convincing both officers that the women had been killed by the same perpetrator.

"Hey," Nia breathed, pulling Drew from his thoughts as she slid into the seat across from him. "Sorry about that. I haven't seen some of those women in years. We had a lot to catch up on. But anyway, thanks again for suggesting this. I cannot tell you how much I needed it."

"Of course. It's the least I could do considering all the great work you put in today. Plus I still owed you after our coffee outing."

"Oh, please. With the amount of wine I'm about to drink? You'll wish you would've covered the coffee date instead—" She froze, a deep shade of crimson coloring her cheeks. "I'm sorry. But did I just refer to our mentoring meeting as a *date*?"

"Yes," he replied, chuckling at her horrified reaction. "I believe you did."

Her mouth fell open, but no words were spoken as she began fanning her face with the specials menu.

"Hey," Drew murmured, flashing a relaxed smile. "It was just a little slipup. Actually it was more like a welcome faux pas. We needed something to take the heaviness off of the day."

Nia's tense expression softened. Reaching across the table, she gave his hand a squeeze, her fingertips teasing his palm. "You're right. Because today was definitely a lot to deal with."

He barely heard her as a tingling sensation shot up his arm. When it snaked below his belt Drew straightened up, turning his attention back to the menu. "So…anything look good?"

"Everything looks good. And I didn't eat a thing today. I'm actually surprised I have an appetite after seeing…"

"Are you okay?" Drew asked after her voice trailed off.

"Yep," she quickly replied, forcing a tight grin before burying her face in the menu. But he could still see the creases of worry lining her forehead.

"I'm thinking of getting the barbecue-glazed salmon with a side of garlic mashed potatoes and roasted asparagus. What about you?"

"I'm going with the bone-in rib eye, loaded baked potato and spring sweet peas."

"*Aaand* I've got that," someone chimed in.

Drew's head swiveled, not realizing the server had approached. After taking the rest of their orders, she rushed off just as the officers' cell phones pinged. Drew grabbed his first.

"Oh, good. We've got an ID on the victim. Her name is Violet Shields. Twenty-six years old. Her parents identified the body at the medical examiner's office."

Biting down on her bottom lip, Nia's eyes remained stuck to her screen.

"Did you receive this text as well?" he asked her.

"No, mine is from Dawn at Latimer Park. And it's not good news. She reviewed last night's surveillance footage. The cameras captured the basketball and tennis courts and the playground. But nothing near the duck pond."

"*Dammit.* I wonder if there's footage of anyone walking past those areas. Unless the suspect entered the park through the back area near the trees, Dawn should've seen him making his way toward the pond."

"You're right. I've already asked that she forward the footage to us so we can review it ourselves, but I'll remind her to do that now."

Drew paused when a server approached with their wood-grilled octopus and drinks. Once she was out of earshot, he said, "Hey, there's something else I want to talk to you about."

"Okay..." Nia uttered. "I'm listening."

"I was talking with Officer Davis this morning before you arrived at the crime scene. He mentioned how much he regretted removing himself from the Latimer Park surveillance assignment. So on behalf of him, myself *and* Chief Mitchell, I wanna apologize."

"Drew, you don't have to—"

"No, no, I do. We really dropped the ball on that. You were the one who initially made that suggestion, and you were one hundred percent right. Had the department taken heed, maybe Violet's murder could've been avoided. So, moving forward, just know that I'll push harder for what you want. Because obviously your instincts are a hell of a lot stronger than some of these veteran cops."

"Thank you for that, Drew. But like I was going to say, there's no need for you to apologize. It wasn't your decision. It started with Officer Davis and ended with Chief Mitchell."

"True." He took a sip of his whiskey sour while Nia filled their plates with octopus. The gesture warmed him, sparking memories of what it felt like being out on a date. The fire it incited within his gut. The excitement, the anticipation of what would come later.

Everything you shouldn't be feeling for Nia...

"Drew?"

"Yep?" he uttered, so buried in his thoughts that he hadn't noticed her handing him a plate.

"Where did you go just now? It seemed like you faded out or something."

"Oh, sorry. I, uh… I was just thinking about Officer Davis," he lied. "And how he swore to never make a rash decision that could cost someone their life again."

"Good. Hey, switching topics for a quick sec. How's Tim doing?"

"He's doing well. Better than the doctors expected, actually. He's out of the ICU, and so far, there are no signs of any brain damage. They're not sure how much longer he'll be in the hospital, but afterwards I'm pretty sure he's going to have a lengthy stint in rehab. They keep saying he's lucky to be alive."

"Any new leads on the driver of the car that hit him?"

"No, unfortunately. Tim didn't get a look at it. And since the accident occurred on a rural road where there were no houses, we weren't able to obtain any surveillance footage." Drew rammed his fork into a tentacle. "I don't know why, but something is telling me that accident was intentional."

"Meaning?"

"I'm wondering if Tim was targeted. And whether the crash is connected to this murder investigation. Because it happened right after Katie Douglas's body was found. Could it have been the killer's way of trying to throw us off, and leave the department with one less officer on the case?"

"Could be. At this point, I wouldn't count any theory out." Nia swiped open her cell and pulled up a photo. "We haven't had a chance to discuss the clue left inside the victim's hand at Latimer Park. What do you make of it?"

Drew studied the image of the wedding invitation Nia had snapped at the crime scene. The thick cream pearlescent stock and gold print was smeared with blood. But he was still able to make out the wording. At the top were two initials, *T* and *I*. The names of the couple set to exchange vows, Terrance Gauff and Ingrid Porter, were printed underneath. The wedding location was at the bottom—the Charlie Sifford Country Club.

"Well, I definitely think it's alluding to what our killer has planned next. And I bet we're on the same page regarding next steps."

"What—that we should set up surveillance at the club?"

"Exactly. Which is why I already spoke to Chief Mitchell and he assigned Officer Ryan to the job. He's patrolling the place as we speak."

Nia held her glass in the air. "Now *that* is some good news I needed to hear. Cheers."

Tapping his glass against hers, Drew's gaze lingered on Nia until the server approached with their food.

"You know what I suggest we do?" Drew asked. "Pause all talk of the investigation and enjoy our dinner."

"Yes, good idea."

Drew eyed her plate, adding, "You know what else would be a good idea? Sliding a piece of that salmon onto my plate."

"Oh, really now," Nia retorted, pointing her fork toward his entrée. "How about we make a trade? A slice of my salmon for a piece of your steak?"

"Deal."

As Drew cut into his rib eye, the tension in his shoulders slackened, which he credited to the change of subject. But underneath that theory lay the fact that Nia's presence had put him at ease.

Yet while the case discussion had ended, thoughts of the investigation persisted. The wedding invitation left at the scene was a stark reminder that the clock was ticking. And it was only a matter of time before the killer would strike again.

Chapter Eight

Nia pulled into the driveway of her tri-level townhome and willed her fatigued legs to carry her to the door. The day had been exhausting—both physically and emotionally. Dinner with Drew did lighten the load of the investigation. But by the end of the meal, she was fighting to keep her eyes open. He'd insisted on ordering key lime pie for dessert, which only exacerbated her exhaustion. Now that Nia was finally home, climbing into bed was the only thing on her mind.

Nia stopped at the mailbox on the way in. Just as she opened the lid, a light flickered inside the house.

She hesitated, peering through the canted bay window's sheer curtains. Every light in the living room was off. Yet the kitchen light was on.

But...how?

She could've sworn she'd turned it off that morning.

You're just tired. You rushed out to the crime scene before 6:00 a.m. Probably left the light on by accident...

Grabbing the stack of envelopes from the mailbox, Nia made her way inside. She kicked off her boots, switched on a lamp and shuffled through the mail.

"Bill, bill, junk, another bill—"

She froze when the last envelope came into view. It didn't have her full name on it, nor her address. The letters *NIA* were handwritten across the middle in bold black letters.

"What the hell is this?"

She tore open the envelope and snatched a thick cream pearlescent card from it. Scanned the beautiful gold print, then dropped it to the floor. Her hands shook as she bent down to pick it up.

It can't be. You're just seeing things...

But upon further inspection, Nia realized her eyes weren't deceiving her. In her hand was an invitation to Ingrid Porter and Terrance Gauff's wedding—the same invitation they'd found at the crime scene. And in the lower left-hand corner was a bloody fingerprint.

"No, no, no..." she muttered.

Nia grabbed her purse, almost ripping the zipper trying to get to her cell phone. With trembling fingers she fumbled through the call log and dialed Drew's number. The call went straight to voicemail.

"Drew! Call me as soon as you get this. I got a wedding invitation in the mail today that matches the one we found at Latimer Park—"

The kitchen light went out again.

Her phone fell by her side. She glanced at the alarm control panel hanging by the door. It had been disabled.

What the...

Terror grabbed hold of Nia's joints as she stumbled against the wall. Without taking her eyes off the kitchen entrance, she reached down and pulled her gun from her purse.

Stay calm. This is what you were trained to do.

Standing straight up, Nia pointed her weapon toward the doorway. "Hey! Whoever's in here, just so you know, I am a police officer. I am armed. And I *will* shoot you. So come out into the living room with your hands up!"

Silence.

She ducked down while inching along the back of the couch. "This is your final warning. Trust me, this is not a game." Curling her finger around the trigger, Nia yelled, "Either come out, or I will—"

"Don't shoot!"

The kitchen suddenly lit up.

"Who the hell is that?" Nia called out right before her sister, Ivy, came bouncing into the living room.

"Niaaa! Hey, girl! Oh, how I've missed you, *seesto*!"

"Ivy! What are you doing here? And why would you scare me half to death like that? I almost shot you!"

"Come on, now. You weren't gonna shoot me."

"The hell I wasn't!"

Ivy jumped into her arms, ending the rant as her wild curls smothered Nia's entire face. Typical Ivy—showering her sister with love to deflect from the issue at hand.

"Anyway, I've missed you, too," Nia said, relenting, before she embraced her sister. But as she grabbed hold of Ivy's bony back, she quickly pulled away. "Wait, what's going on with you? Why do you feel so tiny?"

"Because I *am* tiny." Holding her scrawny arms out at her sides, Ivy spun a three-sixty, showing off the skintight black pleather dress clinging to her rail-thin figure. "I've lost fifteen pounds since the last time you saw me."

"Yeah, well, the problem is you didn't need to lose any weight. Whatever look you've got going on isn't healthy."

"Have you forgotten that I'm in the entertainment industry? You know how it is. The thinner you are, the bigger your chances of becoming a star."

Nia watched through worried eyes as her sister flitted back into the kitchen. Ivy, also known as the black sheep of the Brooks family, had a checkered past that plagued her for years. She'd hung out with a rough crowd during high school and had gotten herself into trouble on numerous occasions.

Those incidents of stealing from local stores for fun, vandalizing the property of people who'd allegedly wronged her and being caught drinking after hours at Latimer Park had left a stain on her reputation. After barely graduating, she'd run off to Los Angeles to pursue a singing career. She and Nia had managed to remain close over the years. But Ivy's erratic behavior remained a point of contention in their relationship.

"So," Ivy said, bouncing back inside the living room with two glasses of wine, "what have I missed since I've been gone?"

"First of all, I don't need another glass of wine. I had plenty during dinner."

"Oh? Dinner with who? Someone special you haven't told me about?"

Plopping down on the couch, Nia replied, "Nope. Just a coworker."

"Hmm," Ivy purred, sliding into the spot next to her. "That's what your mouth says, but that glimmer in your eyes is telling a completely different story. Spill the tea, sis! Tell me all about him."

"There's nothing to tell. Like I said, he's a coworker." When Ivy handed her a glass, Nia turned away. "No, please. Trust me, I've had enough. All I need at this point is a glass of ice water and my bed. I am exhausted. Speaking of which, I wish you would've told me you were coming to town. I wouldn't have stayed out so late."

"Don't worry. There will be plenty of time for

us to spend together since you'll be seeing a whole lot more of me."

"What do you mean?"

"Well…" Ivy avoided Nia's eyes as she picked at a rogue thread hanging from her hemline. "I don't know exactly when I'm going back to LA. So I'll be here for a while."

Judging by the look of Ivy's pouty lower lip, Nia knew what that meant. Ivy was running from something.

"Where are you staying? With mom and dad?"

Suddenly, Ivy's scowl curled into a sugary sweet grin. "That's what I wanted to talk to you about. I was hoping that maybe I could, you know…"

"Oh, no," Nia interrupted, shaking her head so adamantly that her gold hoops slapped her cheeks. "Absolutely not. I was just assigned to a *huge* case that could make or break my career. I do not have time to keep an eye on you."

"Why would you have to keep an eye on me?"

"*Please.* Is that even a real question? Or should I pull up your police report and remind you of all the mess you've gotten yourself into over the years?"

"Can you please stop throwing that up in my face? All that happened forever ago. I'm not the girl I used to be. I've grown up."

Crossing her arms over her stomach, Nia watched as Ivy guzzled her wine, then picked up the second glass she'd poured. "So, tell me, what brought you back to Juniper?"

"I just needed a break. You know how LA can be. Hectic. Grueling. *Expensive*. Plus I got tired of the whole auditioning grind. Singing my heart out day after day, week after week, while working my ass off to make ends meet was getting old. Even though I'd land a few small gigs here and there, they weren't getting me anywhere."

As Ivy slouched down farther into the couch, Nia suspected she wasn't telling the whole truth. Her sister was known to be secretive. She'd always been a wild card, making spontaneous decisions without thinking of the repercussions. So the abrupt move back home didn't come as much of a surprise.

"Well, you should know that now isn't the best time to be in Juniper," Nia warned.

"Why not?"

"Haven't you seen the news? We've got a serial killer on the loose."

"Wait, you've got a *what*?"

Nia tossed her hand in the air for extra emphasis. "There is a serial killer hunting down women in Juniper. He's binding their wrists and ankles, slashing their throats and leaving their bodies on display in public places."

"Oh my God," Ivy moaned, covering her mouth in disgust. "That is…that is *sick*."

"Yes, it is. And I'm assisting the lead investigator on the case—"

"Wait, *you*? But how? You're still a rookie. You just made it onto the force."

"It's a long story. Look, my point is, this partner of mine is a hard-nosed veteran who's working the biggest case of his career, too, and he's depending on me. So I don't have time to be looking after you and making sure you're staying out of trouble."

"And you won't have to," Ivy insisted. "I've already reconnected with several old friends, so if I need anything, I can go to them. Plus I landed a job bartending at the Bullseye Bar and Grill. So I'll be fine."

"Oh, so you told everybody you'd be in town except for me? Even though *I'm* the one you want to stay with?"

Giving Nia's thigh a playful pinch, Ivy squealed, "Yes! Thanks again for letting me crash here."

"Yeah, yeah. Just make sure you stay out of trouble."

Ivy suddenly grew quiet while staring down into her glass. Watching as her sister's eyes filled with tears, Nia didn't interpret the mood switch as a sentimental sign of missing home. It was something deeper. Something troubling.

Knowing Ivy, the more Nia probed, the more she'd withdraw. So Nia decided to leave it be, at least for the time being. She was completely drained. The talk could wait until tomorrow.

"Listen," Nia said, brushing Ivy's bangs out of her eyes. "I'm gonna need for you to be careful. I haven't forgotten about those old friends of yours and how they operate. They weren't the best people. And from what I hear, they've only gotten worse. More importantly, with this killer on the loose, I don't like the idea of you running around town and bartending until the early hours of the morning. Things have changed since you left."

"As hard as it is for you to grasp this fact, I can take care of myself. Stop worrying so much. I'll be fine."

Before Nia could respond, Ivy drained the second glass of wine, then hopped up from the couch.

"Wait, where are you going?"

"To change clothes. I'm getting together with the girls tonight. They're throwing me a little impromptu welcome home party at Army and Lou's Jazz Club. You wanna come?"

"Absolutely not. It's already late and I have to be back at the station early in the morning. How are you getting there?"

Pressing her hands together, Ivy pleaded, "I was hoping you'd let me borrow your car. *Pleeease?*"

"No, ma'am. I highly doubt that you'd bring it back in time for me to make it to work. Can't one of your friends pick you up?"

"I guess one of them will have to, won't they?"

"I guess so."

"Fine," Ivy huffed, charging up the staircase.

"I'll call Madison. Oh, and nice way to welcome your baby sister home."

"Maybe the welcome would've been much nicer had my baby sister told me she'd be here instead of breaking into my house and scaring the hell out of me."

"It's not breaking in when I used the key you gave me!"

"It is when I don't even know you're in town!"

The sound of Ivy's silver cowboy boots pounding the stairs grew louder in response. Nia ignored it and turned on the television, now wide awake thanks to her sister's unexpected arrival.

A flash of sparkly cream cardstock caught Nia's eye. She shot to her feet and ran to the console table by the door. After being startled by Ivy, she'd forgotten all about the wedding invitation left inside her mailbox. Nia had also forgotten about Drew, who'd yet to call her back.

She checked the cell. No text notification from him either. She tried calling again. The call went straight to voicemail.

Dammit.

Nia left another message, snapped a photo of the invitation and texted it to Drew. Once the message was sent, she dead-bolted the door and grabbed her gun off the table. Just as she set the alarm, her phone rang. It was him.

"Are you okay?" he asked the second she picked

up. "I got your voicemail and saw that text. What is going on?"

"*A lot.* I'm fine though. A little shaken up, but I'm okay."

"Good. Sorry it took so long to call you back. I stopped by the gym on the way home because after the day we had, I needed to get in a workout. I didn't realize my phone was on silent. But about that invitation. First of all, do you need for me to come over there? Because I can—"

"No, Drew. You don't have to do that. It's late. And I know you're tired. Plus I've got my Glock right here next to me."

"Okay. Well, if that changes, just let me know. I'm sure getting that invitation was disturbing to say the least. Assuming it was left by the killer, that means he knows where you live. And with that being said, are you *sure* you don't want me to come—"

"I'm positive," Nia interrupted once again, hating the idea of being a burden.

"Look, do me a favor. Put the invitation inside a plastic bag and bring it to the station tomorrow. We'll send it to the crime lab first thing and have it tested for DNA."

"I will." Nia paused at the sound of a glass crashing to the floor right above her head. "Oh God…"

"Wait, what was that I just heard?"

"My sister is upstairs destroying my house."

"Ivy's in town? I didn't know she was coming to visit."

"Yeah, neither did I. When I got home she was already here and scared the crap out of me."

"Nia!" Ivy screamed from the top of the landing. "Do you have any hair mousse?"

"No, I do not!"

Drew's throaty chuckle floated through her ear.

"What's so funny?"

"You and your sister, sounding like two teenagers."

"Interesting you should say that. Because she's acting like a teenager, asking to borrow my car and whatnot. I'm still trying to figure out what she's doing back in Juniper. I have a feeling she's keeping something from me. I'll get it out of her eventually."

"Does she know about this homicidal predator out here roaming the streets?"

"She does now. But Ivy's the type who thinks nothing will happen to her. She's already got me worrying. Especially after hearing that she'll be bartending at Bullseye."

"Look, you've got enough on your plate. I don't want your blood pressure to go up because you're stressing over your sister. I'll talk to the guys and ask them to keep an eye on the bar during her shifts."

"Drew, that is a lot to ask. Are you sure it wouldn't be too much trouble?"

"I'm positive."

"Thank you," she murmured, her quiet tone buzzing with warmth. "I really appreciate it."

"Of course. Oh, and before I forget, I heard back from the joggers who found the victim's body at Latimer Park. They're going to come in tomorrow morning and talk with us. I don't know how useful it'll be since they didn't see much. But sometimes when these witnesses are questioned at the station, they suddenly remember things they'd initially forgotten."

"Good to know. Let's hope that's the case." Nia hesitated when Ivy came clomping down the stairs. "Listen, I'd better go. My sister is getting ready to leave, and I need to give her one more lecture before she heads out."

"Yes, please do. If anything comes up, call me. And don't forget to keep your gun close. Unless you decide otherwise, I'll see you in the morning."

Nia sat there, contemplating whether or not she *should* decide otherwise.

You'd better not. Between all that wine you drank and your vulnerable state, there's no telling what you might do if he comes over...

"Thanks, Drew. I'll see you in the morning."

"Yeah, um…see you then."

There was a tinge of disappointment in his low tone. Nia wondered if it stemmed from his desire to be there with her or the fact that he was just tired. He disconnected the call before she could inquire.

"Okay," Ivy said, strutting into the living room as if she were on a catwalk. "What do you think?"

Nia looked up from her phone and almost fell off the couch. "What in the world are you wearing?" she asked, glaring at the sheer black negligee and glittery platform heels.

"*What?* I think I look good! And according to my nine thousand-plus followers on TikTok, they think so too."

A flash of anger shot through Nia as her sister snapped several selfies. "You aren't taking any of the warnings I gave seriously, are you?"

"Of course I am! I already told my girls about the investigation. Madison is planning on covering the case on her YouTube channel. Oh! And she wanted me to ask if you'd be willing to do an interview with her. You know, on behalf of the Juniper PD. Maybe that partner you mentioned could go live with her, too. Ooh, and what about your boss? Chief Marshall, or whatever his name is."

"It's Chief Mitchell. And, no. None of us are going on some YouTube channel to discuss the case. Besides, I thought Madison's channel was all about makeup and fitness."

"It is. But true crime is really hot right now. A lot of vloggers are doing this thing where they apply their makeup while covering cases. You've gotta keep up, big sis."

A loud engine roared out front.

"Maddy's here!" Ivy exclaimed, teetering toward the door to the beat of a blaring horn. Right before Ivy stepped outside, Nia grabbed her arm.

"Hey, listen. You need to be careful. Keep your eyes open and call me if anything comes up. Don't go wandering off by yourself or get too friendly with every person you see. Most importantly, please don't do anything illegal."

"Yes, *mother.* Now wish me luck. It's open mic night and the winner gets five hundred dollars."

"Good luck. Oh, and try not to stay out all night!"

"Bye!"

As Ivy went bouncing toward a red Toyota Supra, Nia stepped onto the porch and waved. She could barely hear Madison scream her name over the loud house music.

Worry pricked her skin watching the pair speed off into the night.

She's grown, Nia reminded herself. *She'll be fine...*

The night air was cool. And eerily peaceful. Nia eyed the broadleaf evergreen shrubs lining her rock garden, imagining some stranger audaciously invading her space.

The killer had dropped an ominous hint. He wanted her to know that he was aware of her connection to the case. Leaving the invitation was his attempt to extinguish her efforts. But it wasn't going to work. If anything, it would serve as fuel to further ignite her drive.

When she stepped back inside the house, a thought dropped in Nia's head like a hammer to a nail—security cameras were mounted over her front and back doors.

How could you forget that?

She threw her head back in relief and glanced at the top of the door.

"What the…"

The security camera was gone.

Nia rushed inside the house and bolted the door, then grabbed her phone. This time when she dialed Drew's number, he picked up on the first ring.

"Hey, what's up?" he asked. "Is everything okay?"

"No, everything is not okay. I need for you to come to my place. *Now.*"

Chapter Nine

Drew flicked a packet of raw sugar inside his coffee and stared across the conference room table. Nia's distraught expression pained him. The investigation was not going as he'd hoped. And now that she had become a target, it felt as though he was failing her.

The DNA evidence found at Latimer Park matched the evidence from Shelby's Candy Factory. Yet law enforcement still couldn't figure out the suspect's identity since no match had turned up in the national database.

The interview with joggers who'd discovered Violet Shields's body was a complete bust. Not only did they have nothing to report from the crime scene, but they'd brought their children into the station hoping they could tour the facility.

Surveillance footage saved to Nia's computer from the day the wedding invitation had been delivered didn't reveal much. The suspect had not come fully into view after crossing the neighbor's lawn and creeping up onto the porch from the side railing.

From what the officers could tell, he appeared slender and was dressed in all black. A mask covered his face and his head and shoulders were hunched over, making him unrecognizable. The steel rod swinging from his hand, however, was visible. Once he'd reached the landing, the camera shook violently before it went crashing to the ground. Nia's neighbors had allowed her to view their security footage. But none of their cameras were positioned to capture images of her house.

Despite his coffee being steaming hot, Drew took a long sip. The bitter burn on his tongue somehow cancelled the frustration brewing in his chest. The conference room table was covered with every piece of evidence they had collected. He'd suggested they start back at square one and work their way through each crime scene in hopes of stumbling upon something they'd missed. So far, both he and Nia had come up empty.

"This is so aggravating," she said, fiddling with the cap on her water bottle. "All these reports, all the photos, the DNA evidence… But still no suspects. The biggest disappointment was that bloody fingerprint found on the wedding invitation inside my mailbox. I just knew it would link us to our suspect."

"Yeah, same. The fact that it belonged to Violet Shields was just another sinister way for the killer to taunt us. What about that Someone for Everyone app? Have you heard back from the administrator?"

"No, not yet." Nia grabbed her phone and swiped it open. "But I'll check again, just to see if something came through since the last time I looked. I'll also do some online digging to find out who the owners are and get in touch with them directly."

"Good idea. While you do that, I'll have Officer Ryan work on getting a subpoena. That way they'll be forced to hand over the information whether they want to or not. We've waited long enough for a response, which is ridiculous considering our request pertains to a criminal investigation…"

Drew's voice trailed off as Nia smiled at her phone screen.

"What's got you grinning over there like a giddy schoolgirl?"

"Nothing!" She fumbled her cell before sliding it to the side. "I was just—just checking on that response from the administrator."

"Any word from them?"

"Nope. No word yet."

Nia's bottle almost slipped from her hand. She caught it just in time, but not before a stream of water trickled onto the table. Quickly wiping it up with her sleeve, she snatched a report and pointed at the notes. "I've been meaning to ask about Violet's cell phone. Any luck tracking it down?"

"Not as of yet."

Drew watched as Nia's attention remained on the document. He hadn't known her for long. But he knew her well enough to realize when something was off. And she'd been acting strange all morning.

"Hey, is everything all right?"

"Yeah," she uttered a beat too soon. "Everything's fine. Why?"

"You just seem a bit…distracted. Is it that wedding invitation or your security camera going missing? Or what about your sister? I know you were caught off guard after the way she dropped in unexpectedly."

Finally looking up at him, Nia replied, "*Yes*. That's it. I think the fact that Ivy came storming back into town like a tornado has thrown me for a loop. But again, I'm fine. Thanks for asking. Anyway, back to Violet's cell phone. Does her family think they may be able to find it?"

Drew could smell her lie from across the table. Clearly Ivy's visit had nothing to do with the joy on Nia's face after she'd checked the dating app. He was dying to ask what she was hiding. But it was none of his business. Not to mention he shouldn't even be concerned.

So why do you care?

Ignoring the annoying voice in his head, Drew

said, "Violet's family is on top of the search for her cell. They're gonna try and track it down inside her house which, according to them, is a bit of a mess since she had some hoarding tendencies. I've also contacted her phone provider. So even if we can't get our hands on the actual device I'll have a record of her activity."

"Good. Because there is the chance that the killer took it. I'm guessing Violet didn't share her phone's location with anyone?"

"Nope. Nor did she utilize the Find My Device feature. And that's part of the problem. The more I've spoken with her family, the more I realize just how private of a person she was. According to her father, she was also dealing with issues of paranoia. Violet was convinced that if she used any sort of tracking technology, people outside of her family and friend circle would be able to trace her whereabouts."

Nia clicked her tongue while flipping through the photos of Violet's crime scene. "And what ends up happening? Someone still managed to hunt her down and kill her." Stopping on a close-up of the victim's slashed throat, she glared at it, then shoved the whole stack inside the folder. "Where do we go from here, Drew?"

"Great question…"

He rocked back in his black ergonomic chair and scanned the piles strewn in front of him. The documents became a blur of chaos as his mind sought out an answer.

When he leaned his elbows onto the table, Drew's laptop awoke from sleep mode. Katie Douglas's Facebook page popped up. He reached over and enlarged her profile picture. She stared back at him, her head tilted toward the sun while throwing up a peace sign.

"That picture is so haunting," Nia said. "Katie looks so happy and vibrant. And *alive*. To look at her there, knowing she's dead now, is just—just so disturbing."

"Yes, it is…"

Nia's words sparked a fire in Drew that pushed him away from the table.

"I got it," he said, pounding his fist into his palm.

"I'm sorry. You what?"

"I got it! I've got the answer. You and I are going to print out photos of Katie and take them down to Shelby's Candy Factory."

"And do what? Hang them up in hopes that someone will recognize her? I don't know how effective that'll be considering the place is abandoned. And the people who hang out there aren't the type to wanna assist law enforcement."

"Here's what I'm thinking. First we'll use social media to get some intel on when the next underground rave is happening. Once we find out, we'll show up with Katie's photo in hand and ask the attendees about her. Maybe she used to hang out there. Who knows, the killer may even hang out there. Either way, the answers we're looking for might be with the people who party at that factory."

Grabbing her notebook and flipping it open, Nia said, "I like that idea. I like it a lot. On another note, you mentioning a rave brought the whole use of illegal substances to mind, which made me think of the victims' toxicology reports. Have the results come back?"

"No, not yet. But I'm curious to know whether any of them were drugged. I'll put in a call to the medical examiner's office once we're done here and find out when we can expect them. As for now," he continued, pulling up his email, "I'm gonna send Officer Ryan a message asking if he's got intel on the next rave since he's usually up on those types of events."

"You know who else might know something? Ivy. I wouldn't be surprised if some of her old friends were the ones throwing them. I'll shoot her a text now."

As Nia typed away on her phone, Drew peered across the table, taking in her natural beauty. While it was on full display, there was something different. Her eyes, usually sparkling with enthusiasm, appeared dull, almost lifeless. Her lips were never without some shade of gloss. Today, they were bare. While she was still giving her all to the investigation, that fire and drive were missing, as if her spirit had been broken.

"Hey, Brooks," he said, trying his best to sound casual, "how are you holding up?"

Her fingers froze over the phone screen. "What do you mean?"

Those fluttering eyelids indicated that she knew exactly what he'd meant. Drew was slow to respond, empathizing with Nia as he thought back on his days as a rookie cop. They hadn't been easy. The need to appear tough overrode moments of vulnerability. He'd seen Nia the night that invitation showed up in her mailbox and the security camera went missing. She had been damn near inconsolable, falling into his arms the moment he stepped through the door.

But now, as she sat in front of him at the station, Nia was struggling to appear resilient, as if she wasn't being affected by the case. He needed her to know that she didn't have to put up a front for him. Their relationship was a safe space—a soft place to land when everything around her hardened.

"You know," he began, his husky tone laced with sincerity, "you don't have to put on an act for me. You've been through a lot. It's okay to be open and show emotion. You may be a police officer, but you're also human. I just need to know that you're all right. If you're not, I wanna do everything in my power to get you there. I can put a patrol car on duty to keep an eye on your house twenty-four seven. Hell, I'll even stay with you for the time being if that's what it'll take to make you feel secure."

Slowly setting her phone aside, Nia blew a heavy sigh. Her body shifted as she finally looked him in the eyes. "Thank you, Drew. Honestly? I am still shaken up. I don't even go into the kitchen to get a glass of water without taking my gun with me. But I'm working through it. At this point I'm more concerned about Ivy. She's the one who's constantly running around town, coming in at all hours of the night. I've talked her into carrying a can of pepper spray everywhere she goes, so that's made me feel a little better. And the camera your friend installed has helped ease my anxiety, too, so…"

"So, you're hanging in there?"

"Yes. I'm hanging in there." Her pursed lips spread into a faint smile. "I appreciate you looking out for me."

Drew's chest pulled at her gratitude. It was confirmation that his words of encouragement were well received. Nia's response deepened his need to protect her, triggering a surge of emotions that fueled his burgeoning attraction.

Pull back…

He downed a swallow of coffee before grabbing his phone. "I should call the medical examiner's office. Get an update on those toxicology reports."

As he dialed the number, Nia's cell pinged. Her face lit up after checking the notification. A twinge of jealousy stirred in Drew's gut as he wondered what sparked the wave of happiness this time.

Cool out, his inner voice warned once again.

He left the medical examiner a voicemail, then turned his attention back to his laptop, acting as if he hadn't noticed Nia ogling her phone.

"You are not gonna believe this," she said, handing him her cell. "Read that text from Ivy."

"Text from Ivy?" Drew repeated, his neck burning with shame.

And here you were, assuming she was chatting with a man...

He took the phone and scanned the message.

Hey big sis. Funny you asked about the next event at Shelby's. There's a rave happening at midnight tonight. But you DID NOT hear that from me and you'd better not tell your cohorts. If it gets shut down, everyone's gonna assume I snitched thanks to you being a cop. So keep it on the hush!

"Wow," Drew said. "You know what this means? The universe is working in our favor. Tonight is gonna generate some solid new leads. Thanks for contacting Ivy and getting that intel."

"Of course. Thanks for coming up with the idea to pass out Katie's photo at the rave. We make a good team," Nia added with a wink.

The small yet sensual gesture sent a rush of heat straight through Drew's gut that roused below his belt. Forcing his eyes toward the clock hanging above her head, he said, "It's already after twelve. Why don't we figure out tonight's game plan over lunch? Then maybe cut out early. If the rave doesn't start until midnight, we should probably try and get some rest."

"Good idea. These days, I'm never even out until midnight, let alone arriving somewhere at such an ungodly hour."

"Same here. I never had late nights like this unless it was…"

Drew's voice faded as memories of the last New Year's Eve he and his ex-fiancée spent together crashed his mind.

"Unless it was what?" Nia asked.

"Never mind." He slammed his laptop shut and shot to his feet.

"Are you okay?"

"Yep. I'm fine," he told her, despite being far from fine.

Drew wished he had it in him to justify his reaction. To explain why the conversation had turned so triggering. But now was not the time or place to discuss the tragedy surrounding his personal life.

Chapter Ten

Nia and Drew stood outside Shelby's with Katie's flyers in hand, waiting for the partygoers to arrive. They were both dressed in dark, casual clothing and baseball caps in an attempt to blend in with the crowd.

So far, only a few people had trickled inside through a kicked-in side door, carrying lighting and DJ equipment. They'd been less than helpful when the officers flashed Katie's photo, insisting they needed to get inside and set up.

"I'm just imagining all the illegal drugs that are gonna be flowing in and out of here tonight," Nia said.

"Yeah, and unfortunately, we'll have to tackle that problem another night. We're here on a different mission. I don't want anything blocking our road to the killer."

Nia took notice when a group of young men hopped out of a pickup truck. "Here we go," she said, leading with Katie's photo as she approached. "Excuse me, have any of you seen this woman here at the factory? Or anywhere in the vicinity?"

Barely looking at the picture, they muttered an almost inaudible "Nope" before pushing past her.

Spinning around in frustration, she shouted, "Hey!" and followed the men. "You didn't even look at the—"

"Hold on," Drew said, grabbing hold of her mid-confrontation. "Let them go. The night is young. There'll be plenty more people to talk to. This investigation is a marathon, not a sprint. Tonight will be no different. All it's gonna take is one solid tip to lead us in the right direction."

Her arms relaxed within his grip. *Regroup*, Nia thought, feeling less like a lead investigator and more like a newbie fresh out of the academy. She stood taller, straightening the flyers in her hand. "You're right. I'll tamp down the aggression and play it a little cooler."

"Good. But don't lose that fighting spirit of yours. It's one of the traits I admire most about you."

Reassurance permeated within her as Drew's hand slid toward the small of her back.

"I won't…" she murmured.

The candy factory stood far back from the street, with little light surrounding the area. The building's dilapidated wood exterior looked as if it might come crashing down at any given moment. Nia couldn't understand why anyone would want to step foot inside the place. But once it was no longer considered an active crime scene and the police tape was removed, the ravers, drug addicts and squatters began using it again.

"Are you warm enough?" Drew asked when a chilly breeze blew by.

Nia zipped her tan leather jacket up to her chin and hovered closer to him. "I am now."

She took a breath, staring up at the streaks of dark gray clouds scattered across the sky. Her squinting eyes couldn't make out one single star hidden within them. The grim atmosphere was as bleak as the reason they were there. Nia just hoped their efforts wouldn't be in vain.

Boom!

The pair jolted when heavy bass rumbled from inside the factory.

"Sounds like the party is getting started," Drew said.

"Judging by all the headlights rolling up to the curb, we've got some new arrivals, too."

Anticipation swelled in Nia's chest as a crowd began to gather. She held the flyers tighter, slipping one in between her fingers to quickly pass along.

Within seconds, people came rushing toward them like a tsunami, storming past so briskly that the officers hardly had a chance to say hello. They shoved Katie's photo into the partygoers' hands anyway, shouting, "Do you know her?" while praying for a response. Almost everyone blew them off, barely glancing at the picture before tossing the flyer to the ground.

At one point Nia attempted to march inside the factory. But Drew held her back, insisting she remain calm.

"Hey, keep your head," he told her. "I don't want you getting caught up inside of there. It's too many of them and not enough of us. We've just gotta stay patient. And persistent. There's still a ton of people out here. Trust me, we'll find somebody who knows something."

Shuffling her feet to shake the excess energy, Nia nodded. "Once again, you're right."

Techno music blared through the factory's shattered windows as ravers continued to pour inside. Nia's throat burned as she yelled over the blaring drum machines. No one appeared to be listening as throngs of people brushed past her as if she weren't there. Some of them even shoved the flyers back at her. Just when she considered tossing the rest of the pictures in the air and giving up, Drew called out her name.

"Over here!" he shouted after they'd briefly gotten separated. He was surrounded by three men and two women. All of them were dressed in torn black T-shirts, leggings and platform boots, with spiked hair dyed every color of the rainbow.

As Nia scanned the group, Drew said, "Three of these guys said they've seen Katie."

"Here at the candy factory?"

One of the men pointed toward the end of the street. "No. A couple of blocks over at the Green Lizard lounge."

"When was the last time you saw her there?" Drew asked.

Shrugging his scrawny shoulders, he looked to one of the women. "I don't know. Do you remember, Adina?"

"I think it was like a couple of weeks before her body was found."

"So you know about her murder?" Nia probed.

"Um, *yeah*. I think it's safe to say everybody in this town knows. And the word is spreading. This is the first rave they've thrown at Shelby's since her death." She paused, gesturing at the huge crowd. "All these people aren't from Juniper, obviously. But after DJ Onslaught dedicated tonight to Katie, everybody from all over Colorado decided to come out and pay their respects."

Leaning toward Drew, Nia whispered, "Interesting. Most of the people we've talked to claimed to have never heard of her."

A member of the group who was sporting a purple mohawk nudged Adina. "We'd better get inside before they close the doors on us."

As they backed away, Drew called out, "Hey, thanks for that info!"

"So what do you think?" Nia asked. "Should

we stay out here and see who else might know something? Or head over to the Green Lizard?"

He checked his watch, then looked out at the crowd. Partygoers were getting rowdier by the minute, practically climbing over one another trying to get into the factory. "Why don't we head over to the Green Lizard before they close? Maybe someone on the staff or even some of the patrons have seen Katie there."

"It would be even sweeter if they captured her on surveillance video at some point. Then maybe we could see who she was hanging out with, talking to, leaving with…"

"Yeah, that would be nice. Let's go see what we can find out."

Drew offered Nia his arm before pushing his way through the crowd. Her body pressed against his as he led the way, protecting her from the throng of ravers.

She'd gotten so used to looking out for herself that Nia forgot what it was like having a caring, capable man by her side. Despite Drew being a colleague, he was beginning to feel like something else. Something more. And as delusional as that may have been, it felt damn good.

When they reached the car, Drew pulled out his cell phone.

"Who are you calling this late?" Nia asked.

The moment the question escaped her lips she gasped, slapping her hand over her mouth.

"Drew, I—I am so sorry. I shouldn't have asked you that. I mean…obviously you can call whomever you want whenever you want. I don't know what possessed me to be so nosy."

"It's all good," he quipped, his sexy half smile riddled with amusement. "I was actually going to check my voicemail."

"Gotcha," Nia mumbled, biting down on her loose tongue before climbing inside the car.

Please let that be the last time you make a fool of yourself…

BY THE TIME Drew pulled into Nia's driveway, it was almost 3:00 a.m.

After leaving Shelby's, they'd headed straight to the Green Lizard. The lounge was located in a part of town that Nia seldom frequented, so she wasn't familiar with the establishment. When Drew parked in front, she realized why.

The bar looked more like a rundown shack than a place of business with its wrinkled metal roof, weathered wooden planks and foggy glass-block windows.

"Last call was fifteen minutes ago!" the bartender had yelled when they walked through the dented steel door.

"We're not here to order drinks," Drew told the puny, bald-headed man. "We're here on official police business."

The second he flashed his badge, the bartender

dried his crooked fingers on his filthy apron and
called for the manager. She came out from the
kitchen with a towel wrapped around her head,
as if she'd just washed her hair.

"May I help you?" the burly woman barked,
her sparse eyebrows furrowing into her deeply
creased forehead.

Nia couldn't take her eyes off the colorful tattoos running up and down both her arms. Snakes
slithering around bushels of flowers spread from
her wrists to her shoulders. As Drew explained
why they were there, the manager began eyeing
Nia so suspiciously that she stepped away, pulling
out her phone and snapping photos of the lounge.

The seedy establishment appeared more like a
long hallway than an actual tavern. Nia walked
the length of it, the soles of her boots sticking to
the warped hardwood floor. While the red fluo-
rescent lighting was dim, it wasn't dark enough
to hide the cracked vinyl barstools, dingy white
walls and grimy poplar tables. Even though drinks
were no longer being served, there were still several people with beer bottles in hand hovering
around an old laminate jukebox.

It didn't take long for the manager to warm
up to Drew. He had that effect on people—especially women. Nia attributed it to his deep, calming voice, disarming charm and uncanny ability to
come up with the best one-liners at just the right
time. Two minutes into a conversation and strang-

ers felt as though they'd known him for years. The fact that he was devastatingly handsome in a rugged, approachable type of way didn't hurt matters, either.

The highlight of the night occurred when the manager admitted that Katie had been a regular at the bar, then handed over surveillance footage from the last time she'd seen her there. Nia had sung Drew's praises the whole way home for prying that evidence from the prickly woman's hands.

And now, as he walked Nia to the door, she couldn't bring herself to say good-night.

"You know I can't wait until tomorrow to watch that video, right?" she said. "I am *far* too riled up for that."

"You know what's funny? Neither can I."

"Well, then, since neither of us are ready to call it a night, why don't you come inside? I've got a refrigerator full of bar food that Ivy brought home from Bullseye and an unopened bottle of Merlot."

"That sounds amazing, actually. Because I'm starving, my fridge is currently empty and I'm all out of wine."

"Oh, wow. Yeah, you needed this invitation for more reasons than one," Nia joked before leading Drew inside.

All the lights were out, which meant Ivy wasn't home. Nia switched on a couple of lamps before tossing her things onto the console table.

As she sauntered through the living room,

Drew followed closely behind. Nia could feel his eyes roaming her body. The sensation sent a shiver straight to her core.

"Should I pour the wine while you prep the food?" he asked, stopping near the couch while unzipping his camo jacket.

"No, I've got it covered. Why don't you relax. Have a seat. Watch some television while I get everything together."

The suggestion hadn't come from a place of hospitality. Nia didn't trust herself to move about the kitchen with Drew in such close proximity. It was late. She tended to make rash decisions during the wee hours of the morning—especially when it came to her libido.

"Thanks for the kind offer," he told her, "but I'd rather help you instead. That way we can get to the surveillance footage faster, and if you're up for it, maybe watch a movie afterwards."

The suggestion hung in the air like a delectable offering, waiting to be devoured.

"I'd like that," Nia replied with no hesitation.

She hovered near the fireplace as Drew pulled off his coat. She wished he hadn't worn a fitted black T-shirt as it set off his broad chest and bulging biceps.

"I—I, uh…" she stammered, pointing toward the kitchen. "I'm gonna go heat up the food."

"I'm right behind you."

Drew was slow to follow as he eyed the colorful abstract paintings hanging from the walls and black-and-white photos lining the mantel. "I love your place. And this kitchen… Is it newly renovated?"

"It is. I needed a fresh new look. So I switched out the white appliances for stainless steel and replaced the dark wood cabinets for these cream ones. They really brighten up the room, and it all works together to give off the contemporary feel I was going for."

"I agree. Everything looks great." He ran his hand along the granite countertop, brushing up against Nia as she pulled takeout containers from the refrigerator. When her hips grazed his groin, she jumped back.

"Ooh, sorry," he said, palming her back as if to steady her. "I was trying to get to the wine glasses."

Yeah, right…

Ignoring Drew's struggle to suppress a smirk, Nia pointed above his head. "They're in the cabinet to your left."

"And the wine?"

"In the corner next to the coffeemaker."

Nia filled a platter with buffalo wings, truffle mushroom flatbread and onion rings, then placed it in the microwave.

This isn't fair, she thought, watching the food rotate. Having Drew there, inside her home, felt too good. Too right. Their conversation flowed too easily. And the attraction was too strong. This was the first time she'd met a man who seemed perfect in every way. Yet he was off-limits.

"Hey," Drew said, tapping the laptop sitting on the counter. "Can we use this to review the surveillance footage?"

"Yep. Go ahead and start it up."

Once the microwave buzzed, Nia grabbed everything and set up shop on the island.

"Are you sure you've got time for all this?" he asked.

"I do. Why?"

"Well, I've already taken up the majority of your day. *And* night. There isn't anyone special who'd expect to be here with you right now?"

He's fishing...

A long sip of wine fueled her response. "Officer Taylor, are you trying to figure out whether or not I'm seeing someone?"

Nia expected a swift denial. Instead she got a head nod followed by a crooning, "Maybe…"

A tug of silence swirled between them. She turned away and began preparing their plates, taking her time before responding. Taking her lead, Drew busied himself by inserting the USB drive into the computer. His expression was neutral, as if he wasn't pressing for a response. His bouncing knees, however, told her that he was eager for a reply.

"To answer your question, no. I'm single."

Drew's brows shot up toward the ceiling. "Really?"

"Yes. Why is that so shocking?"

"Well, I mean you're beautiful, intelligent, you crack great jokes and are passionate about the things you love. You're family-oriented, and the list goes on. Bottom line, you're everything a man would want in a woman."

His words sent Nia's heart pounding against her ribcage as she slid onto the stool next to his. While she'd sensed their attraction was mutual, she had no clue his admiration ran that deep.

"Wow," she uttered. "That, uh…that was pretty unexpected. But so nice. Thank you."

"You're welcome. I'm just stating the obvious. I can't imagine you haven't heard that from a man before."

"I have. In bits and pieces from different men. It's just surprising coming from you. I didn't think you paid attention to those types of things since all we seem to talk about is the investigation or departmental policies or—"

"Anything that isn't personal?" Drew interjected.

"Yes, exactly."

"You're right. In case you hadn't noticed, it takes me a minute to warm up to people. It isn't easy letting my guard down. Especially when it comes to situations like ours. We were partnered up during a pretty tough time. But now that I've gotten to know you, I've come to realize that you're pretty damn amazing, Nia."

Those words sent her swooning so hard that she almost fell from the stool. Propping her hand underneath her chin, she replied, "Well, I could easily say the same for you. Getting to know you has been a pleasant surprise. Not what I'd expected after the way things went down at that mentorship meeting. Let's just say I'm glad I was wrong about you."

"Thank God I was able to redeem myself," Drew joked before quickly turning serious. "So why aren't you seeing anyone?"

Nia bit into a slice of flatbread, chewing slowly while contemplating her response. "I guess the short answer is I refuse to settle."

"And what would settling look like for you?"

"Getting involved with a man who doesn't want to commit. Who isn't kind and respectful and doesn't work hard. I actually keep a mental checklist of must-haves. And if I can't tick them all off, then I pass. My friends think I'm asking for too much and should reassess my criteria. But I refuse to."

"As you should. Nothing you're asking for is unreasonable." Drew picked up his glass and leaned into her, his touch igniting sparks between them both. "Here's to you finding everything you want and deserve in a partner."

You're everything I want in a partner, Nia almost blurted. Her gaze drifted from his inviting eyes to his soft lips. They parted slightly, leaving her questioning how they'd feel pressed against hers. How he'd feel inside of her...

Shifting in her seat, she asked, "What about you? Are you seeing anyone?"

"Nope. I'm single."

"Hmm, that's not what I expected to hear."

"Yeah, well, my dating life isn't something I normally talk about."

When Drew's lips twisted into a tight expression, Nia hesitated, waiting for him to elaborate. But he didn't, instead draining his glass, then refilling it.

"You don't have to talk about it if you don't want to," she told him.

"I know. But I probably should. Holding it in hasn't been the healthiest way to cope." He picked at the cheese oozing from a mozzarella stick before proceeding. "I was engaged once. To a police detective from Aurora named Ellody. She'd moved to Juniper to be with me and was commuting back and forth while figuring out what she wanted to do with her career. But we soon realized that the distance was what made us work. Once she came here permanently, problems arose that left me questioning whether or not we were even compatible."

"What type of problems were you having?" Nia probed, unable to contain her curiosity.

"Well, when it came to finances, for instance, she was more of a spender while I'm more of a saver. I'm a neat freak, and she didn't mind a lot of clutter. She enjoyed nights out while I'm more of a homebody. Things like that. It got to the point where our differences began to outweigh the good between us. After admitting to that, we decided it would be best to end the relationship."

"Hmm, that couldn't have been easy. Especially when you two were planning on getting married."

"No, it wasn't, but..." Staring down at his steepled hands, Drew uttered, "That's not where the story ends. A few months after Ellody moved back to Aurora, we reconnected. I think we both realized we'd be better off as friends. Just as we began building a platonic relationship, she was killed in the line of duty."

"My God, Drew. I am so sorry. I had no idea..."

"Thanks. Like I said, it's something I rarely talk about. Since then, I haven't really dated. That experience was so devastating that I've pretty much closed myself off to the whole relationship thing." After a long pause, he tapped his hand against the island, then pulled the laptop closer. "But anyway, enough about me. Let's get back to business."

As Drew clicked on the portable drive, Nia pushed her plate to the side, her appetite transforming into a slight bout of nausea. Hearing the news of his ex was tragic. And while she was sympathetic toward his loss, the consequence was duly noted—Drew was not ready to love again.

"Okay, here we go," he said when an image of the Green Lizard's interior appeared on the screen.

The bar was packed. Every stool was occupied. There were rows of people standing behind them, vying for the bartender's attention. The tables were full. Groups of people with drinks in their hands were bouncing to the music.

Peering at the screen, Drew nibbled on a buffalo wing. "Any sign of Katie yet?"

"Not yet. But I'm looking."

Ten minutes into the video, Nia tapped the screen. "I think that's her. The woman in the red sweater and skinny jeans. Isn't that Katie?"

The pair watched as she approached the bar, then turned and faced the crowd.

"Oh, yeah," Drew said. "That's definitely her. Let's see who she's there with."

A group of women approached Katie, embracing her before starting up an animated conversation. As they spoke, two men walked over. One of them was wearing a baseball cap. Nia couldn't make out his face, but he appeared tall and athletic, with wide shoulders and a narrow waist. He hugged Katie tightly, then held her in his arms while whispering in her ear. The twosome began swaying back and forth. Another couple of minutes passed before his friend and the group of women drifted off, leaving Katie and the man alone.

"It's interesting how this guy has his cap pulled down so low," Nia said. "Like he doesn't want anyone to recognize him."

"Yeah, it is. Notice how he's keeping his head down, too. As if he's aware of the surveillance cameras and is trying to avoid them."

"Right. And he's staying glued to Katie's side."

The officers leaned in closer as the man began pulling her by the waist.

"Wait, what is he doing?" Drew asked.

"It looks like he's trying to drag her out of the bar."

The sight of Katie reaching for her friends was unsettling, even though she didn't appear to be under duress.

"This is so eerie," Nia said. "Here Katie's laughing and joking and having a great time. Little did she know she'd be murdered in a matter of days."

Just when it appeared as though Katie and the man were moving toward the exit, the screen flickered, then blacked out.

"Wait," Nia muttered, "What just happened?"

"I don't know."

Drew pounded the Enter and Escape keys. Both officers jolted when a new video popped up. The bar's parking lot came into view. Within minutes, Katie and her companion came back into frame.

"All right," Drew said, "we've got action again.

Now let's just hope we can get a look at the guy's face this time."

The officers watched as Katie approached a large black SUV. The man opened the passenger door for her, then stared down at the ground while walking around to the driver's side.

"Come on," Nia said, both officers leaning in so close that their noses almost touched the screen. "Please look up. Show us your face…"

Suddenly, rain began to pour. The man in the video hesitated, looking up at the sky.

Air caught in Nia's throat as she struggled to process the image on the screen. But as a flash of lightning illuminated the video, there was no mistaking the man's identity.

It was Officer Davis.

Chapter Eleven

Drew pulled into his garage and headed inside the house. Tossing his messenger bag onto the kitchen table, he headed straight for the refrigerator. The half-empty bottle of wine he'd uncorked a few days ago was still sitting in the door. He resisted the urge to grab it and down the remaining malbec.

Just as he reached for a can of sparkling water his cell phone buzzed. A throbbing pain hit his left temple at the sight of Chief Mitchell's name.

"Please, no bad news," Drew mumbled before picking up. "Chief Mitchell. What's going on, sir?"

"Officer Taylor, listen. I just got back into town from my brother-in-law's funeral and wanted to follow up on the Officer Davis situation. Did you and Brooks get a chance to question him about that Katie Douglas surveillance footage?"

"We did, after he finally showed back up to work today. I'm curious about that sudden leave of absence he took."

"I think someone tipped him off about the video, so he knew you were coming for him. What did he have to say for himself?"

"First I asked why he hadn't told us that he knew Katie. He claimed he didn't think it was important enough to mention."

"Oh, come on," the chief grunted. "I don't believe that for one minute. Davis is a veteran officer, for God's sake. He knows information like that is important."

"That's exactly what I told him. After questioning him for almost thirty minutes, he finally admitted to why he hadn't come clean. He thought being connected to a murder victim would be a bad look for the force. Plus he's in a long-term relationship. So he had no business being out with Katie in the first place and didn't want his girlfriend to find out."

"What an idiot," Chief Mitchell bemoaned. "Okay, then. So are we ruling him out as a person of interest?"

"Yes, we are. No one in the department knows this except for Officer Brooks, but I had one of the crime lab technicians compare Davis's fingerprints to the evidence found at the crime scenes. They weren't a match."

"Good to know. And of course that'll stay between us. So what do you and Brooks have planned next? Do the three of us need to sit down and discuss a new course of action?"

Drew set the can of sparkling water back inside the refrigerator and pulled out a bottle of beer. The conversation was going to require something stronger than LaCroix.

"She and I have put together a game plan. We've been spending a lot of time studying the case file trying to figure out what type of person our suspect is. His character traits. What drives his behaviors. Things like that."

"And how exactly are you two doing that?"

"We're following the FBI's method. Evaluating each crime that's been committed, analyzing the scenes, studying each victim and reviewing the police reports with a fine-tooth comb. It's obvious the homicides are linked since the DNA evidence matched up. Plus those ominous clues that are being left with the victims."

"Speaking of which, I'm surprised nothing came of the wedding invitation left at Latimer Park. The nuptial already took place at the country club without incident."

"Yeah, I was shocked by that, too." Drew reached inside his bag and pulled out Violet Shields's autopsy reports. "There's gotta be something we're overlooking. Officer Brooks and I have been over the evidence hundreds of times, yet we haven't come up with any new leads."

"Keep digging, Taylor. I have faith that you two

will get this case solved. In the meantime, if you need me, you know where to find me."

"Thanks, Chief." Drew's cell phone pinged against his ear. "This is Officer Brooks calling on the other line now. We'll check with you tomorrow."

He tapped the Swap button. "Hey, what's up, Nia. Chief Mitchell and I were just talking about—"

"Drew," she panted. "I need you to come to my house. Something is wrong here."

Vaulting from the chair and grabbing his keys, he headed straight for the door. "What's going on?"

"I just got home, and while I was walking up the driveway, I heard some weird, creepy ringing coming from the back of the house. So I walked around to the backyard and saw that all of my deck furniture had been rearranged. And there were two sets of wind chimes hanging from the lamp posts."

"Have you talked to Ivy? Maybe she hung them—"

"No," Nia interrupted. "It wasn't Ivy. I already talked to her and she hasn't touched a thing. And she knows I hate wind chimes, so she never would've put them up. But that's not all. Someone wrote the words *back off, bitch* in red paint across my patio table."

"I'm on my way there now. Are you still outside on the deck?"

"I am. I'm looking around trying to see if any more damage has been done."

"Do you have your gun?"

"Of course. It's right in my hand, locked and loaded."

"Listen to me, Nia. We're dealing with a deranged killer here. I don't want you roaming around out there alone without any backup. Go inside the house, lock up and wait for me to get there. I won't be long."

DREW PULLED INTO Nia's driveway and parked at the bottom near the gate. He climbed out and drew his gun, scaling the fence before entering the backyard.

The lush green lawn didn't appear to be touched. Neither did the pink butterfly bushes and green holly shrubs. But the cream-cushioned wicker loveseat, chairs and ottoman were all sitting in a straight line along the aluminum railing. Drew remembered Nia having each piece surrounding the stone firepit.

An eerie clanging rang out. His head swiveled toward the bronze tiki torch poles. Two sets of shiny blue wind chimes swung from the canisters, creating a deep, sonorous tone that sent a chill straight through him.

After pulling on latex gloves, Drew removed the bells and placed them inside a paper bag, then sent Nia a text letting her know he was there.

Within seconds, the back door swung open and she came charging out.

"Thank God you're here," she moaned, running straight into his arms.

Drew's embrace tightened as she trembled against his chest. "Are you all right?"

"Not really." Nia pointed toward the house. "Somebody tore down the security camera I had mounted over the door."

With an arm securely wrapped around her waist, he led her to the doorway and studied the steel base hanging off the brick exterior. "Have you had a chance to look at the surveillance footage yet?"

"No. I wanted to wait until you got here so we could watch it together." Her head fell against his shoulder. "And that isn't all…"

"What else is going on?"

Without responding, Nia grabbed Drew's hand and led him inside the house. There, sitting on the kitchen counter, was a gift.

"What is that?" he asked.

"A present, I guess. Someone left it on my back doorstep."

Drew stepped cautiously toward the small box, eyeing its elegant silver wrapping and cream satin bow.

"I was afraid to open it," she continued. "It could be a bomb or some sort of poison, like abrin or anthrax."

"Something's telling me this isn't that type of thing. My guess is that it's another clue."

Nia backed away from the counter while shaking her head. "I don't know, Drew. I think we should contact the Postal Inspectors. They've got the specialized screening equipment needed to handle this sort of thing."

"I don't think I can wait that long. I wanna know what's in the box now." He pulled an N95 respirator mask from his bag and covered his face. "Stand back."

She hovered in the doorway while he unwrapped the box and peeled open shimmery tissue paper, revealing some sort of lacy white material.

"I can't just stand here and watch this," Nia declared, reentering the kitchen. "Hand me a pair of gloves and mask."

Drew waited for her to slip on the protective gear before removing the lacy object and holding it in the air.

"Is that…a garter?" she asked.

"Looks like it. Why in the hell would someone leave this on your doorstep?"

"I have no idea."

Several moments passed before Nia finally spoke up, her thin tone tinged with trepidation. "I hope this doesn't have anything to do with one of my exes. I've got a couple who were bitter as hell when I broke things off. When I followed my dream of becoming a police officer, that really set the last one off."

"Would either of these exes happen to know that you hate wind chimes?"

"Oh, absolutely. At some point, one in particular tossed around the idea of us getting married, too, which I immediately shot down."

"Hence him leaving a garter belt at your doorstep, alluding to you missing out on being his bride? If he's keeping up with the news, then he'd know you're one of the lead investigators on the case. He could've done this as a way to throw you off your game."

"Yep. And he was petty as hell, too. So I would not put something like this past him."

Nia cringed at the thought as she reached inside a drawer and pulled out a plastic baggie. After snapping several photos of the garter, Drew slipped it inside the bag along with the gift box and wrapping paper.

"I'll get this to the crime lab first thing in the morning. See if it matches up with anyone in CODIS."

"And in the meantime, I should go through my last ex's garbage to try and find a disposable cup, a straw...anything that would contain his DNA."

"Um, let's wait on the results from the lab before you go doing all that. You never know. This time we just might get a hit. For now, why don't we check out the surveillance footage from the backyard?"

"I'll pull it up."

As Nia launched the video, Drew thought about Ivy. "Hey, you mentioned that your sister has been staying with a friend from work, right?"

"I did. It's just easier that way since she doesn't have a car. She and her friend Madison set their schedules so that they'd cover the same shifts. It's such a relief, because knowing Ivy, she'd be on public transportation or hitching rides with strangers at all hours of the night."

Drew glanced at the back door, reminded of the security camera that had been stolen. "Yeah, that is a relief. For her at least. But what about you? I could put a cop car on the block to keep an eye on your house. I'd feel much better if you weren't here alone though. Is there anywhere else you could stay for the time being? Your parents' house? Or Madison's? At least until we get a suspect in custody."

"Uh, *no*. Madison has at least two other women who work at Bullseye living with her, and that isn't counting Ivy. As for my parents, they've got my uncle Jeffrey staying with them, plus they've somehow managed to hoard every piece of furniture they have ever purchased in life inside that house. So there's no room for me. But don't worry. I'll be fine right here in my own home, with my doors locked, security system on and Glock fully loaded."

When Drew studied Nia's strained expression, he could sense the tension behind her narrowing eyes as they peered at the computer screen. Rather than stress her out further, he took the hint and dropped the subject.

"The surveillance footage is up and running," she said, turning the laptop in his direction. "It was recorded this morning. I left for work at about seven forty-five, so the suspect got here sometime after that. I'll speed up the video until we see some movement."

Several minutes passed before Drew nudged her hand. "Hold on. Go back a few seconds. I think I just saw something."

"Okay. I'll slow it down, too. I think I may have seen a shadow come into view, but I'm not sure…"

The thirty-seven minute mark flashed on the screen when Nia began replaying the tape. Just as she set the view percentage to 150, someone jumped the fence near the driveway, then hid behind the side of the house.

"Did you see that?" Drew asked.

"I did. Let me rewind it again."

After playing the footage back once more, he realized the perp was moving too fast to get a good look at him. He appeared to be wearing a red flannel shirt, black cargo pants and Timberland boots. His head was covered with a red baseball cap, and his face was hidden behind a black mask.

"I'm trying to see what this man looks like," Nia said, rewinding and replaying the footage again, "but he's covered from head to toe. From what I can tell, he looks tall. And slim. Unlike my ex."

"His silhouette is actually similar to the suspect who knocked the camera off the front of your house."

"It sure is. So we're probably dealing with the same person here."

A few seconds later, the film showed the security camera beginning to shake.

"Will you look at this," Nia lamented. "This guy is using the same tactic he did when he stole the other camera."

"And he made sure to knock it down before rearranging the furniture, hanging the wind chimes and leaving the garter. I'll give it to him. The man is going to great lengths to remain unrecognizable."

When Nia dropped her head in her hands, Drew placed an arm around her.

"I'm so sorry," he murmured. "We're gonna catch this guy. That much I can promise you."

"Yeah, but how? And why the sudden attack on me? Is it because I'm connected to the investigation, or is this something more? Something deeper?"

Drew bit his jaw as he stared at the black-and-white static flickering across the screen. "Unfortunately, I don't have the answers to those questions. *Yet*. But I will. Because one thing I don't do is make promises I can't keep."

She nodded, muttering into her hands, "This is such a mess. Did you see the article on the front page of *The Juniper Herald* this morning?"

"I did. And I noticed a few of the guys around the station reading it, then slamming their laptops shut when they saw me. That headline was scathing, too. 'Juniper PD Doesn't Have What It Takes to Catch a Killer.'"

"Yeah, that really pissed me off. More support and less criticism would go a long way here." Nia hesitated, staring at Drew through damp eyes. "But…*do* we have what it takes?"

"Of course we do. You know our motto. This is a marathon. Not a sprint. Like Chief Mitchell once told me, working in the field of criminal justice means playing the long game. And if we work hard enough, we'll get this case solved."

Straightening her back against the stool, Nia replied, "You're right. So where do we go from here? Back to the criminal profile we've been building?"

"I think that would be our best bet. I was just telling the chief that once we have a good understanding of who we're dealing with, we'll have a better chance of apprehending him."

"I'll pull that document up now," she said right before her cell phone pinged.

Drew watched as her tense expression softened, the light suddenly returning to her deep brown eyes. Resisting the urge to peer down at her phone, he said, "Good news?"

"Yeah, that was Ivy. Since we've got this maniac roaming the streets, I've asked her to check in with me a couple times a day, just to let me know she's okay. Surprisingly it's working. She just got to Bullseye and is covering somebody else's shift, so she'll be there until late tonight. She's gonna let me know once she's off and back at Madison's."

"I like that you're keeping up with her."

Or are you relieved to hear that she wasn't communicating with a man?

Ignoring the irritating thought, Drew asked, "Does Ivy know what's been going on here at the house?"

"She does. Which is why she rarely comes back here now. But I told her that whenever she needs to drop in to make sure I'm home first."

Drew's gut urged him to reiterate that it would be good if Nia found somewhere else to stay. At least for the near future. But he refrained. After she'd made it clear that she wanted to remain in her house, he knew he couldn't force her.

"So let's talk about this criminal profile we're building," Nia said. "So far, we've deduced that our suspect is between the ages of thirty-eight and forty-five. He's about six feet tall, maybe a little taller, and no more than a hundred-and-eighty pounds. He is intelligent and well educated, with at least a bachelor's degree. We think he's extroverted and charismatic, and meeting these women in social or public settings, like bars, clubs and gyms. He's familiar with Juniper but probably doesn't live here, and he's definitely killed before."

"Right." Drew swiped open the Notes app on his phone and tapped the bulleted list of profile traits. "He's methodical. Very careful in his planning. Which has a lot to do with why he has yet to be caught. Our suspect is mission-oriented in that he's going after young women and killing them in the same manner. He also enjoys the control he has over the victims once he gets them alone."

"And since the women's toxicology reports came back negative, we know they were fully aware of what was happening to them during their attacks. It's as if the suspect doesn't want them to be sedated because he gets off on their fear."

The clicking of Nia's laptop keys suddenly stopped. She moaned loudly, leaning to one side while clutching her hip.

"Are you okay?" Drew asked.

"I am. I think it's these stools. The sleek Italian lacquer look seemed like a good idea when I was remodeling the kitchen. But they're not the most comfortable pieces of furniture I own." She glanced over at the clock on the microwave. "I'll tell you what. It's dinnertime, and I haven't eaten yet. Have you?"

"No. You called right after I got home from the station. I ran over here so fast that I didn't get a chance to even think about food. But now that you mention it, I'm starving."

Grasping the metal sides of her seat, Nia slowly stood. "Why don't we take this into the living room where we can stretch out on the couch, and I'll order takeout?"

Drew's lips parted. But he failed to respond while watching her dip to one side and knead her gluteal muscles. The move accentuated every curve in her fitted navy slacks, leading to thoughts of those long, lithe legs wrapped around his waist.

"So what do you think?" she asked, looking up at him.

Quickly turning away, he said, "That sounds good," while hoping she hadn't noticed him gawking. "We could do Thai or Mexican..."

"Ooh, yes. Mexican would be perfect." She grabbed her phone and began typing away. "I'll order from Zapata Cove since we both love that place. Can you grab a bottle of cabernet sauvignon from the fridge? Then we'll head to the living room and get back to work."

"You got it."

Drew collected the wine and glasses, then followed Nia out of the kitchen. On the way past the island, he caught a glimpse of the evidence bags.

They were a stark reminder of the imminent danger surrounding her home.

His grip on the bottle tightened. Somehow, he had to convince her that she could no longer stay there alone.

Chapter Twelve

Nia tapped her fingernails against her glass and glanced around The Sphinx Hotel's bar once again. There was still no sign of Shane Anderson.

She pulled her cell phone from her snakeskin clutch and opened the Someone for Everyone app. After scrolling through the messages, she tapped on the last one he'd sent her.

Hello beautiful. I'm so glad you're available this weekend. Can't wait to meet you. I'll see you Saturday night at 7:00 p.m. inside the Sphinx's Solar Lounge bar. Looking forward to it. xx, S

Nia closed out of the app, then immediately re-opened it, deciding to send Shane a message in case he'd forgotten about their date.

Hi there. I'm at The Sphinx, sitting at the bar inside the lounge. Hope everything is okay and you're still able to make it. xx, N

She checked the time. It was 7:41 p.m. She'd give him ten more minutes. If he hadn't arrived by then, she would leave.

"Another pinot grigio, ma'am?" the bartender asked.

"No, I'm fine for now. Thank you."

Nia gripped the stem between her fingertips and twirled the glass along the mahogany bar's shiny surface. The uncertainty bubbling inside her chest had exploded into pangs of anxiety. She'd been looking forward to this evening all week. Thanks to the investigation, she couldn't remember the last time she'd been out socially. As for an actual date, it had been months.

Nia needed this night. Her entire life had begun to center around work. There was no reprieve. The majority of her days were filled with frustration considering the case had hit a wall. No amount of evidence analysis, criminal profiling, interrogating or surveilling had delivered any answers. The clues she and Drew had gathered revealed no new leads. And the DNA left at the crime scenes, which they continuously ran through CODIS, had yet to identify a suspect.

But the investigation wasn't Nia's only concern. There was also Drew. The more time the pair spent together, the deeper her attraction grew. It was getting to the point where she couldn't be around him without blushing underneath his piercing gaze or tingling at the slightest touch of his hand. His presence was beginning to drive her crazy. Yet there was no getting away from him. They had a killer to apprehend. So in the meantime she needed a distraction, and Nia was hoping it would be Shane.

After pulling the neckline of her cream sweater dress over her plunging cleavage, Nia took another look around the bar. This was the first time she'd been there since the hotel had been renovated. The lounge was sleek, with its midnight blue walls, warm crystal pendant lighting and contemporary pewter furniture. The seductive ambience set the perfect mood for a date. But from the look of things, it appeared as if Nia would be going solo.

Other than a few couples scattered about and a rowdy bridal party, the place was fairly empty. She checked the entrance. Still no tall, dapper man dressed in a suit walking through the door to meet her.

Just as she drained her glass, Nia's phone pinged. She almost choked on the last swallow of wine trying to check the notification. Hoping to see Shane's name, she swiped open the screen. Disappointment pushed her back against the chair at the sight of Ivy's message.

Hey! Just letting you know I'm working another double shift tonight then going out afterwards. If you don't hear from me again, it's because I'll be passed out on Madison's couch. Luv you!

For a brief moment, Nia considered stopping by the Bullseye and hanging out with Ivy for a bit. She hated the idea of having gone through over two hours of preparation just to head back home. Somebody needed to see her new dress, wavy curls and perfectly applied makeup.

But by the time she paid for her drink and headed toward the parking lot, all Nia wanted to do was curl up on the couch with a deep-dish pizza and a gruesome horror movie to match her mood.

"I cannot *believe* this man just wasted my time," she grumbled, slamming the car door and revving the engine.

She pulled out of the lot and jetted down the street. The bottoms of her feet went numb inside her tan stiletto boots as she pressed down on the accelerator. Light reflecting off the streetlamps blurred. Lost in her thoughts, Nia was reminded of why she seldom put herself out there. The inevitable disappointment was unbearable.

But she'd grown tired of sitting around the house waiting for someone to come along. As her mother always said, the man of her dreams wasn't going to just come knocking at her door. "Don't waste the pretty," she would tell her. "Get out there and let him find you."

And I did. Just to get stood up.

Nia made a left turn on Dobel Lane, her stomach rumbling with emotion as hot tears stung her eyes. The truth of the matter was right in front of her, but she'd blocked it from her mind. This had nothing to do with Shane or being stood up or putting herself out there in hopes of finding the right man. The right man was already in her life. It was Drew. Yet there was nothing she could do about it. Because Nia still didn't feel comfortable dating a colleague, and Drew was still healing from his tragic past.

"So basically," she whispered, "stop worrying about a relationship and focus on the investigation."

The words burned as they left her lips. All practicalities aside, there was no denying that she wanted love in her life.

As she made a left turn down Mountain View Drive, Nia turned on her high beams. Streetlights on the long stretch of road were few and far between. The lack of sufficient lighting almost caused her to hit a deer last time she'd driven here.

So concentrate, she thought, willing herself to keep her eyes on the street and off the phone as she checked for a message from Shane.

The farther she drove, the more Nia felt as if she were heading down a bleak, never-ending passageway. Loneliness simmered inside her head. Despite having no one to go home to, she focused on curling up on the couch with that pizza and movie.

Just as she turned on the radio, a pair of blinding headlights lit up her car's interior. Nia peered into the rearview mirror. It looked as if someone was trying to get her attention. But then the lights flickered erratically, appearing defective.

Thinking nothing of it, she turned up the volume on a '90's R & B satellite station, bobbing her head as Mary J. Blige's "Real Love" piped through the speakers.

"I'm searching for a real looove," Nia sang. "Someone to set my heart free…"

She stopped abruptly, realizing the lyrics were doing nothing to lighten her mood. Neither did another glance at her phone as there were still no new notifications.

Nia contemplated calling Drew under the guise of discussing the investigation. But she really just wanted to hear his voice. A witty Drew-ism or inside joke would undoubtedly lift her spirits.

The screech of spinning tires squealed behind her. Whipping her head toward the side-view mirror, Nia noticed the car with the flickering lights tailing her.

"What in the hell are you doing?"

She shifted her focus back to the dark road in front of her. Craning her neck, she hoped the intersection would come into view. It didn't. She still had a ways to go.

Nia pressed down on the accelerator. Maybe if she sped up the tailgater would back off. He didn't.

An unnerving sense of panic took hold of Nia's

joints. Her head jerked from right to left. There was nothing but massive ponderosa pines standing guard on either side of her. She faced forward, gripping the steering wheel tighter while eyeing the pitch-black stretch of road.

Vroom!

The revving engine blared loud enough to drown out Nia's music. As the car loomed closer, she reached inside her clutch and felt around for her gun. Just having it in her lap would make her feel more secure. And if she needed it, she'd be ready to use it.

Her eyes darted from the rear-to side-view mirrors as she struggled to keep an eye on the road. "*Dammit*," she hissed, her fingers scrambling over her keys, wallet and compact. But no gun. It wasn't there.

"Where the hell did I…"

Her voice trailed off as she remembered rushing out of the house so quickly that she'd left it inside the hall closet.

A string of curses spewed from her lips as the car rode her bumper. Pounding the voice control button on the steering wheel, she yelled, "Call Drew!"

Please pick up.

On the third ring, he answered.

"Hey, Nia. I was just thinking about you. What's going on?"

Stay calm. Maybe it's nothing and you're just being paranoid.

She blew an unsteady exhale as the sound of his voice soothed her unraveling nerves. "Hey, Drew." Before she got started, Nia took another look in the rearview mirror. The car seemed to be farther away. The sight slowed her racing heart-beat to a semi-normal pace.

"Are you okay?" he asked. "You sound strange."

"I'm—I hope so. I was out at the Solar Lounge, and I'm on my way home now—"

"Wait, you were hanging out at The Sphinx Hotel?" Drew emitted a light chuckle. "Which one of your bougie girlfriends recommended that place? I heard that since the renovation, the drinks start at about thirty dollars a pop and the attire is designer only."

Normally his teasing would've summoned a laugh. But not tonight.

"Nia? You still there?"

"Yes, I'm here. Sorry. I'm on Mountain View Drive and this dark stretch of road has completely thrown me off—"

Her voice broke. Emotions swelled in her throat. Hearing Drew on the other end of the phone sent words dangling from her tongue that she had no intention of sharing.

"I've had a really rough night," she divulged.

"Why? What happened?"

His tone, thick with alarm, disarmed Nia. Tears

welled as she pulled in a rush of air. "I wasn't out with my girlfriends. I was on a date. Or at least I was supposed to be. But I got stood up."

She held her breath, waiting for him to respond. The other end of the line went silent. Nia checked the phone to see if the call had dropped. Reception in the area was known to be spotty.

"Drew? Can you hear me?"

"Yes. I can hear you. So, you were out on a date?"

"I was *supposed* to be on a date. But the guy didn't show up."

"Who's the guy?"

His voice was laced with irritation, leaving Nia wishing she'd never brought it up.

Too late for that now...

"His name is Shane. Shane Anderson. He's new to Juniper."

After a long, awkward pause, Drew asked, "Where did you two meet?"

What's up with the interrogation? she almost blurted. But instead she replied, "We connected through a dating app."

Nia winced at the sound of his repulsed sigh.

"A *dating* app? Really, Nia? So I guess you've forgotten there's a deranged killer running around town. Despite you being a police officer and all, it isn't very wise of you to be hooking up with random strangers—"

"Okay, hold on," she interjected, instantly regretting her decision to call him. "First of all, I'm not *hooking up* with anyone. This man and I have been corresponding for quite some time now, and all we were planning was to meet up for drinks. Secondly, I like to think that I'm a pretty good judge of character. He seemed nice, he's successful… Nothing about him screamed crazed murderer."

"Come on, Nia. You're smarter than that. Do you know how many murderers *seem* nice? Have families? And lead normal lives outside of killing people on the side?"

Curiosity eclipsed her annoyance as Drew rambled on. His genuine concern for her safety was obvious. But his snarky commentary seemed rooted in jealousy. Nia knew she could take care of herself. After living in Juniper her entire life, she didn't need a lecture on how to move around town—nor did she want the investigation to hinder her love life.

But Drew wasn't completely wrong in his sentiments. And she didn't want the night to put a damper on their partnership. So she relented, saying, "Look, I hear you. You're right. You can't judge a killer by his outward appearance."

"*Thank* you. And look, I'm not trying to tell you how to live your life. I'm just looking out for your safety. Because I would hate for something to happen to you—"

Bam!

Nia's forehead banged against the steering wheel. She bounced against the back of the seat, her wide eyes unable to make out the road ahead.

Disoriented, she gripped her pounding head and blinked rapidly, struggling to clear her blurred vision.

"Nia?" Drew said.

Boom!

Her car careened toward the side of the road, skidding along the gravel before spinning out of control.

"Nia!" he yelled. "What the hell is going on?"

The vehicle that had been tailing her came flying toward the driver's door. She pounded the accelerator and jerked the steering wheel. The car missed hers by a few inches. Swiveling toward the back windshield, Nia watched as the car swerved along the shoulder.

"Drew!" Nia screamed. "Somebody hit my car. I—I'm being attacked!"

"Where are you?"

"I'm still on Mountain View Drive."

"Hold on. I'm coming to you now."

As the assailant's vehicle backed away from the shoulder, Nia slammed the accelerator into the floorboard. "Don't bother. By the time you get here, I'll be long gone."

"Listen to me, Nia. Do not go home. Go straight to the police station. Better yet, just come here. My house is closer to Mountain View. My gun and I will be waiting right out front. I'll text Officer Ryan and the other officers on duty and send them your way."

"Thank you," she choked, her fingers cramping around the steering wheel.

Nia's eyes darted toward the side-view mirror. The assailant's car was gaining speed. "I'm trying to get a look at the make and model of this vehicle. But it's so damn dark out here. I think it's some sort of black sedan."

"I'm guessing you can't see the license plate either?"

"No. Not at all."

"Don't worry about it," Drew assured her. "I'll get it when he comes my way. I'm already outside waiting. You've got your weapon in hand, right?"

She gritted her teeth, pissed at herself for leaving it behind.

"*Nia?* Are you still there?"

"I'm here. I, um… No, I don't have my gun. I was so busy rushing out of the house that I forgot to grab it."

Several moments passed before Drew spoke up.

"Don't let that happen again," he warned. "*Especially* when you're going to meet up with a stranger."

"I won't," she told him, her voice small against his commanding tone.

Nia's angst subsided briefly when the intersection appeared up ahead. But just as she reached the corner of the road, those flashing headlights glared behind her.

Trepidation hit as she contemplated what would happen if she stopped—the attacker would ram her into the four-way crossing. But driving straight through could cause an accident.

Pivoting from right to left, Nia saw no cars in the vicinity. The vehicle behind her loomed closer and didn't appear to be slowing down.

Just go!

She floored it, flying through the red light, then making a sharp left turn.

"Where are you now?" Drew asked.

"On Kennedy Boulevard." She glanced in the mirror. The assailant's car was right behind her. "And I've still got company."

"Well, just keep coming this way. Officer Ryan and the rest of the crew are en route."

Nia sat so rigidly that her back began to spasm. She leaned forward, shuddering when the other driver's engine roared. The increased speed sent clouds of smoke billowing through the air. He laid on the horn, causing her to swerve uncontrollably.

"Dammit!" she shrieked, jerking the steering wheel from side to side while struggling to re-gain control.

Gambel Oak Street was up ahead. She was only a couple of blocks away from Drew's house.

You're almost there…

"Talk to me," he said. "Can you still see the vehicle—"

Boom!

"He hit me again!" Nia screamed. "Where the hell is my backup?"

The sound of pounding footsteps beat through her car's speakers.

"That's it," Drew panted. "I'm coming to you. Now!"

"No, just stay where you are! I'm almost there."

The attacker's ultrabright high beams were blinding. Nia angled her rearview mirror until the lights reflected off his windshield. Within seconds, his car went spinning before coming to an abrupt halt.

"*Yes!* I think I may have…"

Nia's voice faded at the piercing screech of tires as the assailant's car skidded along the pavement.

A glance in the mirror sent her chest pounding. Her assailant was back on the road and gaining speed.

Hooking a sharp left onto Belle Lane, Nia huffed, "I'm right around the corner from your house. And I finally hear sirens. Tell the other officers to block off each end of your street so that this maniac will be surrounded."

"I'm on it."

She drove toward another intersection. The light was red. As vehicles heading north drove through their green light, she ran hers, bobbing and weaving through traffic until reaching the other side.

"I'm on your block, Drew!" Nia said after making a right turn down Burr Ridge Avenue.

"I see you. Keep coming this way!"

Relief cooled her burning skin at the sight of him standing in the middle of the road. Cop cars hovered on either end of the street. Nia pulled in front of Drew's house and waited for the car that had been terrorizing her to appear. It didn't.

"Where is this guy?" Drew asked, his head swiveling from one end of the block to the other.

"I don't know. He was—he was just…"

Swallowing the whimper creeping up her throat, Nia climbed out, desperate to apprehend her attacker. Wobbling legs sent her stumbling against the doorframe. Drew caught her, holding on tight as Nia's body collapsed against his.

"It's okay," he assured her. "You're fine. I've got you."

She wrapped her arms around his waist and stared down the street. Officers jumped out of their cars and drew their weapons, covering every inch of the vicinity. The assailant was nowhere in sight.

"He knows," she said, her head falling against Drew's chest. "He knows I was coming to your house. So he kept going."

Drew held her close while calling Officer Ryan. "Hey, the suspect didn't follow Nia all the way here. I need for you all to get back out there and find him."

As he continued giving the officer instructions, Nia closed her eyes. An incoming migraine throbbed over her right eye. The roar of an engine sent her shaking in Drew's embrace. But it was Juniper PD, speeding off in search of the assailant.

"Wow," Drew uttered. "That bastard really did a number on your car."

Nia's eyes shot open. The left side of her bumper was completely hanging off while the trunk had been rammed into the backseat.

The terror that had been pulsating through her joints ignited a fiery anger.

"Drew, it's time to come up with a new game plan."

"It most certainly is. And we will. For now, I'll have forensics analyze your car while we do everything in our power to hunt down your attacker."

Too exhausted to respond, Nia reached inside the car and grabbed her cell phone.

"What are you doing?" Drew asked.

"Calling an Uber. I've been enough of an imposition. I just wanna go home, crawl into bed and—"

"Nia," he interrupted, "are you being serious right now? First of all, you're far from an imposition. You are my partner. It's my duty to be here for you. Secondly, I don't think you need to

go home. You shouldn't be alone right now. Why don't you stay here with me?"

The suggestion eased Nia's bruised emotions. The offer to stay was touching. And tempting. Despite her desire to show strength in the moment, she softened underneath the weight of Drew's concern.

"I'd like that," she whispered. "Thank you."

"Of course. And just so you know, that invitation is open-ended. You can stay here for as long as you want."

With his arm securely wrapped around her, Drew led Nia up the walkway. Her head, no longer throbbing, fell against his shoulder as her mind churned in a hundred different directions.

She thought about Shane standing her up and the violent car chase that followed. Were the two incidents related? And did they somehow link back to the investigation?

"Come on in," Drew said, opening the door and leading her inside. "Make yourself at home. Anything you want or need, just say the word."

The sight of his softly lit living room came into view. The crackling fireplace cast a warm glow over the space. Cream throw pillows lined a chocolate brown leather sofa. Linen drapes hung from the windows. A game of chess sat in the middle of a plush coffee table ottoman. The faint scent of espresso lingered in the air.

Nia exhaled, the tension in her body slowly dissipating.

"You all right?" he murmured, his lips so close to her ear that his breath teased her lobe.

"Not yet. But I will be."

Chapter Thirteen

Drew trudged out of Chief Mitchell's office and returned to his desk, collapsing into his chair. His boss had requested an impromptu update on the case, and it killed him that he had nothing new to report.

It had been almost two weeks since Nia's attack. Police were unsuccessful in tracking down her assailant. With no new leads on the serial killer investigation, the chief was getting frustrated. The amount of pressure that the media and community were putting on the department was becoming unbearable. Chief Mitchell had even asked Drew whether he thought it would be a good idea to let one of the more seasoned homicide detectives take over the case.

"Absolutely not," Drew told him. "Officer Brooks and I are keeping the homicide team up-to-date and welcoming their input. However, we've put a lot of work into this investigation and the momentum is building. Trust me, we're getting closer."

His vow seemed to work as the chief ended the meeting without bumping his lead officer status. But even Drew was getting tired of hearing himself make promises that he had yet to keep.

It's time for some action...

The unsolved case wasn't the only thing bothering him. It had been almost a week since Nia returned home. After days of keeping watch on her house, Officer Ryan saw no signs of suspicious activity. So she felt comfortable enough to go back. Drew, on the other hand, did not—especially now that Ivy was seldom there anymore. He'd expressed that to Nia, even adding that she was more than welcome to keep staying with him. But she'd refused, while promising to remain on high alert at all times.

Drew sensed that Nia felt she'd become a burden staying at his place. What she didn't realize was that her presence filled his home with a comfort he'd missed. Since losing his ex, that void was something he hadn't even acknowledged until Nia came along.

Working and living together had created a deeper bond between them. They'd spend time at the station piecing together evidence while continuing to build their criminal profile. At night they'd hang out at his place, avoiding talk of the investigation while preparing dinner or playing Scrabble. Their organic connection was intoxicating, to the point where Drew found himself imagining Nia being more than just a colleague.

It'd felt like a punch to the gut when she told him she needed to go back home. The news almost caused him to profess his feelings for her. But Drew held back, knowing how resistant Nia was to workplace romances. He did, however, wonder how long he could keep this up. Because at some point he'd have to face a hard truth—he had completely fallen for her.

Drew took a sip of his lukewarm coffee and focused on the computer screen. Katie Douglas's Instagram feed was still on display. He'd been scrolling through it before being called into the chief's office, hoping to get a better understanding of her lifestyle. He studied each post, scrutinizing the captions along with the locations and people she'd tagged.

One thing was for sure—if anybody was looking for Katie, all they'd have to do was turn to her social media to find her. By the time he'd gotten to the third post, Drew knew that she'd worked as a marketing coordinator at Next Level Productions. Her Friday nights were spent at The Golden Standard for happy hour. Every other Saturday, Katie and her sister had gone for manicures and pedicures at Betty's Day Spa. A little further in and he learned she'd been a regular at the candy factory's raves.

As Drew searched for photos taken at the Green Lizard lounge, he realized there were none. There also wasn't any evidence that she'd hung out with Officer Davis. Drew assumed the pair had some sort of understanding since he was in a relationship.

Things had been icy between him and Officer Davis since news of the fling surfaced. Drew couldn't get past the fact that Davis hadn't come clean in the beginning. He could've seen something that may have assisted in the case. In Drew's eyes, any officer willing to put his own personal interest over a murder investigation didn't deserve to be on the force.

A loud clamor and string of "Good mornings" pulled Drew from his thought. He peeked over the top of his cubicle wall, watching as Nia sauntered toward the break room. His eyes weren't the only ones following the officer as several heads turned in her direction.

"Ugh," he grumbled at the sight of their ogling expressions.

The buzz of an incoming text message from Tim served as a welcome distraction.

Taylor! Hope all is well, man. Just checking in with a quick update. I'm doing at-home physical therapy sessions three days a week now. So improvements are happening. Hoping to be back on the

force soon. How are things going with the investigation? Any updates on the jerk that hit me?

Drew swallowed down the sizzle of defeat burning his throat. Not only was the investigation at
a standstill, but they had yet to find the driver
who'd hit Tim.

Just as he began composing a response, footsteps sounded near his desk.

"Drew!"

He spun around and saw Nia standing over him,
a thin sheet of perspiration covering her face.

She shoved her cell phone into his hand. "Look
at this!"

Peering at the screen, he homed in on a photo of
her sitting at a bar. She was all done up, wearing a
beautiful cream dress and sipping a glass of wine.

"Hmph," Drew grunted before handing her the
phone back. "You ran over here in a panic just so I
could tell you how good you look in that picture?"

"*No*," she hissed, jamming her fingertip against
the screen. "Read the text underneath it."

"The what?" He leaned in and eyed the message.

How gorgeous were you on this night?? Too bad
you got stood up. Better luck next time. And another thing. Keep hunting for the Juniper serial
killer and watch the bodies pile up...

"Wait—someone just sent this to you?"

"Yes," Nia confirmed, pulling up a chair. "From an anonymous number. This photo was taken the night I went to The Sphinx Hotel to meet up with that guy from the dating app. I'm convinced he's behind this. Behind *all* of this."

"All of this, meaning…"

"The security cameras being knocked off my house. The wedding invitation, garter and wind chimes. The rearranged deck furniture. The car chase. And maybe even the murders. Keep in mind we connected through the same dating app that was found on Katie's phone. If we get ahold of Violet's cell and find out she was using the app, too, then I think that'll pretty much confirm my suspicions."

"Speaking of that dating app, I need to follow up with Officer Ryan on the subpoena situation. Did you ever hear back from the administrator?"

"No, I didn't." Nia opened Someone for Everyone on her phone. "But you know what's interesting? The day after Shane stood me up, he completely disappeared off the app. His profile is gone and so are all of his photos and the messages we exchanged."

"Yeah, that's very interesting. And telling." Drew paused when he heard Officer Ryan's voice nearby. "Hey, Ryan! What's the latest on the subpoena we sent to that dating app?"

"The administrator objected to it. So I filed a motion to compel. Now I'm just waiting to hear back from the court."

"All right. Keep me posted."

Drew emitted a frustrated groan before draining his cup. "I need more coffee. And some answers regarding this damn investigation."

As Nia stared at his computer screen, he turned it toward her.

"I've been going through Katie's social media trying to figure out her patterns. See where she'd been going. Who she'd hung out with."

"I've been doing the same thing with Violet. And I'm noticing that their Instagram feeds are practically identical. Same aesthetic, same amount of oversharing. Both of their lives were like an open book."

"And that's a dangerous way to live these days. Which is why I mostly avoid social media. The couple of accounts that I do have are set to private."

A knock against Drew's cubicle sent both officers spinning in their chairs.

"Hey, Officer Mills," Drew said. "What's up?"

"I heard you two over here discussing the investigation. Did you get my email?"

"No, I didn't. When did you send it?"

"Early this morning. You know how you'd been waiting on Violet Shields's family to locate her cell phone?"

"I do."

"Well, I reached out to them and got the name of her carrier, then put in a request for the data. The company's working on gathering it now."

"What about a warrant?" Nia asked. "Won't they need that before releasing the information?"

"They will, which is why I put in an urgent request for one this morning. I should receive it later today. Once I turn that over, the carrier said they'd send the data ASAP."

"Mills." Drew gave the officer an enthusiastic high five. "My man. Thank you for doing that."

"Of course. Teamwork makes the dream work. Isn't that what Chief Mitchell always says?"

"Indeed it is. Oh, and speaking of teamwork, could you be sure to include Officer Brooks on any correspondence you send to me? Since we're partners on this case, whatever I need to see, she'll need to see as well."

Officer Mills glanced down at Nia, his grin fading into a sheepish expression. "Sure thing, Taylor. Sorry about that, Officer Brooks. I'll head back to my desk and forward everything to you now."

"Thanks. I'd appreciate it."

Nia gave Drew a look as the officer shuffled off. "I guess some of these guys still see me as the rookie cop, standing on the sidelines while you do all the work."

"Just give them some time to get used to things.

I'm sure once Tim was unable to work the investigation with me, several of these guys thought they'd get his spot. So there might be a little envy happening here, too. But don't sweat it. They'll get over it. Especially after you and I solve this case."

"And even if they don't, I'm grateful that you have my back. On a positive note, I see why you pushed so hard for Chief Mitchell to hire a tech expert earlier this year. Between Katie's and Violet's phone data, we should definitely get some—"

"Officer Taylor!"

Drew and Nia both jumped to their feet at the alarm in Chief Mitchell's voice.

"Where the hell is Officer Taylor?" he asked, scrambling around the middle of the floor.

"I'm right here at my desk, sir. What's going on?"

The officer recoiled when Chief Mitchell turned to him, his pale expression distorted with agony. "I just got a call. There's been another murder."

"There's been a *what*?" Nia snapped. "Where? Please don't say the Charlie Sifford Country Club."

"No. It was at a residence—eight-four twenty-one Birchwood Lane. I need you two to get over there immediately. Officer Davis got the initial call over the radio and he's already en route. I'm right behind you."

"We—we're on it," Drew choked, turning to Nia.

The touch of her hand gave him a shot of re-assurance.

"We got this," she said, somehow knowing that was exactly what he needed to hear.

"Thank you," he whispered before they jetted toward the exit.

Chapter Fourteen

Drew could hear the panic in Nia's voice as they sped down Stoney Drive, then turned onto Birchwood Lane.

"If we're dealing with the same killer here," she breathed, "then he's switching things up on us. Why would he suddenly go from public to private property? Especially after the last clue was all about the country club?"

"Good question. He's probably trying to catch us up. Confuse us so that his next moves won't be too obvious. Either that, or this murder has nothing to do with our investigation."

"I would hate to think that we've got *two* killers on our hands."

The instant Drew pulled in front of the victim's home, Nia hopped out of the car and lifted the trunk. Both officers slipped on their protective gear, grabbed their evidence collection kits and rushed up the walkway.

Officer Adams had already begun cordoning off the exterior of the red brick split-level house.

He nodded, telling them, "Officer Davis and a couple of the homicide detectives are already here. The victim's body is on the third floor inside the primary bedroom."

Drew gave him a thumbs-up and approached the entrance. He paused, checking for signs of forced entry. Both the door and frame appeared to be completely intact as there were no dents or scrapes. The doorknob and locks looked to be untouched.

Upon entering the living room, Drew noticed that nothing appeared out of place. The eighty-inch television was still mounted on the wall. The pristine pale blue sofa and loveseat hadn't been damaged. All of the crystal vases and copper statues were still standing.

The scent of fresh paint mixed with wood and adhesives filled the air. That new construction smell alerted him that the house may have recently been renovated.

To the right of the living room was the kitchen. The home's open floor plan allowed Drew and Nia to see straight into it. Neither of them could make out a speck of dirt on the white marble countertops, and the stainless steel appliances shone from a distance.

"Why don't we head upstairs and—"

Drew stopped when a man came charging through the front door.

"Where's my wife?" he yelled. "Where is my *wife*?"

Officer Adams grabbed him before he made it to the staircase.

"Sir, I'm gonna need for you to step back outside with me. We'll talk on the front lawn."

The man pushed the officer away, insisting, "Get the hell off of me! I want to see my wife."

Drew and Nia waited until Officer Adams convinced him to leave the house before proceeding up the stairs.

"Poor guy," Nia said. "I wish we could've stopped and talked to him."

"I know. But Adams will handle it. We need to get to the crime scene and find out what we're dealing with here."

Drew's breathing quickened as he heard voices coming from inside the bedroom at the end of the hallway. He ran his hand along the back of his neck, a stinging heat kindling around his collar.

They approached the doorway. Sunlight streamed through the half-open venetian blinds, brightening the large, airy space. The coppery scent of blood drifted through the air. As officers milled about, Drew noticed that this room, like the others, appeared to be in perfect condition. The grey velvet king-size bed had already been made, with its silver duvet pulled tightly into each corner and the decorative pillows in a precise line along the crystal-tufted headboard.

Not a piece of clothing or pair of shoes was strewn about the floor. A designer handbag was propped along the edge of a mirrored vanity. It looked to be full and the zipper was securely fastened. Next to it was a porcelain Tiffany jewelry tray, which held a pair of diamond earrings, a platinum wedding ring set, a gold Omega watch and a framed photograph.

Drew bent down, staring at the couple in the picture. They were lying on colorful towels at what looked to be a beach resort. The woman's long, curly hair draped down her back. Her head was nestled against the man's chest—the same man who'd just burst through the front door. At the bottom of the photograph was the caption "Living, laughing and loving on our Bahamian honeymoon…"

"Here's a photo of our victim and her husband," Drew said to Nia.

"Sad. Look at them. They appear to be so in love."

"Yes, they do."

He gave the room another once-over. "One thing's for sure. This doesn't look to be a robbery."

"I agree. Nothing looks to be out of place."

Several officers were gathered in the far right corner. "Let's go take a look at the victim," Drew said.

"Right behind you."

As he walked past the bathroom, Drew noticed

that the toilet seat was up. He found that odd considering the victim's husband was allegedly away from the home at the time of her murder. In that case, the seat should have been down. He made a mental note to dust it for prints, then approached the crime scene area.

Blood spatter covered the pale gray nightstand and eggshell-colored walls behind the victim. Her hands and feet were bound with duct tape. A deep, jagged gash had been slashed across her throat. An enormous amount of blood had poured from the wound, seeping into the cream Berber carpeting and turning her satin lavender nightgown a deep shade of brown.

"This feels like déjà vu all over again," Nia said. "Our victim looks to have been killed the exact same way as Katie and Violet. She's also petite with dark hair. But again, the big difference is this crime was committed inside her home."

Leaning forward, Drew studied the victim's head. "Hey, take a look at her hair. Notice how long it was in that photo we just saw? According to the date on the picture, it was taken recently. And look at it now. It appears to have been chopped off. Literally."

Nia moved in closer. "Oh my God. It does. You can tell by how uneven the ends are. It doesn't even look to have been cut with scissors. If the assailant did this, he must've used a knife."

"Yeah, the same knife he used to slit her throat,

because I can see clumps of dried blood in her hair from here. And look. There are long strands of hair scattered across her body."

"This is so…so *sick*. Is he killing, then collecting souvenirs now, too?"

"Could be. If that's the case, the crimes are escalating. I think our suspect is getting a thrill out of committing these murders—taunting us by leaving clues at the crime scenes and now taking it up a notch. It's like he's daring us to apprehend him before he kills again."

Noticing Officer Davis hovering near the detectives, Drew called out, "Hey, Davis, were you the first one on the scene?"

"I was."

"Who called this in?"

"The neighbor who lives right here on the corner." He motioned to the white-framed casement window, pointing at the house on the left. "The guy told the 9-1-1 operator that he was afraid the victim may be in distress after hearing screams coming through his bathroom window. He let us inside the house, too."

"How'd he let you in?"

"He used a spare key the husband gave him in case of an emergency."

"Did he say why the husband felt it was necessary to give him that key?" Nia asked.

"Yeah, the husband travels a lot for work and his wife is a type 1 diabetic. Since the neighbor is a retired physician, the husband thought it would be a good idea for him to have access to the house in case his wife experienced some sort of health crisis."

"Did you get the impression he had anything to do with this?"

"No, not at all. He appears to be at least seventy-five to eighty years old. The man was dressed in plaid pajamas, a terry-cloth bathrobe and house slippers when he walked over. It looked as if he'd just rolled out of bed."

"All right," Drew sighed, running his hands along his goatee. "Has anyone called the medical examiner's office yet or do I need to take care of that now?"

"I put in a call as soon as I established that the victim was deceased. She'll be here shortly."

Drew gave him a nod of appreciation. It was the first decent exchange the men had shared since the Katie debacle. "Were you able to walk through the house and see if you could figure out the suspect's point of entry?"

"Not yet. I've been up here helping these guys process the scene."

"Officer Brooks and I will take a look around downstairs, then come back up and see what evidence we can collect."

Giving him a slight nod, Officer Davis inhaled sharply, as if he had something to add. Drew waited for him to continue. But he just stood there awkwardly, his mouth opening and closing several times before he backed away and rejoined the detective.

Drew sensed that he wanted to discuss the Katie situation. Now, however, wasn't the time. He had a case to solve.

"You ready?" he asked Nia before leading her out of the bedroom.

On the way downstairs, the victim's husband could be heard wailing out on the front lawn.

"We need to talk to him before we leave," Drew said. "I wonder how he found out about his wife."

"My guess is that the neighbor called and told him. I've been debating whether he may have had something to do with this. But the way he came tearing through the door with that look of fright on his face? I don't know. Plus he and his wife appeared so happy in that honeymoon photo."

"Not to mention he gave the neighbor a spare key in case his wife experiences a diabetic episode. My gut is telling me that he's not involved."

"Yeah, same."

The pair walked through the living room and back to the family room.

"Another area that appears to be untouched," Drew said, eyeing the row of neatly placed navy pillows lining a tan suede sectional and flat-screen television hanging from the wall.

A wedding photo sat prominently on top of the fireplace mantel. He walked over and stared at the black-and-white picture. The couple was holding hands while running through a grassy meadow. Their smiles radiated through the glass casing. Drew could feel their joy, which vibrated throughout the entire house. Yet today, because of some sick bastard, the lives of the groom, their families and friends would be forever shattered.

"Drew!" Nia called out. "Come and take a look at this."

He approached the sliding glass doors that led out onto the backyard deck.

"This door was unlocked and slightly open. I wonder if the victim forgot to secure it, because nothing appears to have been tampered with or broken. The lock is still intact. This may be how our suspect made his way inside the house."

"Or how he exited. Since there were no signs of forced entry at the front door, there's a possibility that our victim knew the suspect and willingly let him in." Drew knelt down and studied the doorframe. "I wish we could figure out the motive behind these attacks. Why these women? I know they've each got their similarities. Katie and Violet were both single, outgoing and pretty heavy fixtures on the Juniper social scene. But this victim is different. She was married. The murder took place inside her home. What's the connection there?"

"Good question, assuming it's the same killer."

"Exactly. We need to know more about this

victim. Starting with her identity. Did you happen to get her name while you were talking with the detectives?"

Nia flipped through the pages in her notebook. "You know, I didn't. We'll find out as soon as we head back up—"

"Hold on," Drew interjected, pointing to the doorframe. "Check this out."

Nia moved in closer as he shone his flashlight toward a partial bloody fingerprint. "Hmm, good catch. I'll see if I can lift an impression of it."

Both officers snapped photos before Nia pulled a bottle from her evidence collection kit.

"What is that you're using?" Drew asked.

"Amido black reagent."

"Nice. That's my preferred chemical of choice for developing blood evidence. I once had a partner who'd use luminol solution, which usually ended up ruining the proteins and genetic markers needed to detect DNA."

"And since luminol is water-based, I bet it diluted the blood impressions, too."

"That's exactly what would happen."

Drew looked on as Nia began applying the reagent to the print. "Where did you learn how to do all this?"

"I minored in forensic science in college and periodically take classes to keep my skills sharp."

"So you always knew you wanted to do this

kind of work, even though you started off in the emergency services department?"

"I did. And working as a 9-1-1 operator gave me a nice head start. Before becoming a police officer, I already had a good understanding of how the radio works, proper protocols, the computer system. Plus I went in knowing how to handle victims and what's expected of law enforcement. Being at that call center really did help prepare me for the streets."

"That's awesome, Brooks. I love hearing about your journey to joining the force." Just as Drew pulled a roll of fingerprint tape from his bag, his cell phone pinged. "Chief Mitchell got held up at the station but he'll be here shortly."

"Good. I'm glad we can report that we've found some evidence. I have never seen him as shaken up as he was today."

"Yeah, neither have I."

Drew looked on as the amido black reagent slowly turned the proteins in the blood a shade of dark blue. Once it had dried, he carefully applied the tape, lifted the print, covered the tape with plastic and placed it inside a brown paper bag.

"That should do it," he told Nia. "Let's head back up and check in with the detectives."

As they walked through the living room, Drew glanced out the window. Officer Adams was still standing on the lawn talking to the victim's husband when the medical examiner's van pulled up. The sight sent the man to his knees. Officer Adams quickly helped him up and sat him inside the squad car.

Drew wished he could do more to ease the husband's sorrow. But there was nothing more important than the task at hand—processing the scene so they could hunt down the killer.

"Hey, Officer Taylor!" Officer Davis called out from the landing. "Can you and Officer Brooks come up here? I need to show you something."

Charging up the stairs, Nia stopped Davis on the way inside the bedroom. "Hey, have you identified the victim yet?"

"I have. Her name is Porter. Ingrid Porter."

"Got it. Thanks."

As Nia began writing the victim's name down in her notepad, Drew noticed her hand freeze on the page.

"What's wrong?" he asked her.

"That name. Ingrid Porter. It sounds so familiar."

"According to one of the detectives," Officer Davis said, "she was born and raised here in Juniper. Maybe you went to school with her or something?"

"That could be it. But I'm not sure…"

"Well, while you try and figure that out, this is what I wanted to show you two."

Officer Davis held up a glossy trifold brochure. Before Drew could make out the wording, his eyes drifted toward the top right side. A single bloody fingerprint was smeared along the edge.

"Hey," he said, pointing toward it. "Did you see that—"

"Wait!" Nia exclaimed, pulling out her cell phone and scrolling through the camera roll. "I remember where I heard that name, Ingrid Porter."

"Where?" Drew and Officer Davis asked in unison.

"She's the woman who got married at the Charlie Sifford Country Club. Look, there's her name on the wedding invitation the killer left at Latimer Park."

Drew stared at the phone screen, tension swirling inside his head. It was all coming together. The invite. The garter. Those clues leading up to Ingrid's murder had nothing to do with the country club itself. They were about the woman getting married there.

"*Damn*," Officer Davis muttered. "Well, now we need to use the clue that was left at this crime scene to figure out the killer's next move."

"Wait, what are you talking about?" Nia asked. "What clue?"

The officer held the brochure in the air again.

"This menu to the Bullseye Bar and Grill."

Chapter Fifteen

Nia awakened to the sound of her pinging cell phone. After yesterday, she had turned the volume all the way up while awaiting Ivy's call. So far, she'd heard nothing and had barely slept.

Opening one eye, Nia grabbed the phone from the nightstand and swiped it open. A text notification appeared on the screen. Finally, a message from her sister.

Hey, sis! Sorry I didn't reach out sooner. The girls and I heard about the latest murder. So tragic! Sounds like she was targeted. No one at Bullseye thinks we're in danger though. STOP worrying about me. I'm good!

Nia sat straight up in bed and replied in all caps.

IVY, THIS IS NOT A JOKE! THE KILLER HAS ALREADY TARGETED ME AND CLEARLY HE KNOWS YOU'RE MY SISTER. SO WHY WOULDN'T HE TARGET YOU?? YOU ARE IN FACT IN DANGER! CALL ME ASAP!!

Nia tossed the phone back onto the nightstand and rolled over. Once her eyes adjusted to the dark room, she gasped, throwing off the comforter. Faint shadows of chairs and floor lamps loomed around her. Nothing looked familiar. She sucked in a panicked breath, confused by the faint smell of coffee.

A knock at the door sent her shuddering against the headboard. And then, it all came rushing back. Yesterday, after finding out Ingrid Porter was their latest victim, then discovering the Bullseye menu at the crime scene, Nia told Drew she couldn't bear going home alone.

"And you don't have to," he'd told her before gently taking her hand in his. "Not tonight or any other night for that matter. You can stay with me for as long as you want."

Nia remembered the plethora of emotions coursing through her mind. Gratitude spun the fiercest. At this point, the feelings she'd been harboring for Drew had blossomed into something more than just a crush. The sentiments ran deep, fusing a mix of admiration, appreciation and deep attraction.

After processing the crime scene, he'd driven her home and waited patiently while she packed a bag.

"This goes without saying," he had told her while setting up the guest bedroom, "but please, let me reiterate that there is no end date to how long you can stay here. You have an open-ended invitation."

A knock at the door pulled Nia from her thoughts.

"Good morning," Drew called out. "Are you up yet?"

"I am!" she lied. "Just one second…"

Hopping out of bed, Nia slipped on her satin lilac robe, ran her fingers through her tousled curls, then threw open the door.

"Sorry about that. Good morning."

"Hey, I hope you're hungry." He glanced down at the cup of coffee and platter filled with fruit and breakfast breads in his hands. "I didn't know what you'd want to eat, so I went to Cooper's and picked up a little bit of everything."

"I see. That was so thoughtful of you. Thanks."

She took the mug and stepped to the side as he entered the room, placing the platter on the desk. Glancing in the mirror, Nia cringed at her disheveled appearance. The plan was to wake up early, shower and pull herself together before Drew laid eyes on her. Yet here she was, fresh out of bed and looking a rumpled mess. It didn't help that he was fully dressed and perfectly groomed.

"Hey," she began, "do you mind if I freshen up a bit, then we can enjoy breakfast together in the kitchen?"

"Of course!" He grabbed the platter and hurried toward the door. "I'm sorry. I didn't mean to bombard you. I, uh—I guess I got a little over-zealous now that you're back in the house. Plus we had such a rough day yesterday, so I figured an early breakfast would be nice. And…well, now I'm just rambling. But you get the gist of what I'm trying to say."

"I do. I appreciate it. *And* you."

As Drew hovered in the doorway, Nia couldn't help but smile. His thoughtfulness, albeit a bit awkward, was quite endearing. "I won't be long getting ready."

"That's fine," he said, glancing down at his watch. "We've got plenty of time before we're due at the station." He turned to walk out, then took a step back. "Hey, were you ever able to get ahold of Ivy?"

Rolling her eyes, Nia went over to the night-stand and grabbed her phone. "Yes, *finally*. But not until a few minutes ago. She and her coworkers are safe. Of course she blew off my warning. Ivy still isn't taking any of this seriously. I'm telling you, the girl thinks she's invincible, just like she always has. She's the type who believes the universe will keep her covered."

"Yeah, well, this time she really needs to take heed. I hope you can get through to her."

The pair fell silent, Drew's gaze remaining on Nia as he stepped into the hallway.

"I'll leave you to it."

The moment he closed the door, Nia hurried to

the bathroom and put a rush on her morning routine. While she made it into the kitchen in less than forty-five minutes, it looked as though she'd taken much longer to pull herself together after putting a little extra care into applying her makeup and flat-ironing soft waves into her hair.

"I just received an email from the crime lab," Drew said once she took a seat at the table. "There was no DNA evidence found on those wind chimes in your backyard or the garter. I'm guessing the suspect must've worn gloves."

"That makes sense. But if he wore gloves then, why wouldn't he have used them while committing the murders?"

"Maybe he did. Think about the method he used to murder the victims. This guy is extremely violent. So violent that he could've worn gloves and torn them while performing the acts."

Nia nodded, spreading her plain bagel with strawberry cream cheese. "You make a good point."

"We'll see what comes of the fingerprint evidence taken from this latest crime scene. Until then, let's keep working with what we've got. Violet Shields's phone records should be coming in any minute now that Officer Mills has submitted the warrant to the carrier. As for Ingrid's cell phone, we got lucky after finding it inside her purse. Mills is going to start downloading the data today."

"You know, I had a theory that all these murders were linked to the Someone for Everyone app. But Ingrid was married. So I doubt she's connected to the killer in that way."

"Yeah, well, you never know..."

Flipping her notepad open to the most recent bulleted list, Nia asked, "What do you mean?"

"I mean, stranger things have happened. People do have affairs, flings, no-strings-attached types of situationships. Hell, a lot of people use those dating apps for quickie one-night stands."

"Something's telling me that's not the case here. But like you said, you never know. I can't help but think about Ingrid's husband though. He was so distraught over her murder. News that she was being unfaithful would tear him apart."

Nia lurched in her chair when Drew jumped up and began pacing the floor.

"What's going on?" she asked. "What are you doing?"

"I just thought of something." He picked up his cell phone and began typing away.

"Um, are you gonna tell me what you thought of?"

"I will," he said, placing the cell back down, then refilling their coffee mugs. "Just let me see what comes of this first."

Within seconds, his phone buzzed. Drew almost knocked it off the table trying to grab it.

"I'm dying to know what you're up to," Nia said, craning her neck to get a look at the cell.

As his eyes darted across the screen, he yelled, "Bingo! See, that's exactly what I thought."

"*What's* exactly what you thought?"

"I just sent a message to Ingrid's husband asking how he and his wife met. I'll give you one guess as to what he responded."

Pressing her palm against her forehead, she rasped, "If I were to say through the Someone for Everyone app…"

"Then you would be absolutely right."

"*Drew,*" Nia shrieked, hopping up and throwing her arms around him. "You are a genius! So Ingrid was on the app, too. See, now we *really* need for Someone for Everyone to turn over the victims' membership information."

"Agreed. It's just a matter of time now that Officer Ryan has filed a motion to compel their objection to the court. At this point, I'm almost certain the administrators have something to hide."

"Not only that, but I'm sure they don't wanna deal with the controversy of having a member who's a serial killer. Whatever the case may be, this is good. We've now got a common thread linking two of our three victims. We'll see what comes of Violet's cell phone data once it comes in."

Drew quickly sobered up as he slumped back

down in his chair. "You mean three out of four. Because unfortunately, you're now included on that list."

IT WAS A little after 1:00 p.m. when Nia and Drew settled in at a table in the back of the Bullseye Bar and Grill. The place was packed with lunchtime patrons as almost every rustic table and booth was filled. Industrial fans whirled from the high exposed ceiling. Jumbo flat-screen televisions hung from each wall, showing practically every sporting event from basketball to soccer to tennis. Nooks hidden within the wood-paneled walls housed dartboards, pinball machines, foosball tables and cornhole boards.

Nia wished she were there for the honey-glazed wings, frothy mugs of beer and a round of pool. But she and Drew were on a stakeout of sorts, looking to see who'd drift in and out during Ivy's shift.

While she tried not to appear as worried as she felt, Nia was actually terrified for her sister. She hoped that by showing up to the bar in person, Ivy would take heed of the danger she was in—especially after refusing to call Nia back that morning.

Sis, you're really killing my vibe, Ivy had texted shortly before Nia arrived at the station. If I wanted to live my life in fear while constantly looking over my shoulder, I would've just stayed in LA!

Nia asked what in the world that last statement

meant as Ivy never told her she was fearful of anything back in LA. Of course the question went unanswered. Typical Ivy—full of secrets and short on admissions.

"Will you look at this girl?" Nia said to Drew while pointing toward the bar. "Ivy is back there just laughing and joking as if she doesn't have a care in the world."

"Well, in Ivy's mind, she doesn't. But that's part of the reason why we're here. Hopefully our presence will prove to her that this is a serious matter, and she needs to move with caution."

"I highly doubt that's gonna happen. She seems to think we're here on a social call. The way she was introducing us to everybody when we walked in, as if we're her guests of honor as opposed to two police officers investigating a serial killer…" Nia paused, grazing her nails against her palms while watching Ivy wiggle her hips as she shook a Boston Shaker high in the air. "She needs to grow up and understand that it's gonna take more than just good vibes and a positive aura to help keep her safe."

"Hey, you never know. Maybe that'll work for her."

"Please tell me you don't believe in all those woo-woo theories, too."

Drew reached inside his beige utility jacket, playfully digging around. "I might. Let me grab my tarot deck and pull a few cards. See what they have to say about all this."

When Nia's expression twisted in frustration, he said, "Look, I get it. You're worried about your sister. But I'm just trying to lighten the mood because there isn't much you can do about her behavior. Just as you've stated time and time again, you cannot control Ivy. All you can do is advise her, which is exactly what you're doing."

"I know, I know." She picked up her fork and stabbed at her Caesar salad, no longer in the mood to eat. Thoughts of her sister becoming the next victim had ruined her appetite.

Glancing around the restaurant, Drew said, "Have you noticed anybody looking suspicious?"

"Yeah, how about everybody in here!" Nia quipped, only half joking.

Her gaze fell on a young man sitting at the bar who was there when she and Drew arrived. He was tall and lean, appearing well-groomed with his freshly trimmed Caesar haircut and goatee. When Nia walked past him, she'd noticed his half-eaten bowl of pasta, indicating he had been there for a while.

"What about that guy?" she asked Drew, pointing at the man as he stood on his stool's footrest and leaned over the bar.

"Which guy?"

"The one in the navy blazer and khaki chinos. He's giving me narcissistic, former frat boy vibes with the constant high-fiving and shoulder bouncing whenever a new song comes on."

"Oh, yeah. I noticed him when we first walked in. He definitely likes attention. I picked up more of a former collegiate athlete, still-living-in-his-glory-days type of vibe off him."

"Either way, something seems off. He's doing entirely too much. And of course my sister, who is a douchebag magnet, has been entertaining him the whole time we've been here."

Nia watched as Ivy rocked her hips back and forth, then poured the shaker's contents into a martini glass. When she slid it toward the man, he blew her a kiss, causing Nia to almost choke on a slice of grilled chicken.

"You know," she said, "when Ivy first got back to town, I told her to be careful and watch who she buddies up with. And look at her. Entertaining every man sitting at the bar. Especially the one who looks like the Preppy Killer."

Tapping his finger against Ingrid's police report, Drew replied, "Well, on a positive note, maybe she can give us some much needed intel since we're not getting anywhere with the evidence that's been left at these crime scenes."

"That would be nice. Notice I didn't even get my hopes up when it came to that bloody fingerprint on the Bullseye menu recovered from Ingrid's crime scene. And just as we'd suspected, it belonged to Ingrid."

"Yep. Another taunt aimed at us. As for Ingrid's husband, Terrance, Officer Adams's notes confirmed that he has a solid alibi. He was at work at the time of her murder."

"And I know the neighbor's officially been ruled out, too. What about the Ring camera footage? I noticed the cameras over the front and back doors. Any word from Terrance on that?"

"Another dead end," Drew grumbled. "Terrance told Officer Adams that the Wi-Fi got really spotty around the time of their home renovation. Plus he and Ingrid were in the process of upgrading the security system. So for the time being, the service was down."

"We need to talk to the neighbors then. See if their cameras captured any footage."

"Officer Adams was on top of that. While we were processing the scene, he interviewed the neighbors to find out if they saw or heard anything. We'll follow up with him once we get back to the station—"

Drew was interrupted when Ivy came strolling over to the table. She plopped down in the seat next to Nia's and planted a kiss on her cheek.

"Hey, big sis!" she squealed, her words a bit slurred. "Hey, big sis's partner."

Nia held her hand to her nose. "*Ivy.* I know that isn't alcohol I smell on your breath. It's barely lunchtime!"

Ivy giggled, tilting her head to one side. "Oop-sies… You've got Gene to blame for that. He and I have been taking shots of whiskey ever since he got here. You know how it is. Hashtag that bartender life!"

"Yeah, how about hashtag you need to slow down," Nia rebutted. "I'm guessing Gene is the guy sitting at the bar who's been vying for your attention ever since we got here?"

"Yep, that's him. Isn't he cute?" She turned and wiggled her fingers at him. He immediately hopped up and began making his way toward them. "No!" Ivy called out, gesturing for him to sit back down. "I'm taking care of some business here. I'll be back soon. Just give me a few minutes!"

He tossed her an exaggerated scowl before returning to his stool.

"Ivy," Nia began, "listen to me. This serial killer investigation is not a joke. Things are really heating up and I'm gonna need for you to start taking your safety more seriously. Now, I'm glad you're staying away from my house. But as for all these wild late nights, the drinking, the taking up with strangers—it's got to stop."

"I agree," Drew chimed in, his eyes softening with concern as he stared across the table at Ivy. "I don't know if your sister has shared this with you, but if not, I trust that you'll keep it to yourself as we can't risk compromising the investigation. But at this latest crime scene, the killer left a Bullseye menu near the victim's body."

"What?" Ivy shrieked so loudly that several patrons turned and stared. "Nia, why didn't you tell me that?"

"When did I have a chance to? I've been trying to reach you since last night, but you refused to call me back!"

Nia looked to Drew, silently urging him to interject before her exchange with Ivy turned into a full-blown argument. He gave her a discreet wink before jumping in.

"Ivy, Nia and I aren't trying to scare you. We just wanna warn you that the streets aren't safe. Your sister is one of the lead investigators on this case, and thanks to all the news media coverage, I'm sure everyone in the community knows that. She's become a target. That Bullseye menu left at the crime scene indicates you may be one as well."

"Oh my God," Ivy moaned, her head falling onto Nia's shoulder.

"Remember when you first got back to town?" Nia asked. "And I told you that Juniper is a different place than it was when you left? Well, this is why. So just watch yourself. Cut out the late nights. Don't go out alone. Be more private on social media. And if you're doing any online dating, cancel your memberships. At least until we get this maniac locked up."

"Yeah!" someone yelled loudly.

Nia watched as the guy at the bar Ivy had been talking to jumped up from his stool and pumped his fist in the air. "Let's go, Buffaloes!"

"What is his deal?" Drew asked.

"He played college football and he's a huge sports fan."

"So he's a friend of yours?"

"We're getting to know one another. He's actually a talent scout in the music industry, and he promised to help me book a few gigs around town. Maybe even something big at one of the venues in Denver. Starting with, drumroll please, the Rose Theater."

"The Rose Theater?" Nia echoed skeptically.

"Yes. The famed Rose Theater, better known as the venue that can make or break a performer's career."

"Um, Ivy?" Drew chimed in. "You do know that place has been under renovation for months, and it may not reopen for another year or so."

"Oh, really?"

"Yes, really," Nia replied, tossing her sister a tight side-eye. "I can't believe you actually fell for the game this man is running on you."

"I didn't fall for anything, little Miss Paranoia. What, you think I just took him at his word? I did do some research. And after looking Gene up, I saw that he has some pretty notable credits to his name. But anyway," Ivy continued quickly before Nia could inquire about said credits, "I'd better get back to work. Oh! And before I forget, Gene is trying to get me on the schedule to perform at Army and Lou's new artists' night next weekend. If he does, you two have to promise me that you'll come."

Drew looked toward Nia, who was slow to respond.

"Pleeease?" Ivy begged, pressing her hands together. "It would mean the world to me. If I get this, it'll be the first real singing gig I've booked in…in *months*. I could really use the support."

"Well, after all that," Nia told her, "how can I say no? Now I can't speak for Drew, but of course I'll be there."

"Nope," he said. "You can speak for me on this one. Because I'll be there, too. As a matter of fact, I wouldn't miss it."

Despite talking directly to Ivy, Drew's eyes were on Nia. She could tell by the glint in his gaze that he knew this was important to her. She mouthed the words *thank you* before turning back to her sister.

"So then it's settled. We'll see you next weekend at Army and Lou's."

"If I book the gig."

"When you book the gig," Nia assured her before glancing at the time. "Listen, it was good seeing you, and I'm really glad we had a chance to talk. But Drew and I should probably get back to the station. We've got a lot of work to do."

"So soon?" Ivy whined.

"Yes, ma'am. As much as we'd love to spend the day here watching sports and playing foosball, we've got a number of murders to solve."

"Ivy," Drew said, handing her his credit card, "it was nice to finally meet you, and thank you for everything."

"It was nice meeting you, too, you're welcome, and please, put that credit card away. Your money is no good here."

"No, Ivy," Nia said. "You don't have to do that."

"Nope. Everything is on the house. Family eats and drinks for free. Now get out of here and go solve your case."

After saying their goodbyes, Nia noticed Drew slip a fifty-dollar bill inside Ivy's hand. She tossed him a wink of thanks, then headed toward the door.

On the way out she gave Ivy's friend Gene one last glance, searching his eyes for that cold, blank look she'd seen in so many killers' mug shots. He didn't have it. When Ivy walked back behind the bar and leaned toward him, he gently covered her hands with his, giving her a bright smile that appeared sweet and genuine.

"So what are you thinking about your sister's acquaintance?" Drew asked.

"I don't think he's our guy."

"Neither do I."

As the pair climbed inside the car, their phones pinged simultaneously.

"Uh-oh," Drew uttered. "Can you check your cell and see what's happening?"

"Yep. It's an email from Officer Mills." Nia swiped open the message. "Oh, *wooow…*"

"What's going on?"

"Violet Shields's cell phone data just came in."

"And?"

"She was an active member on the Someone for Everyone app."

Chapter Sixteen

"Drew!" Nia called out from the guest room.

"What's up?"

"Did I tell you that Ivy texted me about ten times today, reminding me about her show tonight?"

"You did. And you know what I say? Let the woman have her moment. This evening means a lot to her."

Drew fastened his slim-cut gray slacks, leaving unsaid that he was just as excited for the night as Ivy, if not more so.

Toward the end of the week, Ivy had shared the news that she'd booked the gig at Army and Lou's. Tonight would mark the first occasion that he and Nia were getting dressed up and enjoying some time together away from the station in an official social capacity.

The past several days had been nothing short of chaotic. After Ingrid Porter's murder hit the news, Chief Mitchell was forced into defense mode, appearing on every local news channel to discuss the case. The department had been accused of being inadequate and inefficient. The townspeople were insisting they bring in the FBI. A couple of outlets and podcasters even portrayed Drew and Nia as being a pair of bumbling idiots who were being outwitted by their suspect.

The pressure to solve the case was getting to everyone. But no two officers were more affected by the insults and scrutiny than Drew and Nia. At first, she'd told Ivy that they couldn't make it to her show, feeling as though the evening would be better spent working the case. But Drew quickly reminded her that she was still a human being. Focusing on the investigation 24/7 wasn't healthy. Together, he and Nia had put in enough hours that week alone to fill up a month's worth of work for some officers. So when Ivy messaged Nia asking if she'd changed her mind, Drew insisted that Nia RSVP for them both.

After throwing on his blazer, Drew spritzed a few pumps of cologne on his neck, then headed to the living room. Of course he'd beaten Nia there. She had been groaning for the past hour and a half about how she couldn't figure out what to wear and that it was a bad hair day.

Drew blew her off, knowing she was exaggerating. Since Nia had been staying at his place, he'd seen firsthand just how many items of clothing she owned. And when it came to her hair, it didn't matter whether she had it wrapped in a bun or flowing freely over her shoulders. Either way she always managed to look beautiful.

"Nia!" he called out, glancing at his watch. "We're gonna be late. It's already past seven o'clock. Isn't your sister going on at eight?"

"Yes, she is!"

"Well, we'd better get a move on. I'd like to get a good table and order a bottle of champagne before the show starts."

"Ivy already reserved a table for us up front. We'll be sitting in the VIP section, where there's bottle service."

"Ooh," Drew uttered, strolling over to the gold-framed mirror in the hallway and giving himself another once-over. "All right then. Fancy…"

The moment he heard high heels clicking across the floor, Drew spun around, stretching his neck as Nia rushed into the living room. When she came into view, he almost fell against the wall.

While he'd expected her to look nice, he had *not* expected all of this. She was wearing a black strapless leather dress that stopped somewhere in the middle of her thighs. The outfit showcased every ample curve on her slender body. Her hair had been pulled back into a sleek ponytail, and sparkly dangling earrings shimmered along her delicate neck. Her matte red lipstick set the look off, as did the silver stilettos with straps that snaked around her ankles.

"You… I—I think you look…" Drew stammered, completely lost for words.

"I know, I know," Nia said, hurrying over to the coatrack and pulling down a sheer floor-length duster. "I'm late. But I ended up having to throw my hair into this ponytail because it kept frizzing. And the dress I'd originally wanted to wear is at my house, so I had to settle on this one. I hope it doesn't look too snug. And these *shoes*… This is the first time I've ever worn them, so I'm gonna try my best not to waddle around like a walrus when I walk—"

"Nia," he interrupted, taking the duster out of her hands and helping her into it. "You look stunning. Absolutely stunning."

She turned to him, her frazzled look spreading into a slight grin. "I do?"

"Yes. You do. Trust me, you're going to be the most beautiful woman there."

Drew stopped himself. Had he gone too far? Said too much?

Just as he thought to apologize, Nia kissed him softly on the cheek and whispered, "Thank you," confirming that the last thing he needed to be was sorry.

"Just stating the facts," he mumbled, relishing the scent of rose perfume radiating from her neck.

On the way to the car, he couldn't control his ogling as his eyes traveled every inch of her body. His teeth clenched when the stir in his groin responded to the sight. While her hips swayed to the rhythm of her sexy walk, he wondered how much longer he could suppress his growing desire for her.

DREW PULLED OPEN Army and Lou's frosted glass door and followed Nia inside. The moment she gave the hostess her name, they were led down the long wood-paneled hallway lined with black-and-white photos of all the jazz greats who'd performed there over the years.

They stepped down into the dimly lit, intimate main room of the club where the featured performers appeared. The place was already packed as every table and seat at the bar was occupied.

"Follow me to the stage!" the hostess shouted over the house band that was playing a rendition of John Coltrane's "Naima." "Ivy made sure we got you all set up in the VIP area. Once you're seated, the server will be over to take your food and drink orders."

Drew's breath caught in his throat when Nia reached back and grabbed his hand. Practically every man's head turned in her direction as they made their way through the crowded club. Admittedly, it felt good being by her side. And just as he'd told her, Nia was by far the most beautiful woman in the club.

A server approached the table the moment they were seated. Drew ordered champagne and a couple of appetizers to start. If she was up for it, he planned on taking Nia somewhere else for a nice, quiet dinner afterwards.

"I am so excited!" she said, pressing her hands against her voluptuous chest. "I haven't seen Ivy perform in years. Whenever she'd land a gig here or in LA, I was always too busy with work to attend. So tonight is really special." She slid her arm across the black bistro table and clasped Drew's hand. "Especially with you being here. Thanks again for coming with me. It means a lot. I wouldn't have wanted to be here alone because…you know."

"I do know. You don't have to thank me. Being here with you is my pleasure. And I'm happy to support your sister's dream. Plus, like I said before, we both needed a night out. This case is getting to us both, and—"

Nia held her finger to his lips. "*Shh*. You can't do that. You're going against the rules. We're not supposed to discuss the investigation tonight. Remember?"

As her skin pressed against his mouth, Drew resisted the urge to grab her hand and kiss it. "You're right. I'll drop it."

The moment was interrupted when Cynthia and a couple of other 9-1-1 operators approached the table. After chatting for several minutes, Drew tapped open his phone's home screen. It was six minutes to eight o'clock.

He tapped Nia's thigh, then pointed toward the stage. "It's almost showtime…"

"I know!" she gushed, bursting into rapid applause.

When the server came over with their champagne and appetizers, Cynthia and the others said their goodbyes, then hurried back to their table. Nia picked up a glass and held it in the air.

"To Ivy's performance tonight. May it be amazing and lead to all her dreams coming true. And… to us. May we continue to fight the good fight until we catch the killer."

Drew smirked, clinking his glass against Nia's. "I would do to you what you did to me and press my finger against your lips considering you just brought up the investigation. But I won't. I don't wanna ruin your lipstick."

"How thoughtful of you," she teased, blowing a kiss in his direction before taking a sip of her drink.

You'd better cut it out, he almost warned, realizing the evening was bringing out another side of Nia. Thoughts of how it would end ruminated as he readjusted his pants leg.

When the music slowed, Nia reached underneath the table and gave his thigh a squeeze. "This is it. It's time for Ivy's performance!"

While she peered at the stage his eyes remained on her. Drew waited for Nia's hand to slip from his leg. It didn't.

"Okay," she said. "It's after eight now. Where is Ivy?"

"Maybe she's still getting ready, or—"

He paused when a woman came running out from behind a curtain. He'd expected for it to be Ivy. It wasn't.

The woman rushed to the stage and whispered something in the bandleader's ear. He nodded, then pulled the microphone off the stand.

"Good evening, ladies and gentlemen! Welcome to Army and Lou's sizzling Saturday night show-case!"

The crowd broke into applause. Nia wiggled in her seat, then raised her hands in the air, clapping louder than anyone around them.

"If Ivy is peeking out into the audience from backstage," she said, "I want her to see me cheering. You know, just in case she's got the jitters."

"You're such a good big sister," Drew said with a wink before turning his attention back to the man on the mic.

"Thank you for coming out tonight. We've got a roster full of extremely talented artists ready to perform for you. So prepare for some intoxicating rhythm, boisterous blues, vivacious vocals and hypnotic harmonies. First up on tonight's schedule *was* the lovely, talented Ivy Brooks."

"Was?" Nia uttered. "What does he mean, *was*?"

"But I've just been informed that Ivy has yet to arrive. So we're gonna move on to our next rising star, Mario King, then bring Ivy up later tonight. Mario, come on out here and show the people what you've got, my man!"

"Drew, did I just hear him correctly? Ivy isn't here?"

"That's what he said. Maybe she got caught up at work and is running late."

"Nooo..." Snatching open her clutch, Nia pulled out her cell phone. "Ivy wouldn't have missed this for the world. It's all she's been talking about this week. Plus she took the day off. She wanted to make sure she was at the sound check on time this afternoon. She'd even mentioned staying here until tonight so that she wouldn't be late for the show."

"Has she called or texted you?"

"No, not since early this afternoon." Nia turned in her chair, frantically searching the club. "I wonder if any of her friends from Bullseye are here. And that guy who booked this gig for her. What was his name? Gene? He's supposed to be here, too. Have you seen him?"

Drew peered out at all the unfamiliar faces. "No, I haven't."

When Nia jumped up and rushed through the crowd, Drew tossed some cash onto the table and followed her. She stopped at the hostess stand.

"Excuse me," she said to the woman who'd seated them. "Are you involved in scheduling the artists' performances or arranging the sound checks?"

"I am. I keep track of the calendar for the manager. You two were guests of Ivy Brooks, right?"

"Right. She's my sister. Her sound check was scheduled for this afternoon, and she was supposed to perform at eight o'clock. But the bandleader just said that she's not here."

The hostess opened a brown vinyl planner and flipped through the pages. "Hold on. Let me take a look at today's sign-in sheet."

Sensing that Nia was on the brink of breaking down, Drew wrapped an arm around her. "Try and stay calm. I'm sure Ivy is fine. It's been a long time since she's performed. Maybe her nerves got the best of her and she had a change of heart."

"I doubt that. Ivy doesn't get nervous to the point where she wouldn't show up. My sister is the most confident woman I know. Believe me, she wouldn't have let anything get in the way of being here tonight. Unless…"

As her voice trailed off, dread pounded Drew's frontal lobe. In his ten-plus years of being a police officer, that all-too-familiar sensation meant one thing—something was wrong.

"Here she is," the hostess said, pointing at one of the appointments scribbled inside the calendar. "Ivy Brooks. Her sound check was scheduled for two o'clock. But she didn't show up."

Drew felt Nia lean further into him. He held

her tighter before asking the hostess, "Did she call and try to reschedule?"

"No. Which I thought was strange after she'd called several times throughout the week just to confirm she was still on tonight's roster. But no one here at the club has heard from her at all today."

Pulling Drew toward the exit, Nia shouted, "We need to find my sister!"

Chapter Seventeen

It had been nine days since Ivy went missing.

After Nia and Drew left Army and Lou's, they'd rushed to Bullseye, praying that Ivy had had a change of heart and gone to work. But they were told that she never showed up. On the way out the pair ran into Madison. She hadn't seen Ivy since she'd left the apartment earlier that day.

Despite Madison having just left home, Nia begged Madison to take them back to her place. She needed to see for herself that Ivy wasn't there. When they arrived, Nia and Drew spoke to the landlord and learned that the building had no security cameras. None of the buildings in the area looked to have any, either.

Once inside Madison's unit, the officers searched every corner of the cramped one bedroom. There was no sign of Ivy.

Before leaving, Nia went through her sister's things. She'd found a duffel bag filled with what looked to be the things Ivy had planned on taking to the club the day of her performance—a slinky red floor-length gown, makeup bag, curling iron and rollers. Packs of peppermint and chamomile tea to soothe her throat. Her journal.

What was most alarming was the sight of her keys, wallet and cell phone. Ivy never would've left the apartment without those essential items.

That's when Nia and Drew rang the alarm. They issued an alert with Juniper PD as well as the surrounding areas, informing the agencies that it was likely her sister had been kidnapped.

"Hey," Drew said, "how are you holding up?"

Nia jumped at the sound of his voice.

"Sorry," he continued, slowly entering her cubicle and placing a brown paper bag on the desk. "I didn't mean to scare you."

"You're fine. It's me. I've been so jumpy that any little noise sends me leaping ten feet in the air."

"I know. Which is why I've been stuck to your side twenty-four seven ever since Ivy…"

"Went missing," Nia finished for him, struggling to sound stronger than she felt.

He took a seat, propping his chin in his hands while studying her expression. "You're doing it again."

"Doing what?"

"Getting in your feelings. Shuffling through everything you think you've done wrong or could've done differently. Stay out of the weeds, Nia. Fly above it all and keep your head in the now." He pointed toward the bag. "Since you refuse to step away from your desk for food these days, I picked up a turkey club and cup of tomato soup for you from Cooper's. You won't be any good in the search for your sister if you don't start taking better care of yourself."

"I know. But food is the last thing on my mind right now. I'm already sick to my stomach at the thought of what happened to her. Or the idea that she might be—"

"Held captive somewhere," Drew interjected firmly. "And I get that. But still. At least try and take a couple of sips of soup while we go over the recent developments. Chief Mitchell wants an update on the case this afternoon."

Nia reached inside the bag and pulled out the sandwich. The scent of freshly cooked bacon drifted from the foil wrapping. Normally that would've sent hunger pains rumbling through her gut. Today it triggered a bout of nausea.

"So," Drew said, opening his well-worn composition notebook. "Here's what we've got for the chief so far. The rest of the DNA evidence found at Ingrid Porter's house came back from the lab. The fingerprints lifted from the sliding glass door and toilet seat matched that of the suspect's we found at the other victims' crime scenes. After running it through the database once again, we still didn't get a hit."

"Got it," Nia said, typing the notes into her computer as Drew spoke.

"We looked into that guy, Gene, who booked the singing gig for Ivy. His fingerprints didn't match the suspect's, plus he has a solid alibi."

"Right. He'd spent the day with his wife and newborn baby, and wasn't able to leave the house the night of Ivy's performance. Should I add the part where he's a sleazy bastard who was hitting on my sister even though he's married, and—"

"Hold on," Drew cut in. "You're not wrong. But we should probably leave those particulars out of the report."

"If you insist."

Nia continued typing, acting as if she was actually adding the details to the document. When Drew broke into a deep, throaty chuckle, she couldn't help but laugh.

"Wait, is that a smile I see on your face?" he asked. "And did I just hear an actual giggle escape those lips?"

"Yes, you did. You've somehow managed to make even the hardest moments more bearable. That's one of the things I love most about you."

"Ooh, there are things you love about me? Wow, Officer Brooks. You just made my day."

A palpable energy swirled between the pair as they both fell silent. Just when Drew reached for Nia's hand, she cleared her throat and turned back to the computer. "All right, what else have we got?"

Slouching against the back of his chair, he responded, "The court granted our motion to compel Someone for Everyone's objection to the subpoena. So the administrators have no choice but to comply by the deadline."

"Okay, I've got that recorded. Anything else?"

Drew blew a pensive sigh. "Lastly, we need to tell Chief Mitchell everything that you found inside Ivy's journal." He slammed his notebook shut. "But first, you should probably start by telling me."

After saving the document, Nia grabbed the diary and shifted in her seat. She hated having gone through something of her sister's that was so personal. Reading her innermost thoughts and private actions, let alone sharing them with Drew and Chief Mitchell, felt like a betrayal of their sisterhood. But Nia had no choice now that Ivy had gone missing. This was a matter of life and death. And she was willing to do whatever it took to get her sister back.

Nia turned to one of the pages she'd bookmarked with a pink sticky note. "Okay, so, I'll just give you a brief overview of what Ivy had going on back in LA, because I think some of this had a lot to do with why she left the city so abruptly."

"All right," Drew said, cracking open his notebook again and jotting down notes. "I'm listening."

"Earlier this year, Ivy started working for an elite men's social club called Legacy. Have you heard of it?"

"No, I haven't. What's it about?"

"It's basically an underground secret society of sorts. Membership consists of prestigious business owners, judges, attorneys, investment bankers—you get the idea. It's like a brotherhood. These men meet up and unwind over top-shelf spirits, expensive cigars and high stakes poker games while debating politics and brokering business deals."

"Interesting. What type of work was Ivy doing for the club?"

"She was just bartending as far as I know. But the thing is, Ivy was being paid a lot of money. In cash. That part makes sense, because I never could figure out how she'd managed to pay rent on a two-bedroom apartment in a Beverly Hills high-rise. The question is, was she making all that money just serving drinks? Or was there more to it than that?"

"Good question. Because the average bartender definitely isn't making enough money to live in that area."

"Exactly." Nia flipped to a page that had been bookmarked with a yellow sticky note. "I'm thinking that the members were throwing a lot of money at the women who worked for the club as a way of grooming them. Hoping the professional rapport would grow into something more."

"Was there anything in Ivy's journal that gave you that impression?"

"Well, a few months into the job, she'd mentioned that the club's dynamics started to change. Some of the patrons' behavior became dodgy and demanding. Their requests went from business to personal. There was one man in particular whose actions had become downright inappropriate with his aggressive flirting and pleas for a date. I looked through the entire journal for his name, but Ivy never mentioned it. She only referred to him as The Donor."

"The Donor," Drew repeated, rapidly taking notes, then biting down on the tip of his pen. "I wonder if he was one of her big tippers."

"That's what I'm thinking. One name that Ivy did mention pretty often is Coco. She's someone who also worked for Legacy. I found her contact information in Ivy's cell phone and left her a voicemail message. Hopefully she'll get back to me soon. But in the meantime, that's what I've got."

"That's a good amount of information to work with. At least we have a substantial report to turn in to the chief and some solid leads to look into." Drew tossed his notebook onto the desk and slid closer to Nia. "Listen, I know things are tough right now, but I want you to stay positive. And trust that we're going to find your sister."

She nodded, unable to verbally respond for fear that a fresh batch of tears would start to fall.

"Ready to go meet with Chief Mitchell?" Drew asked.

After taking a couple of swallows of soup, Nia gathered herself, then stood. "Yes. I'm ready."

NIA INCREASED THE volume on her cell phone and set it in the middle of the coffee table. She and Drew were sitting on his couch with the latest episode of "Black Cake" muted and their bowls of shrimp risotto only half-eaten.

Their evening had been interrupted when Ivy's coworker Coco finally returned Nia's call.

"So this men's group, Legacy," Drew said. "It isn't based in just one state?"

"No, it isn't," Coco replied. "The members live in California, Nevada, Arizona and Colorado. And they meet in major cities throughout those states. That's what makes the group so difficult to trace."

"Got it," Nia said. "Now, let's get back to Ivy. If she was dealing with all this harassment from the members, well, one member in particular, why didn't she just quit the job?"

"Because the money was too good. But then something happened, and the president of the club fired her. Since she and I were so close, I ended up getting fired, too."

Nia threw Drew a look before he asked, "When you say something happened, what exactly do you mean?"

"I, um… What I mean is, she knew too much."

"What exactly did she know?"

The other end of the phone went silent.

"Coco?" Nia said. "Are you still there?"

"Yeah, I'm here. I just… I really don't feel comfortable talking about this over the phone."

"Well, is there any way we could meet up in person?"

Another long pause.

"Did she hang up?" Drew whispered just as Coco's low grunt rumbled through the speaker.

"Look," she said, "that's not possible. I'm leaving for New Mexico tomorrow night. I've gotta get out of here. After what's happened to Ivy, I just don't feel safe anymore."

Clenching her teeth together, Nia willed herself to keep pressing. "Where are you now?"

"At my parents' cabin in Lake Astor."

"What if we meet you there, before you leave town?" Drew suggested. "I promise that we won't take up too much of your time."

Nia slid to the edge of the couch, balling her hands into tight fists while awaiting the response.

After what seemed like forever, Coco finally uttered, "Fine. Be here tomorrow at two o'clock sharp. I won't have much time to spare. I'll give you thirty minutes, tops."

"Thank you, Coco," Nia told her, grabbing the phone and swiping open the Notes app. "You have no idea how much this means to us. Where is the cabin locate—"

"I'll text you the address."

Before they could say another word, Coco disconnected the call.

"All righty, then," Drew said, staring at the phone screen. "I certainly hope she's more helpful than that tomorrow."

Collapsing against the back of the couch, Nia rubbed her tired eyes. "It's fine. I get it. She's frustrated and obviously scared. I'm just glad that she agreed to meet with us and pray that whatever she knows will lead us to Ivy."

Drew glanced at the clock, then picked up their bowls. "It's getting late. I'm sure you're probably exhausted. Why don't we head to bed? We've got a big day tomorrow."

"I'm right behind you."

Nia turned off the television and grabbed their glasses. On the way to the kitchen, she noticed a slight spring in her step, driven by a boost of optimism. The call with Coco felt like more than just another empty possibility. It seemed like a tangible tip.

After straightening up, she and Drew headed

down the hallway, stopping in front of the guest bedroom.

"You were great today," he said. "We're making good progress."

"Thanks. Just ten minutes ago I was feeling so confident. But now all of a sudden I'm starting to worry about tomorrow. What if Coco gets cold feet and decides she doesn't want to tell us anything? Or what if she skips town before we can even get to Lake Astor—"

"Nia," Drew interrupted, taking her hands in his. "None of those things are going to happen. Coco gave us her word and I believe she'll come through. She and Ivy are close friends. She wants her to be found just as badly as we do. So just relax. Don't put all that unnecessary stress on yourself by running a bunch of fake scenarios through your head."

"You know I have a bad habit of doing that. And I know I need to stop."

Drew leaned in and gently kissed her forehead. Closing her eyes, Nia's hands skimmed his broad shoulders, then rested against the back of his neck. The feel of his lips against her skin was comforting, rousing a stir of emotions deep within her.

The moment intensified when Drew slipped his arms around her waist. As his body pressed against hers, she felt a bulge against her thigh.

Abruptly pulling away, he muttered, "We, uh… we'd better get some rest."

Nia didn't respond, while eyeing Drew intently. Nothing in his lingering stare indicated he wanted to leave.

He brushed several strands of hair away from her face. "I hope you sleep well."

"You, too." She took a step inside the room, hovering in the doorway. "Hey, Drew?"

"Yes?"

"I don't want to be alone tonight."

"You won't be," he murmured, straightening the teardrop pendant on her necklace. "I'll be right next door. If you need anything, just call out my name."

Her body shivered as his fingertips delicately grazed her neck. "Let me put it this way. I don't want to *sleep* alone tonight."

The pair didn't break their gaze as she backed into the bedroom. A deep sense of longing spun through Nia's core when Drew followed, closing the door behind them.

Chapter Eighteen

The rows of dark green Douglas fir trees lining Ensley Lane were all a blur as Drew navigated the winding road. He glanced over at Nia, whose pulsating temples had to be aching by now as they'd been going nonstop since the officers left the station.

"How much longer until we get to Lake Astor?" she asked for a third time.

"About fifteen minutes. Maybe a little sooner since traffic is pretty light."

Drew reached across the console and slid his hand over hers. While she didn't glance in his direction, her fingers intertwined within his. He knew she wasn't in the mood to talk. So he continued to let the smooth jazz flowing through the speakers fill the gaps of silence.

Waking up with Nia lying in his arms felt surreal after their explosive night of lovemaking. They'd poured every pent-up emotion into the moment. Drew could still feel the sensation of her supple skin lingering on his lips. He'd wanted more of her this morning. But the moment she had opened her eyes Nia was all business, anxiously anticipating their meeting with Coco.

Once they arrived at the station, she immediately began digging into the investigation. She'd followed up with Someone for Everyone as the company had yet to submit the subpoenaed documentation. The court-imposed deadline was fast approaching, prompting Officer Ryan to look into having the app shut down until they complied.

At twelve-thirty sharp Nia charged Drew's desk, insisting that they head to Lake Astor just in case Coco decided to leave for New Mexico early. According to the navigation system, they were set to arrive almost thirty minutes earlier than the two o'clock meeting time. Drew just hoped the afternoon wouldn't lead to disappointment.

"In five hundred feet," the navigation system announced, "turn left onto Sandcastle Road. The destination will be on your right."

Nia's grasp on his hand tightened as she leaned forward, staring out the window. "We're almost there."

Within minutes, a two-story cabin deckhouse appeared in the distance. The bright afternoon sun gleamed against the floor-to-ceiling windows. Silverleaf maple trees surrounded the property's vast acreage, with a sizable lake flowing along the side of the home.

As Drew tapped the navigation screen and ended the route, Nia rapped on the window.

"What is going on out here?"

He pulled up to the house's vast front yard, then slammed on the brakes. Yellow caution tape had been wrapped around the lower deck and several nearby trees. Law enforcement officers dressed in hazmat suits were scattered across the front yard. Farther in the distance, a white sheet lay near the edge of the river.

The sight turned Drew's stomach. He peered over at Nia, whose hand covered her mouth.

"I think I'm gonna be sick," she gagged.

"Let's just stay calm," he told her, his steady tone masking the trepidation coursing through his body. "We don't know what's going on here yet."

"I think I have a pretty good idea."

Drew threw open the door and jumped out. "Let me go talk to the officers, then I'll come back and let you—"

"Absolutely not," Nia interrupted, climbing out and following him up the driveway. "I'm coming with you."

Together the pair rushed over to a group of officers. One in particular approached them with his arms in the air.

"Hey!" he shouted. "I'm gonna need for you to get back. This area is closed off."

Drew flashed his badge then extended a hand. "Sir, my name is Officer Taylor, and this is Officer Brooks. We're with the Juniper PD and were scheduled to meet with Coco Campbell here. She told us that her parents own this place."

Despite the detective's face being covered with a mask, Drew noticed his fiery glare soften. "Oh, my apologies. I'm Detective Reynolds with the Lake Astor PD. And um…yeah. I'm sorry to have to tell you this, but Ms. Campbell is dead."

"Oh my God," Nia moaned, doubling over in shock. Drew grabbed her right before she went tumbling to the ground.

"Did you two know her personally?" the detective asked.

"Not exactly," Drew told him. "I'm sure you've heard about the serial killer case we're working up in Juniper. Officer Brooks and I are the lead investigators, and Coco had some information that we were hoping might lead us to the suspect."

Detective Reynolds ran his thumbnail across his brows. "Oh boy. Welp, I wonder if the information she was planning to share has anything to do with her murder."

Nia stood straight up and pulled in a long breath of air. "Coco was a friend of my sister's, Ivy Brooks. She's gone missing." Gesturing toward the sheet covering her body, she choked, "Who found her? And was her throat slashed?"

"A couple of deer hunters were out here early this morning and spotted the body. Judging by the looks of her swollen lips and bruising around the neck, we're thinking she died by asphyxiation. But of course the medical examiner will need to perform an autopsy to confirm that."

"So she wasn't bound at all?" Drew asked.

"No, she wasn't."

Pivoting away from the officers, Nia uttered, "That means we really could be dealing with two killers here."

A couple of men dressed in dark gray suits appeared from behind the house. Alongside them was an extremely petite woman dressed in pink pajama pants and a brown leather aviator jacket. Her shoulders shook as she sobbed uncontrollably, using her long red hair to wipe away the tears.

Detective Reynolds pointed toward the group. "You two may wanna speak with Elena. She was a friend of Coco's. They were supposed to drive down to New Mexico together today. Once she's done with the homicide detectives, I'll send her over."

The officers exchanged business cards, with Reynolds promising to reach out once the crime scene evidence came back from the lab.

As soon as the detective walked away, Nia leaned into Drew. "I have got the worst feeling that Ivy is dead."

"Don't say that. You have got to keep your head in a good space, Nia. If for nothing else, for the sake of your sister. That's the only way you're gonna get through this. We'll be hoping for the best until we can't anymore. Now let's see what this friend of Coco's has to say, all right?"

When she failed to respond, Drew reached down and lifted her chin. His chest pulled at the pain in her eyes. "You heard what Detective Reynolds said. Coco's cause of death is nothing like the other victims. Her murder may not have anything to do with this case we're working." He knew the statement was wishful thinking on his part. But Drew was desperate to say something, *anything*, to prevent Nia from falling apart.

"Hey!" Coco's friend Elena shrieked as she ran toward Drew and Nia. "You're Ivy's sister?"

"I am. You're Elena, right?"

"Yes," she whimpered before collapsing into Nia's arms.

Drew grabbed both women as they teetered back and forth. "Why don't we go sit inside the car and talk?"

"Good idea," Nia told him while they both helped a stumbling Elena across the lawn.

Once inside the vehicle, the officers pulled out their notebooks and turned to the back seat where Elena was sitting.

"I know your sister," she croaked. "Very well. We worked together for Legacy. It's like this high-society men's club. Did you, um…did you know anything about that?"

"I didn't. At least not until Ivy went missing and

I read about it in her journal. What type of work do you do for the club?"

"I bartended at the meetings. Just like Ivy. But I quit and was about to move to New Mexico with Coco, until…" Her voice broke as a low groan gurgled inside her throat.

"We're so sorry for your loss," Drew said. "Can I ask why you quit the job?"

"Yeah," she sniffled, wiping her nose on the sleeve of her coat. "Because just like Ivy, I was sick of all the harassment and gross behavior. The members treated us like we were their property or something. And they were never reprimanded. We were just expected to take it. Which most of us did because the money was so good. I'm actually surprised Ivy didn't fight harder to keep her job when she was fired. She was getting paid more than most of us. But I get it. Ivy was sick of the guys asking for more than just friendly conversations and dinner dates. When she was let go, her plan was to return to Juniper and focus on her singing career."

"Is one of the guys you're referring to known as The Donor?" Nia asked.

"Yep, he's one of them. He's the main one, actually."

"Do you know his name?"

"Yeah. It's Ethan Rogers."

"What do you know about him?" Drew probed. Biting down on her cuticles, Elena mumbled,

"If I get into this, you all have got to promise me you'll keep my name out of it. Because those Legacy members are a trip. And I do not wanna end up like Coco and Iv—" She paused, her head jerking in Nia's direction. "I'm sorry. But, I mean…"

Instead of appearing solemn, there was a determination in Nia's taut expression.

"You have our word," she told Elena. "Now tell us everything you know about Ethan."

Pride erupted inside Drew's chest at her strength. In that moment, he couldn't have been prouder to have her as his partner.

"Ethan," Elena spewed. "Where should I even start. He and Ivy got really cool when she first started working for Legacy. After a while, he started buying her all these expensive gifts and paying her rent. He was there for her as a friend, too. And eventually, as a protector."

"Wait," Nia interjected. "What do you mean as a protector?"

Rolling her eyes toward the roof of the car, Elena emitted a loud snort. "Yeah, so Ivy had a fan club of sorts back in LA that included a stalkerish ex-boyfriend and an overly friendly neighbor. When she and the boyfriend broke up, he wouldn't leave her alone. He kept popping up at her apartment, begging her to take him back. He'd call and text nonstop. Leave flowers and love letters at her front door. She'd made it clear that there wasn't a chance in hell they'd rekindle the relationship. But the man just wouldn't give up."

Drew paused his note-taking and turned to Nia. "Did you know about any of this?"

"No, I didn't. I hadn't read about any of it in Ivy's journal, either." She nodded in Elena's direction. "Sorry, go on."

"Yeah, so as for Ivy's incel of a neighbor… *whew.* That weirdo would magically appear everywhere she went. The grocery store, the gym, her singing gigs. Eventually it got to be too much, and she told Ethan what was going on with both guys. I don't know what that man did. But soon after she talked to him, the harassment just stopped. The next time Ivy saw Ethan, he told her that she wouldn't have to worry about either of the guys ever again."

Both Drew and Nia sat there, neither wanting to ask the inevitable. Several moments passed before Drew finally spoke up.

"What, uh…what exactly do you think Ethan did to the men?"

"Either he beat their asses or threatened to. Because after that, whenever Ivy ran into the neighbor, he'd barely speak, duck his head and keep it moving. As for the ex-boyfriend, he ended up moving to Florida to live with his brother."

"Hmph," Nia sighed. "Well, I'm glad to hear he didn't kill them. But wait, if Ethan was looking out for Ivy and doing all these nice things for her, why did they fall out?"

"Because the more he did, the more he expected. Ivy was content with just being friends. Ethan wasn't. Over time, his feelings for her grew into some sort of twisted infatuation. It became dark. And menacing. I'm telling you, the man was obsessed."

"Do you think he has anything to do with Ivy going missing?"

Elena paused, twisting her hands together as tears welled in her eyes. "I do."

Piercing silence filled the car. Drew's pen stopped in the middle of the page before he expanded the probe, asking, "What about Coco's murder? Do you think he's involved in that as well?"

"I do. Because just like Ivy, she knew too much."

"What did she know?"

"I'm not exactly sure. But it had something to do with him and another club member named Vaughn Clayton. Vaughn is a big-time attorney who's running for senator here in Colorado, and Ethan is the head of his fundraising committee. If you ask me, everything about their partnership is shady. And I think Ivy and Coco discovered a few things that the men didn't want to be known. Exactly what I don't know. But that's just my two cents."

"Are you still in touch with anyone who works for Legacy?" Nia questioned.

"*Hell* no. None of those bitches deserve my friendship. I was so good to all of them. But when I needed backup after complaining to our manager about the way I was being hassled, nobody had my back. They all turned on me. They're all about the money. I'm not surprised though. Those girls have yet to learn that all money isn't good money."

Slamming her notebook shut, Nia thanked Elena for the information, then nudged Drew's arm. "We need to find this Ethan guy and have a talk with him."

"I agree. Why don't we head back to the station and figure out where to—"

"I know where you can find him," Elena interrupted.

"Where?"

"At the next Legacy meeting."

"Do you know when and where it'll be?" Drew replied skeptically. "You know, since you no longer work for the club or speak to your ex-colleagues."

"I still have a couple of connections within the club. I heard that the guys are getting together this Friday night at Richard's Cigar Lounge in downtown Denver. The meeting starts at eight o'clock sharp."

Nia tore her notebook open and wrote down the information. "Good to know. Thank you."

"Oh, and there's one more thing you should know," Elena said.

"What's that?"

"Ethan Rogers sometimes goes by another name. He claims it's for business purposes. But I think there's more to it than that."

Pausing his pen, Drew's eyes drifted from his notebook to Elena. "Oh, really? What's the other name?"

"Shane Anderson."

Chapter Nineteen

"9-1-1. What is your emergency?"

Nia turned up the volume on her phone and held her breath, shivering as the night breeze blew past her. Crouching down behind a row of perfectly manicured boxwood shrubs, she took another look around the vast backyard.

"Hello, 9-1-1," the operator repeated. "Do you need police, fire or medical?"

"I need the police," Nia hissed, barely able to force the words from her constricting throat.

She craned her neck. Stared out toward the massive white pines lining the back of the yard. That shadowy figure she'd just seen darting through the pruned tree trunks was nowhere in sight. Neither was Drew, who should've been there by now.

Juniper PD's plan to raid the Legacy club meeting at the cigar lounge had gone completely awry. And Nia had no one to blame but herself. She was the one who'd insisted that Ethan, also known as Shane, was the only person who could lead them to Ivy. If they confronted him at Richard's, she feared they'd never find her sister. So she insisted they hold off and follow him after the meeting.

Once Ethan and Vaughn left the lounge together, law enforcement trailed the men to the house on Webb Hill Road. Unbeknownst to Nia, who had driven her own car from Juniper to Denver, she'd been the first officer to arrive on the scene. A flickering bulb hanging over the coach house's porch had caught her attention. She'd sent Drew a text letting him know she would meet him there.

Desperately hoping to get to her sister, Nia exited her vehicle and began casing the house's exterior. At one point she could've sworn she'd seen Drew hovering near the coach house doorway, signaling her over. But as she got closer, Nia realized the short, stocky figure dressed in all black was not him.

As she approached, the man lunged at her. She panicked, freezing underneath the grip of his strong, massive hands. Everything happened so fast that Nia didn't have time to draw her weapon. A brief tussle ensued. She'd managed to land a right hook, then slip from his grasp, only to roll her ankle while running to safety.

"I'm sorry, ma'am," the operator said, jolting Nia from her thoughts. "Could you please repeat that? And speak up a bit, if possible?"

"I. Need. *Help!*"

She fell to her knees, her feet aching and head pounding simultaneously.

"What is your location?"

"Forty-two Webb Hill Road."

"Can you tell me what's going on there?"

Covering her mouth, Nia whispered, "I've been attacked. I was able to get away, and now I'm hiding in the backyard. The assailant is still out there somewhere. I'm a Juniper police officer and my team was supposed to meet me here, but we got separated. So now I'm alone, it's pitch-black and I can hardly see a thing."

Frustration stiffened Nia's limbs. She stared up at the gloomy, cloudless sky. Only a few dim streams of light beamed from the scattered stars. They did nothing to break through the relentless darkness blanketing the yard.

"I've got law enforcement heading your way. What is your name, ma'am?"

"Officer Brooks. Officer Nia Brooks—"

Bang! Bang!

"Hello? Officer Brooks? Were those gunshots I just heard?"

"Yes!" Nia screeched into the phone.

"Were you struck?"

"I…no, but I—"

Bang!

Nia hit the ground, narrowly dodging the bullet that flew over her head. A scream threatened to escape her lips. But she bit down on her jaw, knowing one wrong move could end her life.

"Listen to me, Officer Brooks. I'm going to need for you to take cover and stay on the line with me. Denver PD is already en route, okay?"

"Okay. *Please* tell them to hurry."

Blades of grass cut into Nia's cheek as she inhaled the damp, earthy dirt. She thought back on her days of working as a 9-1-1 operator. Being on the other side of danger felt surreal. This moment was eerily similar to the night she'd received the call from Linda Echols. With one exception—Nia was armed.

She unholstered her Glock 22 and squeezed the grip, bracing herself for another round of gunfire.

"Officer Brooks, my name is Sydney. I'll be right here on the line with you until police arrive, all right?"

"Yes, thank you, Sydney." Nia clutched her throbbing ankle, peeking through the bushes as her attacker sprinted across the back of the yard. "How much longer until they'll be here?"

"Just a few more minutes. Hang in there."

A sobering thought crossed Nia's mind—Drew still wasn't there. She wondered if they'd crossed paths with Denver's police department. "Has anyone in your department heard from the Juniper PD?"

"Not as far as I know. But I'll send out a message to dispatch and find out. In the meantime, have you spotted the shooter again?"

"I think I see him lurking in the wooded area behind the backyard. But I'm not sure. I've got my weapon drawn and I'm ready to shoot if necess—"

Boom!

"Officer Brooks! Are shots being fired again?" The phone went silent.

"Officer Brooks, talk to me. Are you okay?"

"Yes," Nia finally uttered through shallow breaths.

Just as another round of shots rang out, someone yelled in the distance, "Officer Brooks! Where are you?"

"Drew!" Nia screamed.

The sound of his voice eased the tension coursing through her body. She hopped to her knees, peering through the bushes while waving an arm in the air. "I'm over—"

Bang!

A bullet ricocheted right past her shoulder.

"Stay down, Brooks!" Drew yelled. "The other officers are surrounding the premises—"

Boom!

Drew's voice faded as a loud thud echoed through the air.

"Officer Taylor?" Nia shouted. "Officer Taylor!"

Another bullet flew past her ear. She burrowed deep within the grass, gripping her chest after what sounded like a body dropping to the ground.

Sirens blared right before footsteps pounded the winding driveway's pavement.

"Police! Drop your weapon and come out with your hands up!"

Nia recognized the voice. It was Chief Mitchell.

"Officer Brooks," Sydney said into the phone, "I'm still here with you. It sounds like the police are on the scene."

"Yes, they're here," she moaned, her tone flattened by the thought of Drew being shot.

I've got to get to him...

Nia slid to her knees. Curled her finger around the trigger while glaring through the brush. The officers' darting flashlights spilled across the lawn. She scanned the yard for the shooter as an urge to call out Drew's name singed her tongue.

Don't do it...

"We need paramedics at forty-two Webb Hill Road!" Sydney yelled through the phone. *"Stat!"*

Dread pricked Nia's skin. An ambulance was probably being called to the scene for Drew.

You cannot let this man die...

Her eyes burned with determination just as she caught sight of the black-clad husky figure she'd seen earlier, creeping toward a sloped rock garden. He hid behind a boulder, then shot at the officers.

"Take cover!" Chief Mitchell commanded.

Nia took aim. Fired one bullet. The shooter fell onto his back.

"We got him!" someone yelled before law enforcement charged the attacker.

Jumping up and running in the opposite direction, Nia's legs went numb right before she crumpled to the ground.

Get on your feet! a voice screamed inside her head.

She dug her palms into the ground, steadied herself and stood, then pressed on in search of Drew.

"Officer Brooks?" Sydney asked. "Are you still there?"

"I am," she panted into the phone. "But I need to hang up and check on my partner."

"Understood. Good luck, Officer."

Disconnecting the call, Nia stayed low while charging across the backyard.

"Drew!" she screamed, spinning in circles while frantically searching the grounds.

Her vision blurred with fear as she peered through the darkness. Chaos reeled all around her. Law enforcement darted in between the trees and bushes. Flashlights beamed in every direction. Gunshots intent on taking down each officer in the vicinity were firing at every moving target.

"Take cover!" Chief Mitchell yelled. "And don't shoot unless you've got a clear shot!"

Ignoring the directive, Nia kept moving, stumbling through the thick patches of grass. Another round of bullets whizzed through the air. She wanted to stop but couldn't. Not until she found Drew.

"Nia! Over here!"

"Drew!"

She sped toward him, almost falling to the ground before collapsing into his arms. "I thought you were—"

"Don't even say it. I'm fine. Now we've got to stay focused. I just saw Ethan and Vaughn run inside the house. I'm gonna have Officer Davis bang on the front door while we force our way in through the back." He paused, staring out at the lawn. "After the way those guys came at us with their guns blazing, I have no doubt they're hiding something in there."

Trembling at the thought of her sister being found dead, Nia stared at Drew, searching his tense expression for a glint of hope. Their eyes met. He pulled her close, the energy flowing within his embrace filling her with reassurance—as if he knew what she needed without having to be told.

For a brief moment, Nia thought about their night together. They'd been so wrapped up in finding Ivy that they had yet to discuss it. But what was understood didn't need to be explained. She knew the opportunity to express their feelings would soon come. In this moment, however, their only goal was to get her sister back.

"It's time to move in!" Chief Mitchell yelled.

As he directed several officers toward the front of the house, Drew shot the lock off the back door. He kicked his way inside with Nia following closely behind, staying low while spreading out inside the dark dining room.

"Police!" he yelled. "Whoever's in here needs to make themselves known. Come out with your hands above your head!"

Nia flinched at the sound of Officer Davis's fist pounding the front door, then fell to the floor when bullets came rushing past them.

Drew grabbed her arm and pulled her behind a stately oak hutch.

"Take cover!" he warned law enforcement as they bum-rushed the living room.

Tightening the straps on her bulletproof vest, Nia rose to her feet.

"There's no one in my line of vision," she whispered, pressing her head against the back of the unit while glancing around the corner.

"Same here. I'm trying to figure out where the shots are coming from."

Officer Davis threw a hand in the air, signaling toward the staircase. Drew gave him a thumbs-up, then placed his hand over his head, indicating he'd cover him.

Just as the officer made a move, a blast of bullets flashed once more.

"The assailant is to the right of the stairs!" Nia shouted.

Together, she and Drew fired back while Officers Davis and Ryan slid underneath the dining table. Glass shattered over their heads as slivers of champagne flutes crashed to the floor. For a brief moment, both sides ceased fire. But the echo of bullets still rang through the air.

"There's another shooter upstairs!" Drew warned.

Nia stooped down, checking to make sure the other officers hadn't been hit. They each nodded before raising their weapons.

"Ethan and Vaughn must have split up," she told Drew. "One is covering the front door while the other is covering the back—" She stopped at the sound of Officer Mills's voice.

"Get down on the floor! Hands over your head. Now!"

An audible gasp came from the room to the right of the staircase, followed by the loud thump of metal hitting the floor. Nia's arms trembled as adrenaline ripped through her body. Repositioning her gun, she pointed it toward the doorway, hoping the shooter would appear.

Drew stepped around Nia and threw the other officers a signal. "That was the shooter's magazine. He's out of bullets. Let's move in!"

He led the squad toward the room just as a man appeared in the doorway.

"Drop your weapon!" Drew yelled. "Get those hands in the air!"

As the officers swooped in, Nia froze. Faint screams filled the gaps of chaos circling around her. She turned her ear in the direction of the pleas. Through the darkness, she was able to make out a door near the back of the dining room.

She darted toward it. Reached for the knob. When the door failed to open, Nia ran her hands along the frame. A metal bolt scraped at her palm. She rammed it to the side and yanked at the door once more. The second it cracked open, a dark figure appeared from behind a curtain hanging from the dining room's windows.

"Dre—" Nia called out right before a gloved hand covered her mouth. The bitter taste of leather grazed her tongue. In one fell swoop she was pulled behind the curtain and knocked to the floor.

Nia's gun fell from her hand and slid across the hardwood planks. She threw an elbow, jabbing her attacker in his side. A chilling grunt rumbled from his mouth.

"You *bitch*," was all she heard before his hand slid from her mouth to her throat.

"Drew..." Nia wheezed, his name dissolving in the air as pressure crushed her neck.

Kicking out at her attacker, she struggled to make contact. But he slid from side to side, making it impossible to land a blow.

Nia's eyes rolled into the back of her head. Shallow streams of breath seeped through her quivering lips. She reached out, her hand shaking as she tried to hit the floor. Grab Drew's attention. Tell him she was in danger.

"Die, bitch," the man rasped. *"Die!"*

Drew... Nia screamed in her mind as the word couldn't escape through her constricting lungs. She struggled to see through the darkness. To catch a glimpse of her attacker. A sheet of sweat covered her face as her body went limp. Everything around her grew hazy, then blackened. A dizzying spell filled her head as she felt herself fading.

"Nia!"

Footsteps pounded the floor as the sound of Drew's voice brought her to. The grip on her neck loosened, then released.

Boom!

A kick to the gut from Drew's boot sent her attacker rolling across the floor. Officer Ryan swooped in and pounced, subduing then handcuffing who she now realized was Ethan.

Blinking rapidly, Nia slowly sat up and clutched her throat. Willed herself to regroup. And find Ivy.

"Nia!" Drew panted, pulling the officer to her feet. "Are you all right? Ethan... He just—he came out of nowhere. And I thought you were right behind me. I should've kept a better eye on you. I am so sorry!"

"It's okay," she gasped. "I'm fine. I just need to get my bearings—"

Faint screams came from the lower level.

"Ivy," Nia said. "I think I hear Ivy!"

Drew held her up as she stumbled toward the door. Throwing it open, Nia screamed out her sister's name.

"I'm down here! In the basement!"

Taking the stairs two at a time, Nia practically skied through the darkness. "Ivy! I don't see you. Keep talking!"

"Hold on, Nia!" Drew called out, pulling her back. "Where's your gun?"

She pressed her hands against her body before pointing toward the ceiling. *"Dammit.* I dropped it when I was being attacked."

He drew his weapon and covered her. "Stay close and let me lead the way. We don't know who may be lurking around down here."

Hovering near Drew's side, Nia called out Ivy's name once again. "Make some noise, Ivy! Where are you?"

"In here!" she yelled as the sound of banging rang out.

Nia ran her hands along the wall in a frantic search for a light switch. "I can hardly see a thing. Drew, *help!*"

Within seconds, the room lit up. Nia looked over and saw him standing across the way, gripping a metal pull string hanging from a lightbulb.

"Thank you," she uttered while eyeing their strange surroundings.

Sheets of plastic dangled from the ceiling, their

edges crumpled against the dusty floor. Exposed wood and insulation lined the unfinished walls. The few pieces of furniture scattered around the spacious area were covered in paint-splattered drop cloths.

"Nia!"

The sound of Ivy's voice sent the officers rushing toward a back corner. A thick, dirty canvas tarp hung across the wall. Nia yanked it to the floor, revealing a narrow wooden door. It was secured shut with an alloy steel padlock.

"Ivy, stand back!" Nia yelled. "Step away from the door!"

Drew took aim and blew off the lock, then kicked down the door.

"Ivy!" Nia screamed, rushing inside. Relief rattled her chest when her sister appeared inside the dimly lit makeshift bedroom.

Stumbling around a gray chest of drawers, Ivy fell into her arms.

"Thank God you found me," she sobbed.

Holding her as tight as she could, Nia said, "Of course we found you. But…how did this happen? How did you get here?"

A guttural moan vibrated against Nia's shoulder as Ivy's body wracked in agony. "I was getting ready to go to the sound check at Army and Lou's, and there was a knock at the door. I thought it was Madison, there to give me a ride during her break at Bullseye. I didn't even look through the peephole before opening the door. When I did, Ethan was standing on the other side. I just knew he was gonna kill me right there on the spot and freaked out. The second I screamed, he attacked, covering my mouth and pushing me back inside the apartment. All I remember is the sting of a needle being jabbed into my arm. When I woke up, I was inside this tiny hellhole."

Nia was overcome by a flood of emotions as she held her sister tighter. "Well, we're here now. I'm just so glad we got to you in time, before…" Her voice broke. She couldn't bring herself to say the words *before he killed you.*

The thought of Coco sprang to mind. Nia couldn't tell Ivy what had happened to her, either. At least not yet.

Tramping overhead alerted the officers that there was still work to be done. Holding on to Nia's shoulder, Drew said, "Keep your sister safe," before turning to Ivy. "We're so glad you're okay. Once we secure this place, we'll get you to the hospital. In the meantime, we need to arrest these bastards."

Chapter Twenty

Drew and Nia entered Chief Mitchell's office, neither of them able to wipe the smiles off their faces.

"Welcome back, Chief. How are you feeling?" Drew asked, pointing at the sling cradling his boss's left arm. During the shootout Chief Mitchell had been hit in the shoulder, landing him in the hospital for a couple of days, then at home for over a week.

"I'm feeling pretty good thanks to a little time off and eight hundred milligrams of ibuprofen every six hours. What've you two got for me?"

"A lot," Drew replied, sliding a copy of the case file across the desk. "Have you been keeping up with the reports we've emailed to you?"

The chief sat straight up and flipped open the file. "I have. But I wanna hear everything I've missed direct from you two. So have a seat and fill me in."

Raising her hand in the air, Nia said, "Wait, before we get started, can I just share with you that my phone, along with Officer Taylor's, has been ringing off the hook ever since Ethan and Vaughn were arrested?"

"And you're not alone in that," Chief Mitchell replied, chuckling into his coffee mug before taking a long sip. "I think every member of this community has called singing the department's praises. It's safe to say they're all breathing easier these days, thanks to you two. But anyway, let's get to it. Give me a rundown of the interrogations."

"So," Drew began, "as you can probably guess, both men turned on one another the second they started talking. Ethan claimed that Vaughn had been misappropriating the funds he'd donated to his senatorial campaign to bankroll his lavish lifestyle, then accused him of being Juniper's serial killer after he'd had multiple affairs with the murdered women."

"Did he mention what his motive would've been?"

"He did. According to Ethan, Vaughn was worried that the women would leak details of their liaisons and ruin his political career."

"*And* his marriage," Nia added. "But as for Ivy's friend Coco, Ethan alleged Vaughn killed her because she knew about the misused funds. He was afraid she'd blow the whistle."

"What about Ivy?" Chief Mitchell asked. "Vaughn wasn't worried about how much she knew?"

"He was. According to Ethan, Vaughn wanted her dead, too. But Ethan wouldn't allow it, and claims he was keeping her safe at his house so that Vaughn couldn't get to her."

The chief reached across the desk and switched on the fan. "So what did Vaughn have to say for himself?"

"Brace yourself," Drew responded, flipping through his copy of the report. "Because Vaughn presented a completely different side to this sadistic story. Officer Brooks and I started off light. We questioned him about the whole misappropriated campaign funds situation first. He claimed that Ethan was the one who'd misused the money by making illegal donations in hopes of influencing policies that would benefit his businesses."

"Then," Nia interjected, "without being prompted, Vaughn went straight to the murders. He called Ethan a possessive, controlling sociopath who met each of the victims through Someone for Everyone and killed them after they broke things off with him. And according to him, Ethan actually *owns* the dating app."

"A fact that he kept hidden after registering the company as an anonymous limited liability," Drew said.

"Hmph," Chief Mitchell huffed. "Sounds to me like both of these men could've had a hand in all this."

Shifting in her chair, Nia said, "Well, just to

add another odd layer to an already twisted story, I actually connected with Ethan through Someone for Everyone. During Vaughn's interrogation, he claimed that since Ethan had been rejected by Ivy, he went after the next best thing."

"Meaning…you?"

"Yes. Exactly. But the night we were supposed to meet up, he was a no-show. Ethan felt as though he'd be betraying Ivy by going out with me. Then when he found out I was one of the lead investigators working the serial killer case, Vaughn claimed that it was Ethan who began stalking and harassing me in hopes of disrupting the investigation."

"Wow," Chief Mitchel grunted. "And the plot thickens…"

Drew threw Nia a look, then slid another report across the table. "Let's get to the good stuff, shall we?"

"What is this?" the chief asked.

"A present from the forensic lab. They processed the evidence in record time and we've already got the results back."

"And?" Chief Mitchell boomed through a widening grin.

"Ethan's DNA matched the evidence collected at the crime scenes of Katie Douglas, Violet Shields and Ingrid Porter. Those footprint impressions Officer Brooks discovered at Katie's and Violet's crime scenes matched a pair of size eleven Lacrosse AeroHead Sport hunting boots that we took from Ethan's house. Blood evidence found on the soles matched both victims' DNA."

"Good work, Brooks."

"Thank you, sir."

"What about Vaughn? Anything come back on him?"

"Oh, yeah," Nia said. "His DNA matched perspiratory evidence found on the body of Coco Campbell. That gave credence to Ethan's claim that she was aware of the illegalities involving Vaughn's campaign, prompting him to kill her before she could expose his illicit campaign activity. *And…*" Nia pivoted in her seat, giving Drew's shoulder a nudge. "I'll let Drew share the rest."

Chief Mitchell looked up from the report. "Go on. I'm listening."

"So, once Ethan's DNA was entered in the criminal database, one of our department's cold cases was cracked. Remember Linda Echols?"

"Of course. How could I forget?"

"Well, the nightgown Linda was wearing the evening she was murdered contained Ethan's DNA. After speaking with her sister, I found out Linda was a member of Someone for Everyone at the time of her death. We didn't figure that out earlier because she used a fake name on the app."

Pounding his fist onto the desk, the chief rocked against the back of his chair and stared up at the ceiling. "This is the best news I've gotten all year!

See, I knew it. I knew you two would somehow get that case solved, too." He shot back up and pointed at Drew. "Aren't you glad that I—"

"Yes," Drew interrupted before Chief Mitchell could finish his statement. "I am *ecstatic* that you insisted I team up with Officer Brooks. Now let's get back to the case before things start getting mushy around here. I still believe that either Ethan or Vaughn caused Tim's car accident due to his involvement in this investigation. But before you even say it, I already know that charge can't be filed since I have no supporting evidence. Nevertheless, I'd be remiss if I didn't at least bring it up."

"Well, we'll continue to keep an eye out. If some sort of evidence does emerge, then we'll file charges. What's the status of the third suspect involved in the shootout?"

"Turns out he was a private security guard hired by Ethan to patrol his home. He's the one who attacked Nia when she first arrived on the scene."

"What's his status?"

"Still in the hospital in critical but stable condition."

Running a hand over his injured shoulder, Chief Mitchell replied, "And once he's discharged he'll go straight to prison. On another note, how did your call go with the district attorney?"

"Great," Drew told him. "She's planning on charging Ethan with four counts of first-degree murder, aggravated kidnapping, attempted murder and conspiracy. Vaughn's being charged first-degree murder, conspiracy, and aiding and abetting. In the meantime, both men are being held without bond."

"Oh, that is *awe*—" The chief groaned, wincing while gripping his shoulder.

"Are you okay?" Nia asked just as his cell phone rang.

"Ugh, I will be. I guess I should've listened to my wife when she told me to stay home a few more days to recuperate. But how could I when all this excitement was happening around here?" He glanced down at the phone. "Speaking of my wife, I'd better grab her call. I'll circle back with you both this afternoon. Thanks again for the great work on this investigation."

"You're welcome, sir."

As Drew followed Nia out of the office, his eyes drifted down to her hips. He shoved his hands inside his pockets, reminding himself that it wouldn't be appropriate to wrap her up in his arms in front of the entire department. Yet in that moment, he felt so full. Emotion was churning inside his chest. With Nia by his side, the pair had managed to solve one of the biggest cases in Juniper's history.

In the midst of it all, memories of their steamy evening together occupied his mind more often than he'd like to admit. As the case continued to heat up, however, there hadn't been time to address that night and talk about whether either of them wanted more.

But now that Ethan and Vaughn were finally behind bars, Drew planned on sitting down with Nia and putting it all on the table, sooner rather than later.

Epilogue

One month later...

Nia pressed her hand against her chest as she approached the door to Army and Lou's. Peering through the frosted glass, she could already tell that she was overdressed. Most patrons were wearing jeans and button-down shirts, or leggings and oversized sweaters. Nia must have missed the memo. She'd chosen a mini tuxedo dress, which she thought would be appropriate since the Juniper PD was gathering to celebrate Drew's promotion to detective.

The moment she stepped inside the club, all eyes were on her. Nia greeted everyone through a stiff smile, squeezing past the crowd of people lining the hallway. She focused on the photos hanging from the wall rather than the ogling expressions on clubgoers' faces.

A loud, familiar roar of laughter echoed from the back of the main room, signaling that her colleagues were gathered near the stage. As she headed that way, a waving hand caught her attention over by the bar.

"Hey, Officer Brooks!"

Nia waved back while Officer Ryan made his way toward her.

"Wow," he uttered, eyeing her from head to toe. "You look…*fantastic*. I don't think I've ever seen you all dressed up like this. Wait, are those real diamonds on your shoes?"

"I wish," she said, laughing as the officer offered her his arm.

"This place is packed tonight," he said. "I'll escort you to the spot where the manager roped off a section for us."

"Thanks, Officer Ryan."

Nia teetered on her heels, struggling not to bump into anyone on the way to their section. The atmosphere was electric as strobe lights shone down on a quartet playing a rendition of Dizzy Gillespie's "Get Happy." The dance floor was packed with couples swinging to the rhythm of the music. And almost everyone there looked to have a drink in their hand and a smile on their face.

Several officers greeted Nia as she approached. While responding with enthusiastic hellos, there was only one thing on her mind—finding Drew.

Her heart stuttered the moment she laid eyes on him. He looked up, as if he could feel her presence. Nia's lips curled into a soft smile. Unlike the other officers, Drew had dressed up, appearing so handsome in his slim-fitting beige suit and crisp white shirt. He tossed her a sexy head nod while his eyes roamed her body. They paused on her arm, which was still nestled within Officer Ryan's. The grin on Drew's face quickly shriveled in a confused scowl.

"We've got a ton of food set up here," the officer told Nia, motioning toward platters filled with buffalo wings, pepperoni flatbread and Philly cheesesteak sliders. "And there's wine, champagne, and of course, beer. If you want a craft cocktail, you'll have to order that at the bar. Or I'd be happy to go over and grab something for you. Anything you want. Just say the word."

Nia's skin prickled as he leaned in closer. She slipped her arm out of his grip and said, "Thanks, but I'm fine for now."

When she walked over to the table and poured herself a glass of ice water, he followed.

"You know," he began, swinging his mug of beer toward the dance floor, "I love this song. Would you like to—"

"Hey, Ryan!" someone called out behind them. "Why don't you at least let Officer Brooks settle in before you try and make a move on her?"

Nia didn't have to turn around to know that it was Drew.

Raising his hands in surrender, Officer Ryan

replied, "It isn't even like that. I was just being friendly. No need to get testy, *Detective Taylor*."

"Ooh, I like the sound of that," Drew retorted. "Thanks, *Officer Ryan*."

Drew wrapped his arm around Nia's waist and led her to a quiet corner. "Damn, that man wasn't even trying to hide the fact that he's got a crush on you."

"Give him a break. He's a nice guy."

Nia's limbs tingled with nerves as several of their colleagues eyed them curiously. But that wasn't the only reason she was feeling anxious. She had yet to talk to Drew about their intimate night together. There hadn't been much time for personal matters. Soon after the killers were arrested, Drew was hit with the news of his promotion. Adjusting to the position and heftier workload practically took over his life. Nia, however, could no longer suppress the things she needed to get off her chest.

Suddenly, the room felt excruciatingly warm. She almost choked on the thick, steamy air circulating around them. Taking a long sip of water, Nia fanned her face before setting the glass down.

"What's going on?" Drew asked. "Are you okay?"

"I, um…" she said right before her cell phone buzzed.

"Let me guess. That's your sister texting you."

Nia smiled and showed him the message. "Of course that's Ivy texting me."

Hey big sis! Just checking in, as you've insisted I do every minute of the day. My audition for I Made It to Broadway is tomorrow morning so I'm heading to bed. Wish me luck!

"Nice," Drew responded. "Tell her I said good luck, too. How's her move back to LA going?"

"Good. Really good. She's happy to be back out there working on her craft."

"Glad to hear it." Drew moved in closer, taking Nia's hand in his. "Can I just say that you look absolutely stunning tonight?"

"Thank you. Listen…" She hesitated, distracted by everything going on around them. After glancing over her shoulder to make sure no one was within earshot, she continued. "There's something I need to tell you—"

"Wait," he interrupted. "You must have forgotten that tonight is my big night. Shouldn't you be holding a glass of champagne in celebration of my promotion?"

"Yes, I should be. But…"

"But what?"

"I can't."

"Why not?"

Nia stared into his inquisitive eyes as perspiration dotted her forehead. "That's what I wanted to talk to you about."

"Uh-oh. You're starting to scare me. What's going on?"

She reached out, straightening his lapel before resting her hand against his chest. "I'm pregnant."

Drew's pecs stiffened against her palm as his eyelids fluttered in confusion. "I'm sorry. It's so loud in here. I actually thought you said that you're *pregnant*."

"I did. I am pregnant."

"Wait," he uttered, taking a step back. "Are you…are you serious?"

"I am."

Between his long pause and twitching eyelids, she didn't know what to make of his reaction.

"Nia, please don't play with my emotions like this."

"I wouldn't do that. I'm being totally serious. But your response is starting to scare me. Could you say something? *Anything?* Are you happy? Is this good news? Or…"

A wide grin covered his face.

"Of course this is good news!" he yelled, sweeping Nia off her feet and twirling her around. "Baby," Drew continued, lowering his voice. "We're gonna have a *baby*?"

"Yes. *Yes!*"

She held his face in her hands as their lips met, sealing the sweet moment with a tender kiss.

"Thank you, everyone!" the bandleader boomed into the microphone. "The Jazzets and I are gonna take a brief break while I turn the mic over to one of Juniper's finest, Chief Bruce Mitchell. Take it away, Chief."

Nia slowly pulled away from Drew. "Maybe we should go back over. I have a feeling our boss might be looking for you considering you're the man of the hour and all."

"Maybe we should. And if he calls me up, I'll try my best not to share the most thrilling news I've ever received before in my life with every-one here."

"Oh, *please* try your best not to do that!"

"I promise I won't." Drew held her chin in his hands, gently kissing her one last time before they returned to the group.

Chief Mitchell grabbed the mic and waved at the crowd. "Thank you, Evan. Hey, Detective Tay-lor, would you mind joining me up here?"

Nia looked on proudly while Drew headed to the stage, clapping the loudest among their cheer-ing colleagues.

"Hey," Cynthia muttered in her ear. "What was that all about?"

"What was what all about?"

"Don't play coy with me. You know what I'm

talking about! I saw you and Drew standing over in the corner all hugged up, making googly eyes at each other and whatnot."

"We'll talk about it later," Nia told her without taking her eyes off the stage.

"Yeah, okay. Just know that you *will* be spilling the tea as soon as Chief Mitchell is done with his speech."

The chief held his hands in the air to quiet the crowd. "Detective Taylor, on behalf of myself and the rest of Juniper PD, I would like to congratulate you on your promotion to detective. This well-deserved position is a testament to the outstanding work you've done for the department. Not only are you an excellent investigator, but you are a leader and the prototype of what anyone working in law enforcement should strive to be. We're all lucky to have you on the force, and for many of us, even luckier to call you a friend. Thank you for all that you've done, and most importantly, for spearheading Juniper's serial killer investigation."

Applause rippled through the room as Drew stepped to the mic, nodding humbly. "Thank you so much for those kind words, Chief Mitchell. I don't know if I've earned all that praise just yet, but hey, you're the boss, right? So far be it from me to disagree."

As the crowd broke into laughter, Drew's gaze drifted to Nia.

Oh no, she thought, that intense look in his eyes screaming *Join me onstage*.

"But seriously," Drew continued, "I certainly didn't solve the biggest case of my career alone. I had the help of this entire department. We were like a fine-tuned machine—everyone played their part. There was, however, one person who stood out from the rest."

Everyone turned to Nia. She crossed her arms over her chest, squeezing tightly while wishing the floor would open up and swallow her. Being the center of attention had never been her thing.

Cynthia reached over and uncrossed her arms. "Hey, relax. This is your moment, too. And you deserve it just as much as Detective Taylor. So enjoy it."

Sucking in a swift breath of air, Nia stood taller and shook out her arms. "You're right," she whispered, bracing herself as Drew proceeded.

"Some time ago, Chief Mitchell decided to implement a mentorship program within the department. I had just been assigned to this case and didn't think I'd have the time nor the patience to serve as a mentor. But the chief insisted, and as you know, what he says goes. So here I was, stuck with mentoring Officer Brooks."

The crowd burst into laughter while Drew's shining eyes homed in on Nia, as if she were the only person in the room.

"Then my partner and good friend, Officer Timothy Braxton, got into a terrible car accident. Thank God he made it out alive and is doing well. But back then, while I was concerned with his injuries and overwhelmed with the investigation, Officer Brooks and I were forced together on a deeper level as we worked to solve the case." Drew paused, then held out his hand. "Officer Brooks, would you please join me onstage?"

Loud clapping rattled her eardrums. She remained frozen in her stance, holding her breath while her colleagues chanted her name.

"Nia," Cynthia hissed, giving her a nudge, "get up on that stage and celebrate your accolades, girl!"

Wringing her hands together, she prayed her stilettos would hold her up as she wobbled toward Drew. He took a step down and extended his arm, then led her to the mic.

"Officer Brooks, it goes without saying that this case would not have been solved without you."

"Well, I don't know about all that, but—"

"No, it's true. I'm just glad that I didn't push back *too* hard. Because I wouldn't have realized that I'd been handed the perfect partner." He paused, slipping his hand along the small of her back. "Or gotten the chance to fall in love with you."

Rippling cheers rolled through the entire club. But Nia barely heard them. And when Drew leaned in and kissed her in front of everyone, she didn't care that all eyes were on them.

The moment their lips separated, she murmured, "I'm in love with you, too."

Nia wasn't sure whether he'd heard it. But judging by the beat of his pounding heart, she was certain that he'd felt it.

* * * * *

A NOTE TO ALL READERS

From October releases Mills & Boon will be making some changes to the series formats and pricing.

What will be different about the series books?

In response to recent reader feedback, we are increasing the size of our paperbacks to bigger books with better quality paper, making for a better reading experience.

What will be the new price of Mills & Boon?

Over the past four years we have seen significant increases in the cost of producing our books. As a result, in order to continue to provide customers with a quality reading experience, the price of our books will increase to RRP $10.99 for Modern singles and RRP $19.99 for 2-in-1s from Medical, Intrigue, Romantic Suspense, Historical and Western.

For futher information regarding format changes and pricing, please visit our website millsandboon.com.au.

MILLS & BOON
millsandboon.com.au

INTRIGUE

Seek thrills. Solve crimes. Justice served.

Available Next Month

The Sheriff's Baby Delores Fossen
Under Lock And Key K.D. Richards

....

Smoky Mountains Mystery Lena Diaz
The Silent Setup Katie Mettner

....

Black Widow Janice Kay Johnson
Safe House Security Jacquelin Thomas

Larger Print

BRAND NEW RELEASE!

A hot-shot pilot's homecoming takes an unexpected detour into an off-limits romance.

When an Air Force pilot returns to his Texas hometown with the task of passing along a Dear Jane message to his best friends ex, the tables are turned and she asks him for a favour…to be her fake fiancé in order to secure her future. But neither expects the red-hot attraction between them!

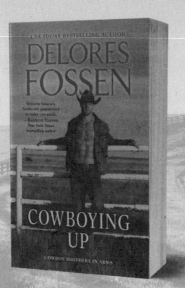

Don't miss this next installment in the Cowboy Brothers in Arms series.

In stores and online October 2024.

MILLS & BOON

millsandboon.com.au

Keep reading for an excerpt of a new title
from the Romantic Suspense series,
CAMERON MOUNTAIN REFUGE by Beth Cornelison

Prologue

The water was rising, along with her panic. She was trapped, and soon she would drown. She banged on the window, desperately trying to get free. To save herself. To save her friends. But she couldn't get out. The water gurgled higher...to her chin, her mouth, her nose. Suffocating. Lungs burning. They would all die. And it was her fault.

Then a giant bee appeared at her window. With his face. Gloating. Sneering. Buzzing. Buzzing. Buzzing.

Jessica Harkney woke with a gasp, her heart racing. Gulping air. She cut a quick glance around her, disoriented. Confused. He'd been there. But where was he now? The buzzing continued...

Clarity slapped her. Nightmare. Again. How long would the same replay of that awful night haunt her dreams? And did she deserve to be free of the nocturnal torture?

The buzzing sounded again as her phone vibrated on her nightstand. Taking a calming breath, she answered the call—her boss—and glimpsed at the time.

Damn! She was late. She tossed back her bedcovers.

"Sorry!" she said immediately. "Horrid night. And I...overslept."

After spending most of the night staring wide-eyed at her ceiling, a parade of worries and regrets tumbling through her head, she'd drifted off around 4:00 a.m., turned off her alarm when it chimed at 6:00 a.m.—and remembered nothing else but the nightmare until now. Eight thirty.

"I was worried about you since…you're usually so punctual," her boss, Carolyn, replied.

And because your life has been such a traumatic mess lately. The words, while unspoken, hovered in her boss's tone.

Raking her raven hair out of her eyes, Jessica groaned. "I know. I—I'll be there in forty minutes."

"Can you make it thirty?" her boss said, firmly but without an edge. "We have a meeting with John Billings at ten, and we need to prep."

Grimacing, Jessica flew to the bathroom, took the world's fastest shower, threw on the clothes she'd laid out last night, whizzed through the kitchen to start her Keurig brewing a cup of coffee, dumped a messy pile of cat kibble in her cat's food bowl, grabbed a banana and a bagel, stuffed her phone in her purse and unplugged her laptop from the charger.

"See you tonight, Pluto! Be good!" she called to her buff-colored feline as she raced out to the garage, feeling like a juggler. She had her bagel in her mouth, her laptop under one arm, the banana under the other, her purse over her shoulder, her shoes in her left hand, her coffee in the right. Opening the door to her rental car with her pinky, she set the coffee in the drink holder and tossed everything but the bagel on the passenger-side seat. Sliding behind the steering wheel, she took a bite of the bagel, then set the rest on top of the dashboard. After she cranked the car engine, she slipped her high-heeled pumps on her feet and strapped on her seat belt.

Only when she reached up to the visor to push the garage remote did she realize her mistake. She hadn't replaced the door opener yet since the accident. With a shudder for the unpleasant reminder of her recent trauma and a grunt at the inconvenience, she unbuckled her seat belt again and climbed out. As she rounded the back end of the rental car, waving away the stink of exhaust, a figure stepped from behind the open storage room door.

She screamed and stumbled backward, away from the man who approached her. When she recognized him, her jaw hardened, and heat coursed through her veins. "How did you get in here? What do you want?" she snarled, then flapped a dismissive hand. "Never mind that. Just…get out!"

"Not until we talk. You owe me that much, Jessie. I saved your life." He took a decisive step, blocking her path back to the open car door. Her purse. Her phone.

She gritted her teeth in frustration. "How many times do I have to tell you, I don't want anything to do with you. Stay away from me!"

"Look, Jessie, stop being so stubborn. I love you! If you weren't so defensive, you'd see—"

When he took a step toward her, she slipped off a shoe and threw it at his head.

"I said stay away from me!" She backed up again, knowing she needed her phone. "I'm calling the police."

His eyes narrowed with menace. "No cops. Just talk to me. I will keep coming back until you see that you love me the way I love you."

With quick steps, she rushed to the passenger side of the rental car and jerked the door handle. Locked. Damn it! Another wave of panic swooped through her. She glanced around for something with which to defend herself. Her tennis racket was on the wall behind him, but she wanted something bigger, heavier. More lethal.

When she turned and darted toward her garden tools, propped against the far wall, he surged up behind her. She seized a shovel as he wrapped an arm around her waist. With a thrust, he threw her to the ground. The shovel clanged down beside her. As she scrambled to get up, he kicked her in the temple, and she saw stars. Blinking, trying to shake off the blow, Jessica rolled to her belly. As she rose to her hands and knees, she put her hand on the shovel's handle. She angled a woozy and wary glance up at him. "Get out."

He glared back, growling through gritted teeth. "You made me do that. If you hadn't—"

She swung the shovel at him, hitting him far too weakly in her injured state to do more than anger him.

He grabbed the shovel, yanked it from her grip and tossed it out of her reach. Then leaning over her, he grabbed a fistful of her hair and bent her head back. "Now you're going to be sorry."

She sucked in a breath, coughing on the collecting exhaust from the idling rental car, then spit in his face.

His face suffused with color, the veins on his forehead bulging. He swiped the spittle off with his free arm, then shoved her down again. His foot connected once, twice with her ribs. Pain juddered through her. With trembling arms, she tried to crawl away from his abuse, but he stomped on her hand. Yelping in pain, she balled herself in fetal position and wrapped her arms around the back of her head, her only thought now of protecting her most tender and vulnerable places.

He kicked her again in the side. The hip. An unprotected part of her head. He stepped back, coughing. Then, getting on his hands and knees, he stuck his face in hers. In a sibilant tone, he whispered, "A restraining order? You thought you could get rid of me? Not a chance. Learn this lesson. Don't piss me off, Jessie."

She heard him grunt as he got back on his feet, heard him stomp across the concrete floor, heard the side door to her garage open and close. And then the only sound was the rumbling purr of the rental car's engine as it filled her garage with poisonous gas.

Subscribe and fall in love with a Mills & Boon series today!

You'll be among the first to read stories delivered to your door monthly and enjoy great savings.

WE SIMPLY LOVE ROMANCE